A CONNECTICUT GUMSHOE IN Sherwood Forest

BY

RANDY MCCHARLES

A CONNECTICUT GUMSHOE IN Sherwood Forest

BY

RANDY MCCHARLES

TYCHE BOOKS LTD.

A Connecticut Gumshoe in Sherwood Forest
Copyright © 2021 Randy McCharles

All rights reserved. No part of this book may be reproduced or transmitted in any form or by any means, electronic or mechanical, including photocopying, recording or by any information storage & retrieval system, without written permission from the copyright holder, except for the inclusion of brief quotations in a review.

The publisher does not have any control over and does not assume any responsibility for author or third-party websites or their content.

This is a work of fiction. All of the characters, organizations and events portrayed in this story are either the product of the author's imagination or are used fictitiously.

Any resemblance to persons living or dead would be really cool, but is purely coincidental.

Published by Tyche Books Ltd.
Calgary, Alberta, Canada
www.TycheBooks.com

Cover Art & Layout by Indigo Chick Designs
Interior Layout by Ryah Deines
Editorial by M.L.D. Curelas

First Tyche Books Ltd Edition 2021
Print ISBN: 978-1-989407-29-5
Ebook ISBN: 978-1-989407-30-1

Author photograph: Leonard Halmrast

This book was funded in part by a grant from the Alberta Media Fund.

This book is dedicated to the innumerable contributors to the Robin Hood mythos. Though the precise origins are unknown, thousands of poets, storytellers, musicians, scriptwriters, directors, actors, and many others have been inspired through the centuries to interpret and expand upon the tales of justice, brotherhood, and intrigue that millions of readers and viewers have come to know and love.

1
PECULIAR TWISTS OF FATE

"Ye there. Stranger. Whit business hae ye?"

It took a moment before Sam Sparrow understood the question. The words had been delivered with a thick Scottish accent, and his ears weren't accustomed to guttural speech. When he finally thought he had it, he carefully considered his response.

What was his business? Sadly, in this kind of situation, it was not unusual for Sam to have no idea what his business was. Maybe he should respond with a question. Should he ask where he was? When he was? Sam had been down this road before. Twice. Both times he'd found himself in King Arthur's Court. Wherever this place was, he didn't think Camelot was just over the hill.

Or maybe he should run? Try to find a way back to Hartford? But he couldn't, could he? He had to find Nora, his partner.

"I'm looking for someone," Sam called back. He reached up and adjusted his fedora to better block the sun from his eyes.

The man, short yet stocky beneath his heavy cloak and plaid kilt, had emerged from what appeared to be a stable. He carried a small round shield in one hand and a long, wide-bladed sword in the other, and looked a little like Mel Gibson from the movie *Braveheart*. "This is King John's land," Mel growled. "Hae ye permission tae be here?"

A Connecticut Gumshoe in Sherwood Forest

King John? Sam rubbed his ear and felt his cheek twitch. Did England, or Scotland considering how the man was dressed and spoke, ever have a King John? Sam couldn't remember one, not that he could list off all the British or Scottish kings. Maybe John had been some inconsequential king no one talked about.

Relaxing his shoulders and pushing his hands into the pockets of his trench coat, Sam slipped his right hand through the tear he had made near the top of the inside pocket. Beneath the flap of his suit coat lay the grip of his Smith & Wesson M&P semi-automatic.

"I'm looking for a woman," Sam said. "Tall. Blond hair. Coat a little like mine."

Mel took several steps, then stopped maybe thirty feet away. "A woman?" A smile spread across the man's swarthy face. "Whit Englishman isnea lookin' fur a wench?"

"She's a friend," Sam amended.

Mel laughed. "A freendly wench. Tell me mair." The man's smile looked more like a leer with each passing second.

"If you haven't seen her," Sam said, "I'll be on my way." He took a step back the way he had come.

"Hold." The smile left Mel's face as he raised his sword. "Who dae ye serve? John or Richard?"

A quiz. Great. Sam slipped his pistol from its holster and held it beneath his coat, aimed at Mel's midsection. The lout may be a small man, but not so small Sam could miss, even with the shield protecting much of his torso. Mel had no idea how close he was to death.

"I'm a foreigner," Sam said. "I have no idea who John and Richard are."

Mel snorted. "Ye dinnae sound lik' a foreigner. Ye speak th' King's English. Nae weel, mynd ye. Urr ye a spy?"

A sigh escaped Sam's lips. "If I'm a spy I'm a bad one. I don't even know where I am."

Puzzlement flashed across Mel's face, disappearing almost as quickly as it had come. "Matters nae how seasoned a spy ye be, a spy is a spy 'n' mist be jailed." Mel took a step forward.

Sam's fingers tightened on the grip of his semi-automatic. "I was afraid you'd say that. Look. Walk away and you'll be fine. We'll just pretend you never saw me."

"Ye call me a coward!" Mel took a step closer and pulled his shield against his chest. "Raise yer weapon, sur. Ah wilnae engage an unarmed man."

Sam was armed, but this fellow didn't need to know that. "I don't have a sword."

Mel paused and pursed his lips. "Na weapon? That wilnae save ye. Ye shall be tied, tried, 'n' hanged. Such is th' fate o' spies."

"I'm not a spy," Sam said. "I'm just looking for a friend."

Mel took another step toward him. "Mibbe ye shall find yer friend in jail."

"I doubt it." Sam flexed his finger against the semi-automatic's trigger. "Last chance to walk away."

Mel gave him an incredulous look, then raised his sword high above his head and rushed forward, a fierce battle cry roaring from his lips.

Damn. Sam had no choice. He'd never shot anyone before. Not shot dead. But as an East Hartford cop, he'd gone through all the training, both practical and psychological. It was kill or be killed. He'd spent countless hours on the target range, countless more in armed tactical exercises. See a threat. Pull the trigger. Don't hesitate. Hesitation was death.

It was more muscle memory than conscious thought as Sam pulled the trigger on his semi-automatic, and tensed for the pressure of the chamber firing so close to his hip. Prepared also for a visual of Mel's eyes going wide in surprise and pain, the sword and shield tumbling from his hands, and the would-be Braveheart collapsing to the ground, a final breath of life escaping his lips.

When Mel continued to scream, reducing the distance between them, Sam realized the man wasn't going down. His finger tightened on the trigger. Again, then again.

Mel was almost upon him, when Sam turned and sprinted through the weeds and tall grass as fast as his Thorogood Oxford dress shoes could carry him.

Mel ceased his yelling and began cursing. "Stand still, ye bugger. Urr ye a man? Only cowards run."

It thrilled Sam to run like a coward. If he could run faster than a coward, that would thrill him even more. His feet motored of their own volition while his brain tried to accept the fact that his gun, the M & P semi-automatic the wizard Merlin had magicked during his first visit in Camelot to never run out of bullets, had done just that. Run out of bullets. What was going on?

Sternwood Castle loomed on Sam's right. He ran toward it, intending to use its tall wall as cover as he raced around to the backside of the stone building. If he could lose Braveheart, find Nora, and get back to Hartford ...

His thoughts were cut off as several men who could have been Mel Gibson's extended family erupted from the castle entrance and headed his way. Now an army was chasing him. "What have I gotten myself into?" he muttered.

Sam lost sight of his pursuers as he ducked behind the wall and raced toward its other end, back to where he had somehow found himself in this unfamiliar version of the Sternwood estate.

Until this moment, he'd had no idea he could have been a track star instead of a cop. Mel had only been a few feet away when Sam began his mad dash. Now at least fifty yards separated them. But he knew motivation was a big factor when it came to speed. As was adrenalin. Sam figured he had a healthy helping of each. He also knew they were only useful in the short term. By the time he reached the back of the castle, his speed had flagged and the sound of pursuit was growing louder.

Sam still had no plan. He'd already tried to find the way he had arrived. The castle wall held a secret door. He knew it was there. He'd come through it, after all. But he'd been unable to find it again, not even after an extensive search. He certainly wasn't going to succeed in the few seconds he had before his pursuers caught up to him. His best option seemed the woods. Maybe he could lose his pursuers, find Nora, circle back, and look again. Yeah, that was a big maybe, but it was all he had.

The woods, which began only a few yards out from the castle wall, weren't especially thick, with lots of room for bushes to grow and Connecticut feet to run. There wasn't much grass beneath the trees, either, kept short perhaps by hungry rabbits and goats. Or maybe there was too much shade. Sam knew he was no arborist. His gaze searched the forest ahead, searching for the best path forward. There were literally dozens of ways he could go.

Shouts rose up behind him, so Sam followed the back wall for a few yards until the castle hid him from his pursuers. Then he took off into the trees, trying to put the thickest part between him and the castle.

When a small white animal, maybe a pig, shot through the

undergrowth practically under his feet, he almost had a heart attack. The jolt pushed him to run faster.

A short distance ahead and above him, a large black bird perched on a thick branch let out a loud croak. Then, with a rustle of feathers, it flew on ahead, weaving among the trees into a thicker section of woods. Sam followed it.

A crow? A raven? A Hartford cop Sam once worked with had claimed ravens were bad luck. He'd also said crows were good luck. Sam was sure he'd seen both varieties, but couldn't say which was which if his life depended on it. He hoped this bird was the lucky kind.

Sam felt himself beginning to tire. His breath came heavier, and his gut was starting to cramp. He knew adrenalin had done all it was going to. Behind him, short men with swords and shields and loud angry voices emerged from around the side of the castle and spread out into the trees. It didn't matter which way Sam went. There were enough pursuers to run him to ground. It was only a matter of time.

Heart in throat, his lungs pumping like a bellows, Sam tripped over something and crashed to the earth. Too exhausted to get up and keep running, he rolled behind a holly bush that hugged the base of a mossy tree trunk. The cover might hide him from seeking eyes if they didn't come too near, but he was certain his huffing and puffing would give him away. What had happened to his magicked gun?

Drawing his knees up against his chest, Sam leaned close against the tree. He pursed his lips and took quick, tiny breaths. To his right, several men with swords rushed past. Two more came up on his left, their heads turning this way and that as they slowed their steps.

"Where'd th' bampot go?"

Sam had no idea what a bampot was, but figured the unusually large man who could have been a stunt double for Arnold Schwarzenegger was referring to him.

The smaller of the pair looked barely out of his teens. Sam decided to call him Red because he sported a thin, red beard that shot out in a dozen directions. Red came to a stop, probably so he wouldn't trip on anything, and crooked his head up. "Mibbe he climbed a tree?"

A third man came running up to them. "How come ye hae

stopped? Laird Furnival say tae bring back th' spy fur questioning."

"Dae ye think th' lout is a spy?" Schwarzenegger asked. "Ah mean, wid a spy wear sae outlandish a cloak? An' his headgear? Ah hae ne'er seen th' like."

"It does nae maiter," the newcomer said. "Laird Furnival wants him. That's guid enough fur me." He gave Red a hard stare. "Why urr ye lookin' at th' sky? Did he fly away?"

"He cuid hae climbed a tree," Red said. "He wis running this way, then disappeared."

The newcomer laughed. "A monkey is he? Mibbe he wull dance."

"Ah dinnae see him in th' trees," Schwarzenegger said. "He mist be up ahead somewhere." The giant man waved a beefy hand and strode forward through the trees.

"Enough dawdling." The newcomer slapped Red across the face to make him stop looking at the sky. "Oor spy is getting awa' while we staun 'ere."

The three men moved on, and Sam realized he'd been holding his breath. He let the stale air out and pulled in a mouthful of much-needed oxygen. Too fast. Too loud. Schwarzenegger came to a sudden stop and turned his face toward him. "Thare!"

Sam froze, his lungs only half-filled with air. Caught. His only weapon a gun that had been magicked by Merlin to never run out of bullets, yet unable to fire. He could run. Again. But these men would be on him in moments. His only option was to raise his hands in the air. Would these medieval mooks even know what that meant?

Rising slowly to his feet, Sam raised his hands. "You got me. I'll come quietly."

Schwarzenegger grinned. "Quietly? Ye shall sleep lik a bairn whin a'm dane wi' ye."

The other two laughed.

The only good news was that all three men were sheathing their swords. Sam decided he'd welcome fists over steel any day and prepared himself for a beating.

The two smaller men stood to either side as Schwarzenegger clenched and unclenched his fists, then flexed his thick neck.

"You do this often?" Sam asked, hoping to delay the inevitable. When Schwarzenegger gave him a blank look, he added. "Beat on people littler than yourself?"

"Gwrtheyrn likes his exercise," Red said.

Sam boggled his eyes and struggled with the pronunciation. "Gwir-cyan? Is that what your parents named you? They must not like you very much."

Red and the newcomer howled with laughter.

Gwrtheyrn cast his companions a look that silenced them, then turned his thick nose on Sam. "Didnea like mah parents much either. Murdurred thaim. Slowly. Whin ah wis ten."

Sam raised his hands a little higher. "Tough childhood. You have any brothers? Sisters?"

Gwrtheyrn smirked. "Sure. I'll introduce ye. After ah knock yer lights oot." He wound up to take a swing.

Sam closed his eyes and braced himself. It had been worth a shot. In his head, he recounted the peculiar twists of fate that had brought him here, and waited for the first punch to land.

2
A CONNECTICUT CASTLE

SAM SAT BEHIND the wheel of his denim blue, 2019 Volvo S60, cruising east along highway 44, maybe thirty minutes outside Hartford.

"This is surprising," Nora said from the passenger seat where she'd been surfing tourism websites on her phone. "It says Connecticut is home to dozens of brick-and-mortar mansions that qualify as castles. The oldest is named Hearthstone and was built in 1899 near Danbury. It's described as a three-storey, battlement-crowned fortress, and was used as a honeymoon cottage for noted portrait photographer E. Starr Stanford. Three years later it was sold to Victor Buck, a retired New York industrialist."

Sam couldn't help but smile. "I guess the honeymoon was over."

Nora ignored him. "Perhaps best-known is Gillette Castle, built in 1914 on the Connecticut River by William Gillette, the famous Sherlock Holmes actor, who lived on the estate until his death in 1937. It was reopened in 2002 after a four-year, eleven million dollar restoration, and now includes a visitors' centre and museum, hiking trails, and a picnic area. Each year it receives 350,000 visitors."

"Never been," Sam said. "Didn't even know about it."

"Ah," Nora exulted. "Here's what I was looking for. The

landscape is about to change, however. Retired four-star general, Obadiah Sternwood of Manchester, Connecticut, has purchased a nine hundred-year-old castle in the countryside outside Sheffield, England, and is having it moved, stone by stone, to an acreage near UConn forest. Experts say the cost of the move is many times what the General originally paid for the castle, and that building a replica would have been much less expensive."

Sam made a guess at the next paragraph. "But the general wanted the real thing because his ancestors lived there during the late seventeenth century."

Nora cleared her phone and slipped it into a pocket of her lululemon trench coat. "You only know that because General Sternwood told us not one hour ago."

Sam shrugged. "So the old man's got some blue in his blood. I'm sure most of us do somewhere along the line. You don't see me buying a castle in Spain and hauling it to East Hartford."

"If you had the General's family fortune," Nora said, "you might."

"Nah. I'd miss all the modern amenities. Besides, it's not like the General is going to live there. He's got his youngest daughter managing the place."

From the corner of his eye, Sam caught Nora wagging her head. "General Sternwood didn't seem too worried about his daughter not answering his calls."

Sternwood's callousness bothered Sam as well, but he always found people with too much money to be as odd as a three-legged duck.

A year ago, Sam would have never dreamed of being hired by one of Connecticut's one-percenters to look into the disappearance of a close friend. A year ago, Sam Sparrow had been a failed private investigator on the brink of bankruptcy. Then Nora Clark entered his life. Sam had never met a more capable woman. It was Nora who kept the business afloat. And it was Nora who attracted big fish clients like General Sternwood.

"As far as I can make out," Sam said, "both Sean Regan and Carmen Sternwood have fallen off the radar, but the General only seems concerned about Regan."

"Concerned?" Nora echoed. "Lost is more like it, like he didn't know what to do without his friend."

Sam decelerated behind a slow-moving van and watched for

an opportunity to pass. "I got the impression the General is used to Carmen dropping out of sight. Vivian Rutledge, Carmen's divorcé older sister, suggested as much."

"Sure," Nora agreed, "but at the same time as the General's friend? The same place? And at a castle, no less. I'm not a fan of coincidences, especially when there's something unusual in the mix. You think this castle is for real? Or is it more of a country mansion? Like Hearthstone Cottage."

"I've got some experience with castles," Sam reminded his partner. "If the General robbed his piggybank to have this thing brought over from England, I'm sure it's the real deal."

"I guess you'd know," Nora admitted, then grew quiet as she sat taking in the summer countryside.

Sam cast his partner a quick glance, then returned his attention to the slow-moving van.

Twice in his life, he had experienced miracles. The first was when the wizard Merlin, and then the Lady of the Lake, magicked him to King Arthur's Court to solve medieval crimes. The second was when he'd returned to Hartford and advertised a partnership position in his failing private investigation agency. Somehow, the gods had smiled upon Sam Sparrow and allowed Nora Clark to answer that ad. He still didn't know which was the greater miracle.

A lull in traffic cleared the oncoming lane, so Sam made a snap decision and hit the gas. The Volvo's engine roared as he crossed the broken yellow line and sped up beside the cumbersome van that seemed to be travelling at only half the speed limit. Sam peered past his partner to get a glimpse of the van's driver, but all he could see was a hat.

"Are we in a hurry?" Nora asked.

"General Sternwood didn't strike me as the most patient of men," Sam muttered, his curiosity divided between the van's mystery driver and the enigmatic retired general he'd met earlier that day. Though in his sixties and confined to a wheelchair, the ex-military man barked when he spoke. "It's not like Sean to not check in. Something is wrong." The growl in the general's voice, and the fire in his deep-set eyes, suggested Sternwood was used to getting what he wanted.

"That's our exit," Nora said, interrupting Sam's reminiscing.

By now Sam had passed the van and was drifting back across

the yellow line. He shifted his gaze and spotted a small sign that marked where Codfish Falls Road split off from the highway. He'd almost driven past it.

Slipping his foot from the gas to the brake, he pressed down, but not too hard, conscious of the van now a short distance behind them. The Volvo slowed, but not enough to leave the highway. Sam continued braking as he pulled the steering wheel into the turn. At the last second, his foot left the brake and prodded the gas. The Volvo leaped onto Codfish Falls Road, barely missing ploughing into the opposite shoulder. Behind him, the slow-moving van leaned on its horn as it puttered past.

"Maybe I should have driven," Nora suggested as Sam swerved the Volvo onto the correct side of the road and slowed down.

"There's something off about Sternwood," Sam said, ignoring the comment.

"Of course, there is." Nora patted his knee. "The man was born with a silver spoon in his mouth and spent most of his days supervising the mass murder of people he'd never met. He married late in life, probably because no woman would have him given his obsession with death. The unfortunate gold digger who finally agreed to tolerate the man gave him two daughters, then promptly died. The young girls were raised by nannies and hardly knew their father."

Sam glanced sideways at this partner. "You got all that from a ten-minute meeting where Sternwood hardly mentioned his family or history?"

"No, I got that from a two-minute conversation with his butler while you were flirting with the elder daughter."

"I wasn't flirting," Sam grumbled. "Vivian Rutledge waylaid me on the way out from the Sternwood estate to express her concern over her missing sister and her father's failing health."

Nora laughed. "Believe that if you want. The woman was hitting on you."

Trouble was, Nora was probably right. Sam had never been good with women. He doubted he'd recognize getting hit on if it came with a solid right to the solar plexus and a left hook to the jaw.

His gaze drifted briefly down to the knee Nora had patted. Had his partner just flirted with him? No. They'd been together for over a year as business partners. That was just Nora being Nora. She was an outgoing woman. She'd even taught him to loosen up himself, just by watching her. Definitely not flirting.

"Whether Ms. Rutledge was hitting on me or not," Sam said, "she told me her younger sister is something of a loose cannon. Carmen Sternwood has been in trouble before. I suspect often."

Nora hummed with amusement. "Then why did the general put Carmen in charge of the castle reconstruction? The girl is only twenty and can't have much experience overseeing anything."

Sam's grip tightened on the steering wheel. Nora had hit the nail on the head. That's what had been bothering him since meeting with Sternwood. Vivian, the older daughter, seemed the better choice for taking on responsibility.

"Is that it?" Nora asked, pointing up ahead.

Since leaving the highway, Codfish Falls Road had rolled through a patchwork of trees and fields. Cows and horses dotted the landscape as well as the occasional small country house. There had been little traffic. Now, off to the right, a stone tower rose above a stand of trees.

As they drew nearer, the trees gave way to wild grass. A white fence traced the boundary of a field, then was replaced by wire. Finally, the fence ended, leaving just a grassy gully.

The castle was fully visible now. What there was of it. The tower and underlying stonework seemed in place, but scaffolding surrounded the remainder of the building. On what would eventually become the front lawn, piles of stone blocks like giant Lego pieces sat in scattered heaps.

At the back of a wide, gravel driveway, a white and black sign announced: Sternwood Castle, a project by Hawks Development Co. In front of the sign sat a red GMC truck with a Hawks logo painted on the side.

"Didn't the General say the castle reassembly had been completed?" Nora asked.

Sam didn't answer. He knew the question was rhetorical.

Slowing the Volvo, he pulled off the road onto the driveway and parked near the truck. Shadows behind a tinted side window indicated someone sat in the driver's seat. A few moments passed, then the cab door opened and a man in his late twenties or early thirties climbed out. He looked fit, though the skin on his face was tanned and weathered. Sandy blond hair fluttered in the breeze. An embossed patch on his work shirt suggested his name was Owen.

Nora and Sam got out of the Volvo. Sam was optimistic Owen would have answers.

"Carmen Sternwood?" The man, who had confirmed his identity as Owen Taylor, an employee of Hawks Development, scratched his head. "Haven't seen her in a couple of days. Normally wouldn't think much of it, except her Porsche 911 is parked in the back driveway. Miss Carmen doesn't usually leave without it."

"How about Sean Regan?" Sam asked.

"Who? No. Well, I might have seen him. Miss Sternwood has men around all the time. Doesn't introduce them. You got a picture?"

Sam pulled out his phone and showed Owen the photo he had taken back at the General's country house.

The Hawks employee squinted at the phone. "Is that a painting?"

Sam suppressed a laugh. "Yes."

The only photo Sternwood had of his friend, who Sam had begun to think might be more than a friend, was a painting that hung on the wall of his smoking room.

Owen shook his head. "Dunno. Doesn't look familiar."

Nora spoke up. "Why has work on the castle stopped?"

The Hawks representative jerked his head away from peering at Sam's phone. "Payments have been held up."

"Payments?" Nora echoed.

"To Hawks Development. The Sternwoods contracted us with payments on some kind of weekly schedule. Cheap bastards. They got more money than God, but dole it out at a glacier's pace. They missed the last few payments. My boss told us to halt work and appointed me to hang on as security. Since we haven't started again, I'm guessing there's still no money."

"We've just come from General Sternwood," Sam said. "He knows nothing about this."

Owen shrugged. "Miss Carmen has been overseeing the work. She's the one my boss negotiates with." He leaned forward and spoke in a whisper. "If you ask me, she's a bit of a flake."

"Could you call your boss?" Nora said. "Ask when he last spoke with Miss Sternwood and if he might know where she is."

"And if he's heard from Sean Regan," Sam added. While the missing daughter was a concern, they'd been hired to find Regan. Sam suspected once they found the General's friend, they'd find Carmen as well.

While Owen tried to track down his boss by phone, Sam and Nora walked past several piles of stone blocks and approached the wall of scaffolding. The castle tower rose above them over a hundred feet, and was made of stone blocks maybe two-foot square. The stones looked ancient, while the mortar holding them together looked new. Scaffolding ran along the entire front wall. And behind the scaffolding, near the centre of the building, they found a wide oak door maybe ten feet tall resting on ornate iron hinges.

"Why the frown?" Nora asked.

"There's no moat," Sam admitted. Since they'd arrived, he'd been looking for signs of a moat. But there was just flat ground and a castle wall.

"Maybe the moat comes later?" Nora suggested.

Sam shook his head. "Instead of this door, there'd be a portcullis—a giant gate made of iron bars that can be raised and lowered. There'd be a drawbridge. This is just a . . . a door."

Nora smiled. "Castle Sternwood doesn't meet your standards?"

"My expectations," Sam corrected. "I don't have standards." Before Nora could make the obvious joke, he added, "Not when it comes to castles."

Nora hummed quietly, then slipped past the scaffolding to better examine the door. "What kind of knocker would you put on the entrance to a Connecticut Castle?"

"I don't know," Sam said. "Something strong, yet tasteful. An eagle?"

Nora hemmed. "This one is metal and appears to be some kind of coat of arms. The plate looks to be a helmet above a shield, with tassels on either side. The knocker is a lion."

Sam joined her and tapped some of the dirt from his shoes. "A lion would be my second choice. I suppose we should knock."

"You think Carmen is in there, and this guy Owen is mistaken that she's missing?"

"Her 911 *is* out back," Sam said.

Lifting the lion knocker away from the door, Nora pushed it back again so it struck the shield plate. The sound it made was deep and heavy. It might scare cows out in the fields, but would the muffled sound on the other side of the thick door be heard by anyone? She knocked twice more before setting the lion to rest against the plate.

Sam waited. And listened. Apart from the breeze blowing dirt against the piled stones in the yard, there was nothing.

"Should we try calling again?" Nora suggested, pulling out her phone.

Sam didn't answer. Nora would try calling the General's daughter again no matter what he said. Instead, he put his hand on the door and pushed.

The heavy oak swung inward, its tall hinges creaking a mournful tone reminiscent of the Addams Family or the Munsters.

"Hello?" Sam called into the wide space beyond the doorway.

The only reply was an echo.

Having connected only to voicemail, Nora put her phone away and let out a soft laugh. "You never told me the castle was haunted."

"I hope not," Sam said. "I'd rather find Regan alive."

"You shouldn't go in there," a voice interrupted.

Sam turned.

Owen Taylor stood a few yards away, his thin blond hair fluttering in the breeze. "My boss is in a meeting. He'll call me back when he's free. But you shouldn't go in there."

"It must be safe," Sam countered. "The General told us Miss Sternwood has been living here."

"Against our advice," Owen said. "But she's the one paying the bills, so what choice do we have."

"We have to go in," Nora told the workman. "Carmen's father hired us to find her."

Not exactly true, but in the private investigation business, true enough.

Owen grumbled and shook his head. "Keep to the north end of the castle. It's as stable as it's going to be. We're still fitting together the south side. It'll take another ten or so days once we get back to work. Then the whole place will need a safety inspection."

"You're really making my day," Sam said.

The Hawks Development employee blew air out between his lips. "Don't say I didn't warn you." He turned and trudged back to his truck.

Nora punched Sam in the shoulder. "You bring me to the nicest places." Then she strode in through the doorway.

Sam hesitated. Was that flirting? First a pat on the knee. Now a tap on the shoulder. And she'd been smiling and laughing. A lot. Sam thought back over the past few weeks. Had Nora been acting that way all along? He didn't think so.

"Coming?" Nora's voice echoed from within the castle.

"Ready or not," Sam said, though he wasn't sure she heard him.

3
A SHAPE ON THE FLOOR

THE INTERIOR OF the castle was, in a word, underwhelming. Sam stood with Nora in some kind of entrance hall. Spacious, with a ceiling maybe thirty feet high. A row of narrow windows lined the exterior wall midway to the ceiling, but they were covered with plastic sheets that let the light in while keeping the wind and wildlife out. Give the place some furniture, art, and maybe a roaring fireplace, and it could be nice. Five-star hotel nice. Right now, the place had the atmosphere of a morgue. Apart from stone and dirt, the place was empty.

To the left, an arched doorway led to the south side of the castle. Like the windows, a sheet of plastic restricted access. To the right stood another arched doorway, and near it a giant fireplace, currently devoid of firewood. Along the back wall, a grand staircase led to a higher level. Beneath the staircase, less extravagant steps led downward into a basement or, more likely, a dungeon.

The doorway on the right was not covered with plastic, so Sam followed Nora in that direction.

Unlike the entrance hall, the north chamber was not empty, though it wasn't the Ritz either. The room stood maybe twelve by twenty feet, with an eight-foot ceiling. A leather couch sat in front of a fireplace shared with the entrance hall. Beside the couch sat a small table holding only a candle set in a stand, and a romance

11

novel. Bookcases and antique-style cupboards lined the opposite wall, except where two windows set with modern glass allowed light to enter the room. The shelves were empty.

The shrewd detective that he was, Sam inspected the candle and saw it was partially burned down. The novel looked used, its cover showcasing a shirtless man who would not look out-of-place on a firefighter fundraising calendar. Someone, probably female, had sat there after sunset, the candle lit, possibly reading the book. Carmen?

The place *had* been lived in. Barely. Maybe. There would have to be a bedroom somewhere else. And a kitchen. If not a kitchen, a pantry.

He looked up as Nora walked over to a small door at the far end of the room.

"Storage closet," she said after opening it. "Empty."

Sam rubbed his ear. "The General said Carmen has been living here for several weeks, ever since this end of the castle was put together." He shook his head. "I have my doubts."

"This can't be all there is," Nora said. "There must be a bedroom upstairs. And a bathroom."

Sam continued shaking his head. "The fireplace hasn't been used. Not once. Rich kids don't live this rough. Carmen's been warming her bed somewhere else."

"She's been lying to her father?" Nora suggested.

"Well, we know she was telling stories about the castle reconstruction being finished. The question is, why?"

Nora snorted. "I want to know why the General gave Carmen the job in the first place. She's obviously ill-suited."

"Maybe he hoped the responsibility would make her grow up."

"Sure," Nora said, sounding less than convinced. "Let's leave that and talk about motive. What reason could Carmen have to tell her father the work is complete when it obviously isn't?"

Sam thought about that. "Money."

"Of course, money," Nora said. "With the wealthy, it is always one of three things: money, power, or sex. The latter two don't seem to apply here. That leaves money."

"Or lack thereof," Sam said.

Nora paced a few steps. "The General gives his daughter funds to manage the reconstruction. The progress is not what she reports. Then she stops answering his calls. Conclusion: she used the funds for something else."

Sam waved his partner over and they walked back out into the entrance hall. "In response, General Sternwood sends his trusted friend Sean Regan to speak with his uncommunicative daughter and ascertain what happened. Only Regan also falls silent." Sam pulled his cellphone from his shirt pocket. "Strong signal." A downed cell tower had been their best theory for the General's calls going unanswered.

"Let's keep looking," Nora suggested, walking toward the stone staircase. "Maybe something will tell us what Carmen was up to. Or where she or Regan went. Up or down?"

Sam ran a finger along the edge of his fedora and felt the familiar twitch of his cheek. "My optimistic side says to search upstairs. The pessimist in me says we go down."

"The basement is probably as empty as this entrance area," Nora said. "Let's go down. We'll get it out of the way and then focus our efforts upstairs."

Sam nodded but almost immediately had doubts. The stairway down was wide but dark. A search along the wall for a light switch yielded only bare stone.

"Maybe there's a pull string," Nora suggested.

"Do people still use those?" Sam asked.

The basement of the small house he had grown up in had been undeveloped. He remembered walking down unlit stairs to a cold cement floor where a string dangled from the ceiling. He'd wave his hand in the air until he found it, then pulled to turn on a bare lightbulb attached to the ceiling. Before leaving, he'd pull the string again and climb the dark stairs. He hoped the General's millions had bought him more than that.

Fortunately, he didn't need to search in the dark for a string. Castle Camelot had taught him a few things. For the past six months, he'd kept a penlight in a pocket of his trench coat. He finally had a chance to use it.

Nora also produced a penlight. Together they traced circles of light along the steps and walls. As they descended, their footsteps echoed loudly in Sam's ears, and it seemed to him the air was growing thicker.

"Musty," Nora said when they reached the bottom step, using a single word to describe the essay Sam had been composing in his head.

No dangling strings or lanterns or anything else to shed light on the castle dungeon. Just an empty corridor ahead of them, with stone walls, floor, and a ceiling so low Sam had to hunch over so as not to hit his head. Having been assembled by Hawks workmen mere days ago, he was surprised by the amount of dust and dirt they encountered.

"Is this metal?" Nora asked.

Sam paused to examine the wall his partner shone her light on. "Looks like the mortar's been reinforced with iron rods. Probably a good idea, though I don't know if the General will agree with the improvement over the original."

"I still feel like I'm in a crypt," Nora said.

Sam laughed. "Crypts have coffins, cobwebs, and mould. Think of this as a wine cellar waiting for the wine to be delivered."

"Like I said, you bring me to the nicest places."

Sam imagined Nora grinning in the darkness. Was it possible his business partner really was flirting with him? He'd recognized how attractive Nora was the day they'd first met. Indeed, it had struck him how much she reminded him of Lady Euphemia Peregrine, Effie, the wizard Merlin's office clerk from Camelot.

Sam found himself letting out a soft sigh. Effie. The first—and last—woman to pull at his heartstrings. One word from Effie and he would have stayed in Camelot, left Hartford and his life here behind. But the feeling hadn't been mutual. Story of his life.

"The corridor branches into a T," Sam said. "Let's go right and see where it goes. If it doesn't loop around, we'll come back and go left. If the main floor is any indication, we're not looking at a lot of ground to cover."

"After you," Nora said.

"Ladies first," Sam countered.

"This is your boondoggle," Nora finished, and Sam knew he'd been bested.

Holding his penlight in front of him, Sam strode forward into the darkness, his steps echoing in the musty air, Nora's footsteps offering a counterpoint behind him. There wasn't much to see. He half expected cells like the ones he had experienced in Castle Camelot's dungeon, but all he found were what he assumed were storage rooms, pantries, and wine closets. All empty.

He sneezed as dust irritated his nose, and at one point threw himself against the cold stones of a wall when movement startled him. A rat? He had no idea what the beast could live off of down here, and assumed it must forage the upper floors. When he resumed walking, he realized he no longer heard Nora's footsteps behind him.

Spinning on his heels, he shone his light back along the corridor the way they had come. The space was empty. "Nora?"

No answer.

Sam charged back along the corridor as fast as his hunched-over gait could carry him, pausing only long enough to flash his penlight into various side chambers. In a matter of seconds, he was back at the foot of the stone stairway.

"Nora!" he called again.

Nothing.

"Stop and think," he mumbled out loud. Your IQ isn't that much lower than Nora's. Search the corridor and rooms again? Go back up the stairs? What else? "Nora!" Nothing.

Then he had it. Grabbing his phone from his shirt pocket, Sam pulled up his contact list and tapped the Call icon next to Nora's name. He listened, but no one picked up. Just before it went to voicemail, he heard a faint sound echoing down the corridor.

Moving his phone away from his ear, he registered one last ring reverberating between the stone walls and ceiling. Then Nora's voicemail message poured out from his phone.

How had he not found Nora as he made his way back to the stairs? It didn't matter. Holding his penlight in front of him, Sam scurried in the direction of Nora's unanswered phone.

He quickly reached the point where he had turned around, with still no sign of his partner. Pulling out his phone, he called again. The unanswered ring echoed somewhere ahead of him. How was that possible? Nora would have had to have gotten past him somehow.

As he continued forward, the bare stone walls seemed to stretch on forever. Had Nora found a cross corridor Sam had thought was a closet? And worked her way ahead of him? But why hadn't she let him know? A tap on the arm would have been enough. Nora was never reckless, and this was . . . reckless. There was no other word for it.

Up ahead, maybe ten feet, the beam from his penlight hit a wall. The corridor had come to an end. Where was Nora?

Sam's worries doubled as he called his partner's number a

third time. The ring sounded loud and directly ahead. Stepping forward, his penlight revealed a shape on the floor. Sam closed the remaining distance, then reached down and retrieved Nora's phone. What . . . ? Where could she have gone?

As Sam stood wondering what to do next, if there was anything he could do, he felt a slight current of air against his cheek. Jamming both phones into his shirt pocket, he leaned forward, holding the penlight close to the wall and squinting his eyes. He ran one finger along the corner where the two walls met. Was that air coming through the seam?

Setting the penlight on the floor, Sam pushed with both hands against the facing wall. Nothing. He put his shoulder into it and felt some give. Nora was tough, but could she push with as much force? Sam took a deep breath, then heaved his shoulder against the wall with every ounce of strength he could muster. Slowly, very slowly, the wall moved, swinging open on hidden hinges.

When the opening grew wide enough that he could see through the gap, what met Sam's gaze was the last thing he expected.

4
I'M NOT IN CONNECTICUT ANYMORE

BRIGHT SUNLIGHT SEEPED in through the opening, partly blinding Sam after the dark interior of the castle basement. Only it couldn't be the basement. The exit came out at ground level. Maybe the acreage behind the castle sat lower than the front. He'd seen a house like that once, where the front entrance was at ground level, but the basement opened out into the back yard. The house had been built on the slope of a hill. Maybe Sternwood Castle did the same thing.

The call of a bird reached Sam's ear, and the sharp smells of plants and earth tickled his nose, clean and sweet after the musty interior of the castle. The heavy stone door pushed back against him, wanting to close, shutting out the sun. Nora's phone was abandoned near the hidden doorway, so she must have gone through. Mustn't she?

Sam's cheek twitched. He retrieved his penlight and began squeezing himself through the opening, his right arm first, then his torso, lastly pulling his legs and left arm through before the wall swung back, closing the gap.

Breathing heavily, Sam sank to the ground and rested against the castle's exterior wall, his gaze aimed out into the trees, his gaze searching for Nora. He tried to call her name, but had little breath after the exertion of forcing open the door.

A large black bird glided down out of a tree, landing on the grass just a few feet away. It cocked its head, eying Sam, dipping its beak up and down as though asking a question. Sam didn't speak bird, so he didn't understand the question, never mind how to answer. The bird cawed once, then flapped its wings and rocketed skyward, flying above the treetops and winging away into the distance.

Sam blinked a few times. There were a lot of trees. A forest full of them. More than he had seen while driving down Codfish Falls Road. The wood looked more like UConn Forest, but that was several miles to the west. He found himself regretting that he and Nora hadn't taken a look behind the castle before entering. Owen Taylor had mentioned there was some kind of driveway and Carmen Sternwood's Porsche. He assumed the Mercedes Sean Regan had driven from General Sternwood's estate might be there as well, but there was no sign of vehicles or driveway.

Brushing dirt from his pants and trench coat, Sam climbed to his feet. His fingers itched for a cigarette, a habit he was still a long way from breaking. To do something with his hands he adjusted his fedora. It did nothing to relieve the itch.

He still couldn't figure how Nora had gotten away from him so quickly. And quietly. Or why. He could only assume she'd found the same secret door he had and was somewhere nearby.

Turning to study the castle wall, he saw no sign of a door. Just stone, dirt, and moss. He'd heard of fortifications having secret tunnels and doors. Escape routes should the fort become besieged and about to fall. He rubbed his ear. Or a means for smuggling mistresses in and out. Could such escapeways have existed in medieval castles as well?

Sam searched with his fingers for a seam or lever, but found nothing, even though he knew the door was there. He didn't remember seeing moss on any of the stonework at the front of the castle. Surely any moss would have died, dried, and fallen off during shipping. But the shaded back side of the castle was covered with healthy, damp moss.

He turned and looked about, seeing forest in every direction. No roadway. No fences. No sign of Man's handiwork anywhere. This wasn't right. Where was Nora? "Nora!"

No answer.

Worried for his partner's safety, Sam walked along the wall to where it ended at a corner. Unlike Castle Camelot, which was round like the table in the knight's council room, Sternwood Castle was more or less rectangular. Trees crowded the horizon on this side of the castle as well. And there was no scaffolding. Wasn't this the unfinished south side?

"Nora!"

Nothing.

Sam continued walking until he reached the next corner, then turned to face the front of the castle. No scaffolding here either. And no piles of stone blocks. The GMC Hawks construction truck was also conspicuously absent, along with its driver. There was just a broad patch of ground covered with mossy grass, trees further off, and fields far in the distance.

Stepping away from the castle wall, Sam looked up to the line of windows running high up along the front façade. No glass, but he noted interior curtains like those he had seen at Castle Camelot. He also saw the small tower rising above the north end of the building. And at ground level, closer to him, the massive oak door entrance to Sternwood Castle, complete with lion's head knocker.

Thirty feet out from the door stood a hitching post, and beyond that a stable. The sound of chickens and horses came from within.

Sam shook his head and mumbled to himself, "I'm not in Connecticut anymore."

Then a man who looked surprisingly like Mel Gibson emerged from the stable. He wore a heavy cloak and patterned kilt and carried a shield and sword. He took a few steps before noticing Sam. "Ye there. Stranger. Whit business hae ye?"

It was the strongest Scottish accent Sam had ever heard.

5
A BETTER PLAN

SAM GRIMACED AS he waited for the blows he knew were coming. He just hoped Schwarzenegger would take pity on him when he failed to defend himself. Defending himself would be a mistake. Bullies were only interested in winning the confrontation. Once it was obvious they had won, they usually let it drop. Sam just hoped he had read Schwarzenegger right, that the man was a bully. If he were a sadist, this could be a beating of a different colour.

Time must have slowed because Sam knew he shouldn't have to wait so long. He could hear Schwarzenegger breathing and the cheers of his two compatriots, Red and the new guy. There was also the chirping of birds and the rustling of wind through the trees.

Sam hoped this wouldn't be his big sleep. When he first signed up as a cop, he knew an early end was more than a possibility. Lots of cops bought it. Most took a bullet. The second leading cause of police death was by vehicle, more from being outside the vehicle than inside. The third was heart attack. Lots of stress being a cop. Assault followed a close fourth. It was surprising how many trained policemen got pummelled to death by idiots strung out on meth. Sam thought he'd put that behind him when he became a private investigator. Well, life was chock full of little surprises.

It would be a shame to die when he didn't know where, or even when, he was. Could it be somewhere near Camelot? Near Effie's father's estate perhaps? If the passage of time was consistent with his first two visits, that would make it six years since he left the last time. Effie would be almost thirty. Virtually the same age as him. Or close enough. A lot could happen in six years. Maybe Effie's feelings had changed. Maybe this time it could work between them. That was, if he survived being beaten and arrested for being a spy.

Sam realized he had stopped breathing and took in a long draw of clean air. So time hadn't stopped entirely, but he still hadn't become the Scottish Conan's punching bag. Was that grunting noise the sound of Schwarzenegger exerting himself? Winding up for the blow of all blows? Sam wondered if maybe he should open his eyes, allow himself to see what was coming, maybe pull away so the blow wouldn't land as hard.

No, that would be defending himself and inviting a larger assault. But he didn't have to open his eyes all the way. Maybe he could just slip one lid open a crack, get a sense of the blow coming so he could ease back with it. Sam wished he had a cigarette. He could almost taste it.

A noise like a soft whistle touched his ears. Then a quiet *thuk* followed by Red's voice. "Whit?"

Sam opened one eye to see an arrow sticking out of the shoulder of Schwarzenegger's punching arm. The giant man stared at the offending length of wood, a frown on his lips. Then a second arrow appeared, sticking out from his chest. The frown widened. Then the big man tipped backward and fell to the ground.

"Och!" Red shouted as Sam turned to watch the smaller man sprint away through the forest. The new guy was already gone, racing back toward the castle. Several additional arrows whistled through the trees, one of them catching Red in the shoulder and another burrowing through his thin red hair. "Och!" he shouted again, still hightailing it after his companion.

Sam stood watching as a half-dozen men dressed in green and brown camouflage melted out of the forest. Each wore calf-length boots and a triangular hat made of green felt. A quiver of arrows rested across each man's back. In their hands, they carried drawn bows.

One of his rescuers was a giant, easily as tall and wide as Schwarzenegger, maybe one of those siblings Schwarzenegger had threatened to introduce Sam to. The others were lean and small, leaner and smaller than Sam, in any case. He recognized one of them. "Robin?"

Robin of Locksley relaxed the drawstring of his bow and lowered his weapon. "Saints preserve us. Sam Spade! Well met, my friend. When we discovered Lord Furnival's men on the hunt, we could not have guessed their prey was the Merlin's pie."

Sam smiled so hard he was sure Robin could see himself reflected in his pearly whites. Six or so years had passed for the youth, while Sam had aged only six months in Hartford. Well, a youth no longer. Sam recognized the young squire from Camelot was now a knight in his mid-twenties. Or was he an archer?

Robin quickly closed the distance and rested a friendly hand on Sam's shoulder, perhaps to ensure Sam was really there and not some illusory phantasm. "What brings you back to us from the land of Connecticut?" Robin asked, apparently satisfied. "The Merlin? Have you seen him?"

One of the other rescuers, the big man who might have been a match for Schwarzenegger, stepped toward them and spoke in a shockingly soft voice. "Robin, there are more of Furnival's men about. We should either hunt them down or return to Sherwood."

"As always, Little John," Robin answered, "you speak truly." Robin then pursed his lips and made a brief whistle that sounded like a bird call. At the same time, he raised his right arm and made some sort of signal with his fingers.

As a unit, his companions turned and faded silently back among the trees the way they had come. Robin and not-so-little John followed after them.

Though desperate to find Nora, Sam figured sticking with Robin and his companions was a better plan than wandering alone in a forest filled with murderous Scotsmen. Besides, Robin could help him search once he explained what had happened. Or tried to explain. Sam had more questions than answers.

He struggled to keep up as Robin's band of men moved through the forest without speaking, flitting silently among the trees. They made hardly a sound with their feet, while their shoulders and hips swayed as they eased around large bushes and protruding tree branches. Sam felt like a bull in a china shop trying to match their skill.

Up ahead, he saw a black bird flitting from treetop to treetop, also making no noise. It moved with Robin's band like it was a pet, or possibly just curious. He wondered if it was the same bird he had followed from the castle.

After maybe ten minutes, one of the men stopped and raised a hand. Everyone immediately froze in mid-step. Sam barely avoided walking into Robin's back.

"Anythin'?" a deep voice called out.

"Na," another answered, shrill in comparison.

"Laird Furnival wull nae be pleased," the deep voice growled.

"Laird Furnival kin kiss mah sorry behind."

The deep voice snorted. "If Furnival hears ye, ye wull hae na behind tae be sorry aboot."

"Let's return tae th' Laird's castle," someone else said. "Mibbe Tamhas or Ailbeart found oor spy."

"We kin hope," the deep voice answered. "Ah hae na wish tae taste Laird Furnival's displeasure."

Several minutes went by as the sound of men crashing through trees faded into the distance. Then a green-clad arm rose into the air and the band resumed its progress.

By now Sam had learned to step softer with less noise, imitating the men in front of him. It felt almost like he was floating above the forest floor. A few times it felt as though the black bird, still flitting from tree to tree in front of them, was watching him, dipping its beak with approval. Though still not superstitious, he figured it must be a crow of good luck rather than a raven.

As they continued to drift silently among the trees, time seemed to expand and contract. Sam had no idea how many minutes had gone by. He wore a watch on his wrist—a Rolex bought after his first trip to Camelot, but he had no desire to check the time. Time wasn't important, not now. Idly, he wondered how close they were to Camelot. Maybe at any moment the trees would part and the mighty city with its broad river would fill the horizon. Then he remembered Little John mentioning going to Sherwood, the forest of Robin Hood myth. Sam had no clue where that was in relation to Camelot.

After a short time, the band again came to a halt and stood in a close circle of trees where several horses had been tied. One by one, Robin's men—his Merry Men according to lore—untied a horse and leaped up into its saddle.

Robin turned to Sam, a grin brightening his handsome face. "You didn't think we were going to run all the way to Sherwood Forest, did you?"

"I hadn't given it much thought," Sam admitted, "since I have no idea where we are."

That seemed to startle Robin. "We're near Locksley Manor. In Yorkshire. We found you but yards from my father's castle."

"Your father?" Something wasn't right. "Your father is Laird Furnival?"

Robin's face went pale and red at the same time. Dark clouds obscured his eyes. "Furnival murdered my father and took my family's lands."

"Oh. That's . . . well . . . that's . . . what can I do to help?"

The clouds parted and health returned to Robin's cheeks. "Nothing. Not with Lord Furnival. He is mine. I do need your help, however, with a greater problem. The Sheriff of Nottingham is plotting insurrection against the King, and I have no idea how to stop him. But there is one thing I do know."

"What's that?" Sam asked.

"That such endeavours are Sam Spade's stock-in-trade."

6
STAND AND DELIVER

BEFORE ROBIN COULD say more, one of his band walked up and pressed the end of a rope into Sam's hand. The man stood taller than most of the others and had thinning, light brown hair. When he spoke, it was in a low, unassuming voice. "We had no thought for freeing captives. Please borrow my mount for our return to Sherwood."

Robin grinned. "Sam, this is David of Doncaster. David joined our cause last winter after the Sheriff's men murdered his wife and father-in-law and burned their farm to ashes. You may remember Squire Vaisey from our time at Camelot. A scoundrel to the core, yet John the Pretender appointed him Sheriff over all of Nottinghamshire."

Sam felt his jaw drop. He wasn't sure this was because of the horrible things Robin described, or the run-of-the-mill way in which he described them. At last finding words, he said, "Vaisey? Yeah, I can picture him in the role of evil Sheriff, but why would he do that to David's family?"

David spat and ducked his head. "As an example of what to expect if you don't pay taxes."

"That's awful," Sam said.

The man ground his teeth. "Taxes have risen each season since King Richard rode off to war. They are impossible now. Had we paid, we would have starved to death. We offered the Sheriff's collector a tithe, as is fair. The Sheriff responded with murder."

"Wait." Robin looked at Sam. "How did you know the Sheriff is an evil man? If you just arrived from Connecticut as you say, would you not assume a Sheriff would uphold just laws?"

Sam smiled and touched the brim of his fedora. "The same way I knew back in Camelot that you should stick to the bow. Your story is not forgotten to history."

"History?" David perked up. "Are you this man Robin has spoken of? The one from the future? Am I also remembered?"

Sam's tongue remained tied for a moment. He'd never heard of David of Doncaster, not that he considered himself any kind of expert. He'd read of Robin Hood, Friar Tuck, and Little John in picture books as a child, and seen a Mel Brooks movie once, though he didn't remember much of the film. But he didn't want to disappoint the man, especially after he had offered up his horse. "Well, all of the Merry Men are famous. Heroes. A bright glimmer of goodness in a dark, dark time."

Both Robin and David frowned, then spoke together. "Merry Men?"

"I have never heard such a term," Robin added. "It sounds . . . , it sounds . . ."

"Not manly," David suggested.

"Oh." Sam searched fast for a way to remove his foot from his mouth. "In my day it's just fine. Merry means you found joy amid adversity. If you haven't yet, you will."

"Joy amid adversity," Robin echoed. "I like it."

"Good," Sam said.

"It means there is hope," Robin added, his expression brightening. "We have certainly found not a single jot of joy thus far. Only loss and suffering. Merry Men means my cause is just and portends we shall succeed. That we shall bring down the Sheriff and his company of criminals, and return England to its former glory, possibly even before King Richard returns."

"Uhm, right," Sam said.

Robin turned to David. "Henceforth, we shall call ourselves Robin and his Merry Men."

Sam interrupted. "Robin Hood. Robin Hood and his Merry Men."

"Hood?" Robin cast Sam a curious look. "You mean like a cowl? I sometimes drape myself in a hooded cloak if I need to move through a crowd without being recognized."

"Uhm . . ." Sam was pretty sure it was hood as in hoodlum. "Is it a green cowl? Forest green?"

David spoke in his quiet voice. "Green is green. Most woodsmen wear green. Sometimes brown. So as to blend in and not scare the game away."

Robin straightened as though making a decision. "I shall examine my hooded cloaks when we arrive at Sherwood. And dispose of any that are not green. Now, we must be on our way if we are to reach our destination before nightfall."

"Of course," Sam said, glad of the change of subject. "Could someone maybe help me up onto this horse? It's been a while." Or never. Sam had never ridden a horse, except maybe a plastic job on a carousel when he was a kid.

"Have you no horses in Connecticut?" David asked.

"We do. I've just . . . well . . . to be honest, I'm not well off enough to have much to do with horses. Horses are a wealthy man's pastime."

As Sam spoke, David intertwined his fingers and hunched over to form them into a stirrup. Sam had seen enough westerns on television to know what to do. Knowing and doing were two different things, however. As David straightened, lifting him up, Sam almost flew over the horse's back. Somehow, he managed to grapple the saddle's pommel and wrestle himself into the seat. Laughter broke out from Little John and other Merry Men. Sam laughed with them, pretending to be the clown.

David's expression remained sober, however. "Too poor to ride a horse. This Connecticut you come from must be a sad, sad place."

Sam sighed. "In many ways, it is." Having served as a Hartford cop, he knew just how sad parts of Connecticut could be. "Are you sure you're all right with me taking your horse?"

David nodded, and for the first time the man's face lit up. "It is naught. I can run as fast as a horse." With that, the man from Doncaster ran ahead and disappeared into the trees.

Robin expertly mounted his own horse, then threw hand signals at various of his men. Finally, he clucked his tongue and his horse moved forward, the others, including Sam's, following suit. Robin Hood and his Merry Men were on their way.

As his horse followed the others, Sam bounced in the saddle

like he was driving over a road that was mostly potholes. The only upside was that he didn't have to do anything, which was just as well. He knew from watching television that he could pull on the reins or kick the horse's sides with his heels, but he wasn't exactly sure what the result would be. Riding a horse was nothing like driving his Volvo.

Up ahead, one of Robin's band separated from the others and disappeared into the woods, probably on a scouting mission. Unlike the rest of the Merry Men, who seemed made of solid British stock, this one had dark skin and wore a headscarf that partly obscured a tattooed face. Sam had no idea Africans had migrated to Britain this early. He didn't remember seeing any in Camelot, except for Jesus Cairo, who seemed more Middle Eastern than African.

The remainder of the band proceeded as a tight group, winding through the forest following some kind of animal track and alternating their pace between a few minutes' walk and a few minutes trot.

With all the jostling in the saddle, in no time at all Sam's keister began screaming at him. He'd heard the term *saddle sore*, of course, but apparently, his notion of sore failed to live up to the reality. What he was feeling was saddle agony. There was nothing he could do for it, however, except grit his teeth and wait for the ride to end, which happened much sooner than he expected.

The forest parted, and Sam's horse stepped out onto a dirt road where it stopped and stood with the others. The scout who had gone ahead sat on his horse facing them. There was no sign of David of Doncaster.

"A half mile," the dark-skinned man said in a concise accent. "No more. It is not far out of our way."

"Okay," Robin said. "You've done well, Azeem. We failed to get what we came for from Lord Furnival. This will be compensation."

"What's happening?" Sam asked.

Robin cocked an eye. "How would you like to see Robin Hood and his band of Merry Men in action?"

"I thought I already had," Sam said.

"What? When we rescued you? Anyone could have done that. What we do is an art. Prepare yourself."

Then they were off at a run. Sam clutched his saddle horn for dear life as his horse galloped to keep up with the others.

After a minute, or at most two, Sam's horse slowed to a trot. It snorted and blew hot air out its nose and mouth. Up ahead on the road, an enclosed carriage was moving away from them. A driver sat up top, his shoulders turned, anxious eyes glaring back at them. He used a whip to encourage the carriage's horse to go faster. It was a lost cause. Even Sam knew that.

Over the huffing of the horses, Sam heard the rasp of arrows being whisked out of quivers and notched against taut bowstrings.

One of the band—a youngish man with long blond hair—called out in a loud voice. "Stand and deliver!"

The driver continued to glare and made no move to slow the carriage.

Little John let his arrow fly. It thunked into the back of the carriage.

The blond called out again. "Stand and deliver!"

Again, the driver made no move to comply.

Sam heard Robin let out a sigh. Then an arrow flew, skimmed the top of the carriage, zipped past just above the driver's shoulder almost brushing his neck, and cut through the reins mere inches from the man's fingers.

At last, the driver responded. Since he could no longer control the horse with the reins, he called out in a soft voice. "Whoa! Whoa up, Rosie!"

The horse must have been well trained. It immediately slowed to a stop, glanced back at the driver, then at the reins dragging in the dirt. It seemed to Sam that it shook its head in disbelief before facing forward again.

"Ronald?" An indignant voice rose from within the carriage. "Why are we stopped?"

The driver let out a heavy sigh. "You have company, m'lord."

Again, the muffled voice from within the carriage. "Don't be absurd. One doesn't receive company on the highway."

"One does today." Still turned in his seat, Ronald looked at Robin and shrugged with his hands.

Robin nodded at his blond band member, who called out a third time. "Stand and deliver!"

The carriage door opened a crack, and the words that came

from within were slightly less muffled. "Don't be ridiculous. I have already paid my taxes."

Then a skinny man wearing a ruffle shirt and narrow shoes stepped out onto the dirt road. His eyes widened when he saw the Merry Men staring down at him from horseback.

"You have not paid the people's tax," Robin said.

"People's tax?" Ruffle shirt appeared baffled. "Don't be absurd. Who are you supposed to be?"

"Are you blind?" Little John said. "This is Robin Hood."

"Robin who?"

"You must have heard of me," Robin said. "I steal from the rich and give to the poor."

"You what? Steal? I thought you said you were a tax collector."

"He's a tax returner," Sam said, jumping in on the fun. "The people have paid too much tax, so now he's returning some."

Ruffle shirt's face grew at the same time white and red. "That. That. I have never heard such nonsense."

"Be the first to tell your friends," Sam quipped.

Little John jumped down off his horse and untied a large canvas sack from his saddle. He strode up to ruffle shirt, who stood two heads shorter than him. "Your valuables, if you please. Nine-tenths of them."

"Nine what? This is outrageous!"

The blond who had called out *Stand and Deliver* aimed a notched arrow at ruffle shirt's chest. "Nine-tenths is the lion's share the Sheriff's collectors are demanding from the poor. Most cannot pay. Those who can will be unable to next time."

"Then take it up with the Sheriff!" ruffle shirt cried. "This has nothing to do with me."

"Tried that," Robin said. "The Sheriff does not listen to us. Perhaps he will listen to you."

"That is—" ruffle shirt began.

"Enough talk." Little John shook the sack. "Fill it, or we will take everything, including your britches. You can walk to your destination wearing the clothes you were born in."

Ruffle shirt's eyes bulged and his cheeks puffed up like balloons. "You will what!"

"Please keep talking," Little John suggested. "Nothing would give me more pleasure than to leave an arrogant nob like you lying naked in a ditch."

Maybe ten minutes later, Robin Hood and his Merry Men galloped down the road, a full sack tied to Little John's saddle.

7
THIS IS SHERWOOD?

THE MERRY MEN didn't stay on the road for long, but turned onto a path through the forest only to come out at another road twenty or so minutes later. This roadway was wider, though still unpaved. Sam heard one of Robin's men refer to it as The King's Great Way.

They travelled south, sometimes passing travellers heading in the opposite direction. No one suggested robbing any of them, and Sam figured that was just as well. His keister and back ached so badly that even threatening someone with murder would prove a feeble distraction.

After a short while, they came to a small town. Or village. Or whatever something smaller than a village was called. Apart from a few humble dwellings along the roadway, it was little more than an intersection of two roads. The village equivalent of downtown occupied the crossroads: an open-air market that was apparently closed, an alehouse, a narrow church, and a broad wooden building with a sign naming it Mansfield Stable.

The Merry Men pulled up to the stable where a short, wiry man agreed to groom and check over the horses. Robin then led the band to the alehouse. Sam hobbled along behind them, his hips and thighs complaining with every step.

The alehouse wasn't much to look at. One storey. A shingled roof with a chimney sticking out the top. Three narrow windows.

The only thing fancy about the place was an elaborate sign beside the entrance naming it the Stag and Boar, and declaring it had been founded in 1170 A.D. To Sam's eyes, the place could have been built last week. Maybe it had. Sam had no clue what year it was now.

The door creaked on iron hinges as Robin pushed it open to reveal a dark interior. When Sam's eyes adjusted, he saw only two occupants. A barkeep. And David of Doncaster.

"Well met," David greeted them quietly. "I have waited here so long, I feared the Sheriff's men had found you."

Little John dropped his canvas bag on the floor near David's feet. "We stopped for a bit of sport."

"Without me?" David let out a soft sigh. "You no longer love me."

"'Twas a matter of opportunity," the big man explained.

"Then you owe me a drink," David said, "and all is forgiven." The quiet man's voice then rose thirty decibels. "Harlson! A round for my friends!"

"As you wish," the barkeep responded. He turned to busy himself behind the bar.

Sam, not confident in his ability to sit after his experience in the saddle, remained standing while the Merry Men drew chairs up around David's table.

"So . . ." Sam waved an arm to encompass the inn and nearby buildings. "This is Sherwood? It's not what I expected."

The Merry Men all looked at him, then Little John let out a roar. "Sherwood Forest is a Kingswood. There is no town. No village. No hamlet. The King, when his royal eminence is not hunting Saladin's Muslims outside Jerusalem, occasionally hunts for game there. And at times, certain criminals congregate there."

Sam let out a weary breath. "So what you're saying is, we're not there yet."

Robin rose from his seat and rested a hand on Sam's shoulder. "Our destination is not far now. My eyes see you are not familiar with a saddle. Only a short distance more, my friend."

The barkeep arrived carrying a wooden tray loaded with heavy metal cups, which he shuffled onto the table. He eyed the canvas bag on the floor. "Has the Sheriff paid tribute again?"

Robin nodded. "Aye, Harlson. Are you willing to distribute the tax?"

"Of course, Robin. I would sooner ride with you, but my leg." The barkeep reached down and patted his thigh.

"We each do our part," Robin said. "Yours no less than mine."

The barkeep nodded and plucked up the bag, hauling it into a back room.

Sam couldn't see anything wrong with the man's leg. He whispered to Robin, "You trust him?"

Robin picked up one of the metal cups and took a long drink before answering. "Harlson is a good man. His father worked for my father before King Richard left for the Holy Land. I helped him get his position here."

Sam eyed the remaining metal cups and picked one up. Sniffed. It was alcohol. Vaguely sweet. It reminded him of the drink Martin Barth, Esquire had drugged him with in Camelot, but was darker in colour.

"'Tis mead," Robin said, reading the question on his face. "It will cure what ails you, I can assure you of that. Just take care not to drink too much. A man's constitution is only so strong."

Sam took a small sip. Between the fire in his throat and the air being torn out of his lungs, he wondered if he'd already had too much. Harlson's mead was much stronger and less sweet than what Barth had given him. He set the cup back on the table and stood flexing his buttocks and lower back, trying to return to them a sense of normalcy.

The Merry Men ignored his discomfort and chatted good-naturedly while drinking from their cups like they contained water. When the mead was gone, they seemed anxious to be on the road again. Sam managed to accommodate two additional small sips, but left his cup mostly untouched, before following them back outside.

The good news was that Sam no longer felt a burning ache in his backside. The bad news was that he couldn't feel much of anything, anywhere. He'd gone numb. Whether it was from the mead, or from standing instead of sitting, he wasn't sure. He brightened at the thought that if he fell out of the saddle and lay trampled on the road, he probably wouldn't feel anything then, either.

After retrieving the horses from the stable, the Merry Men set out along The King's Great Way heading south. David of

Doncaster walked beside Sam's borrowed horse but kept his thoughts to himself. As they passed by the church, Sam noted it looked less busy than the alehouse.

"Where is everyone?" Sam asked. "In this entire town I've seen only two people."

David glanced up at him. "'Tis a village, not a town." Then he sighed. "Even so, the people are scared. Meet a stranger on the road, chances are it is a tax collector or a bandit, not that there is much difference between the two." Another sigh. "It is better to remain out of sight. More than better. It is as much as your life is worth."

Sam recalled what Robin had said about David's wife and father-in-law, and decided to ask no more questions.

They stayed on The King's Great Way for some immeasurable length of time, alternately running the horses and slowing to a walk. David, on foot, kept the same stride and didn't seem to tire. Sam could never have matched that pace. When he returned to Hartford, he'd start an exercise program. Maybe join a gym.

From there, his thoughts wandered to the earlier events of the day. The transplanted castle that should have been reassembled, but wasn't. His near incarceration, or worse, at the hands of Scottish savages. And could he ever find his way back to Sternwood Castle? Or Locksley Castle as it was currently called. Roads were easy enough, but most of the journey had been through unmarked forest. And Nora. Where was she? Had she slipped through time like he had? Or was she back in Connecticut wondering where he had gone? Was she swearing up a storm for him having deserted her?

Eventually, the effects of the alcohol wore off, and Sam's saddle agony came back with a vengeance. He tried to return his thoughts to Nora and what he should do to find her, but he couldn't focus, there was just too much pain. His keister, hips, and lower back felt like they were in a vice.

Just as he thought he couldn't take any more, the Merry Men turned off the road into the trees. Only here the trees were larger and older than what he had seen thus far. Pines gave way to birch, beech, chestnut, and massive oak trees. It had to be Sherwood Forest. It just had to be.

Rather than follow a path or travel in a straight line, the band of riders zigzagged through the woods. Sam figured they were taking a deceptive path to avoid pursuit. They'd probably also already been spotted by lookouts. Odd birdcalls sounded in the air. Single sharp cries rather than repetitive, insistent mating calls. Coded messages. Messages telling Robin the status of the forest, and telling spotters closer to home who was coming.

At last, Robin raised an arm and everyone dismounted. Sam gratefully accepted David's help climbing off the borrowed horse, then stood hunched over, hands on his knees, while he tried not to fall over.

David looked at him in silence a moment, then led his horse over to where the others were being tethered to a stand of birch trees. Sam craned his head and watched as the farmer turned outlaw hung a feedbag beneath the animal's nose.

Feeling awkwardly conspicuous, Sam straightened, and zombie-walked to where Robin and some of his merry band were gathering in a large clearing dominated by a giant oak tree that stood almost as thick as his Volvo S60. It had low, thick branches that looked so knotted, he wondered if it was really several trees fused together.

Sam wasn't sure what he had expected of Robin's camp, but this wasn't it. There were women, children, dogs, and chickens. A giant fire pit, currently unlit, took centre stage. Blankets and canvas sacks lay everywhere. He didn't even know he was speaking aloud when he said, "Refugee camp."

"Yes," Robin said, his voice grim. "But a few of the many displaced by the Sheriff's ambition. Most you see here are family of the Merry Men. The rest are those we have rescued and for whom we have yet to find accommodation."

A large, rotund, balding man came up beside them. "We gather new refugees faster than we can resettle them."

Sam had trouble recognizing the man, but he knew the voice. "Tuck? Is that you?"

The roly-poly man smiled and rubbed his belly. "Less hair and more middle than last we met, but yes, 'tis I, the humble friar. By God's good grace, it is Sam Spade. I had not imagined I would ever see you again."

"And why is that?" Sam asked.

"Why, the fall of Camelot of course. King Arthur's great experiment in democracy has collapsed to ruin. And the Merlin. Why, the Merlin has not been seen in over two years."

A lump filled Sam's throat. Maybe he still suffered some effects from the mead, after all. "Effie. What about Effie?"

"Lady Euphemia Peregrine? I must admit my ignorance, Sam. When the city fell—"

"The city!" Sam couldn't believe what he was hearing. "The whole city?"

Tuck nodded, and tears welled in his eyes. "It was war, Sam. All-out war. The abbot ordered us monks away. Most went to London. Others to Bristol or Oxford. I wanted to leave everything behind me, so I returned to Nottingham to my father's farm, only to discover my father murdered and my mother and siblings gone into hiding."

Sam felt his throat continue to thicken. "That's awful." He was having trouble grasping what he was hearing. "Robin told me Vaisey murdered his father. He murdered yours as well?"

"Or had him killed." Tuck let out a heavy sigh. "Many men's fathers have lost their lives since Vaisey of Nottingham was made Sheriff."

"But," Sam demanded, "why?"

Tuck wiped a hand across his face. "King Richard's brother, John, is making a play for the throne of England while the rightful King is away in the Holy Land. The Sheriff of Nottingham is the Pretender's staunchest supporter."

Of course. That's who Mel Gibson's John and Richard were, and why the Scotsman had mistaken Sam for a spy. Wouldn't you know it? His arrival in the past had dumped him straight in the middle of a coup.

"But you should ask Robin regarding Camelot," Tuck suggested. "Like most of the young knights, he stayed to fight. He can tell you more of what happened than I."

Sam looked at Robin, whose eyes were cold. The green-clad bandit shook his head. "Later. It has been a long day, Sam. Such tales are exhausting and require preparation."

Just then a lovely young woman with sun-bright hair and warmth in her eyes bounced toward them. She gave Robin what was probably the best hug Sam had ever witnessed. The woman looked so much like Effie, Sam had to blink to make sure he wasn't seeing things.

"My hero returns!" the joyful young woman sang into Robin's ear.

When they separated, Robin's expression was no longer dark, but as light-filled as the young woman's cornflower-blue eyes. "I must make introductions. Marian, this is my old friend, Sam Spade. The one I told you about.

"Sam, this is Maid Marian, the light of my life and my soon-to-be bride."

8
MY FRIENDS DO NOT LIKE MY PLAN

"*The* Sam Spade!" Maid Marian practically gushed. "The investigator from the future who visited you in Camelot not once, but twice. To be honest, I was unsure I should put stock in such wild tales." Robin's fiancée ceased speaking and simply stood looking at Sam, as though expecting him to justify himself.

As had happened a few times during his visits to the past, Sam's stomach tightened and the word *imposter* burned a path through his mind. When he first arrived in Camelot and introduced himself to Effie as Sam Spade, one of Humphrey Bogart's most memorable characters, it had all been a bit of flirtatious fun. The Wizard Merlin had charged him with being a Royal Investigator, and the street-smart private detective Sam Spade seemed to fit the bill better than down-on-his-luck ex-cop Sam Sparrow. He'd wanted to impress the young woman and, well, Sam Sparrow wasn't much to make an impression. He still wasn't, though Sam felt he had more going for him now than he did then.

Sam had almost come clean a couple of times, just to ease the guilt if nothing else, but what good would it do? No one in the past knew Spade from Sparrow from Spalding. It would just confuse people. He did that well enough without going looking for it.

He allowed a smile to cross his face, and his left cheek

twitched, Bogart's signature tick in his role as Sam Spade. "I'm not certain I should believe the tales I've heard about you either."

Marian's eyes went wide. "You've heard of me? In the future? In a far-off land?"

Sam nodded. "You. Robin. Tuck. All the Merry Men."

Marian frowned. "Merry Men?"

Robin rested a hand on his fiancée's arm. "I'll explain later."

Sam felt he should backtrack a little, just in case Marian got too excited. "Where I come from, we have stories, histories passed down from generation to generation. I can't be sure how accurate they are, but you and your friends are remembered as the good guys, so I'm pleased to make your acquaintance."

"Well," Marian gushed. "If you say we are the *good guys*, as you put it, then I must believe you. Has Robin told you his plan?"

"His plan?" Sam echoed.

"Now, Marian." Robin again placed his hand on her arm.

She shook it off. "If your friend Sam is from the future, he may know if your plan succeeds or fails. 'Twould be foolish not to ask."

Friar Tuck nodded. "The Lady speaks wisely."

Robin shook his head and gave Sam a hard look. "My friends do not like my plan. They seek to enlist your support against it."

"That is unfair," Tuck said. "For all we know, Sam will tell us his future memories of our time say your plan is a brilliant success."

Sam took a step backward and pushed out with his hands. "Now hold on. I'm no historian. I've heard of you. I-I watched a movie about you. I barely remember it, but I think it was a comedy, so probably not very accurate. And you're remembered as a story, not history. Stories tend to be made up a little. Don't look to me to tell you what side of the bed you're going to wake up on."

All three of his audience gave Sam a puzzled look. Then Tuck said, "I know not the meaning of such words. Perhaps it would be best if Robin lay out his plan."

Robin sighed. "Very well. The Sheriff is sponsoring an archery tournament. The grand prize is an arrow made of purest silver tipped with gold. I plan to be the victor."

"Not for himself," Tuck interjected. "We have a buyer in France. Count Theobald of Blios. The sale of such an arrow will go a long way toward feeding those the Sheriff's greed has displaced."

"Provided I win," Robin concluded.

"Of course, you will win," Marian said, taking Robin into a warm embrace. "There is no greater bowman in all the world, never mind England." She stepped back. "This is how I know it is a trap."

"Of course, it is a trap," Robin agreed. "We simply have to outsmart the Sheriff and not get caught."

"Which he will be expecting," Marian argued.

Tuck pushed himself between the two. "Sam, what say you? You have seen this movie you speak of. What of Robin's attempt to circumvent the Sheriff's trap? Does he succeed?"

Sam worked his jaw open and closed, uncertain of what to say. "An archery tournament. That . . . sounds familiar. Beyond that, I can't remember. I'm sure everything ends well, the Sheriff in a snit and Robin and Marian happy ever after. But you know, a story needs conflict in the middle. No matter what really happened. Happens. Any story I saw had a lot of bad moments in the middle."

Robin rubbed his brow. "That is no help at all."

"What about you, Sam?" Tuck asked.

"Me?"

"Why are you here? If I remember correctly, the first time was to reveal wrongdoings in Camelot Castle for the Merlin. The second time it was to find the Merlin, who had gone missing. Are you here to find the wizard again?"

Sam shook his head. "Ain't got a clue. Those other times I agreed to come. First Merlin brought me here. Then it was the Lady of the Lake. This time I was snooping through a castle outside Hartford and somehow wound up here. That was a whopper of a surprise, I can tell you. I was thinking maybe Merlin could tell me what's going on, but you say he's missing. How about the Lady of the Lake? Maybe she can sort this out."

Tuck glanced at Robin. "No one has seen the Merlin since the fall of Camelot. It is said he left before the fighting. As for the Lady, well, the Lady of the Lake is dead."

9
THE WHITE LADY'S HAND

"Dead?"

Tuck nodded. "It saddens me to say, but yes. Now I think of it, it is the White Lady's death that set everything in motion."

Sam's cheek twitched. "How's that?"

The Friar placed a fist beneath his chin and looked up into the sky, as though searching for memories. "After rescuing the Merlin, you left Camelot rather abruptly. You may not know, Sam, that with the Grail returned to its rightful place and Morgan Le Fay and Mordred the Pretender encased in glass, that both King Arthur's health and Camelot's democracy were restored. All was well for two, three years. Then the Lady of the Lake appeared at court and announced to all and sundry that the end of Camelot was at hand. That the only way to save the kingdom was to execute a certain knight. Unfortunately, Sir Bors was King Arthur's favourite knight."

Sam knew the Lady was a tough cookie, but this seemed a bit much. "What did Arthur do?"

"The King, alas, would not hear of it," Tuck said. "Sir Bors, however, knowing the wisdom and power of the White Lady, volunteered to have his life ended and offered his sword to anyone who would end it for him.

"As you might imagine, King Arthur was flummoxed, both by the Lady's demand and by the knight's offer. As well, the Merlin was angry as I had ever seen him. The wizard argued with the White Lady. Truly argued. Their voices grew loud as thunder, and magical energy thrashed like lightning about the Greater Hall. In the confusion, King Arthur rose from his throne and, taking the sword from Sir Bors' hands, swung it in a mighty arc that sent the blade slicing through flesh, cartilage, and bone.

"Everything stopped. The shouts. The crying. The magic. The Merlin stood there, his jaw on his chest, his mouth agape, his eyes bulging. Sir Bors lay on the floor. Dead, yet his body intact. It was shock that killed the mighty knight, not the blade in Arthur's hands."

"Then, who did Arthur kill?" Sam asked.

"Why." Tuck swallowed. "'Twas the White Lady. At once the court erupted again. Crying. Yelling. Voices raised in wonder and despair. Only the Merlin remained silent. The magician sank to the floor on his knees and took the White Lady's hand in his. The Lady's pale, cooling hand.

"When peace was finally restored, the King remained furious. Furious that his friend had died. He demanded of the Merlin an explanation.

"The Merlin finally stood and gave the King an indecipherable look. 'It is as the Lady said. The end of Camelot.'

"'But Sir Bors is dead,' the King shouted. 'I tried to prevent it, but the blasted woman had her way in the end.'

"The Merlin let out a cold laugh. 'Dead, but not the way the Fates intended. The test was not his, my King, but yours. It was your pride the Lady tested. Which would you put first? Camelot? Or yourself? You failed the test.'

"'But,' Arthur sputtered, 'to kill a man for no reason?'

"The Merlin thrust his hand at the corpse of the fallen knight. 'It was his time. This day was Sir Bors' last no matter the circumstance. But you. You murdered an innocent woman. As you say, for no reason.'

"'But... she... she...' King Arthur's shoulders slumped, and his face took on more weight than its many years had earned. At last, he said, 'What should we do?'

"'Do whatever you like,' the Merlin answered. 'My time here is done. I will see to the Lady, that she receives a funeral worthy of her stature. But my work here is ended.'"

Sam pulled his fedora off his head and stood a moment in

silence. Out of shock or respect, he wasn't sure. "You were there?" he asked Tuck.

The corpulent friar nodded. "The Merlin insisted. And Galahad, also. Afterward, he told Galahad to take the Grail and keep it safe."

"How about you?" Sam asked. "What did Merlin tell you to do?"

Tuck shrugged. "To leave and keep myself safe. And one thing more. He told me a secret. That I'd know when and to whom I should tell it."

Sam flipped his fedora back onto his head. "I take it you think that time is now, and that person is me."

"I do."

"Right." Sam's cheek twitched again. "Give it to me."

The friar cast his gaze about to ensure he and Sam were alone. At the start of his tale, Robin and Marian, already familiar with Camelot's fall, had stepped away. Despite there being no one within hearing distance, Tuck lowered his voice to a whisper. "The Merlin told me that with the Lady's death, magic was done. He was leaving Camelot because he could no longer protect it."

"Well," Sam muttered. "That explains my beanshooter."

"What?"

Sam waved him off. "It's not important. So, Merlin is off on his own somewhere, the Lady of the Lake is dead, and I'm stuck here with no way home. That's just great."

"It does leave me with a question," Tuck whispered. "If magic is dead, how did you get here?"

"How," Sam agreed. "And why."

The crunch of a boot on dry twigs announced Robin's return. When the outlaw caught Sam's eye, he spoke. "Evening approaches. Tuck will find you some food and a place to sleep. On the morrow, we shall speak again."

"Yes," Tuck agreed, amusement returning to his face. "Let us find somewhere to sit, drink some mead, and share happier tales." The friar then slapped his belly. "With all this girth, I grow uncomfortable standing for any great length of time."

Sam wasn't so sure about sitting down, or about the mead, but happier tales sounded grand.

From what Sam could see, there was no organization to the camp. Saddles, sacks, and stacks of gathered wood lay strewn about as though dropped by a tornado. Clothing flapped in the breeze from lines strung between neighbouring trees. Here and there small cook fires burned. Members of Robin's band stood in small clusters or sat on logs, chatting among themselves or organizing their belongings. Some mended shirts or sharpened arrowheads. One skinned a rabbit, a sight Sam hoped he'd never witness again.

The friar led him to a quiet spot on the edge of the camp and promptly sat on a broad stump that served as a chair. Seeing nowhere for himself to sit, Sam piled up a blanket and several empty sacks to use as a cushion, and lowered his aching posterior onto the ground, more or less at the friar's feet.

Tuck nodded his approval before reaching behind the stump to scrounge up two small iron cups and a lidded metal pitcher the size of a coffee pot. After pouring a few ounces of liquid the colour and texture of coffee into one of the cups, the rotund churchman passed it to Sam.

"Made with honey from the apiary at St Mary's Abbey." Tuck's wide mouth stretched into a proud grin. "A brew guaranteed to cure what ails you."

A brief sniff told Sam the drink wasn't coffee sweetened with honey. It was mead. Not as strong-smelling as what he'd been served earlier that day at the Stag and Boar, but strong enough. He was lifting the cup to his lips when he noticed the grin fall from the friar's face.

"'Tis the murderer," Tuck grumbled. Begrudgingly, he reached behind the stump for a third cup.

Sam craned his neck and spotted the approaching murderer just as the newcomer spoke in a heavy, thunderous voice. "So, the prodigal pie has returned."

10
NOT JUST ANY MURDERER

"SAGRAMORE?"

Mystified, Sam watched as a tall, herculean man dressed in brown and black leather strode past him into the trees. A few moments later, the giant returned, hauling a stump of wood that must have weighed over one hundred pounds. He set the makeshift seat next to Tuck's, sat, smiled viciously, and accepted a cup from the reticent friar.

Sam took a small sip of mead, held it in his mouth where it burned his tastebuds to ashes, then let the spiced honey slide down his throat. Sagramore.

The villainous knight looked older than Sam remembered. Since he'd last seen his one-time adversary in Camelot's dungeon, the murderer's once-dark hair had gone grey, and a scar ran down his face from eyebrow to upper lip. The eye beneath the scar seemed to almost glow in the failing light, a pale white orb, blind. Life in Camelot's dungeon must have taken a bigger toll than Sam had thought.

"How are you not in prison?" Sam asked.

The knight scowled. "The dungeon is no more. As is the castle. And the city. The very memory of Camelot has been eradicated from the land."

The image the murderous knight painted was bleaker than the one Sam had gleaned from Tuck's story. "That's some news you're selling. You got anything to back it up?"

Sagramore snorted. "When the traitor Mordred came against Arthur—"

"Let me stop you there," Sam said, interrupting. "Mordred? No, of course. Never mind." It made sense. When magic failed, Mordred and Le Fay would have escaped Merlin's imprisonment. They probably wouldn't have been too happy with the old magician and his friends in Camelot either. Sam waved a hand at the scowling knight. "Go on."

Sagramore took a sip of mead, then cast Sam a cold glare. "When Mordred marched on Camlann with his sixty-thousand redshanks, routiers, and quartered men, King Arthur could see he was outmatched. Raising an army even half that size was a daunting task. As a matter of course, he emptied the dungeon and told us prisoners to stay and fight or leave and never return. Most left."

"Sir Sagramore stayed," Tuck said, though without enthusiasm. "And fought bravely," the friar grudgingly added.

Sagramore traced his scar with a calloused finger. "Sir no more. I am a mercenary now."

"Albeit a brave mercenary," Tuck said, sighing.

The ex-knight waved the churchman off and took another sip of mead. "I fought beside Arthur's knights and any townsfolk who could lift a sword against Mordred's rogues and mercenaries. How the traitor raised so great an army, no one ever learned, though rumour suggested he paid with fistfuls of diamonds.

"Mordred, we soon realized, had but one goal—the complete destruction of King Arthur and everything Arthur held dear. We engaged in battle on a broad field outside the city, but were soon forced to retreat to the very streets of Camelot, and finally to the castle itself. On the fifth day of the siege, Arthur admitted defeat, but Mordred would not accept surrender. The few of us who remained escaped through a secret tunnel beneath the castle and fled to the west. The traitor had won.

"We thought that the end of it, but no, Mordred was not satisfied to hold Camelot, but pursued us all the way to the shores of Avalon. There, in mortal combat, with his sword already blooded from days of battle, the traitor Mordred pierced our great King's noble heart."

"Let me guess," Sam said. "Three women dressed Arthur's

wounds and took him away in a boat."

Sagramore scowled. "Why do you make me recount this tragedy if you already know it?"

"It was just a guess. Go on."

The ex-knight took a sip of mead before continuing. "Your conjecture is on the mark. Witches three, kinfolk of the White Lady, dressed my King's wounds, though the effort was unfruitful. Arthur's injuries, as anyone could see, were grievous unto death. Even so, as they rowed the small boat toward the Isle of Glass, the witches foretold Arthur would one day return and re-establish Camelot."

A forced chuckle escaped Sagramore's lips. "But the witches were mad with grief over the loss of their cousin. All present knew the King's wounds were fatal.

"As I later discovered, so too were Camelot's. You see, the traitor Mordred returned to the city and ordered every remaining stone removed and scattered across the length and breadth of England. He forced men, many of them enslaved citizens, to build dams and alter the course of the river, leaving all of Camelot a desolation, never to recover. His mission accomplished, Mordred vanished from the face of the Earth, so neither I nor any of the others who survived the fall of Camelot, could seek him out and end his life."

Sagramore then leaned back on his stump and drained the remaining mead from his cup.

Sam rubbed his chin, then looked up at the freed murderer. "I thought I'd already heard the worst news of the day. Yours wins hands down. I never liked that Mordred mook."

The ex-knight and the friar bobbed their heads in agreement.

"And what news do *you* bring?" Sagramore asked. "I had thought to never again see your like, yet here you are. Sam Spade. What is your purpose? I hope it is to track down and murder that bearded coward, the Merlin."

Sam took a double take, if that was even possible while sitting on the ground. "What? Mordred's not bad enough? You want to blunt your blade on the magician as well?"

Sagramore waved his empty cup. "The old charlatan was nowhere to be found. Court magician! He could have used his magic to protect Arthur. Protect Camelot. But the mighty magician was fled."

"Right," Sam muttered. It would be easy to tell the irate knight that Merlin had lost his magic and couldn't protect a broom closet, never mind Camelot. But that wasn't Sam's secret to tell. He glanced up at Tuck, who remained silent.

Sagramore also turned his dark countenance on the friar. "Are you going to hoard that mead all night? Or can you spare a pour?"

As Tuck refilled Saggy's cup, Sam noticed the ex-knight was right. The woods beyond the camp had become gloomy to the point where the trees blurred into a solid wall. And the bits of sky he could see above the treetops were now several shades deeper, more purple than blue. In not many minutes, it would become too dark to see.

Born and raised in East Hartford, Sam had never had to deal with getting around in the dark. He'd been spoiled by streetlamps lighting the roads, electric fixtures inside buildings, and when times got tough, a flashlight in hand to get you to the fuse box.

Even in Camelot there'd been page boys with lanterns. Sam hadn't seen a single lantern in the camp and didn't know if he could handle a night in the woods.

He blamed his father for most of the tragedy in his life. A dirty cop murdered in jail when Sam was twelve, Sydney Sparrow had been the world's worst parent. If he had taken Sam camping, just once, Sam might have an idea of how to cope. But whenever the topic came up, dear old Dad had been quick with a "Next summer." Yeah. Right. As if that was ever going to happen. Even if Officer Sydney Sparrow hadn't ended his life on a cold prison floor, he would never have made the time for taking his kid into the woods overnight. Sam's mother had called her husband a workaholic which, looking back, was one of the nicer things she had called him. But Sam figured between legitimate police work and illegal police work, Sydney Sparrow hadn't had much time left for family.

Rubbing his ear, he watched as one of the camp women arranged rags and shaved wood on a patch of cleared ground. A second woman stood by with a stone in one hand and a knife in the other. She knelt by the kindling and struck the knife edge against the stone. Sparks flew, eventually setting the rags and shaved wood alight.

Sam nodded, impressed. He'd heard you could make sparks with rocks, but he'd never seen it done. Still, he thought it odd

Robin hadn't stolen some matches along with everything else he was returning to the poor.

Six months or a year ago Sam would have had matches or a lighter in his pocket. Starting a fire would have been child's play. Now all he had were nicotine patches.

Since he was a young boy, Sam had idolized Humphrey Bogart. He'd watched *Casablanca* so many times he could quote Rick Blaine almost word for word. Bogart's performance as Charlie Allnutt in *The African Queen* made him long to visit Africa. Then there was *The Maltese Falcon*. Sam's resentment toward his criminal father had prevented him from seeing the film until recently, but Bogart's delivery in the film of a cunning yet flawed Sam Spade had only raised Sam's already high opinion of the actor. It was at best unfortunate that Bogart had been a chain smoker and an alcoholic.

At the tender age of nineteen, Bogart had been expelled from high school for the measly crime of enjoying alcohol and cigarettes. As a screen actor, Bogart had made smoking cool, and Sam Sparrow had not been immune. Sam had started combing his hair like Rick Blaine and puffing on cancer sticks at every opportunity. In no time at all he was up to two packs a day. It wasn't until five or so years later that Sam learned his idol had been killed in the prime of his career by esophageal cancer. Since then, Sam had spent more years trying to quit than he had enjoying the habit.

He'd tried everything from chewing gum to hypnosis. Nothing worked. This was his second go with nicotine patches. His first attempt had been while he was still a cop. They'd made him irritable, gave him headaches, and wonky dreams had kept him up nights. But maybe that had just been from being a cop. He'd decided to give it another shot. So far, it hadn't been too bad. After a week, or almost a week, his fingers twitched less and he'd only felt occasional nausea. In a month, when he ran out of patches, he'd either be cancer-stick-free or jonesing for a hit. The latter could be a problem. He had no idea how to score a smoke in a bandit-infested forest.

Thinking about cigarettes made Sam's fingers twitch. He addressed the problem with the only vice at hand. Raising the metal cup to his lips, he took a second small sip of fermented honey. The liquid burned as hard as it had the first go as it passed his lips, tongue, and throat. When it settled in his stomach, it became heartburn. Sam had never been good at drinking on an empty stomach. Food. He needed something solid.

Looking up at Sagramore, Sam saw the ex-knight had finished half his refilled cup. The murderer stared at Sam with his one good eye. "You haven't answered my question, pie. Why are you here in Sherwood Forest?"

Sam took a deep breath. "I wish I knew. Could be I'm here by accident. Just dumb luck. I was working this missing person's case at this partially reconstructed castle back home. One minute I'm there. The next I'm here. Maybe the person I'm looking for also ended up here. Fellow goes by the name Sean Regan. He was last seen headed for the same castle. And I got separated from my partner Nora Clark. I'm pretty sure she ended up here as well."

Sagramore seemed to consider this, then shook his head. "You are a confusing man, Merlin's pie."

The sky continued to darken, and it surprised Sam how little light the cook fire generated. There were more of them now, all throughout the camp. The one he had watched being lit now included an assembly of thin sticks that held the skinned rabbit he had seen earlier. The flayed animal looked awful, but the aroma of meat cooking only made him hungrier. He hadn't eaten since breakfast. That felt like a year ago.

"I must go seek my supper," Sagramore said, rising from his stump and handing his empty cup to Tuck. He gave Sam one last look. "I suspect we shall have more to discuss on the morrow." Then he was gone.

Tuck snorted. "Not even a thank you."

"I take it you and Saggy aren't buddies," Sam suggested as he climbed to his feet. Carefully, he stretched some of the ache out of his backside before taking the ex-knight's place on the makeshift seat.

The friar let out a long, deep breath. "I know not the meaning of the word *buddies*, but if you suggest we are not friends, you speak truly."

"And why is that? You seemed impressed that he stood up for Arthur at Camelot."

"Yet he is a murderer," Tuck hissed. "And not just any murderer, he murdered a brother knight."

Sam smiled. "If you're gonna hold that against him, you

should know he's also an adulterer. Lancelot's wife, no less."

The churchman sniffed. "Show me a nobleman who is not an adulterer, and I shall show you a nobleman who has never been wed."

"Yeah," Sam said. "I see your point. But maybe you should cut Saggy some slack. He spent a decade in a dungeon, then fought to protect the king who put him there. There's not a lot of men who would do that."

The friar took Sam's mostly still-full cup, downed its contents, then set the metal utensil behind his seat. "What you say has merit. I shall think on it. Are you ready for a bite of supper?"

"I could eat a horse," Sam admitted.

Tuck's jaw dropped. "Only pagans eat horseflesh. Is this Connecticut you come from godless?"

"We've got churches," Sam said, "though I read somewhere that Connecticut ranks as the eighth-most godless state in the union. Not something to be proud of, I suppose. But I wasn't speaking literally. Hungry enough to eat a horse just means I'm really hungry."

"So, you don't eat horseflesh?" Tuck insisted.

Sam glanced over at the cook fire. "I don't even eat rabbit, but if that's my only choice, I'll give it a whirl."

11
NO KISSES FOR SAM

SAM SLEPT BADLY.

He didn't think it was from the nicotine strips. He just wasn't used to sleeping outdoors under an open sky, an entrée for insects. The ground was hard, and his body still ached from his time in the saddle. The mead Tuck had given him alleviated some of the discomfort, but the contents of the tiny cup only went so far, medicinally. Then there was the cacophony of snoring from others in the camp, enough voices to make an orchestra. By the time the sun cracked the sky and his fellow campers began preparing breakfast, Sam wasn't sure he'd slept at all.

In a half-asleep stupor, he emerged from his borrowed blanket and sat on Sagramore's stump until Tuck thrust a bowl into his hands. "What's this?"

"Porridge." The friar sat on his stump holding his own bowl. "Not as tasty as last night's venison, but it fills the stomach."

"Is that what that was?" Sam hadn't questioned the mystery meat when the camp women roasted it over the fire and brought it around. He hadn't eaten since breakfast an ungodly number of hours earlier and would have eaten anything.

Sam stared at the bowl Tuck gave him. "How am I supposed to eat this?"

The friar grinned, then stuck two fingers into his own bowl and shovelled a portion of sticky goop into his mouth.

"Terrific," Sam muttered.

Porridge had never been Sam's favourite, but he could stomach the stuff. The contents of the bowl, however, looked nothing like porridge. It was dark, gooey, and had the texture of stucco. His fingers told him the mash was warm, and he lifted a small amount to his mouth. To his surprise, it tasted like porridge. And mead. "Honey?"

Tuck laughed. "Of course. Unsweetened porridge is hardly edible."

"I can agree with you there."

Though not exactly starving, Sam had no idea when or what he'd eat next, and figured he should get while the getting was good. After licking the bowl clean, he contemplated asking if there was more.

Tuck, however, snatched away the empty bowl. "We are leaving forthwith. If you wish to visit the bushes . . ."

Sam didn't need to ask for an explanation. By the time he was done, Tuck had joined Robin, Little John, Sagramore, and several others where they stood in a loose huddle. One of the men was the young blond fellow who took part in robbing the carriage the previous day. Despite his golden locks, the men all called him Will Scarlet.

"We cannot take the horses," Robin announced to his Merry Men. "The Sheriff's agents will be on the alert for us. We must needs walk afoot into Nottingham in twos and threes, with the air of simple folk. Rough men with neither heavy purse nor familiarity with horses."

"I certainly qualify," Sam quipped. He was still feeling yesterday's hours in the saddle and figured a brisk walk would work out some of the kinks.

Robin failed to crack a smile and kept his serious gaze focused on his men. "Should we find ourselves obliged to hide along the way, it will be easier if we don't have horses to hide as well."

Little John expelled a loud harrumph. "If you insist on going ahead with this foolhardy plan, we must depart at once. Should we need to avoid the Sheriff's patrols, our journey will take longer than it would otherwise."

Tuck had been standing only a few minutes, but sweat rolled down his cherub face. "I shall only slow you afoot, yet I wish to be nearby in the event I am needed. I shall ride out, alone, to the

Hospital of St John the Baptist to help tend the sick. Should you require aid, you will find me there."

"That is perhaps for the best," Robin agreed. "The Sheriff knows you and will be sure to have given your description to his men."

Tuck laughed and rubbed his belly. "I am a hard man to miss."

Sagramore stepped forward and slapped the friar on the back. "I shall walk in your stead. That little snot Vaisey will not recognize me. Instead of defending Camelot with Robin and the other young knights, he ran back to Nottingham with his tail between his legs. He was a page when last we crossed paths. And I, well, I have changed much since then." Like the previous evening, the aging ex-knight fingered the scar that ran down his face.

The friar seemed no more accepting of the murderer than the night before, but Sam noted Tuck didn't complain about the familiar contact.

"We can well use your assistance," Robin told the ex-knight. "If there is trouble, you will be more help than you know."

Sam believed it. The first time he'd visited Camelot, Saggy had stood among the three most capable knights in the kingdom. Though a dozen years had passed, and life behind bars had not been kind, Sam doubted any of Vaisey's men could stand against the ex-knight. That, and while most of Robin's Merry Men carried bows, Saggy wore a scabbard at his hip.

Without further ado, Robin raised two fingers to his lips. At the call, people moved, grabbing cloaks and bags they could hang from the waist or shoulder. Most of the men slipped a leather quiver across their back that held an unstrung bow and a bundle of arrows. Several of the camp women hugged their men and kissed them farewell.

No kisses for Tuck, however, as the portly friar retrieved a sack from behind his stump and struck off toward where the horses were tethered.

No kisses for Sam either.

His cheek twitched as he found himself wondering where Nora might be, if she was lost somewhere near Locksley Castle, or if she was still in Hartford wondering what had happened to him. He shook himself. Why did kisses make him think of Nora? She was his business partner. Important to him, of course. But there had never been romance. Even the flirting he had wondered about the day before could have been innocent. Was probably innocent. Was for sure innocent. They worked together, that was all. Still, he envied the looks exchanged between the men and women of the camp.

Sam had been a loner his entire life. The few attempts he'd made at dating had been a disaster, and he'd quickly given up. The closest he'd come to having a special someone was with Lady Euphemia Peregrine when he was in Camelot. The daughter of a duke, who had been his assistant and who was as intelligent as she was beautiful. They'd flirted, or at least he'd thought they had. Effie's father had given his blessing. Then Sam had discovered his feelings weren't returned, that Effie couldn't return them. It wasn't in her nature.

"You coming, pie?"

Sam shook himself again and saw Saggy waiting for him. The Merry Men had already gone ahead, out of sight.

Dressed in his trench coat and fedora, Sam realized he was as ready as he could be. There was no sack for him to grab from behind the stump that sat next to Tuck's. Not even a box lunch for later in the day. He didn't like feeling unprepared, but that was all he'd felt since squeezing through the bolthole of Sternwood Castle. That his magic beanshooter was no longer magic was maybe the worst of it. That, and having no idea how to get home.

Sam shook himself one last time and mentally girded his loins. Whatever happened next, he'd make the best of it. After all, there wasn't much else he could do.

"Right behind you," Sam called to the waiting ex-knight. "Right behind you."

12
THE PERFECT STRANGER

As ROBIN HOOD and his Merry Men ghosted through Sherwood Forest, Sam found himself half-walking and half-running to keep up. His hips and legs ached from his time in the saddle the previous day, but the thrumming pain eventually faded to a kind of background noise, overtaken by blisters forming on his toes and the soles of his feet. His previous visits to the past had had their share of challenges, but this time he just wasn't catching a break.

Sam tried to distract himself by counting trees, picturing in his head scenes from various Bogart films, and trying to remember the plot of that Mel Brooks movie he had watched as a teenager. He remembered the title now. *Robin Hood: Men in Tights*. Well, Brooks got that part wrong. Most of Robin's men wore wool pants, dyed, as David of Doncaster had said, green or brown or a mix of the two colours. How much else had the movie gotten wrong? Sam also remembered there had been an archery tournament. He couldn't remember the details, but he didn't think Robin had walked away with a fancy golden arrow.

At some point, Sam grew too exhausted to think about distractions. Robin had to stop soon. Right? For a rest if nothing else. Sherwood Forest couldn't go on forever.

Apparently, manly men from the days of yore didn't believe in rest breaks. It wasn't until the forest gave signs of ending that

Robin slowed their pace and they came to a stop.

"This is where we part ways," Robin said. "Does everyone understand their part?"

A chorus of "Aye" and nodding heads greeted their leader.

Most of the men wore clothes other than their forest garb, disguises to pass as villagers and farmers come to watch the contest. Dark pants, white shirts, and wool tunics. Several wore hoods, which they now pulled up over their heads, casting their faces in shadow.

Sam had no disguise, but wore his trademark tan trench coat and fedora. He would have felt better about it if his gun were still magic, but you had to play the hand you're dealt. His job was to enter Nottingham first, alone, and grab the attention of the Sheriff's soldiers and spies. A distraction. Not only was his attire distinctive, but few, if any, inhabitants would have seen him years earlier at Camelot. He would be the perfect stranger.

"Walk in that direction," Robin said to Sam, pointing through the remainder of the trees. "After a few yards you will come to The King's Great Way. Go south until you cross the Day Brook Bridge. A short distance after, you will come to the Mansfield Gate of Nottingham Township."

Robin turned to the big ex-knight, who stood out almost as much as Sam did with his head-to-toe leather mercenary outfit and three-foot sword. "Sagramore, you will follow just out of view. Should Sam find himself in danger, go to his aid. Otherwise, your height and your sword should distract anyone who doesn't follow Sam into the town."

The Thief of Sherwood Forest stood back and folded his arms across his chest. "This diversion will work best if you stay away from the tournament until Kevin of Gunthorp is called to the line."

"How will we know when that is?" Sam asked.

Little John laughed. "There will be criers in the street, announcing the lineup and the results. Most of the folk coming to town will only be interested in contests they have money on."

"I get it," Sam said. "Kind of like the races back home." He and Nora had been hired several times by clients wanting evidence of their spouses' gambling habits.

David of Doncaster thrust a leather wineskin into his hands. Sam raised it to his lips thinking he'd finally caught a break; mead wasn't really his thing. But the skin contained only water. Sam sighed and passed it back. Maybe he could scrounge beer or wine or something more to his liking in the town.

Sam set out and soon found the road. It looked much the same as the one where they had robbed the carriage, just a wide dirt track. With no one in sight, he left the trees and began his trek toward town. Almost immediately, a pair of young men on horseback came up behind him and slowed to take in his unusual attire.

"Where do you hail from?" one of the young men called to him.

Sam searched for a response, settling finally on, "France."

"Do all Frenchmen dress as you?" the other called.

Sam shook his head. "Only the more fashionable ones."

"Fashionable?" The two men cast each other confused looks.

Taking in their plain pants and shirts, Sam added, "Nothing you'll ever have to worry about."

The two men frowned, then kicked their horses in the ribs with the heels of their boots. Sam choked on dust as they shot ahead of him. Maybe he shouldn't have added that last bit.

Additional traffic appeared on the road, people riding on horseback or in carriages or wagons. All but a few travelled toward Nottingham, some with goods, others with little more than good spirits. Sam guessed this archery tournament must be a pretty big deal.

Invariably, the travellers gawked at Sam. Some, like the two men on horseback, tried to engage in conversation. Saying as little as possible seemed safest, so they quickly let him be. Sam didn't feel too bad about it. He wasn't here to make friends.

Of course, he had no idea why he was here at all. Sure, to help Robin Hood benefit the poor by winning an archery contest. But why was he here in Sherwood Forest, and not in Connecticut? What had happened to bring him thousands of miles and hundreds of years from home? Or who had happened? It took magic and some kind of intelligence to move someone across the centuries. It couldn't be a coincidence he'd been brought to Robin and Tuck.

Three trips across time. Six months apart for him, and six years for everyone else. Despite what Tuck and Sagramore had told him about dire events in Camelot after he had left, and magic failing, someone with magic must have consciously brought him back again. And must have done it for a reason.

If Merlin no longer had magic, and the Lady of the Lake was dead, then it had to be someone else. But who? Was there someone from the Robin Hood story who had magic? Sam couldn't recall anyone. It seemed more likely that Merlin had found magic somewhere and had made this happen. If so, the old wizard must have a plan of some kind. But what?

Maybe Merlin was somewhere in Nottingham and all would be revealed. That seemed the most likely explanation of why Sam had arrived here and not somewhere else. But why hadn't the old goat brought him to Nottingham directly? Or met him at Locksley Castle?

Sam knew all he had was wild speculation. Wishful thinking. But searching Nottingham for the wizard, and for Nora—she could be there as well—would give him something to do while he waited for Robin to enter the tournament.

As the morning wore on, he kept checking his watch. Four hours passed before he came to what he figured was Day Brook, though sluggish water and grassy embankments made the waterway seem more like a manmade canal. A dusty wooden bridge with no side rails and in desperate need of repair allowed The King's Great Way to cross to the other side. Sam couldn't see any buildings up ahead, so he figured he still had a way to go. Which was disappointing, as his feet were killing him.

The air felt hot and humid, just like back home in summer. Though he was no longer in Sherwood Forest, and much of the land had been cleared for farms, there were still plenty of trees. Sam could almost believe he was in Connecticut, Wickham Park or one of the farms outside Bolton.

Sweat trickled down his forehead and into his eyes, and blisters burned the bottom of his feet. Sam was used to walking. As a cop he'd been a flatfoot, spending most of his time pounding a beat rather than driving a cruiser. And as a PI he did his share of walking the streets of Hartford. But those experiences were nothing like this endless trek through forest and along a hardpacked dirt road. Civilized people took breaks. They sat in cafés drinking coffee, and leafed through newspapers and magazines in waiting rooms.

Sam couldn't help but laugh. Civilization hadn't been invented yet. He should count himself lucky he had a good pair of shoes.

Thinking back, he realized he'd been subconsciously looking for a place to stop and rest. A bench. A rock to sit on. But there'd been nothing. Besides, if he stopped, he might not start again. Nottingham had to be just up ahead. He'd get there soon enough.

The sound of birds made Sam crane his neck. The sky was clear, hardly a cloud in sight and no wind to speak of. Perfect weather for an archery tournament, he supposed. A flock of grey and white birds landed in the branches of a spreading tree, leaving a single black bird circling above. The bird looked suspiciously like a crow. Surely not the same crow from his escape from Locksley Castle?

Sam watched as it swooped down and flitted onto a branch that hung over the road just ahead of him. The crow cawed and looked at Sam, then ruffled its black feathers. It sure looked like the same bird Sam had seen while fleeing Mel Gibson and his clan. But didn't all crows look alike?

"Thanks for the help yesterday," he told it, just in case.

The crow cawed again, then flew off toward Nottingham.

After a few more minutes of walking, Sam finally saw in the distance what looked like a building blocking the end of the road. As he drew closer, he realized it wasn't a building, but a wall that extended in both directions, obscured to either side by clusters of trees. Soon he made out battlements where archers could shoot from between the crenels. What kind of town was Nottingham? He'd expected a quaint little village. Maybe two streets of shops surrounded by a few rows of houses. And a field for football games and archery contests. But here was a fortification wall and a guarded gate.

Sam spied a gathering of people, including carts and carriages that had passed him on the road, waiting to enter the town. As he joined the back of the line, he looked along the wall, which seemed endless, and saw a dirt path separated it from the forest. And to the east, what looked like people milling in front of another gate.

He scrutinized the wall, the battlements, the dirt track, and the trees lining the path, but didn't see any soldiers. Why would someone fortify a town, but not man the fortifications? Or were the soldiers hidden, and this was all part of Vaisey's trap?

A tide of whispers rose, then went silent as the people in front of Sam began to notice him. One by one, everyone turned, until all eyes were on Sam. Most seemed curious. Other shocked. Some appeared entertained. Sam smiled and touched the edge of his fedora, all to show that he not only dressed funny, but could exhibit odd behaviour as well.

A young boy, maybe nine years old, stared at Sam. "Are you an angel?"

"No, kid, I ain't no angel. I'm a foreigner."

The boy thought about that. "Are not angels foreigners? They visit us from a land called Heaven."

Exhausted from the long walk, Sam rested his hands on his knees and leaned forward, bringing his face closer to the boy's. "I'm from a place called Hartford. I've never heard anyone call it Heaven."

"Maybe you are an angel and do not know it," the boy suggested.

Sam chuckled. "That would be nice if it were true."

"Hey! You there. Leave my boy be." A woman in a bulky array of flowing cloth appeared from the mob, took the boy by the arm, and pulled him a yard or so away from Sam.

"We were just passing the time," Sam said.

"Siward, you know better than to talk to strangers," the mother scolded her son.

"Or angels," Sam shouted as she pulled the boy deeper into the crowd.

Now that Sam had been well and truly rebuked, the rest of the mob seemed content, apart from odd looks and the occasional stink eye, to leave him alone.

As the line moved slowly forward, new arrivals crowded behind him. Sam was struck by a moment of déjà vu from his last visit to the DMV. He was hot, sweating beneath his trench coat, suit coat, and hat. The soles of his feet burned, and his fingers itched for a cigarette.

With the hasty departure after breakfast, Sam had forgotten to replace his nicotine patch. He was hours overdue, and his body had leached every last milligram of chemicals from the square on his shoulder. As soon as he entered the town, he'd have to find a quiet place and apply a new one.

Eventually the shuffling line brought Sam close to the gate, where he spied the leather coats and caps of soldiers. There were four of them, and they looked to be inspecting each visitor. Not a body search or anything, just a good look at their faces and dress, and anything they carried. He could just imagine their reaction when it was his turn. In his mind he heard Jack Nicholson's voice as the Joker from the *Batman* movie: "Wait till they get a load of me."

All was not going well, however. Before letting each person into the town, the guards were demanding some kind of payment. A toll? A bribe? Most visitors seemed willing to offer a coin for entry, but the soldiers were holding out for several. Sam watched as a thin man dressed in rags haggled, eventually opening the heavy bag he carried and handing over a chicken.

When Sam's turn came up, he realized he had no coins. Or chickens. His wallet held a few greenbacks, not that Washington, Lincoln, or Jackson would mean anything to medieval soldiers. Nor would the shiny new VISA card he'd applied for after Nora helped him clean up his credit rating.

He wasn't completely without coins. There were two in his pocket: an American Silver Eagle dollar, and the slightly larger silver Pendragon he kept as a souvenir from Camelot. Sam didn't think he could bring himself to part with either.

"Five pennies," a soldier spat at Sam after looking him up and down. The soldier took a longer look, then frowned. "No foreign coin neither. Short-cross pennies only."

Well, that solved the problem of parting with his coins.

"Five pennies!" Sam blurted, knowing from observation that this was the expected response. "That's robbery."

The soldier regarded him. "That be the price. If you have no coin, mayhap you have somewhat tucked away in that fancy dress of yours for trade."

Sam realized he'd have to wrap this up quick, then try to climb over the wall somewhere. His job was to distract, and he'd done that. Getting arrested by the soldiers wouldn't be any help.

Even so, he couldn't resist upping his game. He sucked in a lungful of air and let out a dramatic huff. "I'm not wearing a dress. It's a suit."

"And a fine suit at that," announced a gruff voice from behind him.

Sam turned and found Sagramore towering over the rest of the crowd.

The scarred ex-knight grinned. "Watching your comic

exchange is well worth the price of five pennies." He tossed several coins toward the soldier, who scrambled to catch them. Before the man could regain his balance, Sagramore tossed five more. "You have there ten pennies, and more than I pay in a month to enter other towns. I shall not be visiting Nottingham again any time soon."

The soldier stood counting coins as Sam and then Sagramore shuffled past him, through the gate, and into a crowded street.

"I appreciate the loan," Sam said to Sagramore. "I don't suppose you could spot me beer money?"

The old knight snorted. "What I gave the guard was my own beer money. I fail to understand how Vaisey has not already come to an untimely end."

"Is that why you're really here?" Sam asked. "To help Robin deliver retribution on the man who murdered his father? Or is there another reason?"

Sagramore ran a finger along his scar. "A worthy question. What I truly seek is to make amends for the murder that put me in the dungeon."

"Lancelot?"

The knight nodded. "At the time, my brother knight was so dishonourable in his behaviour, I felt justified in what I gave him. A decade in prison has granted me a new perspective."

"So, Lancelot didn't deserve death for his philandering?" Sam suggested, just to make sure he was hearing the old murderer correctly.

Sagramore snarled his upper lip. "Oh, no. The scoundrel deserved that and more. But it was not my place to be judge, jury, and executioner. Nor was it honourable to allow someone else to take the blame for my act of hubris."

"You know," Sam said, "when we first met, you insisted I call you Sir, but I wouldn't do it. Where I come from, Sir has to be earned, not from a king, but from behaving like a man who deserves the honorific. From what you said just now, I am happy to call you Sir Sagramore."

"But . . ." the old knight took a step back. "I am no longer a knight. My title was stripped from me when I was sent to the dungeon."

"You never had that title from me," Sam said. "Now I give it to you. From now on, in my eyes, you are Sir Sagramore."

"I—I do not know what to say."

Sam passed his gaze along the cobblestone street that led into the heart of Nottingham. A small sign on the wall named it Cow Lane, and it did seem wide enough to lead a cow, though maybe not a fat one. A raised sidewalk ran along one side, but it was so uneven and constricted as to be unusable. Instead, people, carts, and horses all dodged each other as they plodded along in both directions along the narrow lane.

"I know what you can say," Sam suggested. "Say you have some idea where Merlin might hide if he were spending time in this backwater town."

"The Merlin?" Sagramore seemed taken aback. "Why would the wizard be here?"

"He probably isn't," Sam admitted. "But if he is, I'd like to find him."

Sagramore shrugged. "I have seen much of Nottingham since coming here in the aftermath of Camelot, but not all. Still. There is a street of shops near the east wall that caters to the more learned among us. That may be your best hope for finding one such as the Merlin."

"Terrific. I'll do that. Then I'll see you later at the tournament. What are you going to do before then?"

A wide grin stretched across the ex-knight's face, intensifying his ugly scar. "Near the north wall is a street of shops that caters to the less learned among us. While I no longer have coin to dampen my throat or sharpen my blade, perhaps I may yet trade for the opportunity."

"Trade?" Sam asked.

"Information, perhaps. Or unpaid bill collections. I have recently accumulated some experience in that regard."

Sam nodded. "Oh yes, I can see that career working out very well for you."

13
MORE BEAUTIFUL THAN I REMEMBER

SAM GLANCED OVER his shoulder a few times as he navigated Cow Lane toward the centre of Nottingham, dodging visitors and townsfolk alike who gawked at his tan trench coat and fedora. He figured there were at least two men following him. Mid-twenties, dressed in clothes that were common enough, but looked brand new or had been washed and pressed that morning. Most everyone else on the street looked like they'd been wearing the same clothes for a week. Maybe slept in them as well.

Cow Lane ended after one city block, revealing a crowded open market on the right and a street called Great Smith Gate on the left. Sam turned the corner. After a minute he looked back to find the two men still tailing him, only there appeared to be three of them now. He wondered how many were following Sagramore.

Half a block along, his path merged with another lane and changed its name to Swine Green, which changed again to Goose Gate after crossing Stoney Street. There were fewer people, so the men tailing him had to hang further back. The next street didn't seem to have a name, and the one after that was called Halifax Lane. It was all but deserted and twisted south parallel to the town wall.

Sam had a good feeling it was the street Sagramore had mentioned. Maybe a dozen narrow shops stood built against the wall, with another dozen standing opposite. Storefronts offered signs like Aesop's Apothecary, Quality Candles, and The Hattery. But one caught Sam's eye—Pallium's Parchments.

A wooden sign above the door stood engraved with the two words against a background of what Sam assumed was an image of parchment paper. Back in Merlin's office in Camelot, the old wizard had kept very few possessions, but Sam remembered they'd included a number of dusty books and parchments.

After standing in the middle of the street for a moment, rubbing his jaw, Sam glanced back the way he had come and spied the three who had followed him lingering at the side of the lane, pretending they had no interest in him. They looked so conspicuous he almost laughed. But he and Sagramore had done their job. Hopefully, there were now fewer such men at the town gate to follow the Merry Men into Nottingham.

His favour for Robin accomplished, he now had his own job to do: find Merlin so he could figure out why he was once again wandering about the days of yore. He figured Pallium's Parchments was as good a place as any to start. Stepping up to the door, he took hold of the handle and pulled it open.

The shop's musty interior stood cloaked in darkness. Sam had noticed the proliferation of shutters on the windows but assumed they would somehow let some light inside. He was wrong. The only light seemed to consist of what he was letting in through the open doorway. Was the shop closed due to the tournament?

Squinting into the shadows, Sam saw what appeared to be a large table taking up the centre of the room. Sheets of parchment or thin books lay side by side around the table's perimeter. There also appeared to be bookshelves along the walls to either side, but he couldn't make out their contents. A long counter occupied the back of the room, its surface littered with more side-by-side parchments or books. Someone leaned against the wall behind the counter, but Sam could make out no details. He assumed this to be the proprietor.

Allowing the door to swing shut, sending the shop back into near-total darkness, Sam reached into his trench coat pocket and took a firm grip on his penlight. If things started to go sideways, he'd turn it on and blind the proprietor. Sometimes a twenty-dollar penlight from Walmart was all you needed to diffuse a situation.

He waited a few moments for his eyes to adjust enough to

avoid the table, then stepped up to the counter.

"Not much of a book shop, is it?" he said by way of greeting, borrowing from Monty Python's infamous cheese shop sketch. "How am I expected to find a particular book if I can't see to find my way among the shelves?"

"You are here to buy a book?" The voice was female, crisp, and oddly familiar.

"This is a book shop, isn't it?" Sam countered.

"Sam?" The voice was definitely familiar.

"Effie?"

"Oh, Sam, what are you doing here?"

"I could ask the same thing."

Sam couldn't believe it. How was it possible? The first door in Nottingham he walks through just happens to be where Effie is working? "Lady Euphemia Peregrine! This shop is a far cry from clerking for a crime-fighting wizard."

Effie's laugh permeated the darkness. "There are no more wizards. Have you not heard? Magic is lost."

So, Tuck wasn't the only one who carried that little secret. "Did Merlin tell you that?"

"The Merlin? No. But, is it not obvious? I have seen not one work of magic since before the Merlin left Camelot."

"Someone must have magic," Sam suggested. "They brought me here."

He heard movement. Footsteps. Then Effie was on his side of the counter, crushing him in a huge embrace, which he gladly returned.

"I've missed you, Sam."

"Uh, you too, Effie. Though for me it's only been six months."

Effie released the hug and stepped back. Sam could barely make out her outline in the darkened room.

"Six months." Effie echoed his words. "So strange. Every several years I see you for a few days, during which time you turn my life upside down. Then you are gone again."

"Not by choice," Sam said. "We're both pawns in other people's games of magic."

"Only there is no more magic," Effie insisted. "But you are right. How is it you are here otherwise?"

"As usual," Sam said, "I'll be the last to know."

Six years since Effie had seen him, making her almost as old as he was. Could that be why fate had brought him back? Maybe a relationship was meant to be now their ages weren't mismatched. But was Effie still . . . a ladies' woman?

"Are you with someone?" Sam asked.

"With someone?" Effie echoed uncertainly. "Do you mean married?" She laughed. "You see true despite the poor light. I am an old maid now. But I told you I would not marry. Could not."

"Of course. And your father, the Duke?"

"Gone these many years," Effie said. "Before the fall of Camelot, fortunately."

"Effie?"

"Yes."

"Why is it so dark in here? I can hardly see you."

More movement. Then Effie was back behind the counter. A light flared as she lit a match and set it against a wick, then another. The candles burned like twin suns, illuminating the counter and Effie's face. Sam made out the familiar noble nose, wide-set eyes, and flowing blonde hair. Her jaw stood firm and strong, her mouth round with full lips. The brave woman he remembered from his two visits to Camelot.

But there was something else. A long scar much like Sagamore's, only finer, ran up her right cheek, past her ear, and into her hairline. Tears glistened in Effie's eyes as she read Sam's gaze.

Sam smiled. "You're more beautiful than I remember."

14
A REAL NOTTINGHAM BOOKSTORE

EFFIE DID A repeat performance of running around the counter and throwing her arms around Sam. Her breath was hot on his cheek as she whispered, "But I am hideous."

Sam laughed. "Where I'm from, you'd be a much-beloved heroine in an action movie. Besides, your scar has nothing on Sir Sagramore's."

Effie pulled herself away. "*Sir* Sagramore? The knight who lost his title and was confined to the dungeon?"

"That's the guy," Sam said. "Only, he's earned a title from me. He's here in Nottingham."

Confusion creased her forehead. "Sagramore is in Nottingham? Did he not die in Camelot's dungeon?"

"No. They let him out to fight Mordred's army. Unfortunately, it wasn't enough to save the city. He got the scar as a souvenir."

"As did I," Effie said.

"You fought at Camelot?" Sam asked.

"Of course, I fought. Well, actually I did not do any fighting. I was a spy in Mordred's camp. But, oh, enough of me. Why is it you are here?"

"No idea," Sam said, though he wanted to say it was for him and Effie to live happily ever after. "I'm hoping to find Merlin so he can answer that question."

"The Merlin?"

"I figured if he was anywhere near Nottingham, he'd visit this book shop. While in Camelot, I noticed he had a fondness for books."

"Books," Effie echoed.

"Have you seen him?" Sam asked. "Merlin?"

Effie pursed her lips, then looked at the ceiling. "Here is the thing, Sam. Pallium's Parchments is not, in truth, a book shop."

"It isn't?"

"No. Well. Occasionally someone buys a book or a parchment. But that is not why they come here."

"Okay."

Effie stared at Sam a moment.

Sam stared back. He hoped with all his heart she wasn't going to tell him the place was a brothel. "So why do they come here?"

"To . . ." Effie let the word linger in the air. "They come here to—"

She had been about to tell him. Sam knew she was going to. But just then the door to the shop opened and a man stepped inside, closing the door quickly behind him.

"Oh," he said, noticing Sam standing at the counter. "You are with another customer. I shall return anon." Even in the poor light cast by the two candles, Sam could see the man's face flush red before he fled back through the doorway.

"Drat," Effie said. "Mr. Geiger will not be pleased."

"Is Geiger your pimp?" Sam asked, his heart sinking. Things had been going so well up to now.

"Pimp? I am unfamiliar with the word. Arthur Geiger is the owner of the shop. I am his clerk."

"Clerk," Sam echoed.

"Well, more than a clerk. Mr. Geiger is never here, so I more or less run the shop."

"I don't see how he'd be much use," Sam said, unable to help himself.

"Oh, he can do the job," Effie replied. "He taught me how to do it. Even with some of the more difficult clients."

"I don't think I need any details," Sam said.

"With the tournament this afternoon," Effie added. "I have had a busy morning. Once the tournament starts, I shall be run off my feet."

"What is it, exactly," Sam asked, the images in his mind

wreaking havoc, "that you do for Arthur Geiger?"

"Oh, I thought I said. I take bets for him."

"Bets?" Sam felt relief rush from his ears all the way down to his blistered toes. "You're a bookie?"

"Is that what you call it?"

"Geiger gives you a list of odds for a sporting event. Five to one if Joe Schmo wins. Joe wins, you stuff your pockets. Joe loses, you get nothing?"

A relieved smile washed across Effie's face. "You have done this before."

"No, but I've arrested people for doing it."

Effie lost her smile. "Oh."

"It doesn't matter. That was back in Connecticut. The laws are different here."

Effie's voice fell to a whisper. "It is illegal here as well."

"Then why are you doing it?"

Effie pointed at her scar. "Because I am hideous. No one is hiring hideous."

"You're gorgeous," Sam said. "I'd hire you in a heartbeat."

"I am available if you are hiring," Effie said, excitement in her voice. "Working for you in Camelot, though brief, was gratifying. Some days—most days lately—I have wished I could go back in time."

"It's not what it's cracked up to be," Sam said. "Maybe if I find Merlin, I can find out why I'm here. If it is permanent, I'll have to set up some kind of business. Then of course I'll hire you."

"I have not seen the Merlin, Sam," Effie said, "but..."

"But?"

"I have seen someone odd. A woman. She arrived in Nottingham some weeks ago, alone, confused, completely out of place. Even her clothes. Well, her clothes reminded me of you."

"Can you describe this woman?" Sam asked with perhaps too much excitement in his voice. Could Effie have encountered Nora?

"Of course. Somewhat shorter than you. Blond hair to her shoulders. Eyes of blue. Her features, well, somewhat similar to mine."

Sam sighed and reached into his shirt pocket to pull out his cell phone. Nora was taller, not shorter. And weeks ago was too long.

When he powered it up, the phone's low battery indicator came on. He didn't waste any time clicking the gallery icon and swiping images before showing the display to Effie. "Is that her?"

"What? Why, yes. That is a very good likeness. What painter made it?"

"Not important." Sam powered down the phone and put it away. "What is important is that I find her."

"I have only her first name. For Mr. Geiger's books, you understand."

"Carmen," Sam supplied.

"Why, yes. That is right. Mr. Geiger would know more. He would have required more information before allowing her as a client. Oh!" Effie raised a hand to her mouth. "But he would never give you that information, his business being what it is."

"Carmen Sternwood is one of Geiger's clients?" Sam asked.

"I shouldn't be telling you this," Effie said. "But, yes. And with the tournament this afternoon, she is sure to come in sometime today."

Effie blinked as the door opened.

A male voice from the doorway said, "Oh."

"That's okay," Sam said. "I'm done here."

He winked at Effie, then whispered, "I don't want to see you lose your job until I find you a better one. Who knows? Maybe we'll open a real Nottingham bookstore."

15
A CORPSE ON THE FLOOR

FROM HIS SHAPE, Sam could tell this was a different client than the one who had fled the bookshop earlier. As Sam brushed past him on the way out, the man turned his face away. As if that would help, had Sam been the law. Although, it probably wasn't the law the man was worried about. More like he was afraid of blackmail, a threat to tell his wife or employer about his gambling habit. Idly, Sam wondered if there were any private investigators working in Nottingham. If there weren't, he might have the entire field to himself should he set up shop.

But that wasn't it. Everything he'd heard so far suggested the Sheriff was the biggest criminal in town. Sam didn't see why a little nickel action would worry anyone unless they were in competition with the Sheriff. But he didn't see how Effie's boss, Arthur Geiger, could be in business at all without paying Vaisey a percentage. Pallium's Parchments was just a little too out in the open to operate without the Sheriff learning about it.

As he stepped out onto the street, Sam blinked, the sun bright in his eyes after the shop's dark interior. While he took a moment for his eyes to adjust, he noted how few people were about. Just the three mooks who'd followed him from the gate, still lurking at the end of the street, and an old man who stood contemplating entering one of the other shops.

Of course, this close to the tournament starting, everyone who was anyone would be at the village green or seated at one of the nearby alehouses. There were no alehouses on Halifax Lane. No drink or food dispensaries of any kind that Sam could see. He also realized the businesses along the street catered to the wealthier townsfolk, some of whom, according to Robin, left town when Vaisey was appointed Sheriff. Sam couldn't decide if they left because they were well-known supporters of Richard, or because they didn't want to pay the higher taxes. Maybe both.

Sam rubbed his ear as he wondered what to do about the three men following him. He also wondered how he'd find his way to the tournament once it started. He'd been told to wait until Kevin of Gunthorp was announced by criers. But would there be a crier on a deserted street like Halifax Lane?

Kevin of Gunthorp. Was that the name Robin had used to enter the tournament?

He wished he knew more about how all this worked. Robin had asked if Sam thought his plan would succeed. Right. Everything Sam knew about medieval archery tournaments he could write on a square of toilet paper. With a crayon. A thick crayon. Maybe he should just keep out of it.

Sam's gaze swivelled along the street. Directly across from Pallium's Parchments stood an operation named St Paul's Haberdashery. A wide eave along the roof cast significant shade over a bench that sat against the wall. A shady bench sounded like the best idea he'd had all day. Just thinking about his feet caused them to ache.

A sign hanging from the door handle said CLOSED. Below that, in smaller letters, were the words UNTIL FURTHER NOTICE. Perfect.

Easing himself onto the bench, Sam decided his keister had mostly recovered from its intimacy with a horse's saddle. Well, maybe not mostly. It still took considerable effort to reach down and untie his shoelaces. Even more effort to slip off his shoes.

His socks smelled like a men's locker room, but Sam rejected the idea of peeling them off. He might not get them on again. He also wasn't sure he wanted to know the state of his heels and toes. Blisters could be bad. Or they could be worse than bad. Best just to leave them be. Let his feet breathe while he could.

Leaning back against the bench, Sam wiggled his toes and waited. Effie had suggested Carmen would place a bet on the tournament. All he needed was to sit and wait. Then he could confront her about Sean Regan. Find out what she knew.

After a few minutes, the customer who had entered the shop to not buy a book stepped outside. Sam sat still and didn't think the man even noticed him as he looked left then right before beating a hasty retreat down the street.

Once the man was out of sight, Sam resumed wiggling his toes and watching Effie's shop.

Effie. He couldn't believe he had found the woman he had met in Camelot and lost his heart to. Or that Effie had encountered Carmen Sternwood. That was one mystery solved. Carmen must have found the bolthole in Sternwood Castle just as he had, only a day or so earlier. That meant she would have arrived at Locksley Castle around two weeks before Sam had. Carmen must have escaped Lord Furnival's Scottish savages, or sweet-talked her way out. Or maybe Furnival hadn't arrived yet. Sam had no idea when Robin's father had been murdered. It could have been a day or a year ago.

Had General Sternwood's friend, Sean Regan, gone through the bolthole with Carmen? Or followed after her? And Nora? If Nora had proceeded Sam back in time, she couldn't have arrived more than an hour before him. But there had been no sign of her. Unless Braveheart had grabbed her before he showed up.

Of course, if any of that were true, it shot down Sam's *Sam the Hero* theory. Maybe there was no mastermind behind his third trip to the Dark Ages. Maybe the act of moving Locksley Castle to Connecticut had ripped a hole in time and space, and Sam was just one of many to fall through it. Completely by accident. Carmen. Regan. Nora. And lastly, himself.

At least Sam knew Carmen had been spotted in town. Maybe Regan and Nora had also found their way to Nottingham. Or were they being held as spies in Locksley Castle's dungeon?

Maybe after Robin finished this tournament, Sam, Little John, Sagramore, and anyone else they could round up, would storm Locksley Castle and see who needed rescuing. Drat! Wasn't that what Robin's Merry Men were doing before he got in the way? If Nora, and maybe Sean Regan, were rotting in a dungeon or being interrogated by this Furnival character, who seemed such a monster, was it Sam's fault?

A large, black bird landed on the eave above Sam's head and

peered down at him. It cocked its head to one side, then the other, as though asking Sam what he was doing. Then it cawed loudly and ruffled its feathers.

"Come on," Sam grumbled. "Can't I rest my feet for a moment?"

The crow cast him a hard, piercing stare, let out a miserly squawk, then winged its way up the street.

Sam followed with his gaze until it disappeared around the corner where Vaisey's mooks had been lurking. Had been. Vaisey's mooks were gone. Had they lost interest? Or had the smell of Sam's feet reached them and they'd moved in search of a position upwind? More likely they'd decided he wasn't here for the tournament and had nothing to do with Robin Hood. That made sense. He'd gone to the opposite end of town from the village green, and now was whiling away the time sitting in the shade.

Well. There was nothing Sam could do about that. Maybe if he did hear a tournament crier, he'd stay on the bench despite the crow's harsh opinion. There was nothing he could do to help Robin anyway, even if his feet were working properly. His Smith and Wesson automatic now, if that were still magicked, would have made Sam a good man to have in a fight. As it was, he'd be no more use than cannon fodder.

The scrape of a shoe against stone drew Sam's attention. Slinking up the street from the other direction, a heavyset man wearing a broad-brimmed straw hat that obscured his face, meandered toward Pallium's Parchments and slipped inside. A few minutes later, he slithered out of the shop and sidled back the way he had come, his head bent low. Sam figured the locals took committing crime seriously.

Effie a criminal. Sam couldn't believe it. She was the daughter of a Duke. Clerk for a wizard, in Camelot no less. And now here she was, hiding in the dark, taking book from suspicious characters. It had to be the scar. She'd called herself hideous, but the scar was nothing. It couldn't hide her beauty. Not on the outside. And definitely not on the inside. All Effie needed was a little confidence.

More movement caught Sam's eye. He turned his gaze to see the woman of his dreams slip through Pallium's Parchments' doorway. Effie turned back toward the door and hung a sign on the handle before glancing up and down the street. She didn't look across the street. Or if she did, she failed to see Sam sitting in the eave's shadow. A scarf covered her hair. She adjusted it to ensure it covered her scar as well. Then Effie walked away, fast, heading the direction the crow had gone.

Sam hastily slipped his aching feet back into his shoes and heaved himself off the bench. Effie was still in sight, so he crossed the street to read the sign she had left. BACK AT HIGH NOON. What did she think this was? A western?

Despite the agony in his feet, Sam followed at a fast walk, not wanting to lose sight of her. Effie hadn't mentioned anything about leaving the shop.

Rather than turn onto Goose Gate toward the market, Effie continued up the next street, which also ran along the town wall.

A small sign said this new street was called Laverne Terrace. No shops, just stately houses that, unlike others Sam had seen in Nottingham, included small yards planted with trees, bushes, and flowers. The homes themselves appeared vacant, though the occupants could have been away at pre-tournament festivities.

As he hobbled past the houses, Sam spotted the occasional face peer out from an open doorway or curtained window. None held smiles. Sam had the impression the Sheriff's reign of terror had polarized the town into two factions. Those whose loyalty Vaisey had bought, and everyone else.

Effie looked neither left nor right as she hurried past several houses, then turned toward one. Her knock on the door was firm, firm enough for Sam to hear it despite the distance between them. He watched the door open and Effie slip inside, but was at the wrong angle to glimpse whoever she was meeting.

He walked a bit closer before settling himself behind a holly bush that occupied much of a neighbouring yard. Then he waited for Effie to come out. He wasn't sure what he would do when she did. Was this an innocent lunch break? Or did part of Lady Peregrine's making book include house calls?

After less than five minutes, a woman's scream erupted from inside the house.

Sam was off like a shot, stumbling around the bush, his sore thigh muscles forgotten, the blisters on his feet unimportant. He raced across the street, pushed open the door of the house Effie had entered, and burst inside. Almost immediately, his gaze found Effie slumped in a wide chair, her long blonde hair freed from its scarf and fanned across her face. She couldn't be dead! Sam crouched and checked her pulse. He let out a long, slow breath. She was alive. Merely unconscious.

Sam brushed back her hair and lifted her chin, hoping to find the cause of the scream and Effie's current condition. What he saw sent him rocking backward. The woman wasn't Effie. It was Carmen Sternwood. General Sternwood's missing daughter.

Sam quickly rose to his feet to look about the room. Where was Effie?

It was only then he saw a corpse on the floor. That of a thickset man, hair slightly grey, tailored clothing. Even before pressing his fingers against the man's throat, Sam knew he was dead. There was too much blood puddled on the floor near his head. Of Effie, there was no sign.

Realizing time was of the essence, Sam searched the house. Effie had to be somewhere. But there was no one else. He did, however, find a rear door that led to a tiny yard set between the house and the town wall. Built within the wall, a metal gate stood unlatched and open. Sam stepped through and found himself in a narrow tunnel that ran inside the wall in both directions. Similar small gates, that apparently opened into neighbouring yards, provided the only light, but enough to make the tunnel navigable.

Rushing back into the house, Sam lifted Carmen in a fireman's carry, something he had learned as a cop, and returned to the tiny yard with its open gate. Behind him, the sound of running feet approached the house. Sam hadn't been the only one to hear the scream, Carmen's or Effie's, he didn't know. All he did know was that Effie must have escaped out the back.

After pulling shut the gate, Sam chose a direction that should lead him back toward Effie's shop and ran along the tunnel as fast as he could with Carmen's dead weight hanging from his shoulders. He had no idea who the corpse on the floor was, or who had killed him. He couldn't make himself believe Effie had done it. It had to have been Carmen, his client's daughter. Or someone else who had also run out the back.

Effie might know what had happened, unless she'd left via the back way before the murder. Carmen definitely would know. Sam had all but convinced himself it was Carmen whose scream he'd heard. Carmen Sternwood might be the only witness. And no one was going to question her before he did.

16
A BACK DOOR

THE TUNNEL SEEMED to run the entire length of the town wall, with gates opening into the backyard of each of the upscale houses, a perk for the more affluent citizens who could afford to live adjacent to the wall. The tunnel probably served as a way to come and go unseen by the general populace. Perhaps for the transport of contraband. Or mistresses.

The tunnel didn't seem to have an exit onto a street or alley, but for the tunnel to be of any practical use, it must. Vaisey's men had to know about the back exit. If not, they'd find it as quickly as Sam had. With the house empty except for a bloody corpse, they'd be looking for the woman who had screamed. The absence of hysterical women in the street would send them to the tunnel. That wouldn't take long. Sam expected to hear footfalls and shouting from behind at any second.

Then again, any shouting he heard could easily be his own. The blisters on the soles of his feet screamed in protest as he ran, the howls rising up through his chest and struggling to reach his lips. Carmen was a petite woman, but her additional weight wasn't doing him any favours. And she seemed to be growing heavier by the second.

He paused to catch his breath and looked back the way he'd come, all but expecting to see a trail of blood seeping through his Oxford shoes. There wasn't one, but he suspected it was only a matter of time. He was going to need to get his feet looked at.

Antibiotics and bandages. Could they even do that in medieval England?

Sam forced himself to keep moving and distracted his thoughts from his burning feet, aching hips and legs, and the worry of being caught, by wondering if Effie had come this way or gone the opposite direction. He had no idea which was the better route to the book shop: the near-empty street out front or the tunnel passageway out back. But why had Effie arrived one way and departed the other? Had she fled out the back because the killer blocked the front door? Or was Effie herself the killer? Fleeing out the back way so no one would see her?

No. Sam couldn't see Effie as a killer. But whoever had killed that man had done it recently. The blood still seeped from his body. It must have happened just before or shortly after Effie entered the house. Had Effie witnessed the murder, then fled? Or had she been taken hostage and forced out the back way?

Speculation was getting Sam nowhere. He needed more information. He needed to get Carmen somewhere safe, wake her up, and find out from his employer's younger daughter what had happened. It was the only way to discover if Effie was in danger. Or was herself a killer.

The more he thought about it, however, the more he had to believe it was Effie who had screamed, not Carmen. Carmen couldn't have screamed, then fainted. People don't do that, do they? Except on television. But that would mean Effie had discovered Carmen unconscious on the couch and the thickset man dead on the floor, screamed, then run out the back. Would she do that? And where had the killer gone?

He paused to look back a second time. Still no pursuit. Maybe the man's neighbours were curious enough to investigate a scream, but not curious enough to chase a killer down a shadowed tunnel. Sam wondered how long that would last. Surely they had gone to fetch the Sheriff's men. Or whoever one fetched to chase killers down shadowed tunnels.

Sam adjusted Carmen's weight on his shoulders and moved forward again. Up ahead, the tunnel looked darker than normal. Maybe the house gates there were blocked. Or maybe that's where the tunnel ended. Sam almost suffered a heart attack when he realized it could be a dead end. There was no rule saying the tunnel had to go anywhere. Maybe it just connected a bunch of residents' houses.

He let out a sigh of relief as he realized the tunnel wasn't ending. He could see light beyond the darker section. Even so, he slowed, wondering what made this part of the tunnel different. There were no house gates for one thing. He turned his gaze to the outside wall and found a tall, narrow, wooden door. A drop bar the size of a railway tie lay across it, suspended by giant brackets embedded in the wall on either side. How about that. Nottingham had a back door.

Sam stood for a moment, breathing hard. He needed to leave the tunnel. Ideally, he needed to get to Effie's shop and make sure she was okay. But he had no idea how to get there. The metal gates all led to the yards of houses. He had an unconscious woman draped across his shoulders. And pursuit could catch him at any moment. He glanced along the tunnel in both directions, then turn his gaze to the wooden door. For now, it seemed the only option.

Grunting, Sam lowered Carmen to the tunnel floor. Then he tried lifting the drop bar from the brackets. The thing wouldn't budge. Bending down, he wedged his shoulder underneath and lifted by straightening his already smarting thighs. It was painful, but since he already hurt all over, he didn't care. The wooden beam moved, scraping against the door. When he felt he'd raised it high enough, he pivoted away from the door and let the beam tumble from his shoulder onto the ground, where it landed mere inches from his feet.

Amazed he had succeeded without injuring himself, he bent over and dragged the beam further away so it no longer blocked the exit. Grabbing the door's handle with both hands, he felt a latch disengage, then blinked in the sudden brightness as he pulled the door open toward him.

His bleary gaze took in a wide field growing wheat or some other type of grain. To his relief, no one was working among the tall stalks. Maybe the time of year was wrong. Or maybe the workers were inside the walls for the tournament. Whatever the reason, Sam counted himself fortunate. Fewer witnesses to watch him sneak out of town.

Ducking back inside the tunnel, he slung Carmen once again over his shoulders and stepped outside, pulling the door shut behind him. Or as shut as he could get it; there was no handle on the outside.

Then he ran through the field as fast as he could, the yellow heads of grain slapping against his knees, a still unconscious Carmen Sternwood bogging him down like so much dead weight. At last, he hit the treeline and hid in the forest where anyone on the battlements atop the wall would be unable to see him. Not that he thought there was anyone on the battlements. The crenels looked deserted.

Taking his bearings, Sam figured he was east of the town and south of the northern wall where he had entered through the Mansfield Gate. Further south he saw what looked like a river winding past the town. So now what?

Robin and his Merry Men were sure to all be inside Nottingham already. There was no way Sam was going to carry Carmen all the way back to Sherwood Forest.

Then he remembered. Tuck was outside the wall. The portly friar had gone to a place called St John the Baptist Hospital. Hospital! That was just what Sam needed. Where had Tuck said it was? Outside Nottingham somewhere, but nearby. Hadn't Robin mentioned it being northeast of town? That would be just north of where Sam was now. It had to be close by.

After once again adjusting Carmen's weight, Sam began following the treeline north, staying just inside its shadow. He could still see the town wall, as well as a dirt path that followed along the wall, probably for whoever worked the fields to come and go.

He tried to ignore the complaints from his body, concentrating instead on the sound of his breath. In. Out. In. Out. Eventually, the wall turned westward and the dirt path widened. Sam kept to the treeline, which now also ran westward. After maybe ten minutes, he spotted a low building set among the trees. Outside the building, several monks worked a small garden.

At this point, Sam didn't care if he'd found St John the Baptist Hospital or not. His legs felt like Jell-O and his back and shoulders had gone numb. Too exhausted to do anything else, he shouted at the monks. "Help!"

The burlap-clad men straightened and looked at him.

Sam smiled and took a step. Then the strength left his legs and he crashed to the ground.

17
I DO NOT LIKE IT

"I'M ALL RIGHT," Sam muttered before realizing he must not be all right. One tonsured monk held him by his wrists, and another by his ankles. They hauled him between them like a gunnysack of potatoes. Sam's head lolled on his shoulders, causing everything to bounce like he was on a trampoline. Stone walls. A ceiling. A floor. He didn't recall going inside a building. Last he remembered, he'd been standing at the edge of the forest, his back broken, his legs missing, and his feet on fire. "Okay, maybe I'm not all right."

The monks set him on a small cot that didn't feel much softer than the stone floor looked, then backed away.

"My friend," a voice said, "do not expect them to speak with you. They have taken a vow of silence."

Sam felt he should know that voice. He swung his head to one side and saw the bulk of Friar Tuck leaning against a wall, the rotund man's thick arms crossed over his chest and resting on his substantial stomach.

"Silence?" At least Sam's tongue worked. "Why?"

"The Bishop of Hereford," Tuck answered, "who oversees this hospital, requested it."

"And why did he do that?"

The friar's face remained passive. "His Excellency the Bishop has not said, but I suspect it is to curtail unwanted comments from churchmen regarding the Sheriff's behaviour."

Sam watched as the silent monks gave barely perceptible nods. "The bishop and Vaisey are tight, I take it."

"If by tight you mean the Bishop of Hereford is eager to do the Sheriff's bidding, regardless how offensive to God, the Church, and human decency, then yes, they are tight."

"Then it's probably best you don't tell him I'm here."

A wide smile stretched across Tuck's round face. "Who is there to tell him?"

The two monks again nodded.

"I am curious," Tuck said, "How is it you are here at St John's with an unconscious woman across your shoulders and yourself on the verge of collapse. I do not recall this being part of Robin's plan."

A woman? Carmen Sternwood. How could he have forgotten? Sam took a deep breath and let it out slowly. "It's possible the woman killed a man. Or Effie did."

Tuck's eyebrows rose against his forehead. "Lady Euphemia Peregrine? Surely not."

"Apparently Effie works in the town. As a clerk." Sam wasn't sure why he felt the need to clarify her work.

"And Lady Peregrine killed someone?"

Sam shook his head. "I don't know. It could have been Effie. Or Carmen, the woman I brought with me. Or someone else entirely. I need to question Carmen when she wakes up."

"Know you what ails this Carmen?" Tuck asked.

"I think she fainted." Sam glanced toward his feet and saw a curious monk carefully untying the laces of his Thorogood Oxfords.

"Fainted?" Tuck echoed. "But any woman would have woken from a swoon long before now."

"You'd think." Sam gasped as the monk worked the shoe off his foot. He wiggled his toes while the monk inspected the shoe before passing it to Tuck.

"Curious," the friar said.

"What's that?" Sam listened for the reply as he watched the monk peel back his sock.

"This shoe," admitted Tuck. "It is made from the finest quality leather. Nay, finer than any leather I have seen. Thick. Not just the sole, but the entire shoe. And these laces. Not leather at all.

Jute? Only softer. But what is most curious is the shine. I have witnessed the glint of the finest quality boiled leather, but this shoe almost glows."

"I'm glad you like it." Sam's foot was free of the sock, and the monk had started on the other shoe.

"Oh, I do not like it," Tuck said. "Yes, the construction of the shoe is remarkable, but it is hardly fit for wearing. Your very feet testify to that. The leather does not breathe. And it constricts the toes and heel, nay, the entire foot. It is a wonder your feet are not worn to the bone."

"Thanks," Sam said, not knowing what else to say.

"And you carried this woman from the town," Tuck continued. "In these shoes? It would have been better had she carried you from the town."

"I would have appreciated that," Sam said.

Tuck clicked his tongue, then bent forward to study Sam's feet, both of which were now liberated of sock and shoe. "Not good. Not good at all. The soles of both feet are black and filled with puss."

"Thanks for the lovely imagery," Sam said.

18
PERHAPS YOU SHOULD QUESTION HER ABOUT THE MURDER

THE PASTE THE monks applied to the soles of Sam's feet felt like heaven. Cool against the burning blisters. Calm against the throb of angry nerves. And something else. Something. A certain euphoria. Part of him hoped the paste didn't contain any psychedelics, while another part figured a brief vacation from his body might be just what the doctor ordered.

Sam closed his eyes and stretched his head back, coming as close to a swoon as he'd ever found himself. "Tuck. Can you tell me what's in this stuff? It would be a miracle cure back home."

"'Tis but a simple salve," the friar answered. "I shall have one of the monks write it down."

"Yeah," Sam mumbled. "You do that."

He heard rather than saw another person enter the room. He opened one eyelid just enough to see the newly arrived monk flash Tuck a hand signal.

"Your witness is awake," Tuck said. "Should someone bring her here to you?"

"I don't think I can go to her." Sam shook himself, trying to clear his head. "But be careful. She may be dangerous." If Carmen had committed the murder, who knew what she was capable of?

"If care is required, I shall escort her myself," Tuck said.

The portly friar left, returning a few minutes later dragging a kicking and screaming Carmen by the arm. "Mr. Spade, you failed to mention your woman is a wildcat."

"I am not," Carmen spat, "anyone's woman." Then she saw Sam and stopped struggling. "Your clothes. You're not from here."

Sam smiled. "No, I'm from Hartford. Your father sent me to find Sean Regan."

"Sean!" If Carmen was angry before, now she was on fire. "You're saying Daddy Dearest sent you to find his chauffeur, but not his daughter?"

Sam lost his smile. "Chauffeur? Your father told us Regan was a close friend."

Carmen laughed. "My father doesn't have friends. I suppose Sean is as close as it gets."

"In your father's defence, I don't think he knew you were missing, just that you weren't answering your phone."

Carmen pulled an iPhone from some kind of apron at her waist. "You mean this phone. There's no signal. And after a few days, the battery died. I don't know why I still carry it around."

Not really the issue, Sam thought. "Your father suggested you have a habit of ignoring your phone."

The young woman snorted. "Only when he's calling. Daddy only ever calls to tell me to stop what I'm doing. Or to start doing something I'm not. I have my own life, you know. Or I did before I wound up here."

"Excuse me," Tuck interrupted. "Is this young woman from your land? Connecticut?"

"I'm afraid so," Sam admitted.

"Well, I for one am relieved," Tuck said. "I now understand her curious demeanour. But perhaps you should question her about the murder."

"Murder?" The young woman's mouth opened into a large 'O', and her eyes went wide.

Sam could tell it was just a show. As a cop he'd seen more feigned innocence than he could stomach. "Yes, murder. The one that caused you to scream and faint."

Carmen worked her jaw for a moment, saying nothing. When she finally spoke, it was another lie. "I didn't scream."

"Look," Sam said. "I heard the scream. Now I've heard you

talking, I know it was you who screamed. It's the same voice. And when I ran into the house, the only one there was you, standing over the body."

"Body?"

"Okay, you weren't exactly standing over it, but you would have been if you hadn't fainted."

"I fainted?"

This was going nowhere fast. "Look. Did you see who killed the guy or not?"

Carmen's voice rose to a shout, shrill and ready to break. "I didn't see anyone kill anyone. All I saw was—" She stopped.

"All you saw was what? Go on."

"I saw Arthur," Carmen admitted. "One minute he was alive and speaking with that scarred up bookie of his, Euphoria—what a silly name—the next she was gone and he was lying dead on the floor."

So, the corpse was Effie's boss. Not good. "And then you screamed," Sam suggested.

"Hmm. Maybe I did scream."

"And then you fainted."

"I suppose I did. I don't remember. I don't remember coming here, either. Where is here, by the way?"

Sam rubbed his ear. "That's a long and complicated story. We'll hash that out when we have more time. Right now, I need to know what Geiger and Effie—Euphemia—were talking about."

Carmen scrunched her face. "How should I know? Arthur was secretive about his work. He made me hide in a back room when *Euphoria—*" her lip curled as she purposefully re-mispronounced the name, "—arrived. When I came back out, *Euphoria* was gone and Arthur was dead. *Euphoria* must have killed him."

"That's one theory," Sam said, though he found it a hard one to swallow. "Another is that you killed Arthur Geiger and you're pinning it on his bookie."

Carmen didn't even flinch. "Why would I?"

"Why were you at his house?"

She hesitated. "Business."

That was a lie. "What kind of business? I know you're one of his clients. Were you placing a bet on today's tournament?"

"Sure." Carmen crossed her arms against her chest. "That's

exactly what I was doing."

"Then why weren't you doing it through Geiger's bookie, at his place of business. Why were you in his house?"

Carmen turned her face away. "I don't have to answer to you."

Sam was getting tired. Maybe the salve on his feet was making him sleepy. Or maybe he was just fatigued by a young woman's arrogance. He'd seen this before. Too many times. The children of wealthy parents figuring they can get away with murder. Perhaps literally this time. "No, you don't have to answer to me. But Effie will tell me everything. Between what I heard and saw, and what she'll tell me, I'll know exactly what happened."

Carmen turned her head even further, then performed the definitive entitlement move. She stuck her nose in the air.

Sam leaned his head back into his pillow. "Tuck, can your monk friends see to it that Carmen is kept comfortable, the operative word being *kept*. It's possible she's a killer. We don't want her running off on us."

Carmen let out a big huff before allowing a pair of monks to lead her away.

When she was gone, Sam let out a huge breath of air, sat up in bed, and began pulling on his bloody socks.

"What are you doing?" Tuck asked.

Sam gritted his teeth. The dried, blood-soaked cotton felt like sandpaper scraping over his swollen feet. "You and I have to return to town. Geiger was dead, but I don't know how he died. Learning that may help us figure out who did what to who."

Tuck let out a low-pitched chortle. "Are you suggesting I carry you into Nottingham? I must tell you, Mr. Spade, that feat is well beyond my poor talents. Also, they will arrest me on sight. I cannot do as you ask."

"You won't be arrested," Sam said through clenched teeth as he pulled on a shoe. "I found a back way in."

"Really?" The friar rubbed his double chin. "That could prove useful."

19
IS IT LUCK? OR DESIGN?

A FEW YEARS earlier when Sam was still a cop, he and other members of his unit were tasked with security at an event put on by the city. They'd called it *Hawaii in Hartford*. There'd been a luau complete with tiki lamps, hula dancers, ukulele music, and a dozen pigs roasted in a pit. The city had charged a thousand dollars a plate, and no one ever did find out where the proceeds went. The part Sam remembered most was a ten-foot bed of hot coals laid out along a sidewalk where one of the performers had taken off his shoes and walked the entire length in bare feet. The memory hurt Sam's teeth just thinking about it.

His teeth hurt now as well as he slowly walked from the cot to the entrance of the small room. The stone floor was exactly how he had imagined the hot coals must have felt. Only he had more than ten feet to walk. There was the forest, the field, and the tunnel to Geiger's house. And he had to hope he and Tuck got there before Vaisey's men moved the body.

Tuck eyed Sam critically. "Perhaps it would be best to wait here for Robin."

Sam shook his head. "We don't know how long they'll leave the body at the house." In Hartford, they'd have to wait for the forensics team to collect evidence and the coroner to sign off. Since the Dark Ages didn't have photography, fingerprinting, or DNA sequencing, that left only the coroner's okay.

"Does Nottingham have a coroner?" Sam asked. "Or do they have to bring someone in from somewhere else? London maybe?"

The friar's expression went flat. "Coroner?"

"The person who examines a body to determine cause of death."

"Ah, yes!" Tuck's face brightened. "That used to be one of the Sheriff's responsibilities, but then King Richard sent us a man to take on that task. I believe he was called a coroner."

"Was?"

The smile vanished. "The Sheriff had him detained. I am unsure of the charges. No one has seen him since his arrest."

Sam rubbed his ear. "So, it will be Vaisey signing off on the body. We might find him at the house when we get there."

Tuck shook his head. "The Sheriff will be at the village green, busy with tournament preparations. A simple death will not deter him, especially if the tournament is a trap of his design for Robin."

"Yes," Sam agreed, "you're right. This is Vaisey's big day."

Taking a tentative step into the hospital hallway, Sam tested his weight on his feet. Grimacing, he let go of the stone wall and hobbled a few paces toward what looked like the hospital's entrance. Grunting between clenched teeth, he told the friar, "The tournament. Itself. Will buy us time. To examine the body."

He noticed Tuck casting a critical eye at his progress and shaking his head. "The Sheriff will have men watching the house."

Sam ignored the large man's visual and verbal objections, but leaned against the doorjamb as he took a steadying breath. "We'll talk our way past them."

"Humph." Tuck pulled a walking stick from a vaselike pot just inside the entrance and handed it to Sam. "Your optimism is an inspiration to us all."

The friar grabbed a second stick for himself, then Sam led the way outside.

It took only a moment for Sam to get his bearings.

The hospital was smaller than he'd expected, two-storeys and built of stone blocks much like Sternwood Castle. Small windows lined the walls, letting in plenty of light and fresh air. It was not intended as a fortification. Several stone benches sat near the entrance, and the herb garden he remembered from when he arrived lined the southern wall.

Trees surrounded the structure, but he could see a path leading west and another going south to where it ended at the track running along Nottingham's town wall.

Sam rubbed his jaw. Following the dirt track would shorten the distance considerably. The temptation was maddening, but reason won out, and he opted to stay within the forest. He was in no shape to run if a soldier on the wall or along the track spotted them.

Tuck said nothing about the decision, but followed beside Sam when the forest allowed, and behind when necessary. The friar's unspoken doubts about what they were doing worried Sam more than words could.

"The way I see it," Sam said into the silence, "a man's gotta do what a man's gotta do."

"No matter how foolish?" Tuck asked.

Sam had no answer for that, and they trudged along in continued silence.

He had to agree the walking stick was a good idea. Mostly because deciding where to place it with each step was a handy distraction from everything his body was complaining about. Miraculously, his feet weren't the worst grievance. Something in the monks' paste had numbed the nerves. It might be like walking with bricks for feet, but at least the bricks weren't on fire.

Over time, he grew used to the lack of feeling and more proficient with the walking stick. Soon he was setting a pace that left Tuck huffing and puffing and trailing behind. Sam found himself slowing to allow the friar to catch up.

"Are we almost there?" Tuck asked as he paused to lean against a young tree, causing it to bend noticeably.

"Almost is a relative term," Sam said.

"What does that mean exactly? Relative term?"

"Look." Sam pointed across the wheat field toward the town. "You can see the back entrance from here. That dark smudge in the wall there."

Tuck squinted, then nodded his sweating head. "Then why do we yet slog through the forest, and away from the entrance? Should we not cross the field to your secret door?"

"There's no cover in the field," Sam pointed out.

The friar wagged his head. "We must cross the field sometime. As well here as directly across from the entrance."

Sam considered that. Sure, they would be exposed a minute or so longer, but it would shorten the trip. "You may have something there."

As when Sam had crossed earlier, the wheat field was deserted. He'd assumed any workers would be at the tournament preparations, but now wondered if the Sheriff had recalled them as part of his plan to trap Robin, if indeed there was such a plan. Vaisey would have difficulty arresting Robin at the tournament if he and his Merry Men couldn't sneak into Nottingham. Sam's chief concern now was that Vaisey might have men hidden on the battlements watching the field, so they could report Robin's approach. If someone recognized Tuck, they might make a report. Of course, that would be another distraction from Robin's real plan, and Sam did need to get back into Nottingham. "Let's cross and see what happens."

Whether anyone saw them or not, Sam and Tuck arrived at the town wall unmolested.

"It is not much of a wall, is it?" Tuck muttered, looking up. "I mean, it would be a simple thing to toss a grappling hook up onto the battlements and scale the beast. A child could do it." He looked down at his portly waist. "But alas, I could not."

"I'm no expert on fortifications," Sam said noncommittally.

Tuck returned his gaze to the battlements. "I suppose bowmen atop the wall would be a deterrent. In times of war, archers man the crenels. Scaling a wall is more challenging when arrows are flying at you."

"It's good we're not scaling the wall, then," Sam suggested.

Tuck shrugged. "We are equally vulnerable standing here below the wall where rocks or scalding water could be thrown down on us."

"Then we should find that door as quickly as possible."

It took maybe ten minutes to follow the track along the wall to where the back door to the town stood slightly ajar, just as Sam had left it. Tuck pushed his considerable weight against the door, and it swung inward. The length of rough timber lay inside the tunnel exactly where Sam had left it.

"Another bit of luck," he said. "No one replaced the barricade."

"Is it luck?" Tuck asked. "Or design?"

Sam felt his cheek twitch. "If Vaisey left the door open in hopes of catching Robin, he'll be disappointed. Robin's not here. But we can still use this back entrance to our advantage."

Tuck glanced up and down the tunnel. "Remarkable. How is it no one knows this is here?"

"People know," Sam said. "People in the know, know. Follow me."

Wielding his walking stick before him like a third leg, Sam set off in the direction of Arthur Geiger's house.

Something he hadn't considered was how to identify the correct gate. They all looked much the same, and there were no address numbers or family names. As it was, Sam was forced to pause at several likely gates and peer into the yards, hoping to recognize the one he had fled through carrying Carmen over his shoulder. Fortunately, each small yard was significantly unique, offering different arrangements of plants, fountains, and even statuary.

"This looks like it," Sam whispered after examining several possibilities.

"Are you certain?" Tuck cast the tiny yard a suspicious glance, then paused to listen. "I hear no sounds from the house. Surely the Sheriff's men would make some noise."

Sam shrugged. "As certain as I can be."

The metal latch was surprisingly quiet as he lifted it upward and pushed open the gate. He looked again at the arrangement of the yard. The bushes all seemed the right shape and in the right place. Geiger hadn't had a fountain or any statuary. The place felt right.

Tuck followed as Sam shuffled across the small yard and eased up to the house's narrow back door. He pressed his ear against the polished wood. After a moment he whispered, "I don't hear anything."

Tuck said nothing, so Sam reached for the handle and pulled the door open.

The interior of the house greeted them with silence.

Glancing about, Sam recognized the furniture he'd seen earlier. There were still no sounds. The place felt empty. Cautiously, he led Tuck to the front of the house, and though he half-expected Geiger's body to be gone, he was still startled to find no sign of the recent murder. Not even a bloodstain on the floor.

Tuck stood at Sam's shoulder gazing into the empty sitting room. "You are certain there was a body?"

"Yes."

"Then the Sheriff's men have it."

20
WHAT THE SHERIFF OF NOTTINGHAM SAW

SAM CREPT FORWARD to the window next to the front door and peered out past the curtain. Like before, the street was empty. Everyone was indoors, or at the village green for the tournament. Testing the door, Sam pulled it open a crack and stuck his head outside. No police. No police tape. No medieval equivalent of either of those things. Nothing.

He ducked back inside and eased the door shut. "Where would they take the body?"

Tuck pursed his lips. "If your corpse dwelt in this house, then he was a man of means if not import. The Sheriff's men could not simply dispose of the body. Relatives might protest. No, they would have remanded your corpse to Nottingham Gaol."

"The lion's den," Sam suggested. "Of course."

"I cannot go there," Tuck said. "I would be arrested. Neither should you go. Vaisey knows and despises you."

"The feeling's mutual."

"Be that as it may," Tuck said, "the Sheriff has the keys to the cells. You do not."

"Good point. But if Vaisey's at the tournament, he won't be at the jail."

Tuck nodded his thick chin. "You make a sound case."

"I take it you know where the jail is?" Sam asked.

"Of course. The Sheriff's Keep lies on Castle Road, opposite the village green."

Sam's cheek twitched. "Where the tournament is. That's just dandy."

Once again opening the door, Sam stepped out into the street and looked in both directions for the Sheriff's men. There didn't appear to be any. Just a few regular townsfolk maybe a dozen houses away, though they did cast curious glances at Sam's trench coat and fedora. When Tuck joined him, the corpulent monk received his own share of looks.

Sam laughed. "I came into town to distract Vaisey's men from searching for Robin. Looks like I'm still doing my job, and you're doing it with me."

Tuck grinned. "Yet I am known and loved by many, while you, Mr. Spade, are the oddest of strangers. I suspect I shall fair better than you on a journey through Nottingham township."

"So long as no one arrests you," Sam amended.

"Or you, my friend, though that is one way of arriving at the gaol."

"Arrested? On what charge? I haven't done anything."

Tuck shrugged. "Dressing, speaking, and moving in a suspicious manner? You need not break any law to be arrested."

"Well, let's try to avoid that, shall we? I'd rather walk into the jail of my own accord. Which way is it?"

Tuck waved a hand in the opposite direction of Geiger's shop.

Sam needed Effie's account of what happened in the house, but that would have to wait. "Lead on," he said.

After maybe six houses, a narrow side street called Fair Maiden Lane broke away toward the centre of town. Sam followed the friar, each of them hobbling along with the aid of a walking stick. The bricks that were Sam's feet seemed to be regaining some feeling, but not a good feeling. At first, it was as though his feet had fallen asleep, a stubborn tingling sensation. But before long it escalated to walking on sharp stones, then broken glass.

"Are you in pain, Mr. Spade?"

Sam glanced at Tuck, whose gaze was focused on Sam's guarded steps. "Only when I breathe."

"Even should you suffer for righteousness' sake, you will be blessed," Tuck quoted. "First Peter 3:14."

Sam gritted his teeth. "I hope Peter knew what he was talking about."

The friar snorted. "Saint Peter was the first pillar of the Church. The first Bishop of Rome. And the first Pope. He was martyred in similitude to our saviour, yet was demeaned by being tied on the cross upside down."

"So . . . ," Sam said. "I guess I shouldn't complain about my feet?"

Tuck shrugged. "Complain all you wish. It is Man's lot in life to complain."

"In that case, my feet are killing me."

The churchman appeared unmoved. "You ignored my counsel to remain at hospital."

Sam shook his head. "My lying in bed wasn't going to help anyone."

Tuck cast him an appraising look. "Then your suffering *is* for righteousness' sake. In the end, you shall be blessed."

"All the blessing I need," Sam suggested, "is to find Nora and make sure she's safe."

"Nora?" Tuck asked. "Who is Nora?"

"A friend from back home who might also be here," Sam explained. "Like Carmen."

"Not too like Carmen, I hope," the friar said.

"No," Sam agreed. "Nora is nothing like Carmen."

As they neared the marketplace Sam had skirted that morning, the streets became busy with people, horses, and carts. A man walking along the crowded street shouted, "Oliver of Hyson Green has outscored Edward of Netherfield. Next up: Liam of West Bridgford followed by William of Watnall."

"The tournament is already underway," Tuck whispered. "Robin will be on the line very soon."

"What should we do?" Sam asked. "Continue to the jail, maybe hope to pull away some of the Sheriff's men to keep an eye on us? Or go to the tournament and hope to draw their attention that way?"

Tuck considered for a moment, then shook his head. "We have come to the crucible. The crux upon which Robin's fate lies. To the tournament. We shall be more able to help, should we know what is happening."

As much as Sam wanted to inspect Geiger's corpse and speak with Effie, he knew Tuck was right. Besides, he'd never get the Merry Men to help him storm Locksley Castle if Robin was dead or in jail. "Lead on, Macduff."

"Who?" Tuck asked.

"You."

"Mr. Spade, sometimes you speak in the strangest of ways."

Pushing their way through the crowds to the village green was a fight, but an unfair one. All Tuck had to do was lean in a direction, and it would part to let him through. All Sam had to do was follow in the friar's wake.

The green, when Sam could see it, was underwhelming. He'd expected something like a football field, with a grandstand crowd of onlookers. What he found was a small grassy area surrounded by mobs of standing people, all shouting and laughing. At one end of the narrow field stood several tents, maybe five feet in diameter and seven feet tall. A length of cloth held in place by several stones marked the shooting line. To one side, a platform had been erected and set with several chairs. A dozen or so dour-looking men dressed in colourful tunics and cloaks sat in the chairs or stood beside them.

Sam recognized one of the seated men, not so much by the black clothing he wore or the jet-black hair that fell across his eyes, but by the eyes themselves—dark, foreboding, and filled with hate. Vaisey. The six years that had passed since Sam last saw him had done Squire Vaisey no favours. He'd put on a few pounds. Lines creased his cheeks. And his scowl was deeper than Sam remembered.

Standing near the platform, a dozen men dressed in leather with swords or bows in hand watched the crowd with hawk eyes. Sam assumed they were among the Sheriff's best soldiers.

Movement caught his attention, and he watched as a young man dressed in loose clothing emerged from one of the tents and stepped up to the shooting line. The man held a bow in one hand and a single arrow in the other. There was no quiver on his back. A crier near the platform read from a length of paper that threatened to roll up on him if he didn't hold it just right. In a loud voice, he called out, "Kenneth of Tollerton. Last year's winner of the tourney at Leicester."

Sam half-expected the archer to grin at the audience and take a bow. Instead, he took no notice of the crier or the crowd, but fixed his gaze upon the circular target mounted on a wooden easel at the opposite end of the green.

Having shot at enough targets at Wolf's Indoor Range and Shooting Centre back in Hartford, Sam knew the circle would be difficult to miss, even with a bow. But he figured hitting the target wasn't the goal. No. The exact centre of the circle was the goal, and at that distance, wind would be a factor. Fortunately, there was little wind. Still, even with a perfect shot, a gust could blow up and push an arrow off the mark. It was a terrific gamble Robin was taking, coming here today.

The crowd hooted and hollered as Kenneth of Tollerton studied the target. Many had placed bets. If not with Geiger through Effie, then with other bookies, or even simple friendly bets with friends and family.

Vaisey stamped a staff, not unlike Sam's own, against the wooden surface of the platform. The crowd immediately quieted. In the stillness, the archer notched his arrow and drew the bow, pulling the string to position beneath his jaw. The crowd waited, failing even to breathe. Then the arrow flew, moments later making a *thuk* sound as the arrowhead pierced the target. A spattering of applause filled the square, but not much considering the number of people.

Sam continued watching as a man with a string walked up to the target followed by another man who seemed to be observing. After placing the string, the two men held a brief discussion. Then the observer raised his hand and signalled with his fingers. A man standing next to Vaisey's chair observed the fingers closely, then bent down and whispered into Vaisey's ear. The Sheriff nodded, and the man turned and whispered again into the ear of a young boy who stood waiting. The boy ran to another man and whispered into his ear. Then that man straightened, filled his lungs with air, and shouted, "Three and one-fifth inches. No win. The current record is two and one-quarter inches held by Rodney of Scunthorpe."

Other criers took up the message, and word spread out from the square to those not close enough to hear the first crier.

Kenneth of Tollerton, for his part, frowned and spit into the grass before marching back to the tent he had emerged from.

"Next up," the first crier yelled, "Marius of Yorkshire. A new challenger with no awards."

The crowd burst out laughing as a tent opened, revealing a lean frame dressed in forest green, a simple bow in one hand and a simpler arrow in the other. Sam couldn't see the archer's face because he wore a dark green hood that kept his features in shadow.

A buzz moved through the crowd, and Sam looked up to see Vaisey leaning forward in his seat, a smirk barely held in check on his lips.

The new archer strode up to the cloth marker and readied his bow. He did not pull down his hood. Again, the crowd laughed. Vaisey's staff stamped against the platform, and the jeering stopped.

Silence as the archer pulled back the string. Then he let loose, and again Sam heard the *thuk* of the arrow embedding itself in the target. No applause this time.

The two measuremen marched up to the target, but before the fellow with the string could do anything, his companion turned toward the platform and shook his head. Vaisey was already nodding, angrily, before his man could whisper. The boy stood helpless, not knowing what to do, then the crier shouted, "No contest. Marius of Yorkshire has hit the target, but too far from the leaders to be worthy of measurement."

The archer pulled down his hood revealing long blond hair, cornflower-blue eyes, and a face that was obviously female. It was Maid Marian who had made the shot. The crowd erupted in applause and catcalls. Grinning, Marian curtsied and returned to the tent.

"Is that normal?" Sam shouted at Tuck over the noise.

Tuck laughed. "No. Women have their own tournaments, the few there are who wish to compete. Had Marian's shot been measured, and had it beaten any of the men's, there would be trouble."

"Yeah," Sam said. "In my day as well, sad as that is."

On the platform, Vaisey was growling at several of his men, a look of annoyance on his cruel face. When he finished, he nodded at the crier with the paper scroll, who shouted, "Next up, Kevin of Gunthorp. A new challenger with no awards."

Vaisey almost jumped up out of his seat when a tent opened and another hooded archer stepped out. This one was dressed head to toe in black, except for a red scarf tied at his left bicep. He carried a bow of reddish-brown wood that glistened in the sunlight. Sam watched him move, trying to see if this, too, was a woman, but gave up. The archer moved with the grace of an athlete, as had Marian.

The crowd was going crazy. Two unknown contestants in a row. Sam had the sense this was more than unusual.

Vaisey stamped his staff, and leaned forward in his seat, scrutinizing the archer harder than Sam had. The crowd quieted, and the archer notched his bow. In one swift motion, he drew the string to his jaw and released. The arrow seemed to strike the target almost before it was launched.

The two measuremen jumped into action. The one with the string seemed agitated while taking a measurement. His companion leaned in close, so Sam couldn't see what they were doing. Then they seemed to argue. The one with the string kept waving it in the face of the other, then threw it on the ground and stalked off. The other stared at the string, then raised his head and stared at the target. Finally, he lifted his hand and performed some hasty, agitated signalling.

The watcher on the platform hesitated, then whispered cautiously to Vaisey, who jumped out of his seat and pointed a finger at the archer. "Arrest that man!"

The entire crowd exploded. Some applauding, but most forming their lips in a circle and howling, "Boo!"

Several of Vaisey's men advanced on the archer, who stood as though stunned. One of the soldiers took away the red bow, while two others grabbed the man's arms. Vaisey himself stepped down from the platform and pulled the hood back from the archer's head. What the Sheriff of Nottingham saw did not make him happy. The archer was not Robin Hood.

21
AN ODD HAT THAT SERVES NO FUNCTION

"FIND HIM!" VAISEY shouted.

All but the two soldiers holding blond-haired Will Scarlet dashed into the crowd, swords drawn and bows at the ready. Bystanders stepped back, causing a ripple effect as people stumbled out of the way.

"We must be gone," Tuck said urgently, already backing away several steps.

"I thought Robin was supposed to win the contest," Sam said, too dazed to move. "Who knew Will Scarlet was such a good shot?"

Tuck laughed. "Young William is artless with a bow. Robin is teaching him."

"But—"

"Did you not see?" Tuck inquired. "Robin and Will are of similar size and are dressed alike. Robin shot the arrow, then backed into the tent while the Sheriff and the rest observed the measuremen. Will stepped out to take his place."

"Oh," Sam said, at last forcing himself to follow the friar. "I guess I was watching the measuremen as well." He hastened his step as one of Vaisey's men broke through the crowd and turned toward them.

Tuck also saw the soldier, and changed course, pushing sideways into the mob. "The Sheriff's men hunt Robin, but lesser criminals are also fair game. Come!" He grabbed Sam's elbow and dragged him further into the crowd.

Sam looked back to see if the soldier followed them, and was surprised to see the man turn and race back toward the Sheriff.

"Wait," Sam called to Tuck.

"I fear waiting may be our last mistake," the friar called back, still tugging Sam's elbow.

"Something's happened," Sam said, breaking free of Tuck's grasp. "Vaisey's man is no longer chasing us."

"That is not good," Tuck said. "We must determine why."

The portly friar's bravery startled Sam, and he had to run on his abused feet to keep up as Tuck forced his way toward the platform through the now diminished crowd.

When they returned more or less to the place where they'd watched the tournament, Sam saw two men in black being held by the Sheriff's men. One sported blond hair, the other dark.

"They must have checked the tents," Tuck whispered. "And captured Robin before he escaped. We must rescue him!"

"Sure," Sam said. "But not right now. If you haven't noticed, the two of us are grossly outnumbered."

The friar sighed, watching as several of the Sheriff's men returned to take position around the captured outlaws. "You speak truly. We must retreat and form a plan."

Retreating was easier said than done. Though the Sheriff had successfully baited and trapped Robin Hood, snaring Will Scarlet in the bargain, he still had several soldiers wandering through the crowds searching for the remaining Merry Men. Fortunately, they were busy congratulating themselves over Robin's arrest, and their efforts were half-hearted.

Street by street, Sam and Tuck made their way to Mansfield Gate where a crowd of angry farmers was demanding a refund of their five pennies.

"The contest ended mid-stride," one of the farmers shouted.

"No winner was proclaimed," called another.

"'Twas five pennies to enter Nottingham," a guard argued. "Ye entered. Leave in peace, or ye shall pay another five pennies."

In the confusion, Sam and Tucked slipped unnoticed past the guards, hobbled a short distance down the road, then turned into the trees.

"We are to meet the others at the Hospital of St John the Baptist," Tuck said, reminding Sam of Robin's instructions from that morning. Was it only that morning they had left Robin's camp? It seemed like days ago. At least they didn't have to walk all the way back to Robin's camp in Sherwood Forest. Sam thought he would die first.

After less than twenty minutes of stumbling through the forest, across another road, and through another brief stand of trees, they arrived at the hospital. Tuck rushed them inside to a large common room with a central table surrounded by chairs, where they met Little John, David of Doncaster, Reynold Greenleaf, and Much the Miller's Son. A few minutes later, Gilbert Whitehand, Azeem the Moor, and Maid Marian joined them.

"My Robin has been taken by the Sheriff," Marian exclaimed, her cheeks wet with tears.

Alan-a-Dale, a roving minstrel who had recently joined the Merry Men, tried to console her, but failed.

"We shall get Robin back," Little John declared. "The Sheriff will have taken him to the gaol. I need three men. We shall storm the keep, put the Sheriff and his men to the sword, and return Robin to Sherwood Forest."

Azeem shook his head. "The Sheriff will expect such an attack."

Once again, Sam was impressed by how well the Moor spoke English. The tattooed foreigner spoke it better than many of the locals.

"Then I will need four men," Little John countered.

Tuck pulled Sam aside. "Such planning is not for the likes of us. Let us give them space. Once they settle on a plan, we shall listen and tell them why it is doomed to fail."

Sam's cheek twitched. "Well, aren't you a ray of sunshine?"

"There are too few of us," Tuck said. "No matter what attempt is made, the Sheriff's men shall cut us down."

"Then we need more men," Sam suggested. "Where should we get them?"

Tuck just shook his head, much as Azeem had done. "And I have worse news."

"Spill it," Sam said. The last thing he needed right now was worse news.

"I have spoken with the silent monks. Your friend from Connecticut has escaped."

"How did that happen?" Sam demanded.

The friar's expression grew red. "The monks pantomimed an explanation until I bid them stop. I, too, have vows to keep."

Sam could imagine what tricks Carmen Sternwood might have pulled on the innocent monks. "Don't worry about it. When I questioned her, all she did was lie. I doubt she'd know the truth if it jumped up and strangled her. I'll still have to take her with me when I find a way home, though."

"I will help in any way I can," Tuck said, his expression still darkened by guilt.

Sam pushed the problem aside so he could focus on the larger issue. Who was there who could help them rescue Robin Hood? He struggled with what he remembered about his childhood stories of Robin Hood and his Merry Men, but all that came to him was a few men in green tights camping in the forest, the evil Sheriff living in what seemed a very small castle, various farmers paying outrageous taxes, and guarded carriages on the roadways waiting to be robbed. It hardly seemed like a functional economy. Was there no one else?

At the sound of approaching boots, Sam looked up. It was Sagramore. At his side stood a young boy.

"Sagramore," Tuck said, seeming almost happy to see his detested murderer. "Thank the one and only God you are safe. Who is your friend?"

The ex-knight cast his gaze about, as though making sure no one else was in hearing distance. "The lad calls himself Bob. Says he has a note for a foreigner known as Sam Spade."

Sam said nothing, but looked more closely at the boy. He might have been eight years old, possibly younger, and wore worn and ragged clothing. His face was smudged with dirt and lacked the barest hint of cleverness.

"I have heard tell of this Sam Spade," Tuck said. "Perhaps if Bob gives me the note, I may find a way to deliver it to him."

The boy blinked at Tuck, then turned toward Sam. "You are Sam Spade."

"Oh," Sam said. "How do you figure that?"

"I was told the foreigner wore a long coat the colour of deer hide, and an odd hat that serves no function." The boy dug a hand into his pocket and pulled out a slip of rough parchment. He offered it to Sam.

Sam took the note. "I'm curious what a man who would insult my hat has to say."

Everyone watched as he unfolded the parchment. The penmanship was poor but legible. Sam read it aloud. "I saws who kilt Artur Geiger. For money, I will tell thee and forgoet."

"Who gave you this?" Sam asked, looking up from the note. But the boy was gone.

22
THIS SO-CALLED WITNESS

"Apologies." Sagramore wagged his head sheepishly. "I was watching you read the letter."

"As was I," Tuck said. "It is an intriguing message. But how do we act on it?"

"That's okay," Sam said. "There's more." He looked back at the note. "Meet me at midnite at Pallium's Parchments."

"It smells of a trap," Sagramore said.

Tuck nodded his agreement.

Sam rubbed his ear, then rubbed it again when no nuggets of wisdom came to him. "Sure it's a trap. But whose? This doesn't feel like Vaisey."

"No," Tuck agreed. "The Sheriff has men of letters who would write a better note."

"I need to check this out," Sam said. Before anyone could object, he added, "I'll be careful."

Tuck shook his head, and Sagramore frowned.

"Look," Sam said. "The worst that could happen is I'll end up in jail with Robin. When you rescue him, you can rescue me as well."

"Methinks that is not the worst that could happen," Sagramore said.

Tuck wasn't convinced either. "Unless we find more men to help us—a great many more men—there will be no rescue."

"Well." Sam pulled off his fedora, turned it in his hands, then put it back on. "We're in such a pickle now, how can it get any worse?"

"Things are never so bad they cannot be made worse," Sagramore suggested.

Sam chuckled. "Sir Sagramore. I never knew you had such a way with words. If you don't mind, I'm gonna steal that line from you."

Bafflement clouded the ex-knight's one-eyed face. "They are but words. How does one go about stealing them?"

"Where I come from," Sam said, "it's a crime. Hey, let's get something to eat. If I haven't talked myself out of going by then, you'll have won your argument."

Tuck grinned. "I am glad you mentioned nourishment. I am on the threshold of collapse from hunger."

Sagramore snorted. "You are always on the threshold of something from hunger."

"Such is my lot in life," Tuck said.

The sun was setting as silent monks lit candles and arranged a plain white cloth on the long table. The Merry Men stepped out of the way as jugs of wine that was dark, thick, and syrupy, and smelled of cinnamon were set out, followed by wooden platters of meats, cheeses, and several kinds of bread. The bread came as small, whole loaves, and the cheeses were round and the size of small pumpkins. The meat was cut into strips or chunks, and some still contained bones. Sam couldn't tell by look or smell what animal or animals they had come from.

"Isn't this a conference room?" he asked Tuck.

The friar looked at him. "I know not what that is. This is the refectory, where we have our meals."

"Yeah, I got that."

As the Merry Men sat themselves around the table and began tearing into the bread and meat with their fingers, Sam realized he was witnessing what might be the oddest candle-lit dinner in history.

Tuck found them two available chairs and poured himself a drink from one of the jugs. While there were cups, there were no plates, just cloth napkins.

The wine and food seemed to help Robin's men lose some of the bleakness they'd carried since returning from the tournament, but the meal failed to interrupt Little John's argument with Azeem and a few of the others. Most of the disagreement centred around what Tuck had pointed out. There were too few Merry Men to go up against the Sheriff.

Sam's stomach growled, and he realized he hadn't eaten since breakfast. Now was not the time for grazing. Taking a knife from one of the platters, he slit open one of the small loaves of bread, then sliced cheese from several of the rounds. Into the folded open loaf he piled on alternating layers of meats and cheeses. Finally, he squeezed the bread back together and began chewing from one end. The bread was tough, but the meats were tasty and the cheeses flavourful. He closed his eyes to relish the experience. When he opened them again, he saw that everyone had stopped eating and were staring at him.

He swallowed what was in his mouth before speaking. "It's called a submarine sandwich."

"What is a submarine?" Azeem asked.

Tuck was more direct. "What is a sandwich?"

"Well, it's . . ." Of all the things Sam thought he might be called upon to explain, this was not one of them. "It's this." He waved the sandwich at them.

"I think I see," Tuck said. "You use part of the meal to hold the rest of the meal together."

Sam thought about that. He had to admit it was about as good an explanation of a sandwich as he had heard.

By the time he took another bite, Tuck had cut open a new loaf and was stuffing it with meats. Others watched, but in the end, only Sagramore followed suit. Evidently, the Merry Men decided they could never eat a whole sandwich. It didn't seem to occur to them that a sandwich could be shared.

His hunger appeased, Sam stepped outside the building and sat on one of the stone benches, eager to take some weight off his feet. Tilting his head back, he looked up at the sky. The night was now full dark, the stars glowing like fireflies across the heavens. A full moon offered enough light that Sam could make out the monk's garden and the trees beyond. He had no idea what time it was, or when it would be midnight. He glanced at his watch, but the Rolex told him it was 8 p.m., Hartford time.

"How do you ever know what time it is?" he asked Tuck, who joined him on the bench.

The friar, apparently sated after eating an entire submarine sandwich on top of his earlier grazing, shrugged. "What does it matter the time?"

"I have a rendezvous at midnight," Sam said.

"I had hoped you had forgotten."

Sam shook his head. "The more I think about it, the more I have to go. How would this so-called witness know I'd be interested unless he saw me there. I think it's the real deal."

Tuck scowled. "Do you have funds for the ransom?"

Sam reached into his coat pocket and retrieved the Pendragon coin he had kept from Camelot. He had no idea how much it was worth here in Nottingham, but six years ago it had been worth a king's ransom in Camelot.

"Put that away," the friar said. He ground his teeth, then grunted as he rummaged through the folds of his robes, retrieving a small, cloth bag. After loosening the string that secured it, he spilled out some coins. "How much coin do you believe this extortionist requires?"

"I have no idea."

Tuck ground his teeth some more, then spilled out several additional coins. "The only currency of worth in Nottingham today must bear King John's likeness. By order of the Sheriff."

"Who is this John?" Sam asked, accepting the coins.

"A scoundrel."

"So, Vaisey's BFF," Sam said.

The friar glowered at him. "I know not what that means. John Lackland is Good King Richard's younger brother, who seeks to usurp the throne by way of murder and robbery. Vaisey, though evil and notorious in his own way, is John's tool in Nottinghamshire. The taxes Vaisey extorts go to pay John's redshank mercenaries as they raze the countryside."

That was a bigger fish than Sam wanted to fry. "Forget I asked. Thanks for the loan, though. Unless things go sideways, I'll return with the information and your money."

"Do not worry yourself," Tuck said. "Should Little John's rescue attempt succeed, we shall also liberate the Sheriff's taxes. Vaisey keeps his horde in a locked chest, in a locked cell, in the gaol. Should the attempt fail . . ." The friar paused. "None of us shall have need of money."

"Well, we don't want the rescue to fail. Make sure Little John doesn't do anything stupid before I get back."

Tuck smiled. "As Little John does everything I ask, that shall not be a problem."

"Good," Sam said.

Tuck continued smiling.

"That was sarcasm, wasn't it?"

"Your wisdom knows no bounds, Sam Spade."

There was nothing more Sam could do about Robin or his Merry Men, so he climbed unsteadily to his aching feet and retrieved his walking stick. For the few moments he'd been sitting, he'd forgotten all about his feet. What he really needed was more of that salve and a good night's rest. Not yet, though.

Sagramore stepped out of the hospital and let out a heavy sigh. "You are meeting with your writer of parchments?"

"I don't have much choice," Sam said.

"Then I shall accompany you."

"I'd like that, believe me. But I need you here."

The ex-knight arched a brow. "Oh?"

"Someone needs to keep Little John from going off half-cocked. Tuck claims not to be that someone."

Sagramore trained his good eye at Tuck, who shrugged. "Then of course. I shall keep Little John in his place."

"You think you can?" Sam asked.

"If they are to succeed," the ex-knight said, "the Merry Men will require my help. Bows are fine weapons, but slow and unwieldy in enclosed spaces. Any rescue will have need of my sword."

Sam nodded. "Good thinking. If Little John gets restless, tell him he needs to figure out how to get more men. The Sheriff has an army. Little John has a bridge club."

Sagramore wrinkled his brow. "If you say it is so, then it is true."

"I'll be back as soon as I can." With that, Sam hobbled toward the dirt track that followed the wall toward the town gates.

23
A DEAD MAN'S MONEY

SAM HAD CONSIDERED going the other way, through the forest, across the field, and into the secret tunnel inside the wall. But even if he didn't lose himself in the darkness, and the door hadn't been rebarricaded after the Sheriff captured Robin, he had no idea how to get to Pallium's Parchments from there without going through Geiger's house. Too many ifs. That, of course, meant he had to deal with the gate guard.

The dirt track was lonelier than an East Hartford alley at 3 a.m. A terrific place to get mugged. But it was a short walk to the easternmost gate he had glimpsed earlier that day from the Mansfield Gate. A sign posted on the wall and illuminated by torches declared the entrance as York Gate.

Two soldiers lounged outside the wall looking bored as no one currently was entering or leaving the town. They seemed surprised to see Sam and gave his trench coat, fedora, and walking stick a long look before making a tired demand for five pennies. This time, thanks to Tuck, Sam had the coins. The soldiers seemed satisfied and waved him through.

The town was only slightly better lit than the road outside the gate. Candlelight, and perhaps the light from cook fires, escaped through the occasional shuttered window, accentuating the starry night. If the sky had been cloudy, Sam doubted he could travel at all without using the penlight in his pocket, or a lamp like the ones he had used in Camelot.

The streets seemed quieter than they had that morning. After the abrupt end of the tournament, Sam doubted any planned revelry had proceeded. Visitors had left for their farms and villages, townsfolk had returned to their homes, and the sidewalks had been rolled up. Just another quiet night in medieval Nottingham.

He chuckled to himself at the thought of those who had bet on the tournament, only to have it fall apart midway through. He suspected a lot of people had lost their shirts and were now crying into their beer in Nottingham's various inns and taverns. Maybe some of those disconsolate men could be convinced to help with Little John's rescue.

Ignoring the complaints from his feet, Sam hobbled eastward from the gate, taking narrow, mostly deserted streets. Had the town been as large as Camelot, he would have gotten lost, but the whole of Nottingham felt no larger than Bridgewater, Connecticut, a small resort town that catered to wealthy New York tourists, where as a teenager he had found work one summer because no one knew who he was or that his father had died in prison, a convicted dirty cop. Sam had to say one thing about his life—it had never been boring.

When he reached Halifax Lane, Sam sat on the bench opposite Geiger's betting house and took a few steady breaths as the pain in his toes and heels dulled to a steady ache. It felt good to be off his feet. Or at least not as bad as being on them. With careful concentration, he wiggled his toes within his shoes. The movement hurt, but it was a good kind of hurt. It told him his toes were still attached and probably still alive. He should have had the monks apply more salve before leaving the hospital, but dreaded the thought of taking his shoes and socks off and putting them back on again.

Forcing himself, he left those thoughts alone and focused his attention on Geiger's book shop. With the shutters closed, it was impossible to tell if anyone was inside. Sam had no idea of the time, but the lights in the houses he had passed suggested the occupants were still awake. He had to figure midnight was still a good way off. Which was perfect. He wanted to check the area and be in a good vantage spot before his witness showed up.

Before he got too comfortable, Sam figured he should get back on his feet and see if Pallium's Parchments was occupied. The note said to meet at the shop, but surely the place would be closed for business well before midnight. If the shop was open, he still needed to speak with Effie. Since finding Geiger's corpse, he'd assumed she had returned to her job at the shop and everything was all right. He still hoped that was true. If she hadn't left for the day, he'd soon know.

Bracing himself, Sam rose from the bench and hobbled across the street as fast as his walking stick and aching feet could carry him. The shop looked just as dark up close as it had from a distance. He tried the door handle and almost fell down in disbelief. The door opened.

"We are just closing up," a voice from behind the counter said. Effie.

"I'm not here to buy parchments."

"Sam?"

He walked up to the counter. Since it was night outside, his eyes adjusted quickly to the dark interior. He could easily make out the outline of Effie's face and hair in the gloom. "I have to ask you something."

"What?"

Was it just him? Or was Effie not being talkative? "Was it you who sent the note?"

"Note? What note? Sam, you are not making sense."

"Okay. What were you doing at Geiger's house earlier today?"

"You *were* following me." Effie let out an undecipherable humph. "I thought I saw you."

"Never mind that. Why were you there?"

Effie's voice was hard as she answered. "Arthur Geiger is my boss. I delivered bet money to him. He prefers not to keep monies in the shop where any tomfool might try to steal it. I make deliveries twice a day."

As an ex-cop, Sam questioned Geiger's security policies. Tomfoolhardy is exactly how he'd describe them. "Did anything unusual happen during that delivery?"

"Sam, why all the questions?"

"Humour me."

"No," Effie admitted. "Not really. Well, yes actually. Mr. Geiger said he was alone, but I'm pretty sure someone else was in the house."

"You heard someone?"

"No, but he acted strangely. Seemed overeager for me to leave, then told me to go out by the back way. He had never done that before."

"You didn't see or hear anyone as you left? No unusual sounds from the house once you were outside?"

"No. Sam, what is this about?"

Sam didn't think Effie could tell him anything more, so he decided to share what he knew. "Shortly after you left, a woman in the house screamed."

"What?"

"I thought it was you, so I rushed inside."

Effie leaned forward over the counter. "What did you find?"

"Geiger. On the floor. Dead."

Effie raised a hand to her mouth.

"And Carmen Sternwood, unconscious on a couch."

"Carmen Sternwood?" Effie sucked in a breath of air. "The Carmen whose image you showed me? Was this the woman who screamed?"

"I assume so. I was hoping you could tell me more of what happened in Geiger's house."

"It seems you know more than I," Effie said. "But I can tell you one thing."

"What's that?"

"The house does not belong to Arthur Geiger. It belongs to someone else. I don't know his name, but I believe Mr. Geiger works—worked—for him."

"Does Vaisey own the house?"

"The Sheriff? Why would you think that?"

"Just a feeling," Sam said.

Effie set her elbows on the counter and buried her face in her hands. "What am I to do? The day is ended and I am to deliver this afternoon's betting money to Mr. Geiger. Only Mr. Geiger is dead."

"No one has come to you?" Sam asked. "Given you different instructions?"

Face still in hands, Effie shook her head.

"Well, Vaisey has been busy. He might not have gotten around to it."

Effie looked up. "Why do you insist that Mr. Geiger worked for the Sheriff? What Mr. Geiger does—did—is illegal. It is the Sheriff's job to arrest him."

"The current Sheriff of Nottingham has his own agenda," Sam said. "And it doesn't include upholding the law."

"If what you say is true," Effie stood up straight, "then all this time I have been working for the Sheriff." Effie reached below the counter and retrieved a bag that rattled with coins. The sack looked heavy and was about the size of the sandwich Sam had eaten for dinner. "What am I to do with this?"

"That's a good question," Sam said, eyeing the betting house's afternoon proceeds.

"There is not usually this much money," Effie said, dropping the heavy bag onto the counter, where it clunked and rearranged itself as coins shifted. "With today's tournament, there were more and larger bets."

"What time is it?" Sam asked.

"Time?" Effie seemed surprised by the question.

"How close to midnight?"

"It is almost midnight now. Technically, midnight is when I close the shop."

Sam laughed. "Nottingham, the town that never sleeps."

Effie gave him a peculiar look, but before she could speak, the shop door opened and a man stepped inside. In the darkness, Sam couldn't make out a face.

"Ya have me money?" the man said.

"What money?" Effie demanded. "I know you haven't won a bet, because Mr. Geiger cut you off."

"You know this man?" Sam asked.

"His name is Joe. Joe Brody. He was one of Mr. Geiger's clients before he was caught trying to rig the results of an archery tournament. He paid the measuremen to ensure his bet would win."

Brody snarled and took two steps into the room. He stopped when he bumped into the table that filled the centre of the shop. "The measuremen lied. They had their own plans, then lied to shift the blame to me when they was caught."

"Either way," Effie said. "Your name is not in the book. Mr. Geiger owes you nothing."

Brody grinned. "Mr. Geiger need no longer worry 'bout who he owes."

"So you know he's dead," Sam said. "I take it you sent the note?"

Brody nodded.

"And you know who killed him?"

Again, Brody nodded.

Sam reached into his pants pocket and fingered the remaining coins Tuck had given him. "How much is that information going to cost?"

Brody nodded a third time, only with his chin aimed at the sack of coins on the table.

Now it was Sam's turn to grin. "I don't think so. That's not my money to pay with."

Brody snorted. "'Tis a dead man's money. Geiger no be needin' it."

"Even so," Sam said. "Your information isn't worth that much." He emptied his pocket onto the counter. A dozen pennies. They looked like flat stones in the pale moonlight that seeped in through the open doorway. "This is all you'll get."

"I can sell what I know elsewheres," Brody growled.

"Go ahead. I never knew Geiger. Couldn't care less who killed him."

"Then why was ya outside his house?"

Sam laughed. "I can sell you the answer to that question. How about a trade?"

Brody shuffled over so the table no longer stood in his way. Sam could see a fighter's stance forming. The fool was going to try to attack him. Normally that wouldn't be a problem. Sam knew how to handle himself. Only, in his current condition, he wasn't sure he could win a fight. His entire body ached from his lower back on down. His shoulders weren't doing well either after carrying Carmen across England's back forty. Best nip this in the bud.

Sam tightened his hand on his walking stick and kept his gaze focused on Brody's midsection. When the man made his move, Sam flicked the stick up, catching Brody in the stomach with its business end.

The would-be thief let out a half-oof, half-awk, then turned and stumbled out of the shop, not bothering to close the door.

"I believe you have done him an injury," Effie said.

Sam turned and threw Effie a wide smile she probably

couldn't see. "Nothing he didn't deserve."

"Are you not curious of what he knows?" she asked.

"Doll, as long as you didn't kill Arthur Geiger, I don't really care who did."

Effie's eyes widened. "Of course, I did not kill him. Why would you think that?"

Sam swept his pile of pennies off the counter and returned them to his pocket. "Only two people were with Geiger shortly before he died. You and Carmen Sternwood. I have a hard time imagining either of you doing it, so there must have been someone else in the house. I'd hoped to find out who from this Brody character. After meeting him, though, I'm not sure I'd trust a word he said. For all I know, *he* killed Geiger."

Effie looked down at the sack of coins. "What do you suggest we do with this?"

Sam rubbed his ear. "Unless you want people to think you stole it, I think we should head over to Geiger's house."

"But, if Arthur is dead . . ."

Sam shrugged. "How are you supposed to know that?"

24
A LAUGH A MINUTE

SAM WATCHED AS Effie hung a CLOSED sign on the shop door before returning his gaze to the empty street. There was no sign of Joe Brody, or anyone else for that matter. The street was dark, the moon and stars offering the only light.

"You step with a curious gait," Effie remarked as they headed up the street. "And that stick is more than a weapon. It is an aid for walking. Are you ill?"

"A temporary setback," Sam explained. "I've been walking more than I'm used to."

Effie nodded. "There is a hospital outside the town wall. I am told the monks there work miracles."

"The monks," Sam said, "have already worked their magic. They're the reason I'm able to walk at all."

"Magic?" Effie stopped and looked at him in the darkness, though Sam wasn't sure how much she could see. "But there is no magic."

"A miracle, then. Sometimes it's hard to tell the difference between miracles, magic, and science."

"I am unfamiliar with that word," Effie said. "Science. It rolls pleasingly off the tongue."

"Let's see," Sam said. "I'm no philosopher, but I'll give it a whirl. A miracle is something you can't explain, so it must come from a higher power. Magic you can't explain either, but you understand it well enough to see some rules and figure maybe a higher power isn't necessary. Then, when you finally know how something works, or at least think you do, it's science."

Effie stared at him. "Perhaps you should keep your philosophy to yourself. The Church holds much sway in Nottinghamshire."

"You might be right," Sam said. "Look, why don't you walk several steps ahead of me. You don't usually have company for this trip, do you?"

"No. I am always alone."

Sam's heart fell. The way Effie said it, he was sure she meant alone in more than just the current context. "You shouldn't be alone." He meant that in more than the current context as well.

"I can take care of myself," Effie said.

And you have been, Sam thought. For years now. "Okay. You walk ahead and enter Geiger's house like you normally do. Stick to your routine. I'll keep an eye out here and listen for trouble coming from the house. Just so you know, someone removed Geiger's body and cleaned up. You won't have that ugly experience to look forward to. But if there's trouble, yell, and I'll come running."

Effie's lips moved, but no words came out. Then she walked on ahead.

Sam waited until she had gone maybe ten yards, then hobbled after her.

He had no idea what she would find at the house. Would it be empty? Geiger forgotten while Vaisey amused himself with Robin in custody? That is, if the Sheriff had anything to do with Geiger's business. It was a good theory, but he'd yet to have proof. Or had someone taken Geiger's place, and was waiting for Effie to arrive with the afternoon book?

Sam figured the latter. As a cop, he'd dealt with criminals. They were like cockroaches. Step on one, and another was waiting to take its place. That's why he couldn't just show up with Effie. There'd be questions. And it might put her in danger. Best that Effie just follow her routine. If something went sideways, Sam could get there soon enough, even with raw feet.

There was also Joe Brody to consider. Where had he gone after leaving the book shop? Was the mook hiding in the shadows, following them? Had he gone ahead to Geiger's house, where he waited for Effie to show up with the coins?

Too many questions. Not enough answers.

As Effie strode up the short walk to Geiger's door, Sam hobbled next to a tree and leaned against it, using its branches to block most of the moonlight. No one had tried to rob Effie on her journey between shop and house, more evidence that Geiger had been connected, if not to the Sheriff, then someone else. Nottingham's criminals knew to leave Effie and her deliveries alone. Or maybe everyone but dumb onions like Joe Brody.

Effie knocked.

Sam wasn't surprised when the door opened and she disappeared inside.

He had a better angle than earlier in the day but still couldn't see who stood inside the doorway. His gut, however, told him it was a woman.

He resumed walking as the door swung closed, intent on getting closer to the house in case there was trouble. Vaisey didn't seem the type to employ a woman to take Geiger's place. Sam didn't like the look of this. Not one bit.

There were no screams. No yelling. But Sam wasn't about to wait outside. Something didn't smell right. He was almost at a run when he reached the door and pushed it open.

Light momentarily blinded him. He counted five, no, six candles. Possibly more he couldn't see right away. His vision adjusted quickly, however.

Effie stood maybe three feet further into the room, the bag of coins cradled like a small child to her chest. The woman standing in front of Effie, reaching for the sack, was none other than Carmen Sternwood.

"It's my money," Carmen growled. "Art owes it to me. I earned it." Her hands froze in mid-reach as she noticed Sam's arrival.

"Earned it how?" Sam asked as he pushed the door closed.

The young woman added a scowl to an expression that was already disturbingly savage. "None of your business."

Sam leaned against the door. "That's a pretty weak argument for convincing Effie to give you Geiger's money."

Carmen placed her hands on her hips. "That I now own Art's business should be argument enough."

"You?" Effie asked. "You are but a simple client of Mr. Geiger. A minor one at that. How is it you now own his business?"

"I—Well, you'll just have to take my word for it."

Sam let out a soft laugh. "If you think that by killing a man you inherit his property, you're sadly mistaken."

"I told you before," Carmen spat in what was almost a shriek. "I didn't kill anyone. A man named Joe Brody killed Arthur Geiger."

"And you know this how?"

"I saw him do it. They were arguing." Carmen pointed at Effie. "Right where she's standing. Then Joe took something out of his pocket and smacked Arthur on the head with it."

"Something?"

"I don't know. A blackjack or something."

Sam smiled. "I don't think blackjacks have been invented yet."

"A rock, then, maybe."

"I'm sure he could have found a better weapon than a rock."

Carmen lifted her nose in irritation. "I don't know what it was. All I know is Art dropped to the floor, I screamed, and Joe went running out the back. Then, well, then I must have fainted."

"You told me earlier today that you didn't see a thing before you fainted."

An unladylike snort sounded from the young woman's nose. "Why would I tell you anything? I don't even know who you are, though you're obviously not from around here. Are you the one responsible for bringing me to this backward place?"

Before Sam could think of a reply, the door swung open, hammering him in the back. The only thing that stopped him from landing on his face was his quick reflexes and his borrowed walking stick that he dug into the floor like a third leg.

With the grace of a drunken horse, he spun around and found himself face-to-face with a stout man dressed in polished leather. A glance downward confirmed Sam's suspicion that he was armed with a sword. The soldier glowered at Sam and the two women, then stepped back outside. He was replaced by someone Sam remembered well.

"L-Lord Sheriff," Effie muttered.

Vaisey nodded. "Lady Peregrine." His eyes drifted to the sack of coins clutched to her bosom. "Good. You have Arthur's proceeds for the afternoon."

"W-Where is Mr. Geiger?" Effie asked, doing exactly what Sam had told her, though it might be a bit late now that Miss Sternwood had just described Geiger's death.

"Arthur Geiger has gone on to a new position," the Sheriff lied smoothly. "I shall appoint his replacement in the morning." He returned his gaze to Sam.

"But," Effie continued, "this woman claims she is Mr. Geiger's replacement."

Vaisey sighed and turned his attention on Carmen. "Do I know you?"

Carmen swallowed. "I work for Arthur Geiger."

Vaisey dismissed her with a glance. "Not anymore. Present yourself to his replacement when I appoint one. If he deigns to hire you, then so be it."

Sam gawked as Carmen curtsied. Doing so must have galled the entitled brat.

The Sheriff once again turned his attention to Sam. "Well, well, well. The Merlin's pie." Vaisey snickered. "You are the last person I expected to see in Nottingham."

"I'd heard you'd done great things with the place," Sam said. "Had to come see for myself."

Vaisey lifted his hand to his chin and pulled on his beard. If his moustache had been longer, Sam was sure he would have twirled it. The Sheriff of Nottingham raised his voice so he could be heard outside. "Guy, come collect from Lady Peregrine the proceeds from this afternoon's book."

A tall, skinny man with receding hair squeezed in through the doorway and around the Sheriff, who didn't move to unblocked his way. Even without Vaisey calling his name, Sam would have recognized Page Guy, despite the passage of a dozen years. Guy of Gisbourne still looked like a snivelling sycophant, just a taller, older one.

"Hurry up, you incompetent fool. I have no desire to still be here when the sun rises."

Guy said nothing, but took the sack from Effie and scurried back outside.

"No desire to be here," Sam said to Vaisey. "But I thought you owned this house."

The Sheriff snorted. "I own many houses. I do not sleep in all of them."

"But you do own this house?" Sam said.

"Of course. Why do you ask?"

"No reason. Just curious."

Vaisey's left eye twitched. "That is one of your many problems. You are too curious for your own good."

"I won't say you're wrong," Sam said.

A frown pinched the Sheriff's lips, and he turned his head. "What are you really doing in Nottingham?"

Sam shrugged. "Just passing through."

"On your way to . . ."

"London," Sam said. "There's a bridge and a clock tower I've heard a lot about."

"Then you are not on your way to Camelot?"

"Camelot? Yesterday's news."

"I see. Were you not a friend of Robin of Locksley?"

Sam's cheek twitched. "The boy with the bow? I'm not sure you'd call us friends."

"Very well." The Sheriff seemed to relax a bit. "Am I correct in saying that if I asked why you were following Lady Euphemia Peregrine along the street outside; you would have a good answer for me?"

Sam smiled. "You were asking about friends. You could use that word for Effie and me. She was my clerk for a time back in Camelot. We grew close. Didn't we, Effie?"

When there was no answer, Sam turned, only to discover Effie was nowhere in sight. Neither was Carmen. "Oh. They appear to have run out on us."

Vaisey smiled. "The womenfolk fled out the back of the house while we were conversing. No matter. Women are of little consequence."

"If you say so," Sam said. His inner voice continued with, *you little weasel.*

"Do you plan on staying in Nottingham long?" Vaisey asked.

"I'm not staying in Nottingham," Sam said. "I came in for today's tournament. That kind of blew up in our faces, didn't it? No. I have a small camp down the road. I'll sleep there tonight, then continue on my way to London in the morning."

Vaisey stared at him for several moments, then sniffed. "Very well. I expect never to see you again. If I do, you will not be a happy man."

Sam smiled. "That's what I like about you, Vaisey. Always a laugh a minute."

25
THAT WAS NEVER THE PLAN

THE SHERIFF'S MEN cast Sam cold looks as he hobbled out of Geiger's house and into the street, none colder than Guy of Gisbourne's. Vaisey's toady stood like a wraith among the half-dozen armed men, his thin fingers clutching Effie's sack of coins like it was worth more than his own life. Perhaps it was.

Unlike Camelot, where the knights clanked around in armour, Vaisey's soldiers wore leather or cloth, or a combination of both. There seemed to be no standard uniform. No one bore a badge or a coat of arms on their chest. Sam was pretty sure none had earned one. These soldiers looked like lost souls, who in Hartford would be panhandling in alleyways or collecting empties from garbage bins. Risking their lives to serve Nottingham's Sheriff was probably a career of last resort. He doubted they'd amount to much in a fight and figured Sagramore could take them on six at a time.

But Sagramore wasn't there. It was just Sam on his own, and, as Effie had pointed out, somewhat crippled. His semi-automatic handgun wouldn't shoot a single bullet, never mind the endless quantity Merlin had magicked it to. Sam figured he might be able to handle one of Vaisey's men, even with a wooden stick against sharpened metal, but two or more would be suicide. The best move was to walk away. He just hoped they'd let him walk. At any moment, Vaisey could give the order to cut Sam to ribbons. The town gate couldn't come soon enough.

The street with Vaisey's men was otherwise deserted, but as Sam left Geiger's house behind and walked closer to the centre of town, Nottingham seemed to come alive. Lights appeared in windows, and people wandered the streets. Where had they come from? Had the bars all closed for the night?

Rough-looking men roamed in twos and threes, many of them laughing at whispered jokes. Couples walked quickly, their heads down and not speaking a word. There were even a few bands of women, travelling in packs no fewer than six, hurrying along, crossing away from any men who came too near.

One such pack was on a collision course with Sam and veered to the opposite side of the street. Sam wondered what would happen if he drifted in the same direction, then stopped and stood where he was. Isn't that? It couldn't be.

Resuming motion, he began hobbling toward them. The pack of women slowed, then veered back the other way. Sam adjusted his course, and the women slowed again. He could now see scowls on each of their faces, despite the darkness.

"Ladies," he said. "Might I have a word?"

One of the women, the oldest by the look of her—he assumed Effie and Robin would call her a matron—spoke in a forceful voice. "Men do not speak with women after dark. If you would have a word, find us after the sun rises."

Well, that was odd. "But I know you," Sam said. "Well, I know one of you. Nora?"

Though dressed in Nottingham style—a white underdress with a dyed woollen overdress—the taller woman among them could have been Nora's twin.

"Is *Nora* a name?" demanded the matron. "If so, you are mistaken. None of us go by that name. Please, I must adjure you. Leave us be or we shall be forced to call upon the Sheriff's men to have you arrested."

The women began moving again, shifting to the far left to go around Sam. The woman who looked like Nora cast Sam an appraising look, but there was no sign of recognition. Sam had to be wrong. How could it be Nora? Nora would have answered him.

Even so, Sam watched as the pack of women slipped past him and worked their way further along the street. At the first alley they came to, they turned.

Sam was dead tired. It had been a tricky two days since he'd found himself in Sherwood Forest. His entire body ached, and his feet were murder. And just minutes ago, Nottingham's Sheriff had threatened worse punishment should he see Sam again. The smart move would be to return to St John the Baptist Hospital and get some sleep.

He shook his head and mumbled into the darkness. "Why do I never make the smart move?"

Hobbling as quickly as his walking stick and abused feet allowed, Sam shuffled down the street in the direction the women had gone. When he turned at the corner, he discovered the alley to be a constricted street that accessed shanty-like rowhouses on either side. Up ahead, the pack of women drifted in the moonlight like ghostly shadows. Sam paced himself to close the distance, then paused when one woman split off from the group and entered one of the narrow houses. She was not the one who resembled Nora, so he resumed following the others.

Soon, another woman split off and approached one of the skinny houses. She was taller than the rest. Though Sam couldn't make out her face in the dark, he was certain she was the one who resembled Nora.

The pack continued on while Sam hobbled toward the shanty the tall woman had entered. When he reached the door, he rested his ear against it. The wood was thin enough that he could hear voices inside. Arguing, though he couldn't make out the words. Then he recognized one of the voices.

Sam grabbed the flimsy handle and pushed the door open, almost ripping it off its hinges. "Effie?"

Inside the house, a single candle illuminated a room almost devoid of furniture, and small enough that its three occupants made the place feel crowded. Effie and the woman who looked like Nora stood confronting a man Sam had recently met.

"Joe Brody? What are you doing here?"

The would-be extortionist allowed a broken-toothed grin to further mar his unpleasant features. "I be askin' the same. This be my house. What do ya here?"

Sam cast a questioning look at Effie.

"What? I—" The whites of the startled young woman's eyes glowed in the candlelight. "Carmen brought me. We needed a place to hide where the Sheriff's men would not think to look. I was as surprised as you to find Joe Brody here. How did you escape the Sheriff?"

"It wasn't that difficult," Sam said, brushing aside the question. "But let me get this straight. Carmen brought you to Brody? *Brody*? I'm not sure you're any safer. Where's Carmen now?"

"I know not," Effie said. "She spoke of looking for her sister."

"Her sister? I'm pretty sure Vivian Rutledge is a long way from Nottingham."

The other woman, the one who looked like Nora, chose that moment to speak. "Vivian." She said the name loudly, in Nora's voice.

Sam stared at her. "Nora?"

"Vivian," she said again, almost at a shout. Then she reached into a fold of the ratty dress she wore and produced a business card.

Sam took the card and held it near the candle flame. The name on it said Vivian Rutledge. It was the card Nora had accepted at the Sternwood estate when they had met with the General. Vivian had given Sam a card as well, only the General's older daughter had paused to write her personal phone number on the back.

Sam returned the card to Nora and gave her a closer inspection. He reached out to touch a bump on the side of her head. Nora shied away at the touch. "Owie."

"I hates to break up a party," Brody said, "but ya have not answered me question."

"This is my business partner Nora," Sam said. "I've been looking for her."

"Is she now?" said Brody. "According to Carmen, this be her sister Vivian."

"The one she went looking for?" Effie asked.

Brody nodded. "Miss Carmen be me houseguest these past days. We be havin' our own business arrangements."

Sam found himself at a loss for words. Nora injured and given another woman's identity, then left at the mercy of an unsavoury character. The missing words were quickly replaced by anger. Before Sam could act, however, the door opened.

"Vivian! There you are. I went to Ye Olde Salutation to fetch you."

Carmen Sternwood marched into the house, only then seeing

Sam occupying part of the dimly lit and crowded space. She froze, her mouth gaping open.

"Terrific," Sam said. "Now that we're all here, why don't we discuss Arthur Geiger?"

"What about Mr. Geiger?" Effie asked.

"As in," Sam clarified, "who killed him." He pointed at Brody. "Earlier tonight, you were going to tell me. All for the small price of Geiger's sack of coins."

Carmen shifted her gaping mouth to stare at Brody.

"And you," Sam said, pointing at Carmen, "felt that with Geiger dead, the sack of coins somehow belonged to you."

"I . . ." Carmen began but said no more.

"We had an agreement," Brody snarled at Carmen.

"What is happening here?" Effie asked.

Carmen ignored her, keeping her attention on Brody. "You tried to take the coins before Art's stooge brought them to me?"

"'Twas safer that way," Brody said.

Carmen waved her hands at Sam and Effie. "You would have told them that *I* killed Art, then run off with the coins while I rotted in jail."

Brody's face contorted into a sneer. "Ya see an opportunity, ya take it."

"It was him!" Carmen pointed at Brody. "He killed Art. I was supposed to take Art's place and collect the coins from this woman." She moved her finger to point at Effie. "Then we were to split the coins equally and flee Nottingham before anyone even knew Art was dead. That was the plan."

"That was never the plan," Brody retorted. He threw Sam an anxious look. "I be a thief, not a murderer. These women be new in town. Some days ago, this Carmen woman sees me put out at Geiger's book shop. She tells me she needs a place. And money. I tells her I know of money to be had. Offer a place to stay and introductions. Arrange everything. Arthur was never meant to die. I be there. At the house. Hidden. Carmen's part be to distract Arthur. Mine to subdue him. Hit him on the head. Tie him like a roast pig. Then we take the coin, Carmen and meself. Flee Nottingham as she said.

"But Arthur be uneasy. Carmen be a poor actress. He knows there be something amiss. He sends his woman out the back way. Is on his guard. Even so, I comes up behind and hits him. He goes down. The plan is a success. But then Carmen also hits him. With a stone in her hand. 'What be ya doin'?' I demand. 'There be not enough coin,' she says. 'This be the midday coin. We need matins coin as well.' I check Arthur. The man not be unconscious. He be dead. 'Ya kilt him,' I say. 'He be an evil man,' she says. Then she raises her hand with the stone at me."

"I was never going to hit you," Carmen growled.

Brody shook his head. "Ya wanted more coin. What better way than to kill ya partner? I wrestle the stone from her hand, and the bloody woman screams. The worse thing ta do, what with a dead man on the floor. So I hits her and takes the coins. Then I escapes out the back way, the secret way."

"I've yet to receive a penny," Carmen grumbled. "You still owe me."

Sam rubbed his eyes. As a cop, he'd seen his fair share of stupid criminals. Brody fell into that category. Carmen Sternwood was another matter. She had no clue how to be a criminal. He sighed. "Where are the coins now?"

"With that Sheriff-guy," Carmen said. "You were there. If you hadn't interrupted, I would have had them and escaped out the back before the po-po arrived."

Effie shook her head. "I would never have given you the coins on your say so."

"The other coins," Sam said, barely keeping the exasperation from his voice. "From this morning."

"I have 'em," Brody admitted. "That be why ya all be here, is it not? To take me coin?"

"They're my coins too," Carmen growled.

Sam had had enough. There were too many chefs in this kitchen. "Effie, you know where St John the Baptist Hospital is outside town?"

"Of course," Effie said. "I have never required their service, but I know where it is."

"Please escort Carmen and Nora there. I'll catch up shortly."

"Nora?" Effie and Carmen spoke at the same time.

Sam cast a quick glance at his partner, who under other circumstances he might think was high. Nora would never take drugs voluntarily, but something had happened to her. The apparent blow to the head might explain it, but why was Carmen going along with the story that Nora was her sister. "Vivian, then.

The town isn't safe right now. Not for any of us."

"I'm not leaving without my money," Carmen said.

Sam smiled. "You can stay if you like, sister, but you're guilty of either murder or conspiracy to commit murder. And the victim was one of the Sheriff's employees. He'll be looking for not just the missing coins, but retribution as well."

Carmen frowned and headed for the door. Nora, apparently believing she was Carmen's sister, followed. Effie squeezed Sam's arm and was last out the door.

"Now what?" Brody demanded. "Ya gonna threaten me if I don't hand over the coin?"

"You may find this hard to believe," Sam said, "but not everyone's end-all-to-beat-all is a meagre pile of pennies."

The ugly thief cocked his head. "I don't know what ya just said."

"Forget the coins. You accused Carmen of killing Geiger. She accused you. Who should I believe?"

Brody snorted. "The woman be a liar. Been a liar since she arrived in Nottingham. Not a true word has left her lips. That sister o' hers? She be no sister. They look nothin' alike. Sure, their locks be honey. But they have strangers' eyes. And the bones o' the face. Strangers."

Sam thought for a moment. That the two women weren't sisters was the one fact he knew. "Carmen seems to care for her, though."

"Care." Brody laughed. "Carmen told me she needs the woman. For what, she never says."

That made an odd kind of sense. Carmen must think Nora knew how to get back to Connecticut. She probably also knew why Nora was acting so strange. He'd have to get them all back to the hospital as quick as possible and make Sternwood's daughter talk.

"Okay. Let's say I believe you. What are you going to do now?"

"What do ya think? Get meself as far from Nottingham as possible."

"Sounds like a plan. A better plan than you had concerning Geiger."

Brody snorted. "That plan would have gone fine if that woman Carmen not be crazy."

"You could be right," Sam said.

There was no point sticking around, so Sam slipped out into the street and began hobbling toward York Gate. He couldn't believe he'd found Nora. The good news was he wouldn't have to rescue her from Furnival's dungeon at Locksley Castle. The bad news was that something had happened to her. Probably a blow to the head. One bad enough to cause amnesia. Sam hoped it was temporary. Amnesia caused by a head injury usually was, but it could last for days, maybe weeks.

The sound of a door opening behind him made Sam turn. It was Brody's house. He watched as the self-proclaimed thief shut the door and peered up and down the street. His movements stopped when he spotted Sam.

Sam reached up to tip his fedora, then froze when Brody suddenly jerked and toppled to the ground.

26
HOGWASH OR HALF-TRUTH

SAM PEERED DOWN the dark, narrow street, listening, hoping for some idea of what had happened. But there was no movement anywhere. Brody lay where he fell. No one ran off. Then a sound caught his ear. Sam's gaze darted to a roof opposite Brody's hovel. There. A man running. Skipping across the rooftops. In a moment he was gone.

Who? And how? Were those buildings even sturdy enough to support someone running across them?

Hobbling with his walking stick, Sam limped back to Brody's unmoving form. The night was so dark he could barely make out the arrow sticking from the man's chest. Brody was certainly dead. There, beside him, lay a sack of coins. The cloth bag was smaller than the one Effie had turned over to Vaisey's toady, but maybe there was enough to hire a few mercenaries to help rescue Robin.

As Sam reached down to retrieve the bag, a thought occurred to him. Carefully, using both hands, he snapped off the feathered end of the arrow. He'd seen enough westerns to know the feathers could sometimes indicate the arrow's origin. And sometimes that could tell you who fired it. Old-school forensics. Before forensics was even invented.

He stuffed the piece of arrow into a pocket of his trench coat, then retrieved the coin sack and stuffed it into the opposite pocket. The coins were heavy, causing one side of his coat to hang down lower than the other, and his collar to chafe a bit. Sam ignored the discomfort as he hobbled away from the scene of the crime.

Brody's street remained quiet as Sam put distance behind him. No one shouted an alarm. None of Vaisey's sword-wielding policemen showed up. Sam saw not another soul until after he turned onto Stoney Street and could see the outline of York Gate in the moonlight. Midway down the street, a man in a dark cloak stood watching. One man, Sam could handle. He'd rather a confrontation than be forced to walk further through town to the Mansfield Gate.

Whoever the shadowed nightbird was, however, skulked away before Sam got close. Just as well. At the gate, the guards barely gave him notice, which he barely returned before hobbling down the dirt track toward St John's.

When he arrived at the hospital refectory, he found mayhem. Or rather, two mayhems.

"We should attack now!" Little John insisted. "The Sheriff and most of his men will be asleep. His gaol will have but token resistance."

Sagramore shook his head. "Such an attack is exactly what Vaisey expects. The guard will be doubled. No, tripled. It is a trap no less obvious than the tournament itself. Look, there is Sam Spade. He will agree with me."

That was the last thing Sam needed. What he needed was rest. More salve for his feet. And a new nicotine patch. The one he still wore had expired two days ago.

"Tell him, Sam," Sagramore insisted.

Sam sighed. "I saw the Sheriff an hour ago. Maybe less. He and his men are out in full force. And yes, he'd be a fool not to expect an assault on the jail."

"But we must assault the gaol," Little John said. "Robin languishes there."

Sam rubbed his ear. "Sure we need to break Robin out, but we'll need help to do it." He pulled the sack of coins from his trench coat pocket and tossed it to Little John. "How many mercenaries will that buy?"

Little John opened the sack and peered inside. Then he dumped the coins onto the table where he could better see them.

"Who did you rob?" the big outlaw asked.

"It's a long story, but technically, I robbed Vaisey."

Little John grinned. "We can hire a dozen men with swords. Two dozen if they are desperate enough for coin."

The second mayhem now joined the first.

"Those are my coins!"

General Sternwood's youngest daughter stood in the doorway to a side room or hallway. Her eyes bulged slightly and her jaw was clenched. Not a good look for her. She stepped into the refectory. "What did you do? Did you kill Joe?"

"Brody's dead," Sam admitted. "But I didn't kill him."

"My apologies," Tuck breathed, huffing and puffing as he came up behind Carmen. "Your Connecticut friend has trouble staying in one place for long."

Sam sighed. "Carmen is not my friend. She's a client's daughter. And this—" Sam pulled the feathered end of the arrow from his coat pocket and held it up "—is what killed Joe Brody."

Tuck blinked. "Who?"

"A thief and a scoundrel," Sam said. "Do you recognize the feathers?"

The friar took the broken arrow shaft from Sam and stared at it. "Chicken. I could not tell you which breed."

"The colours," Sam said. Lord he was tired. "Don't different arrow makers colour their feathers differently?"

"Some," Tuck agreed. "But I see no discernible pattern in the fletching. What do you hope to accomplish?"

"I'm hoping to figure out who shot this arrow."

Tuck handed it back. "But why? If this Brody fellow was a scoundrel . . ."

Sam felt his cheek twitch. "Habit."

Tuck nodded. "Shame you did not retrieve the arrowhead. Arrowheads are often more telling than fletching."

"What about my money?" Carmen insisted, losing patience.

Sam's cheek twitched again. "Forget the money. It was never yours, and now it's going to a good cause. Come with me. We need to talk."

Carmen squawked as Sam grabbed her arm and dragged her out of the refectory. Little John, Sagramore, and the others ignored them. The Merry Men were more interested in sharing ideas of where to find mercenaries.

"Let go of me, you, you, you . . ."

"Brute?" Sam finished. He kept one eye out in case the General's daughter produced a stone from somewhere. Joe Brody may have been a disreputable thief and extortionist, but Sam believed him when he said Carmen had murdered Geiger. Sam had only a vague impression of how the young woman had managed her life in Connecticut, but he could well imagine an escalation into violence here in Sherwood Forest, especially if Carmen was forced to live as a pauper.

Once they were outside, with only the moon and garden for company, Sam stopped walking and let go of Carmen's arm.

She spun on her heels. "What do you want from me?"

"I want you to tell me how my partner, Nora, became your sister Vivian?"

"Your partner?"

"Your father hired us to find Sean Regan, last seen at the castle whose reconstruction you were overseeing."

Carmen frowned. He had already told her this.

"Let me spell it out for you. When Nora and I arrived at your father's castle, we found the reconstruction unfinished, you not there, and Regan not there. While searching the castle's lower level, Nora and I were separated. When I found myself here in medieval England, I figured all three of you had arrived ahead of me."

Carmen huffed. "You're taking this rather calmly. When I figured out I was lost in the middle ages, I freaked."

"This isn't my first rodeo," Sam said. "I'm getting used to it."

Carmen's eyes widened, then she leaned so close against him she was almost sitting in his lap. "You've done this before? You know how to get home?"

Sam sighed and backed away several inches. "It's different every time, but I will get us home. If you want to see Connecticut again, maybe you should start doing what I tell you instead of running away."

Carmen pressed her hands against Sam's chest and pushed him back another inch. "You sound like my daddy. He doesn't allow me to do anything except exactly what he says."

"Well, I'm not your daddy. But from what I can tell, you've done nothing but get yourself in trouble since you got here. Now tell me about Nora. How did she end up masquerading as your sister?"

The young woman remained silent for a moment, her moonlit expression a mixture of annoyance and anger. At last, she said, "I found your partner wandering through the forest."

Sam figured this was a lie, but decided to let it go. Whatever tale Carmen spun would have to hold some truth. She wasn't that good a liar. "When? When did this happen?"

"I don't know. Two? Three days ago? At the time I was so relieved to find someone wearing proper clothes, I could hardly think. I'd been here for weeks and hadn't seen a soul who wasn't a backcountry yokel. I could tell right away she didn't belong here. Just like I don't belong."

"Okay, so you found Nora wandering through the woods. What next?"

"Well, I asked her her name, of course? She just gave me a blank look. Said she couldn't remember. Together we searched her pockets and found my sister's business card. 'Oh,' she said, 'I must be Vivian Rutledge.' I knew that was the one person she couldn't be, but telling her that wouldn't be helpful, so I didn't."

"What happened to her own identification?" Sam asked.

"She didn't have a purse when I found her."

Sam knew that much was true. "Nora doesn't carry a purse. She keeps a wallet in her coat. How about her weapon? A Glock 19. What happened to that?"

Carmen shook her head. "All she had was my sister's business card."

Sam figured most of what Sternwood's daughter said was either hogwash or, at best, a half-truth. He'd try again later. See how many lies he could catch her in. He was worried about the Glock, though. Someone, somewhere in Sherwood forest, was walking around with a loaded handgun.

27
AT ONCE BRILLIANT AND ABSURD

BY THE TIME Sam got to sleep, it was almost sunrise. When Tuck woke him a short time later, he was tempted to tell everyone to go on without him. Then the friar reminded him that Little John's attempt at rescuing Robin was doomed to end in disaster.

Sam sat up and rubbed his eyes. "Do me a favour. Ask those monks of yours for more salve for my feet."

Tuck grinned and went in search of the monks.

While Sam waited, he took off his shirt and peeled away his depleted nicotine patch. After applying a new one, he sniffed the underarms of his shirt. "Damn." Well, he doubted anyone smelled much better. He'd just finished replacing his shirt when the monks arrived with their miracle.

Sam had been too exhausted to remove his shoes before falling asleep, so he gritted his teeth and clenched his fists as the monks undid the laces and worked loose each shoe. He gritted his teeth even harder as they peeled away his socks, probably taking half the skin off his feet in the process.

"They look better," Tuck opined.

Sam forced his jaw open. "They what?"

"Your feet. I see no infection." The friar leaned down for a closer look. "The skin has toughened. There is much redness yet and some dark areas between your toes, but overall, I am happy with the result."

"You're kidding."

Tuck frowned as he straightened. "How are goats giving birth relevant?"

Sam forced himself to sit up. "Goats? Never mind." He hauled one leg up over the opposite knee so he could see what the friar was describing. It wasn't pretty, but it wasn't near as bad as he had expected. "I still have ten toes."

"Is that important to you?" When Sam stared at the friar, Tuck added, "Most men are unhampered by missing toes."

"I'm not most men."

"That much is true," Tuck agreed.

Sam lay back as the monks applied salve and forced his blood-stiffened socks and dusty shoes back onto his feet. Before they could leave, however, he retrieved a handkerchief from his suit coat and scooped up a dab of salve from the metal pot they carried.

"What is that for?" Tuck asked.

Sam carefully folded the cloth and replaced it in his coat. "Insurance."

After a short hobble around the small hospital room, Sam decided his feet felt better than they had, or at least no worse. He wandered out to the refectory in search of breakfast and found Little John and Sagramore arguing about mercenaries. He assumed they'd been at it the entire night.

"We have sufficient bowmen," Sagramore said. "Their job is to subdue whatever men the Sheriff has stationed outside the gaol, and to hold that position until we are ready to make our exit. The bulk of the Sheriff's men will be inside the gaol. We need swordsmen to enter, subdue them all, and break into the cells. Right now, we have but one swordsman. Me."

Little John shook his head. "Most of my men handle the sword as well as the bow. I cannot ask them to wait outside while strangers rescue Robin. No, we must hire mercenaries to subdue the Sheriff's men stationed outside the gaol, and hold that position while the Merry Men enter to rescue Robin."

Sagramore threw his hands in the air, then noticed Sam and Tuck. "Friar, you tell him. The Sheriff's men are better with the sword than Robin's. What Little John plans is madness."

Tuck lowered his bulk into one of the chairs at the table. "I am no fighter, but Sagramore is correct. The Sheriff's men outnumber us ten to one. Twenty to one. And most are career swordsmen and mercenaries. Madness is a generous description."

Both Little John and the ex-knight frowned.

"What say you, Sam?" Little John demanded. "Robin spoke highly of your acumen."

That took Sam aback. He could guess at what acumen meant, but wouldn't bet on it. "He did?"

Sagramore laughed. "Little John, put aside your blunt plans for rescue. Sam Spade is a man of unusual craft. He will think of a better plan that is at once brilliant and absurd. It will baffle the Sheriff and the Sheriff's men, and distract them while we free Robin from his chains."

A pause lingered in the air after this statement. All three men stared at Sam.

"No pressure," Sam said. He rubbed his ear, and his cheek twitched. "I might just have an idea. Let me mull it over for a few minutes while I have a bite to eat."

He helped himself to the contents of the table. He'd always thought it was only the French who drank wine with every meal, but maybe in olden days it was a broader custom. Even so, he poured himself just enough to wash down a serving of bread, cheese, and eggs.

The refectory, though crowded, was silent as a tomb. The Merry Men sat or stood, watching Sam eat while his mind tried to formulate a scattered idea into an executable plan that didn't have too many holes in it. Sam wasn't a man-with-a-plan kind of guy. Nora was better at it. He usually left that side of the business to her. Only Nora thought her name was Vivian, and had limited herself to one-word sentences since he'd found her. So it was up to him.

With his plate empty, Sam drained his wine cup and looked at Little John. "Okay, here's what we're going to do."

28
WE WISH TO REPORT A MISSING PERSON

ABOUT AN HOUR later, Sam, Maid Marian, and Nora left for the Sheriff's Keep in the township of Nottingham. The keep was probably the last place in the world Sam should go, but he saw no other way to make a rescue attempt without getting Robin's entire band of Merry Men killed. He also had no idea when the word *reconnaissance* came in to use, but he was using it today.

In the yard outside the hospital, they found Friar Tuck waiting. Sam figured the churchman was going to give them some kind of blessing. Maybe a benediction invoking St Francis, the patron saint of fools.

Instead, the friar was more direct. "You cannot possibly believe this will work."

"It's got risks," Sam admitted. "Where's Effie? I couldn't find her after breakfast, and I'd like to see her before we leave."

"Lady Euphemia Peregrine? Is she here?"

"She arrived last night with Nora and Carmen," Sam said.

"The two sisters, yes," Tuck said. "They arrived. But I did not see Lady Peregrine."

Sam heard laughter and turned to see Azeem the Moor sitting on a stone bench near the garden.

"The churchman is blind," the Moor said. "Three young

women with yellow hair arrived in the night. One ran wild through the camp. One sat still as a mouse. The third felt it her duty to safeguard the quiet one."

Tuck cast Azeem a scowl, then turned to Sam. "I saw your friend, Carmen, last night, and yes, she flitted about the hospital causing all manner of mischief. In the end, I shooed her to a private room and stood guard outside her door."

Again, the Moor laughed. "You did not stand. You sat guard. Then you sat sleeping. Azeem sees all."

The friar pretended to ignore him. "The only other woman I saw was Maid Marian. Then this morning, I saw Carmen's sister, Vivian."

"Nora," Sam said. "And she's not Carmen's sister."

Azeem laughed a third time. "The one who safeguarded the quiet mouse left us early this morning, claiming to have business in the town."

"I suppose Effie went back to the bookstore," Sam said. "Geiger's dead. But Vaisey told her she'd have a new boss."

Tuck let out a sigh. "I am saddened to have missed Lady Peregrine. Hers is a welcome face." He cast a dark look at Carmen, who skulked in the hospital entranceway. For the second time in two days, Sam was leaving the troublesome woman in the friar's care.

"We'll try not to be too long," Sam told Tuck.

The friar snorted. "You shall have little choice should the Sheriff decide otherwise."

Sam hated to admit it, but Tuck was right. He'd tried to think of a better plan, but what he had in mind still seemed the least risky. He sighed. Then, with Nora and Maid Marian for company, he took up his walking stick and headed for Nottingham.

Despite the monks' miracle salve and the walking stick, Sam hobbled along the path through the trees, favouring his feet. Still, he felt he was setting a decent pace. Neither of his companions complained, though Marian frequently surged ahead, then waited for them to catch up. Nora, by comparison, may as well have been sleepwalking.

When Sam explained his plan to Nora, back inside the hospital, his partner had stared at him with vacuous eyes and uttered not a word. But she had come along quietly enough when he took her arm to coax her out of her chair.

Taking the shortest route from the hospital to the Sheriff's Keep, they turned onto the track along the town wall, walked past the York Gate, and entered Nottingham through the Mansfield Gate. Sam wasn't interested in stealth. This was an information-gathering mission. How many men could they spot in the battlements along the wall? None. How many guards manned each gate? Four during the day. Two at night. How many soldiers walked the streets between the Mansfield Gate and the keep. Only six. Officially. He was sure there were more. Out of sight, or dressed as townsfolk or visiting farmers.

When they arrived at the village green, Sam saw that the platform, tents, and target from yesterday's tournament had been removed. Most of the people were also gone, leaving just a few mothers chatting with friends while their children played together, and a few townsfolk cutting across the green on their way to or from the market.

"Stop and observe," Maid Marion said.

"That was kind of my plan," Sam agreed.

Robin's fiancée raised an arm and pointed a finger south down Castle Road toward an extravagant building. "Nottingham Castle."

Little John had mentioned the castle while arguing how to rescue Robin. The fortress sat on a rocky promontory at the southwest corner of town and was a residence for King Richard when he visited Nottingham or, according to the current Sheriff, when King John visited. Sam figured it was kind of like the White House. Whoever happened to be the current President, stayed there.

Across from the castle, the street was lined with buildings, including several large houses and a church whose bells rang out calling parishioners to mass or whatever medieval folks did at nine in the morning.

Returning his gaze to the castle complex, he focused on the north end, locating what must be the Sheriff's Keep. Though less ostentatious than the castle proper, the keep was no less a fortress, complete with battlements and its own portcullis. He hoped Nora was taking note. This was what a real castle should look like, not the cinderblock mansion General Sternwood had bought.

He had already asked little John about approaching the keep

from the west, but was told the promontory on that side couldn't be climbed. In their favour, the castle didn't have a moat, though Robin's lieutenant said an outer bailey and dry moat would be added at some point. Sam had no idea what those were, and since they weren't an issue today, didn't ask.

He wondered how Nora was faring and turned his head to see his partner wasn't even looking at the Sheriff's Keep, but instead watched a group of children playing on the green. Well, he wasn't sure how much help Nora would be anyway in gauging the keep's defences. She was less familiar with England's Dark Ages than he was. Which was why he'd brought Marian.

Returning his attention to the keep, Sam saw the portcullis was raised, revealing a courtyard that separated the gate from a broad doorway made of dark timber. He could only see two guards, though more could be hidden behind the gate wall. He had no idea how wide the courtyard was.

Along the keep's battlements that ran to either side above the gate, two men paced with bows at the ready. Two more bowmen stood behind crenels on the roof that rose above the courtyard.

"What do you see?" Maid Marian asked.

"I see a problem."

She turned to look at him. "How so?"

Sam sighed. "I'd hoped the Merry Men could take control of the castle battlements, but I don't see a way to do that without getting past the portcullis and into the courtyard first. I assume there are steps leading up on either side behind the wall, but the soldiers above and on the roof will rain arrows down on Robin's men. It'll be like shooting fish in a barrel."

Marian creased her brow. "Shooting fish?"

"That's not important. I'm also worried there's no way up to the roof from the courtyard. Even if the Merry Men do take the lower battlements, they'll have no protection from the archers on the roof."

"I would not worry overmuch about archers," Marian said.

"Oh? Why is that?"

"See how they are dressed?"

Sam rubbed his ear. "They don't look like the soldiers I saw yesterday. Wait a minute. Is that man wearing a kilt?" The guard in question paced the courtyard, exposing his bare and slightly sunburned knees and calves.

"They are redshanks," Marian said, as if that should explain things.

"Redshanks?"

"Celtic mercenaries," Marian explained.

Sam took a longer look and spotted a round wooden shield leaning against the courtyard wall. The sword at the nearest guard's hip was also shorter and a bit wider than the ones Vaisey's men had carried. But it was the kilt that was the giveaway. He glimpsed another kilt as one of the men on the lower battlements crossed between two crenels. "They look like Lord Furnival's men."

"John Lackland," Marian said, "the King's brother and, incidentally, my useless cousin, hired mercenaries from Scotland to support his bid to usurp the throne. Though most of the King's army is in the Holy Land, those left behind who can wield a sword or bow remain, for the most part, loyal to Richard. Lord Furnival and our Lord Sheriff both employ redshanks to support Prince John's cause."

"Okay. So why shouldn't we be worried about Scotsmen on the battlements?"

Marian smiled. "The Scots are merciless with the broadsword, claymore, or halberd, but are awkward with the bow. There!" She pointed to a man with flaming red hair who walked the upper battlements. "See the bow he carries?"

"A bow is a bow," Sam said.

"Not at all. The Scots could never master the longbow. Theirs are short, and shoot lighter arrows, with less force and accuracy. From the height of the roof and battlements, many will miss their target. Those that score will do little damage unless the shot is a lucky one."

"So, what you're saying is the Merry Men can storm the castle and receive only a few scrapes and cuts."

"I am saying that if we rush the gate before the portcullis closes, and ascend to the lower battlements, we shall suffer few casualties."

Sam shook his head. "I'm looking for a zero-casualty solution."

Marian gawked at him. "We are at war. There are always casualties."

"Call me a pacifist."

"I am unfamiliar with that word."

"I don't think it's been invented yet." Sam's cheek twitched. "What about the roof?"

"With a simple grappling hook, David or Gilbert will take the roof."

Sam continued watching as the Scottish mercenaries paced their positions. "I'm only seeing a half-dozen soldiers. Two at the gate. Two on the lower battlements. And two on the roof. Does that strike you as odd?"

Marian snickered. "Peacetime numbers. It is for show. The Sheriff knows Robin's Men will attempt to free him. There will be another twenty mercenaries hidden out of sight. And the Lord Sheriff will have his personal guard of English soldiers with him. At least ten armed men."

"That makes forty, or thereabouts."

Sam had brought Maid Marian along for three reasons. First, because she had insisted. Robin's fiancée needed to ensure he was being well treated. Second, because she said she had an eidetic memory and could accurately report Vaisey's defences; Tuck had vouched this was true. The third, because she knew better than him how castles, sheriffs, and the whole medieval schtick worked. So far, the last reason seemed the best.

Since he had Marian for company, Sam had figured having another woman along would help ease tensions with the Sheriff. How threatening could one man in a trench coat and two women in fine dress be?

Before leaving St John the Baptist Hospital, Marian had found Nora some better clothes to wear and had helped clean her up. They both looked ready to appear at court, while Sam, well, Sam looked like a gumshoe who had trudged through a filthy alley for three days.

He also had an ulterior motive for bringing Nora. Besides not wanting to leave her alone with Carmen, he hoped a little time together would help restore Nora's memories. But so far, his partner had kept her silence, despite any hopeful cajoling on Sam's part. At least she hadn't complained about tagging along.

"Well, no sense in dillydallying," Sam said. "Let's go say hi to his Lordship and see what the inside of his man cave looks like."

Marian gave him a confused look but didn't ask for clarification.

They continued walking along the green until they stood directly across from the keep gate. Then they crossed Castle Road and stepped beneath the raised portcullis into the courtyard. Sam glanced around, spotting steps leading up to the battlements, but could see no additional mercenaries.

"Whit business hae ye wi' th' Sheriff?" one of the redshanks demanded.

"He's expecting us," Sam said.

The Scotsman grinned. "Then gang oan in." He waved a hand in invitation.

"Security is tight," Sam murmured to Marian.

"Departing may be more challenging than entering," she countered.

Before Sam could reach for the broad handle on the heavy door to the keep, the other redshank guarding the courtyard took hold of it and heaved the giant door open.

Sam paused to glance at Marian. "Normally I'd say Ladies first, but maybe I should take a little look-see."

"If you wish," Marian said. Nora made no comment but stared curiously at the redshank mercenaries, maybe puzzled by their Scottish accents.

The inside of the Sheriff's Keep was not what Sam expected. As an ex-cop, he was used to police stations. And as a fan of western movies and television, he'd familiarized himself with sheriff's offices, which were gross oversimplifications of modern ones. He'd expected Nottingham's Sheriff's Keep to be an even greater oversimplification. The last thing he expected was a throne room.

"Oh."

Sam turned. That was the first word Nora had spoken since they'd left the hospital.

He smiled as his partner turned her head this way and that, taking in the wagon wheel chandelier high above their heads, the rich tapestries adorning the walls, the shadowed galleries that lined two sides of the spacious room, a firepit the size of a small wading pool and, most important, the grand throne that dominated the room. Between the firepit and the throne stood a life-size statue Sam recognized as Squire Vaisey from Camelot, only older and uglier.

Despite the open doorway and a multitude of lit candles, the place was still darker than a barn at sunset. Shadows everywhere. The gloom made it difficult to count the number of English soldiers and Scottish redshanks who stood almost shoulder to shoulder along the walls, each with a sword pulled half out of its scabbard. Not one of the men made a sound, though they all looked confused and uncertain, confronted as they were by two women and an oddly dressed foreigner who, with his walking stick, might be a cripple.

Maid Marian broke the silence. "We are here to speak with the Sheriff."

"Speak."

Sam looked at the throne, which was so large he had missed seeing the diminutive man in black sprawled across the seat, the statue come to life.

Marian seemed undeterred. "We wish to report a missing person. His name is Sean Regan, and is a good friend of the Sternwood family." She turned to Nora. "This is Vivian Rutledge-Sternwood. As you can see, she is very concerned."

Squire Vaisey, now six years older and appointed the Sheriff of Nottingham, pursed his lips. Then he stuck a finger in his ear and wiggled it. "Missing person?"

"Yes." Marian nodded. "He has not been seen in days."

"Missing person," Vaisey repeated. "I cannot say I am familiar with the term."

"Have people never gone missing?" Marian asked.

Vaisey smiled. "All the time. No one reports it."

"Well, I am reporting it."

Vaisey slipped down off the throne and stepped over to a small wooden desk that was stained so dark Sam could barely see it in the poor lighting. From a towering stack of parchments, the Sheriff pulled a single sheet. Then he lifted a quill from an inkwell and wrote on it. After replacing the quill, he stepped over to a dark-stained wooden wall beyond the desk and, using some kind of dart, pinned the parchment next to several others. Sam's eyesight was keen enough, even in the heavy gloom, to read what was on it. Sean Regan. And below that: Missing.

"Oh," Vaisey said. "I should have asked. Is there a reward?"

Marian sighed. "Sadly, no. I wish it were otherwise, but the Sternwoods have not two pennies to rub together."

Vaisey sniffed. "Indeed. Sad. Sam Spade, is that you hiding

behind the skirts of these two fine ladies?"

Sam lifted a hand and waved. "I didn't realize I was hiding. I thought I was standing in plain sight."

Vaisey pursed his lips again. "And I thought you were on your way to London. Change of plans?"

"You know how it is." Sam removed his fedora and doffed it toward the ladies. "Damsels in distress. Met them on the road outside town. They were falling all over themselves with grief over their missing family friend, desperate that I had seen him, or knew of his whereabouts. Unfortunately, being a stranger here, I had no information to offer. Then it occurred to me that the Sheriff of Nottingham was the man they should speak to. Who better to know the ins and outs of the area?" Sam's cheek twitched. "They were shy about approaching your eminence, so I offered to escort them."

Vaisey brought his fingers up to his beard and fingered the short black hairs. "That is quite the story. I cannot decide if it amuses me or not. What say you, Guy? Mortianna? Are you amused?"

"I have heard better," Guy of Gisbourne drawled. The sycophant deputy stood leaning against one side of the throne.

The woman named Mortianna stepped out from behind a wall of soldiers. Sam recognized her immediately. Six years had passed since he'd last seen Morgan Le Fay. For part of that time, she'd been encased in glass, punishment for her attempted overthrow of Camelot. Sam already knew she and Mordred had escaped imprisonment when magic failed. Sagramore had told him Mordred's fate, that he had raised an army, razed Camelot, then vanished. Sagramore had made no mention, however, of the bastard hedge knight's co-conspirator.

"Sam Spade." The charlatan of Camelot's voice was loud and domineering, not the demur speech of the gentle Lady who had once begged Sam to rescue her non-existent sister. "Why am I not surprised to see you?"

In their previous encounters, Le Fay had repeatedly pretended to be someone she wasn't. That she now had a new name and persona came as no surprise. Mortianna wore a flowing black and red dress, with golden bells and tassels running along the folds. Ribbons of red silk had been woven through her night-black hair, though no longer quite black; Sam could clearly make out streaks of grey.

"Who are you supposed to be now?" Sam asked. "A fortune-teller?"

Vaisey sniffed. "Mortianna is a close friend. And one of my advisors. A soothsayer. I have found her advice indispensable. What do you advise now, good lady?"

Le Fay sashayed past the crowd of soldiers and halted in front of Nora, who stood two heads taller than the faux clairvoyant. Sam's partner had never said, but he assumed she was of Viking heritage. "This one is nobody," Le Fay said, looking up at Nora. "Probably sent to confuse us."

She stepped in front of Sam. "This one is trouble. Here to scout your stronghold and measure your strength. He is in league with your enemy, Robin of Locksley."

Lastly, she stood in front of Maid Marian. "This one. Ah. A cousin to King John. Interesting."

Vaisey's dull eyes perked up. "A close cousin?"

A cat-like smile touched Le Fay's lips. "John knows of her. Acknowledges her. But has no love for her."

"Well," Sam said, "I have to admit your soothsayer's story of who we are and why we're here is more interesting than mine. But really, we only came to report a missing person. So if you don't mind, we'll be on our way." He turned to leave, but redshanks with wild red hair and round shields immediately blocked his way.

"Not so hasty," Vaisey said. "We have yet to hear from my other advisor. The Bishop of Hereford."

From behind the throne emerged a weasel of a man dressed head to foot in purple silk. Perhaps in his sixties, his face was like wax and his tonsured hair the colour of rotten wood. He placed his hands in front of him and paraded himself through the crowd of guards. When he arrived in front of Sam, Sam saw the weasel was even shorter up close than he looked from a distance.

"Well, well, well," Sam said, his cheek twitching. "A priest and a mystic. I have to hand it to you, Vaisey. You've got your bases covered no matter which way the cosmic winds blow."

The Bishop sneered and regarded Sam with dead eyes. "It is as Lady Mortianna says. They have come to spy out your defences."

"Of course they have," Vaisey said, pounding his fist on the small table of parchments. "Any fool can see that. The question is, what should I do about it?"

The Bishop wagged his head at Nora. "Keep this one as a hostage."

"Wait a minute," Sam said.

The Bishop turned to Sam. "Send this one back to bargain with Robin's men."

Then he leered at Maid Marian. "And this one. This one is the bargain."

29
MAKING CONVERSATION

IT WAS ALMOST noon by the time Sam made it back to St John the Baptist Hospital. Alone.

Tuck, who had been keeping watch, was first to see him. "Sam Spade! Thank the one true God you have returned. But . . . where are the others?"

"It appears my plan was more absurd than brilliant," Sam admitted. "Vaisey is holding Nora hostage, and Maid Marian, well, Maid Marian is to become his wife."

The friar's face turned several different colours as surprise, shock, amazement, and finally, anger took turns wreaking havoc with his blood pressure. In the end, the churchman had to sit down and shake his head. "Do not blame yourself. I have known Vaisey since childhood. I should have foreseen this."

"That'd be fine if it was Vaisey's idea, but it's your overdressed Bishop of Hereford who gets the credit."

Tuck looked up. "The Bishop? So, he is more than just the Sheriff's tool. He is a confederate?"

"Vaisey called him an advisor," Sam said. "Oh, and you'll never guess who his other advisor is. Morgan Le Fay."

"The witch?" Tuck shook his head. "Is there no end to Vaisey's wickedness?"

The rest of Robin's Merry Men took the news less well than Tuck. After several minutes of shouting, fist-waving, and colourful expletives, Azeem the Moor called for order.

"Children, children, cease your squabbles. No amount of wailing will undo what has already been done. Instead, we must behave as men, and decide what measures are required to remedy the situation."

"What the Moor said," David of Doncaster agreed in his soft voice. "Sam Spade, you were with the Sheriff. What is it we should do to get Robin and Marian back?"

Sam rubbed his ear. "Well, the problem as I see it, is that Marian agreed to the marriage—"

The room immediately came alive with shouts and cries of disbelief. Sam raised a hand in the air and left it there until the Merry Men ran out of steam. "Under duress," he finished. "And in exchange for Robin's release."

Little John swore. "You cannot believe the Sheriff will keep his word. Under no circumstance would he release Robin. Not ever. Robin is the Sheriff's sworn enemy."

"I know that," Sam said. "You know that. I'm sure Marian knows that. But right now, the Sheriff has Robin, Marian, and two additional hostages. Rescuing all four of them is going to be near impossible."

Everyone stopped speaking when Tuck let out a huge belly laugh.

"What is it, churchman?" Little John demanded. "What is it you find so funny?"

"Why," Tuck answered. "Do you not see? Nothing has changed. Sam Spade's plan is still the best we have. We have work before us yet to accomplish it. Remind me, Sam. You did not see Robin when you met with the Sheriff?"

"No," Sam admitted, "but his keep is a big place."

"There," Tuck said. "Sam must return and visit the Sheriff again. And this time, Sam, you must ascertain the location of Robin, Maid Marian, Will Scarlet, and your friend from Connecticut."

"Nora," Sam said.

"Of course, Nora. Once we know where the Sheriff is keeping them, we may move forward with your plan."

"Fine. Fine." Sam threw both hands in the air. "Let me rest my feet and have a bite of food. Then I'll go back and see Vaisey. Again."

Sam sat at the refectory table as Little John rose from his seat and left with Sagramore to hire mercenaries. David of Doncaster also left, saying he knew some people who might help. Much the Miller's Son volunteered to go with him. The rest of Robin's men—Gilbert Whitehand, Reynold Greenleaf, and the others—set out for Sherwood Forest to collect additional arrows and other supplies they'd need for the rescue.

That left Tuck and Carmen Sternwood for company, until one of the monks beckoned the friar away. Then there was just Carmen.

Sam would have liked to share his lunch with Effie, but Merlin's former clerk was in Nottingham working in Geiger's book shop with the shades drawn. It had been good to see her again. Sam's blood always raced when they met, sometimes when he merely thought of her. How could he let someone do that to him? Effie gave new meaning to the idiom *so near, yet so far*.

A throat cleared, and Sam looked up.

Carmen stood hovering at his shoulder. Now there was a woman who made his blood boil rather than race. Look up entitlement in a dictionary and you'd see Carmen Sternwood's scowling face. Currently, she wasn't scowling, which meant she wanted something.

"I understand you attempted suicide this morning by visiting the Sheriff, and you're going to do it again this afternoon. Are you a glutton for punishment?"

Sam set down his sandwich. "I don't have much choice now, do I? The Sheriff is holding three of my friends."

Carmen set her lips in a pout. "But only your partner Nora is from Connecticut. The others are from here. How can they be your friends?"

Sam shook his head. "If you have to ask . . ."

And there it was. The scowl. "You aren't more than just friends with Nora, are you?"

Sam cast her a chill look.

"I only ask because, well, maybe I shouldn't say."

"Go ahead. You know you want to."

The scowl softened. "Well, I was helping Nora in the town, you know. Finding her a place to live. To work."

"She was living with that lowlife, Brody. And I think you mentioned her workplace was an alehouse."

Carmen shrugged. "Hard for a single woman to find any other kind of work around here. I had to live with Brody myself. Don't worry. Nothing happened. I paid our rent by promising him a payoff from Geiger's business."

Sam had to admit the woman had been helpful to Nora, provided what she said wasn't more lies.

Carmen leaned closer even though there was no one to overhear. "It's Nora, you see."

"What about Nora?"

"I've seen her a few times. You know. Getting friendly."

Sam felt a scowl of his own coming on. Since finding Nora, his partner had been little more than a zombie. Hardly saying two words. And doing what she was told, provided it wasn't too complicated. Nora Clark had a brilliant mind. He couldn't bear it if she didn't return to her old self. And now she was Vaisey's prisoner. "Friendly?" Sam echoed.

"You know." Carmen's hand pressed against his shoulder, and her voice became a sibilant hiss, probably much like the snake when it suggested to Eve that apples were good eating. "Sidling up to men. Whispering in their ear."

Sam shook off the hand. "What are you talking about?"

Carmen sat in the chair next to Sam's. "I've seen Nora with men. Well, a man. The Sheriff. They were, you know, being friendly." Carmen nudged him with her elbow. "Do I have to spell it out for you?"

Sam shifted his chair away from the annoying woman, the wooden feet shrieking loudly against the stone floor of the refectory. "Why would Nora be anywhere near the Sheriff?"

"She's with him now." Carmen widened her eyes.

"As a hostage."

"Is she, though?" The words came out as a purr.

Sam sucked a breath in through his teeth, then let it out slowly. He knew Carmen was lying. Making up a tall tale and playing mind games. Carmen Sternwood could give Morgan Le Fay a run for her money. Still, the lie disturbed him more than it should have. "Where did you see Nora and Vaisey together?"

"Vaisey? Is that the Sheriff's name?"

"Where?"

"I can't remember. Was it on the village green? No. Maybe the alehouse where Nora worked."

Sam couldn't imagine Vaisey spending time in either place. And certainly not with Nora. "What are you trying to do here?"

"Do?" Carmen pouted her lips. "Nothing. I'm just making conversation."

"Well, make it somewhere else."

A deeper pout. "But I thought you should know. I mean, when you go see the Sheriff again. Or maybe you shouldn't go. Maybe you and I should just go back to Connecticut. Forget all this."

So that was her game. "You think we should leave Nora behind? And Sean Regan?"

"Sean!" Carmen swatted Sam with her fist. "Sean! Why do you care so much about Sean? You've never even met him. He's not a nice man, you know."

"I care because your father hired me to find him."

Carmen leaped to her feet. "But Daddy Dearest never hired you to find me!" Then she ran from the room, almost knocking Tuck off his feet as they crossed paths in a doorway.

Sam didn't think he'd ever met a crazier young woman.

30
DOWN IN THE DIRT

"Are you certain you wish to go alone?" Tuck asked. "Who knows what the Sheriff will do next?"

Sam clenched his teeth as he pulled up a sock. Because going back to bed hadn't been an option, he'd asked for another dose of the monks' salve. This was his second walk of the day into town, and he'd only just finished lunch. When the sock cooperated, he answered. "We can't afford any more hostages."

The friar nodded. "This is true."

Sam noticed Tuck looking more nervous than usual. "What is it?"

The corpulent churchman paced a few steps. "Little John grows impatient. He may not wait until you are ready before assaulting the castle. The Merry Men are fond of Maid Marian and have no wish to see her wed to the Sheriff."

"Really?" Sam let out a heavy sigh. Was he the only one who could think about this with his head instead of his heart? "There won't be a wedding. You know Marian loves Robin. She would never marry another man."

Tuck halted his pacing. "Not even to save Robin's life?"

Sam dipped a foot into one of his shoes. "You can believe that if you want. But then you'd have to believe Vaisey is an honourable man."

"He is anything but," Tuck agreed. "But why would Maid

Marian agree to any of this?"

Tying the laces was the easy part. Even so, Sam grunted as he answered. "It was the best. Choice. She could make. At the time. Had Marian said no. All three of us would have been kept as hostages. And another thing. As long as Vaisey thinks she's being sincere, he won't lift a finger against Robin. Her agreement was a bid to keep everyone safe and to allow me to return here with what I saw of Vaisey's defences. There's also a good chance the Sheriff now believes the Merry Men will wait for the wedding and Robin's release rather than attack."

"Then the Sheriff is a fool."

"On that, we can agree."

Sam stood and tested his weight. His feet were pleasantly numb, but it felt like he was walking on balloons. He'd have to watch his step.

Tuck handed Sam his walking stick, then pressed a heavy hand on Sam's shoulder. "Be careful, my friend. Take my prayers that the Lord may preserve you."

"I'll take any help I can get," Sam said.

The sun had begun its slow descent as Sam entered Nottingham for the second time that day. By now he was used to the short trek back and forth between the hospital and the town, but he was getting low on pennies to pay the gate tax. He'd have to get more from Tuck, or from the coin bag he'd given to Little John.

Once inside the wall, he decided not to go straight to Vaisey. He'd check on Effie first. Make sure she was okay and find out if she had learned anything.

He reached Pallium's Parchments without incident and was pleased to find Effie working inside.

"Do you have a new boss yet?" Sam asked after stepping into the doorway.

"Sam." If Effie smiled, it was hidden by the darkened shop's gloomy interior. "A man named Carol Lundgren. He seems to have little interest in the work and was more than pleased to accept my offer of help. But what of you? Was your scouting of the Sheriff's Keep successful?"

"I wish I had better news." Sam worked his way to the counter, then explained how things had gone awry and that he was on his way to meet Vaisey again.

"Oh, Sam! Do you believe that wise? The Sheriff harbours no love for you."

"Wise or not, I still need to find out where he's holding Robin and the others." Sam rubbed his ear. "I'm sure he'll put up with me as long as I'm useful."

"Then I too shall attempt to be useful," Effie said. "When I meet with Mr. Lundgren later today, I will attempt to ascertain his feelings toward our Lord Sheriff."

"That sounds dangerous, angel. If anyone discovers you're working against Vaisey . . ."

"You forget I was a spy in Mordred's camp." Without seeming to know she was doing it, Effie fingered the scar on her cheek.

"Just . . . be careful," Sam said.

He hated leaving Effie alone in the darkened shop, but he had work to do. He'd messed up taking Nora and Marian with him to see Vaisey. It would have been better if he'd just gone alone. Bluffed his way to discovering where Robin was kept, then bluffed his way back out of the keep. His stupidity had put two people in danger. And not just any two people. One of them was Nora. If anything happened to her or Maid Marian, it would be on him.

Bright sunlight hampered Sam's vision as he left Geiger's shop and peered up and down Halifax Lane. Was it just his imagination? Or was there more foot traffic than when he'd arrived? The street had been deserted during the tournament, but today people had somewhere to go. He paused to take a long look at each person in the street. A mother and child marched stately toward a nearby shop. Their clothes were clean and looked new, so possibly they belonged. A man dressed in dark pants and an even darker shirt lounged idly against a shop wall maybe a hundred feet away. Was he waiting for Sam to leave so he could place a bet? Another man, dressed like a farmer, sauntered down the middle of the cobblestone road.

Sam shook his head. He wasn't familiar enough with the town or its customs to know who may or may not belong. But he was smart enough to realize the biggest danger to Effie might be Vaisey's men watching him enter and leave her shop. Once again, he'd been an idiot. He should never have come here.

Stepping into the street, he placed his walking stick before him and hobbled off in the opposite direction he usually took. He kept his head down, but glanced left and right as well as he could from the corner of his eye. When the street ended, he made the only available turn and realized he was on course for where he needed to be, the Sheriff's Keep.

After passing a few houses, Sam spied an unmarked section of wall. He hobbled over and leaned against it, pretending to rest. Well, maybe not so much pretending. Peering out from beneath the brim of his fedora, he scanned the street for any familiarly dressed characters. The street was busier than Halifax Lane, but he didn't think he had been followed.

Across from where he rested, an alley ran between two buildings. Sam squinted. The streets in Nottingham were already narrow. What he was looking at now was even narrower. Unlike the streets, no sign provided a name.

Resigned that he couldn't rest forever, Sam hobbled to the alley entrance and saw the ground was dirt rather than cobblestone. The two-storey buildings on either side left the pathway masked in shadows, but the light of another street glimmered at the far end. If Sam had a tail, this was as good a way as any to shake it. If anyone did come that way after him, it would confirm the Sheriff was having him followed.

Almost immediately after entering the alley, Sam stepped into water. He shook his shoe and stepped closer to one of the walls, but after a few more steps hit water again. So, not so much an alley as a drainage ditch. He looked back the way he had come. Should he turn around?

Well, his shoes were already wet. Damage done. He kept going.

About halfway through the alley, the ground rose slightly and there were fewer puddles. Sam paused again to see if he was being followed, and couldn't see anyone in the gloom. Maybe Effie was safe after all.

He took several more steps, then something hard thumped him in the small of his back. Sam spun, raising his walking stick, and slammed it against something. No, someone. Sam could see him now, despite the poor light between the buildings. The goon was small and wiry, dressed head to toe in dark clothing, and spoke not a word as he threw blow after blow at Sam.

Sam used his walking stick as a shield, but the bullyboy didn't seem concerned and managed to get in every third or fourth blow. He watched for opportunities to strike out, but the goon was fast on his feet, ducking out of the way and following up with a quick punch. If this continued, Sam knew who was going to win this fight, and it wasn't him.

He was trying to figure out a new strategy when another blow slammed into his back. He spun. Now there were two hard numbers. Where had this one come from? Before he knew what was happening, the first goon had his walking stick and threw it down the alley. Then both bullyboys came at him, fists flying.

Sam blocked and punched as best he could, but being outnumbered, stood no chance. Before long he was down in the dirt, curled up in the fetal position with his hands covering his head. The goons now used booted feet as weapons. Sam curled up as much as he could in an attempt to protect himself. At some point, he lost consciousness.

31
A SHOW OF GOOD FAITH

SAM HAD NO idea how long he had been out. Every inch of his body quivered in pain, even the soles of his feet, which had been numb since leaving the hospital. As he uncurled himself, he groaned like a derelict ship at sea. Finally, he lay on his back and opened his eyes. He was still in the alley. Turning his head left, then right, he realized he was alone. Well, that was something.

Since there was no imminent threat, he lay there for a good long time, slowly stretching his fingers, hands, arms, legs, and torso, checking for broken bones. The bullyboys who had attacked him knew their business. Every inch of him was bruised or bleeding, but not a single bone was broken.

He couldn't lay in the dirt all day, however. Using a wall for support, Sam climbed to his feet and checked his pockets. Nothing seemed to be missing. Not a robbery. Again, no surprise. The bullyboys had been Vaisey's men, sent to teach Sam a lesson.

His fedora lay a few feet away. Sam hobbled toward it, circumventing a deep puddle, and almost found himself again in the dirt as he bent down to retrieve it. Still using the wall to keep himself vertical, he dragged himself back the way he had come, and let out a sigh of relief when he spotted his walking stick still in one piece. He doubted he could walk without it.

Walking stick in hand, or rather being used as a crutch, Sam hobbled the rest of the way through the damp alley and came out on a relatively wide street not far from a church that was much larger than the one near Nottingham Castle. How about that, Nottingham was a two-church town.

A street sign said he was on a road called High Pavement. Noises from a market a couple of blocks away reached his ears, and beyond that, the main tower of the Castle brooded over the town. At least he couldn't get lost.

As he neared the market, the aroma of baking bread and roasting meats clashed with the stench of human and animal waste. Sam was glad he'd already eaten lunch, and that it had been a small lunch. He hobbled past as quickly as he could.

The street narrowed and changed its name to Low Pavement, then widened again and called itself Castle Gate. Ahead, the castle tower and parts of the roof grew larger as Sam hobbled closer. Soon he was on Castle Road, with the church he had seen the day before behind him and the village green up ahead.

While the people he had passed near the market pretended they couldn't see him, those outside the entrance to the Sheriff's Keep were of an entirely different mind. Most stopped what they were doing and appeared to take great pleasure in gawking at him. One small boy, who reminded Sam of the bully Nelson from *The Simpsons*, pointed and laughed. Sam was in no mood for a confrontation, so he reached up and tipped his hat. The boy stood there staring as Sam made his slow way along the cobbles toward the keep gate.

The same two redshanks stood guard in the courtyard, but Sam could now only see two archers on the battlements. Maybe the missing pair were taking a siesta. As Sam hobbled beneath the open portcullis, the guards made no attempt to conceal their glee.

"Hud ye a tussle in th' mud?" one asked, taking in Sam's cuts, bruises, and wrinkled clothing.

"It looks lik' th' mud won," the other said, then laughed as he pushed open the keep's heavy door.

Sam ignored them and limped into the gloomy interior of Vaisey's domain.

"I'd like to report an incident," Sam shouted, his voice echoing.

Fewer soldiers than he had seen that morning filled the cavernous hall. Vaisey probably felt he no longer needed them now he had more hostages. And, of course, because of the message Sam had delivered to Robin's Merry Men. Good. Overconfidence was a weakness.

The Sheriff of Nottingham slipped down from his throne and sauntered across his audience hall. He smirked as he looked Sam up and down, taking in the fresh cuts, scrapes, and bruises. "What sort of incident?" As if he couldn't see.

Sam buried the anger he felt and spoke in his friendliest voice. "There's an illegally parked carriage next to the green."

Vaisey's eyes widened.

"Oh. And I was assaulted by a couple of bullyboys."

The Sheriff sniffed. "Only two? I thought you were a man who could handle yourself."

"They got the jump on me," Sam admitted.

"Do you have a description?"

"Nothing useful. I don't expect them to be arrested or anything, I just wanted to let you know they'd done their job."

Vaisey smiled. "I cannot say I understand what you are telling me."

"If you say so," Sam said. "I really just came to check on Nora. I'm sure you're treating her well, but she's recovering from an injury, so I thought I'd better drop by."

"Nora? Oh. The tall woman. Injured, you say? That could explain her . . . oddness."

"If one of your men could take me to see her?"

Vaisey's smile stretched into a grin. "I can do you one better." The villain snapped his fingers and Guy came running forward from behind the throne. "Fetch the woman."

"The woman?"

"Don't be a fool. The quiet one."

Guy grumbled and wandered toward the back of the hall.

"You're letting her go?" Sam asked.

"A show of good faith," Vaisey said. "Maid Marian is cooperating nicely. This is her reward."

"Might I see Marian?" Sam peered past Vaisey's shoulder hoping to see where Guy had gone, but the hall was enormous, poorly lit, and there were too many soldiers blocking his view.

"All in good time," Vaisey said. "Return here tomorrow and we shall see."

"Marian's friends are worried," Sam suggested. "It will ease their minds if I could report she is being well treated."

A frown darkened Vaisey's expression. "Of course, Maid Marian is being well treated. She is to be my wife. Should any of my men treat her beneath her station, they would find themselves at the wrong end of a very pointy blade."

"Even so, if I could say I saw her . . ."

"Your Nora can say she saw her. That is why I am releasing your friend. Good faith, remember? Guy! Where are you, you dolt?"

While they waited, Sam took a closer look at the vile man he had first met in Camelot as a tyrannical page, then later as an entitled knight-in-training. The years had been kind to Vaisey in some ways. He seemed to have lost his baby fat, built up some muscle, and even appear dashing in an Alan Rickman sort of way. He did have one flaw, however.

"It's taller than you," Sam said.

Vaisey glared at him. "What do you mean?"

"The statue." Sam pointed at the Sheriff cast in stone a few feet away. "It's taller by two inches. At least."

Vaisey straightened his back and lifted himself on his toes. "You are mistaken. That statue was made to my exact measurements by the renowned Londonshire craftsman Taggart Wilde. To say otherwise is to insult the artist."

"You're probably right," Sam said, knowing he wasn't. "Maybe it's just the bad lighting in here."

Vaisey grunted and returned his gaze to the back of the hall. "Guy! Where are you? You bumbling dolt!"

A wall of soldiers parted, and Guy slunk forward with Nora in tow. Sam's partner looked no worse than she had earlier that morning, but no better.

When Nora saw him, her lips parted in a tight smile. "Sam?"

"Are you okay?" Sam asked.

"I'm fine. Are you taking me with you?"

"Yes. We'll go find you some fresh air. And sunlight."

"Find her a bridesmaid's dress," Vaisey suggested. "A nice one. It shall be the wedding of the season."

A frown crossed Nora's face. She looked at Sam more closely. "Are *you* okay?"

"Nothing that a month on a sandy beach won't fix," Sam said. It was a relief to see Nora talking again. And she had recognized him. Even called him by name. Sure, it had taken her a while to notice his injuries, but she had noticed. That was a good sign.

32
THE SOUP CANNOT WAIT

THE WALK BACK to St John the Baptist Hospital nearly killed Sam. His feet were only part of it. The beating he'd received was the other part. Bruises on the outside were one thing. His bruised muscles on the inside were another. He felt like he'd been hit by a truck. Repeatedly. He only made it back because of the walking stick and Nora's shoulder. If he'd had the pennies for it, he would have hired a carriage.

Nora spoke little during the trip but seemed to know something was wrong, as well as how to help. She was inches taller than Sam and hunched down without being asked in order to support his weight.

"Heavens!" Tuck shouted as he ran out from the modest building and wedged himself under Sam's other arm. "Vaisey did this to you?"

"Not that he'll admit, but it was his men."

"You must lie down," Tuck said. "No, we must bathe you first. Then ointments. And soup. I have a special soup."

Having returned Nora to safety, Sam sank into some kind of half-awake state where he barely noticed what was being done to him. He remembered the hot water of a bath. And hands. Men's hands. He assumed they belonged to the silent monks. The heat from the water changed the pain he felt throughout his body. It didn't remove it, or reduce it, but changed it to something different and slightly more bearable. He vaguely remembered being lifted from the bath and carried to his bed.

When he woke, he found himself covered in bandages, with pungent odours leaking from beneath the layers of thin cloth. He remembered Tuck saying something about ointments, a likely source of the smells.

"Good. You are awake," the friar said from where he sat in a chair next to the bed. "I shall fetch the soup."

Soup sounded good. Sam was starving. He wondered what time it was. How long since he'd eaten. But he couldn't check his Rolex. His watch was no longer on his wrist.

The sound of approaching footsteps perked him up. Soup. But it wasn't Tuck who entered his small room. The hulking figure in the doorway was Robin's chief lieutenant, Little John.

"What news?" Little John demanded. "Your tall friend from Connecticut said little, but that Robin and Maid Marian were both well. Pardon my saying, but she does not seem right in the head."

"I'm sorry, Little John," Sam said, "but I was unable to see either of them. Nora was brought out from wherever she was kept. I suspect Vaisey is holding them somewhere in his keep, but they could be somewhere else nearby. I'll speak with Nora. Maybe I can get her to remember something."

Little John frowned, then concern softened his expression. "The Sheriff did this to you?"

"Not that he'll admit, but yes."

The big man shook his head. "Not a minute longer. We must stage our rescue now. If Robin is being held outside the keep, we will put the Sheriff's men to the sword until they tell us where."

"Little John—," Sam began.

A fierce grin split the big man's features. "We have hired mercenaries. Swordsmen. And a few additional archers."

"That's good," Sam said. "But is it enough?"

"It will have to be," Little John growled. "The Sheriff cannot be trusted."

"Let me look for Robin one more time," Sam suggested. "The Sheriff asked me to return tomorrow. He said he would let me see Robin and Marian. I'll have a good chance of finding out exactly where he's keeping them."

"Tomorrow?" Little John said. "Or do you mean today?"

"Today?"

The big man pursed his lips. "You returned to us yesterday afternoon. You have been asleep most of the morning."

Sam tried to sit up, then thought better of it. He lay back against the bed's pillow and took a deep breath. "I have to go."

"Not before your soup," Tuck said, nudging Little John aside as he entered the room. The churchman carried a deep bowl in his hands.

"Soup can wait," Sam said. "Vaisey is expecting me. Who knows what he'll do if I don't show up."

"The soup cannot wait," Tuck argued. "If you do not eat the soup, you will not take ten steps toward Nottingham."

"That's gotta be some soup," Sam said.

Tuck set the bowl on a side table and helped Sam sit up. The friar then placed the bowl in Sam's hands. "You tell me."

The heat from the fired clay bowl felt good as it warmed Sam's fingers. And the smells rising from the thick, yellow-green liquid weren't horrible. Peas? Beans? Carrots? "What kind of soup is it?"

Tuck ladled some of the liquid and made to spoon-feed Sam. "Split pea."

Sam laughed. "I hate to break it to you, friar, but we have split pea soup in my day and it doesn't have any magical healing properties."

"Neither does this," Tuck said. "Not magical in the way of the Merlin. But it will give you a much-needed boost."

Sam opened his mouth and took a swallow. "Not bad."

"Soup does a body good," Tuck suggested.

Sam laughed. "You should get a job writing slogans."

The friar snorted. "You would reduce me to the vocation of a bard? I shall try not to take offense."

"No offense intended. Where I come from, slogan writers make a good living."

The churchman grunted and force-fed Sam another spoonful.

As much as Sam appreciated the attention, he was beginning to feel like a child. He shifted the bowl into one hand and took the spoon from Tuck. "I can take it from here."

His two visitors watched in silence while Sam ate. When the soup was gone, he realized he was still hungry. "Is there more?"

"Yes," Tuck said, taking the empty bowl, "but you should not have more now. When you return from Nottingham, perhaps, if you wish."

Sam could have argued, but the friar did have a point. "Right. I'm late for a meeting. Help me get dressed."

"You do not need help." Tuck nudged Little John, and the two men left through the doorway.

"Well," Sam said to the empty room, "isn't this swell."

After swinging his feet onto the floor, he climbed out of bed and stood without the aid of a wall or walking stick. His body still ached, but he felt energized. He spotted his clothes folded into a neat pile on a bench. They looked to have been laundered. Even his trench coat. He checked the pockets and found nothing missing. The monks must have taken exceptional care.

Leaving his bandages in place, Sam applied a fresh nicotine patch. The monks must have removed the old one from his arm when they bathed him. He tried to think of when he last craved a cigarette—a real one—but couldn't place it. Maybe the patches were working this time. Or maybe the meat grinder he'd been going through since arriving in Sherwood had confused his body so much it didn't know what it wanted. Either way, he'd take it. However he broke his cravings for cancer sticks, he'd call it a win.

Even though his feet felt a bit better, Sam grabbed his walking stick from where it leaned against the wall in the corner of the room. Who knew how soon he'd need it?

Outside the hospital, he found most of the Merry Men waiting for him.

"We are attempting to decide who should go with you," Little John said. "One, more than one, or all of us?"

"None of you can go with me," Sam said. "Vaisey would arrest you on sight. I'm surprised he hasn't tracked you here yet."

"It is doubtful the Sheriff knows we are here," Tuck suggested. "He has few friends among the common folk, and the monks would never tell, even were they permitted to speak."

"Besides," Little John added, "the Sheriff cannot split his forces. Were he to send men outside Nottingham's walls, that would leave his keep vulnerable to attack. No, the man is a coward, and hides in his fortified web waiting for us to come to him."

"Maybe," Sam said. He looked past the Merry Men and saw Nora standing with Carmen. "I'll take them with me."

"The women?" Little John asked. "Why?"
"For one thing, Vaisey isn't likely to arrest them."
"And the other reason?" Tuck asked.
"We have business to discuss."

33
IT WORKED FOR CLAIRE RANDALL

"Business?" Carmen asked once they were on their way. "What business?"

Sam glanced at General Sternwood's daughter. "I need you to tell me where Nora's gun is."

"Gun? What gun?"

"Okay, let's back up. Where were you when you found Nora?"

"I already told you. In the forest."

"What forest?" Sam asked.

Carmen blew air out from between her lips. "I don't know. There were trees."

"Let's try it this way. How long had you been in Nottingham before Nora showed up?"

Silence.

"And how did Nora get hit on the head?"

Carmen threw her hands in the air. "How am I supposed to know the answer to these questions?"

"How about an easier one? What happened to Nora's clothes?"

"What?"

"You said when you found her, Nora had your sister's business card in her pocket. Nora would have been wearing her original clothes from Connecticut."

"Uhm, yes," Carmen admitted. "But she wasn't fitting in. I had to destroy her clothes like I did mine."

"Where?"

"What?"

Sam silently counted to three. "Where were you when you destroyed Nora's clothes?"

"What does it matter?"

"Look. Do you want to get back to Connecticut?"

Carmen's face went pale. "What are you saying? That we can't go back unless we're wearing the clothes we arrived in?"

Sam knew from experience that wasn't true, but he didn't have to tell Carmen that. If she was going to lie to him, maybe a little tit-for-tat was in order. "The clothes might not be a problem, they can burn or degrade relatively quickly. But Nora's gun, well, that's a modern chunk of metal that can hang around for centuries. It's just possible it could tie us here."

Again, Carmen went silent.

Into that silence, Nora spoke. "Are you all right, Sam?" Those were her first words since leaving the hospital.

Sam took Nora's hand in his and squeezed. "All right for now, angel."

As they walked, it occurred to Sam that those were the exact same words she had spoken the previous day after registering that he had taken a beating. Had her thoughts gone anywhere in between? Was this a sign that she'd suffered brain damage? Maybe permanent brain damage? Or was it a sign that Nora was getting better? That she recognized him. Recognized that he had been beaten. And could remember it a day later.

Carmen interrupted his thoughts by at last deigning to answer his question. "It was a farmhouse, somewhere between Nottingham and Bestwood."

Sam threw her an expectant look.

The young woman sighed. "Let me start at the beginning. When I first got here, after finding myself in a forest outside Daddy's castle, I tried to make sense of where I was. I could tell the castle was the same, but it looked like it had never been taken apart. Then when I saw soldiers outside the castle, I figured I was living Claire Randall's life."

"Who?" Sam asked.

"Claire Randall. The heroine in Diana Gabaldon's *Outlander* novels."

Sam had no idea who Carmen was referring to, but he got the

gist of it. Carmen had realized she wasn't in Connecticut anymore.

Sternwood's daughter continued. "Not wanting to deal with the soldiers, I made my way through the forest. Eventually, I found a party of women gathering herbs and told them I was lost, that I needed to speak with the police. It took them a while to understand me, but eventually I got directions, first to a village called Bestwood, and from there to Nottingham, where I would find a Sheriff.

"I was hungry, so I helped them gather herbs and they shared a meal with me. I got lost looking for Bestwood, so by the time I found it, my clothes were filthy and torn. I stole some clean ones from where they were drying on a line and made my way toward Nottingham.

"I never did see the Sheriff. What would be the point? Instead, I got myself settled, and returned to Bestwood every now and then to steal more clothes, and sometimes food. On one of those trips, I found Nora.

"Imagine my surprise when I found another woman in Connecticut clothes wandering down the road. She had a bump on her head and blood on her face, and couldn't remember who she was. She stood there like a crash test dummy as I searched her pockets, not saying a word as I transferred her wallet, holstered gun, and other items to the cloth sack I carried. The last item I found was my sister's business card. Up until then I was doing pretty good. When I saw that card, I freaked."

"Why did you take Nora's belongings," Sam asked, "and destroy your and her clothes?"

"You never read *Outlander*, did you?"

"I have to admit, I have not."

"You have to fit in," Carmen said. "You can't stand out. I mean, look at you. Dressed as you are. Yesterday you were beaten to within an inch of your life."

"I'm not sure how much that had to do with how I'm dressed," Sam said.

"Well, it worked for Claire Randall in the books."

"You were telling me about Nora's gun." Sam didn't believe the part of Carmen finding Nora already injured, but he could deal with that later.

"Right." Carmen took a deep breath. "After Nora suggested

she must be my sister, I told her that was true, and that we were going to Nottingham to find help to get us home. Nora told me she couldn't remember home. Anyway, I knew I had to get rid of her things before we reached Nottingham, so I kept an eye out for a landmark. When we came to a farm by the side of the road, I found a large stone with some kind of animal hole running under it, and stuffed the sack in there."

"You remember where this farm is?" Sam asked.

"Of course."

"Then we'll go there when we're done with Vaisey."

Carmen glared at him. "You'll have us walking all day!"

"If I can do it," Sam said with a wave of his walking stick, "so can you."

34
SKILLED AT GIVING ADVICE

"I SEE YOU brought bodyguards again."

The Sheriff of Nottingham lay sprawled on his throne with one leg dangling over an arm of the oversized chair. He twirled his moustache while leering at Carmen and Nora. Okay, maybe not twirling—there wasn't enough moustache for that. Vaisey stroked his moustache.

Sam resisted the urge to draw his handgun and shoot the villain. Not that it would make any difference. His Smith and Wesson M&P semi-automatic had no bullets. Someone needed to take Vaisey down a peg, but it wasn't going to be Sam Sparrow. Not today.

Resisting an urge to march up to the throne and slap the Sheriff silly, Sam said, "I thought it prudent to bring bodyguards since I can't seem to protect myself,"

He noted there were fewer soldiers in the keep than the previous afternoon. Was the man's overconfidence growing? Or was he setting a trap? Perhaps hoping Robin's men would attack before the wedding.

"No, not bodyguards." Vaisey rearranged himself on the throne into a more dignified position. "Advisors, perhaps? A cheap imitation of my own?" The smug man in black raised two fingers to his lips and let out a whistle. In response, Le Fay and the sycophant Bishop stepped out from behind the massive chair.

Sam felt like he was in a bad movie. "I don't mind taking advice from time to time. I prefer it, actually. Getting a second opinion never hurts." Why was Le Fay grinning like a Cheshire cat?

"Advice." Vaisey slipped down from the throne and strolled toward Sam. "Perhaps you yourself are sometimes skilled at giving advice. Perhaps you have dissuaded Little John and his cohorts from attempting something rash? I am a peaceful man and have no desire to see my guards test their blades. Rather, I would make a truce with Robin and his men."

Sam felt his cheek twitch. How did Vaisey know what he had accomplished with Little John? Or was it a guess?

The villain in black grinned. "I see you are surprised. Why is that? I am the Sheriff. My job is to uphold the peace." Vaisey waved a dismissive hand. "I expect no answer. No doubt Little John has told you some tales. But know this, once Maid Marian and I are wed, if Little John brings the fight to me, he brings it to Marian as well."

"You mean Robin," Sam said.

"Pardon?"

"Since you are releasing Robin at the wedding, it would be Robin, not Little John, who brings the fight to you."

Vaisey dipped his head. "As you say."

"Speaking of Marian and Robin, you told me I could see them today."

"Ah!" Vaisey's eyes widened. "I was prepared to earlier, but you are late in coming. I am afraid a visit at this point is out of the question."

"How can I be late?" Sam demanded. "We never set a time, just a day. This day."

Vaisey spread his hands. "Be that as it may. Return tomorrow, and I guarantee you will see at least one of them."

Sam's cheek twitched again, and he rubbed his earlobe. "What kind of game is this?"

"No games. But I am a busy man. I cannot spend all my time catering to the whims of foreigners. Now, I have business to attend. You can find your own way out?"

"I'm sure I can," Sam said. "The door is right behind me."

"So it is. Goodbye then." With that, Vaisey turned and strolled back to his throne.

"What was that all about?" Carmen asked once they were back in the street.

Sam scowled into the afternoon sun. "Vaisey accomplished what he intended, and got rid of us."

"He did? I thought he was supposed to let us see these friends of yours."

"That's what he told me yesterday. But it seems what he really wanted was to show us fewer soldiers guarding the Sheriff's Keep. He's setting a trap."

"A trap? He said he wanted peace."

"True, but the only way the Sheriff of Nottingham can get peace is to have all the Merry Men dead or in prison."

"Then we should go," Carmen said. "Back to Connecticut, I mean. Whatever beef this Sheriff has with your friends has nothing to do with us."

Sam turned to study Carmen's face. Was that fear? Or was she just eager to get back to her life of leisure and entitlement? "We can't leave until we recover Nora's gun. Let's go to that farmhouse you mentioned."

Carmen huffed out a breath. "More walking. Fine."

Nora turned abruptly to Sam. "Are you all right?"

"I will be, Nora. Are *you* all right?"

Nora sucked on her lower lip. "I will be, Sam."

"Then I guess that's all we can hope for right now."

35
JUST DOWN THIS ROAD

BY THE TIME they left Nottingham through the Mansfield Gate, travelling north along The King's Great Way, it was well past noon. The sun sat high in a clear blue sky, and there was hardly a breath of wind. Sam's handkerchief was soaked from wiping sweat from his forehead. He wasn't used to wandering around the great outdoors all day, and almost wished he'd left his trench coat with Tuck at the hospital.

A thick forest lined the hardpacked dirt road on the right, while fields of yellow grain spread out to the left. Sam watched as a large black bird fluttered out from the trees and winged its way across the fields, disappearing into the hazy distance.

He was beginning to think maybe they should return to the hospital. Have a rest. And soup. The friar had said he could have more soup later. He could leave Nora with Tuck, and take Sagramore to the farm instead.

But he wanted to keep an eye on Nora. He felt sure she was making progress. Maybe he was being optimistic, hopeful even, but he'd sensed slivers of recognition in the occasional looks she'd given him. Maybe it was his company, some familiarity with her past before her injury, that was bringing Nora back.

When they crossed Day Brook Bridge, Sam noticed narrow tracks branching off to the left and right. He figured the right track could take them through the shaded forest to St John the

Baptist Hospital, provided he didn't get lost. The left track followed the canal-like brook for maybe a hundred yards, then veered off through the fields.

"The farm is just down this road," Carmen said, pointing to the track by the brook.

"How far?" Sam asked.

Carmen didn't look at him. "Ten minutes. Twenty at the pace you're setting with that walking stick."

Sam stretched his back and tried to clear his head. If Carmen was playing him, he needed to keep an eye out. With the farm that close, returning to the hospital made no sense. But what if she was lying?

Fatigue won out. His feet had no desire to walk to the hospital and back again if they didn't need to. "Fine. I'll try to walk faster."

Farmland stretched out before them for as far as he could see. Here and there, workers studded the fields. Sam wasn't sure what they were doing. Perhaps looking for clogged irrigation ditches. Or filling in rabbit holes. There were few buildings, but after a while Sam could make out a long one-storey house set near the dirt track. And near the house, just off the track, stood a white boulder the size of an automobile.

"Is that your stone?" Sam asked, watching the young woman's eyes. You could often tell from the eyes if a person was lying.

Carmen nodded, then gasped.

Sam returned his gaze to the boulder and saw Vaisey's lackey, Guy of Gisbourne, standing next to it. The scarecrow stooge wore a stupid grin on his face. Sam had the feeling he was in for another beating. Two more of Vaisey's hatchet men stepped out from behind the boulder, confirming his fear. He didn't think he could run, not in his current condition, but he did know the ladies could.

"When I give the signal," Sam whispered, "run."

Carmen whispered back. "What signal?"

"Run!" Sam shouted.

Carmen was off like a shot, sprinting back the way they had come.

Nora, however, just stood there. Sam grabbed his partner's arm and began dragging her after Carmen, but she moved at barely more than a walk.

Then, up ahead, Sam saw several soldiers rise up from where

they had been concealed among the tall wheat. The armed men waded through the yellow grain until they stood on the dirt track, blocking any escape.

Carmen saw them as well and bounded like a frightened rabbit into the wall of tall wheat that grew south of the track. One of the soldiers raced after her, but Carmen ducked down, making her path through the field harder to follow.

Sam slowed to a stop. He knew he and Nora would never get away. Not with him hobbling like a cripple and Nora almost sleepwalking. Better to take the punishment. They'd probably leave Nora be. It was him Gisbourne wanted.

Turning around and using his walking stick for more support than necessary, Sam limped toward the skeletal wraith. Nora walked with him a half-step behind. Maybe he could talk his way out of whatever Vaisey's lackey had planned for them.

Gisbourne, however, wasn't in a talkative mood.

"Did Vaisey send you?" Sam asked. He thought he detected a slight left to right movement of that stupid grin, but then the back of Sam's head exploded, and he couldn't detect anything.

36
A GUN IS A FINE THING

SAM'S ENTIRE BODY ached, but the back of his head hurt the most. He tried to keep his torso still while testing his hands and feet. It was as he had thought. Someone had tied him to a chair.

"So glad you could join us," a female voice said.

Sam opened his eyes.

Morgan Le Fay stood leaning against an interior wall. She wore the black and red dress he had seen before that made her look like a gypsy. The golden bells and tassels glittered, and the grey in her hair appeared almost white.

He risked turning his head and saw why the room was so bright—a pair of uncovered windows. He also saw a long table and several empty chairs and figured he must be inside the farmhouse.

"Where's Nora?" he managed to whisper.

"Nora? You mean the puppet. She is here."

"You'd better not have hurt—" Sam turned his head the other way and saw his partner standing near the wall opposite the windows, her eyes gazing off into space.

"What have you done to her?" he demanded.

"I?" Le Fay seemed honestly confused. "I thought her peculiar state was your doing. You mean it is not? I may be wasting my time."

The fog in Sam's head was beginning to clear. "Vaisey's

marriage to Maid Marian. That's *your* scheme, isn't it? Not much different than what you tried to pull in Camelot."

Le Fay grinned. "You must admit it is a good plan. Marrying into power is the easiest way to attain it. And our Lord Vaisey, he certainly likes his power."

"Speaking of power," Sam said, "What do you know about magic?"

"That," Le Fay said, her expression darkening, "was my question for you. You have returned from that distant land of yours, but how was it accomplished? How did you arrive here? When?"

Sam laughed, then grimaced as the back of his head rebelled. "Well, I guess that makes two of us who don't know anything."

Le Fay left the wall and came to stand in front of Sam. "Do not play the fool with me. Twice before someone with magic has summoned you to this land. Who was it this time? And what is it they would have you do?"

"Honestly," Sam said. "I have no idea."

Le Fay straightened. "Guy of Gisbourne is a quiet man. But he has a cruel streak. He will make you talk." The witch-woman cast a glance at Nora. "And your friend will watch."

"Leave Nora out of it." Sam flexed his hands against the ropes tying his wrists, but found no give. "She's suffered enough."

Le Fay let out a girlish giggle. "Perhaps Guy should practice his art on your woman, while *you* watch. Would that loosen your tongue quicker?"

"I'm telling you," Sam said. "I don't know anything."

"We shall see." Le Fay stepped across the room, paused to run a finger along Nora's jaw, then exited through a doorway.

Sam immediately resumed struggling with his bindings. They felt more like cloth than rope but held just as tight.

"Are you okay, Sam?"

He stopped struggling.

Nora had crossed the room and now stood almost directly in front of him, blinking her eyes.

"Can you loosen these bindings?" he asked her, his voice a whisper.

Nora's eyes moved, taking in all of Sam and the chair. Her gaze stopped at his ankles, which he knew were tied together and also fastened to the chair legs.

"My hands would be best," Sam said.

Nora returned her gaze to his, then stepped around behind the chair. By the sound of her movements, he figured she had knelt. Then he could feel her hands working on his bindings.

It seemed to take forever, but Sam finally managed to pull one hand, then the other, through the loosened bindings.

"Go back to where you were standing," he told Nora.

Nora straightened and moved back against the wall.

Sam went to work on his ankles, pausing when voices were raised in the next room, then worked even faster. He was running out of time.

Once he freed his ankles, he looked around the room and spotted another door. The tall, narrow window beside it told him it led outside. Escape. Despite his body aches and the throbbing in his head, Sam made a run for it, though *limp for it* was a more accurate description. He'd have snatched up his walking stick, except he couldn't see it anywhere. And there was nothing he could do for Nora. Not yet.

Sam yanked open the door, then heard a shout from Gisbourne somewhere behind him. Then he was outside.

Further along the side of the house, Sam saw one of Vaisey's hatchet men. From inside, he heard another shout from Gisbourne. "To arms! To arms!"

Sam ran from the house, unsure how far he could get before the nearby soldier or his cohorts would catch him. He hoped he could at least make it as far as the white boulder.

Gritting his teeth, he fought against the aches in his body and the fire in his feet and the merciless throbbing in his head, and ran faster than he thought possible. He fell and slid behind the boulder like he was making a home run, then searched for the hole Carmen had said was beneath it. The General's younger daughter was a compulsive liar, but he hoped she hadn't bent the truth too much about the farmhouse.

Besides being tall, the boulder was long, with numerous shaded crevices along the ground, probably burrowed out by animals. Sam poked and prodded, hoping to find no one home, until he touched soft cloth. He pulled at it until he hauled it out of the crevice. A cloth bag. Something inside had clanked against the side of the boulder. Sam was sure it must be metal.

A shadow cut off the sun, and Sam looked up to see one of

Gisbourne's hatchet men. The man rested a hand on the pommel of a sword. He hadn't drawn it. Not yet. Sam fumbled with the bag as Gisbourne strode up behind the soldier and glared down at him. Gisbourne's sword *was* unsheathed. The vile wraith looked eager to use it.

"Hold on a minute," Sam said. "Ah. Here we go." He'd managed to free Nora's gun from its holster and disable the safety. Now, provided neither Nora nor Carmen had shot or removed the bullets, he was in good shape.

Another sword-wielding hatchet man joined Gisbourne and the first soldier.

"Right then," Sam said. "Who'd like to go first?"

"Move aside," Guy of Gisbourne snapped. "This dog is mine."

"Excellent," Sam said. "A volunteer."

The two hatchet men stepped away as Vaisey's stooge loomed over Sam. "I tire of chasing you," the scarecrow said. "How quickly, I wonder, can you run without toes?"

"You won't find out," Sam said, waving Nora's Glock at him.

Guy narrowed his eyes. "That is an amusing rock you hold. Perhaps I will take it from you after I remove your toes."

"This?" Sam said. "This isn't a rock. But it throws rocks. Tiny ones. Would you like a demonstration?"

Guy's lips sneered with amusement. "Show me."

"If you insist." Sam took aim at Guy's left thigh and fired.

Vaisey's henchman's scream was loud, but not as loud as the retort from Nora's Austrian-made handgun. Sam figured they could hear it back in Nottingham.

Private investigators didn't believe in silencers. If they were ever called upon to fire their weapon, they wanted as many people to know about it as possible. Especially the police, if any were nearby.

Guy shrieked and danced on one leg while clutching his thigh. Then he toppled into the dirt.

"Right," Sam said. "Who's next?" But when he looked around, the other two hatchet men were gone.

Ignoring his many and varied aches, Sam climbed to his feet and hobbled back toward the house. There was no sign in the yard of Morgan Le Fay or any of the soldiers, but they could be hiding inside. Leading with Nora's Glock, Sam re-entered through the same door he had exited, taking precautions to avoid anyone waiting just inside the doorway with a sword, or across the room with a bow.

Nora, thankfully, stood right where he had left her, apparently unharmed.

Sam cleared the house to make sure there were no surprises, found his walking stick, and returned to his partner. "Are you all right?"

Nora smiled. "I am now, Sam."

Sam also smiled and gave his partner a hug. They'd known each other for a year and had lived through some harrowing experiences, but this was the first time they had exchanged a hug. He stood back, feeling awkward as a schoolboy. "You," he mumbled, "have no idea how glad I am to hear that."

As they stood there, Sam's mind flashed back to a few days earlier when Nora had patted his knee and touched his arm. He'd wondered then if she had flirted with him, or if it had just been his imagination. He looked into her eyes now and saw . . . nothing. Le Fay had called Nora a puppet. It was an apt description.

Sam shook himself. They weren't out of the woods yet. "Wait here."

After checking the yard outside by peeking through the windows, he came back and collected Nora. They left the farmhouse and hobbled over to the boulder, where he collected the sack with the rest of Nora's belongings. Apart from a blood trail leading into a wheat field, there was no sign of Guy of Gisbourne.

Sam took one last look around, saw no one, then led Nora back along the track that would take them to Day Brook Bridge, and from there to St John the Baptist Hospital.

All the way, Sam felt exposed. At any moment, an archer could rise up from among the tall wheat and shoot an arrow at them. A gun is a fine thing, but worthless if an arrow took you by surprise.

They had only made it a short distance past the bridge and into the forest when a band of archers blocked their way. Sam had been about to hustle Nora into the protection of the trees, when he noticed how tall and broad the lead archer was. "Little John?"

He waited as the band moved closer and he could make out more faces. There was Tuck. And Sagramore, his long sword at his side. David of Doncaster. And Azeem the Moor. Then he made out Carmen. How about that? The general's bratty daughter had not only found her way to St John's, but she had called out the cavalry.

"Sam Spade," Tuck cried. "We were just coming to rescue you."

"Much appreciated," Sam said, "but we managed to escape on our own."

"How?"

Sam let out a heavy breath and felt his shoulders slump. "I'll tell you after another bowl of your special soup. And this time you'll tell me your secret. Split peas may be good for you, but no vegetable is that good."

Tuck looked at his companions, then drew Sam to one side. "Can you not guess? You encountered my secret ingredient once before. In Camelot."

Sam searched his memory, but couldn't remember sharing any meals with the friar during his earlier visits, and certainly not soup. "Give me a hint."

Tuck shook his head in disbelief. "A hint? Very well. At the time it was your jeweller friend in need of energy."

"Jeweller?" Sam had forgotten all about the wannabe bard who had helped him in Camelot. "Whatever happened to Hammett?"

Before Tuck could answer, he figured out what the friar's secret ingredient must be. "Cocaine? You put cocaine in my soup?"

"Just a pinch," Tuck said. "Thomas Hammett was years ago. I have refined my measurements since then. You shall suffer no ill effects, I assure you."

"Friar!" Little John called. "Do not monopolize the man. Others wish to bend his ear."

"Once we return to St John's," Tuck answered. "Mr. Spade requires medical attention. And I would rather we were not found on the road."

Sam thought about mentioning that Vaisey probably knew they were staying at the hospital, but he had no real evidence of that, and he didn't think an attack on the Merry Men was in the Sheriff's plans. Vaisey had spent days preparing a trap at his centre of power. He wasn't going to waste that effort.

Little John grumbled as he offered Sam a shoulder, which was too high for comfort. Sam accepted it anyway. Sagramore took up the other side, and Sam felt he was being carried more than being helped along.

After a change of bandages and a dinner of soup—one that did not include cocaine—Sam wanted nothing more than to sleep for a week or two. But couldn't, because he once again had to explain to Little John why the Merry Men couldn't just run into Nottingham, storm the Sheriff's Keep, and rescue Robin and Marian.

"But we have mercenaries," Little John complained. "They are camped a short distance along The King's Great Way and await our summons."

"It's a trap," Sam repeated. "Each time I visit the Sheriff's Keep fewer men are guarding his throne."

Little John's eyes widened. "Then the time to strike is now!"

"The men aren't by the throne because they're hidden in the balcony above it, bows at the ready and with a mountain of arrows. Each time I visit, there are more people in the street. At least half of them have swords at their belts or stashed in carts or hidden in the bushes. Vaisey wants you to attack. He's ready for you. He's invited me back twice now so I can report to you how weak he appears."

Little John's beard bristled. "We cannot just sit on our hands and do nothing."

"We aren't doing nothing," Sam said. "Not quite. I'm working on a plan."

"You are? What is it?"

"Too early to share. And until I know exactly where Robin and Maid Marian are being held, we can't make a move."

Little John blew air out between his lips. "So how do we learn this information?"

"For that, I do have a plan I can share. Tomorrow I'll visit Vaisey again. Afterward, if I still don't know where he's keeping his hostages, I'll corner one of his bullyboys and extract the information from him."

Little John nodded. "At last. A plan I can understand."

37
A VERY COMPLEX MAN

IT WAS MIDMORNING by the time Sam rolled out of the hospital cot he'd been using as a bed. His body ached from the hairs on his head to the tips of his toenails, and he was tempted to call upon Tuck for a bowl of his special soup, but he settled for replacing his nicotine patch instead.

Like the day before, Little John offered to join him for his confrontation with Vaisey.

"I have to go alone this time," Sam said.

"Oh?" Tuck asked. "Yesterday you took the womenfolk with you."

"And you saw how well that turned out. I can't put them at risk again. Besides, if I have to get brutal with Vaisey's men to find out where Robin and Marian are being held, I'm not sure I want Nora or Carmen as witnesses."

Neither Tuck nor Little John commented.

Sam considered leaving his walking stick behind. Despite his body aches, he didn't feel he needed it anymore. The soles of his feet had formed a layer of nerveless, bloodied calluses that made fitting them into his shoes a battle. A few more days of mistreatment and they might turn into hooves.

In the end, he decided to take the stick. He pictured himself entering the Sheriff's fortress, alone except for his long coat, his hat, and his staff. The archetypical pilgrim. Besides, if the stick got in the way, he could ditch it.

"Sam Spade." Vaisey's tone rang cold and deafening in the near-empty fortress. The few soldiers Sam could see stood just inside the entrance, clustered beside him and at his back.

"What? No clever welcome today." Sam stood with the walking stick in his left hand, his right hand deep inside his trench coat pocket, through the tear he had made when he first bought the coat, and gripping the handle of his Smith & Wesson M&P semi-automatic. He'd drawn the weapon from his hip holster before entering the Sheriff's Keep. That morning at St John the Baptist Hospital, he'd transferred the remaining 16 nine-millimetre bullets from Nora's Glock to his own weapon, ten in the magazine, one in the chamber, and the five extra bullets in his coat pocket.

"I am vexed with you," Vaisey announced. "After leaving here yesterday, you injured my deputy. An assault on one of my own is an assault on me."

"Yes, well. Excuse me if I'm fond of my toes. I wasn't about to allow your man to cut them off with a sword."

Vaisey sucked on his lower lip. "Your toes. Are you saying Guy threatened to do you an injury?"

"More than threaten. He was already swinging that oversized toad stabber of his."

The Sheriff of Nottingham ground his teeth. "I shall speak with him."

"Then you should speak with your soothsayer as well. It was her idea."

"Mortianna? You must be mistaken."

"Oh no. She's the one who threatened me. Then she sent Gisbourne to carry out the threat."

Vaisey blew out a lungful of air. "Mortianna! Guy!"

The spiritual advisor and Vaisey's number one henchman appeared from behind the throne more slowly than they had in the past. Guy of Gisbourne, because he hopped out on a makeshift crutch. Le Fay because she was just being slow. Both of them looked ready to duck for cover at a moment's notice.

"Sam Spade accuses you of going against my wishes. What say you?"

Silence ensued. When Gisbourne failed to answer, Le Fay said, "Sam Spade stands before you, does he not? If I see him correctly, he still has all ten of his toes."

Vaisey pondered that a moment. "Yet you did waylay him, did you not? Why?"

Again, Gisbourne remained silent. Le Fay continued frowning, then a smile crept across her face. "Sam Spade is a foreigner. He is not here by accident. I sought to discover his motives."

Vaisey tapped a finger against the arm of his throne. "Could you not see his motives in his countenance?"

"Not fully," Le Fay said. "Sam Spade is a very complex man."

"What see you now?" Vaisey demanded.

"That the woman—the puppet—the one called both Vivian and Nora, is of import to him."

"What sort of import?"

"That is among the things I attempted to ascertain."

Vaisey ceased tapping his finger. "The weapon used on Guy. I understand it is a slingshot of some kind. I must see it."

Sam blinked. "Slingshot? I hit Guy with a sharp rock."

"A rock? His thigh is pierced."

"A very sharp rock."

Vaisey leaned forward in his oversized seat. "Guy's leg turns purple as a mulberry tart."

Sam shrugged. "The rock was lying in the dirt. I didn't have a chance to clean it before I hit him with it. You may want to have someone clean his wound with hot water."

Vaisey shook his head. "Enough. I bid you leave us and return on the morrow."

Sam waited while Gisbourne cast his master a scathing look, then he raised his voice at Vaisey. "Hold on. You said I could see Robin or Marian today."

"Yes." A smirk creased its way across Vaisey's thin lips. "Unfortunately, this news of my trusted deputy acting without instruction has soured my mood." Vaisey shot up his hand. "I will hear no complaints. No doubt Little John will be enraged that you have once again failed to ascertain the health of his friends. But here is some good news you may deliver. The wedding shall take place tomorrow at the peak of the sun. Should you choose to attend, you will see both Marian and Robin. Marian by my side as Holy vows are spoken. And Robin as he is released from custody following the wedding."

"Of course, I'll attend," Sam said. "I wouldn't miss it for the world."

Vaisey grinned. "Excellent. Bring your lovely companions. Nora and—what was the other's name?—Carmen? My Lady Marian has requested both as bridesmaids."

Sam stood there, the realization kicking him in the teeth that he had run out of time.

Vaisey smirked and waggled his fingers at him. "Go on. Go. I shall see to it that Guy fails at sending assassins after you. For a few moments, anyway."

38
A PERFECT PLACE TO HIDE A HOSTAGE

INSTEAD OF HEADING for the York Gate, Sam made a beeline across the village green to the open-air market on the other side. He knew Vaisey had men outside the keep watching him. He just didn't know how many. And who knew how many moments Vaisey would wait before leaving Gisbourne to his own devices, devices that likely included revenge of some kind.

Sam moved fast. Faster than he had in days, pumping his arms to give himself momentum. Once he reached the stalls, he turned to see who else was crossing the green. Only a dozen or so men. If that's all there was, he could deal with it.

After making a speedy zig-zag among the stalls, hopeful that goods, piled sometimes six feet high, obstructed the view of at least some of his pursuers, Sam ducked into an open tavern. Being late morning, the place wasn't busy. Maybe half a dozen customers. A portly man wiping down a dry counter with a dirty rag took in Sam's trench coat and fedora, frowned, and asked, "What be your pleasure?"

Sam didn't have much time. He also didn't see what he was looking for. Adopting a speech pattern he assumed a foreigner in medieval times might have, he said, "I am a stranger to this land. What is your best local brew?"

The barman's frown softened. "As everyone in Nottinghamshire knows, our best ale is from St Mary's Abbey."

"Very well. I am eager to test my palate. But first, is there a commode where I might relieve myself?"

A nod and a wag of the barman's head directed Sam to a narrow door half-hidden behind a staircase.

"My thanks."

Sam reached the door in just a few strides and was relieved to find it was exactly what he was looking for. Not a water closet, but an exit to a tiny yard that contained grass, bushes, trees, a privy, and a gated fence.

He hustled as fast as he could toward the gate and lifted the latch which allowed him to escape.

Finding himself in an alley similar to the one where he had been mugged two days earlier, Sam dashed around puddles and mudholes until he reached one of Nottingham's narrow streets.

A church took up most of the next block. It was much larger than the other two he had seen, with a crenelated tower capped with a tall steeple. Battlements also capped the high stone walls, and there were few windows, making the place look more like a fortress than a church.

Voices called somewhere behind him, so Sam figured he should get off the street. In his *mean streets* getup, he stood out like a drunkard in a tea house.

The front entrance sat on an open square crowded with people, so he hobbled down a sloped side street until he spotted what looked like a service door. A breath of relief escaped his lungs as the handle turned and the door swung open. Stepping quickly inside, he closed the door and slid a latch that would keep anyone from following.

Organ music from deep inside the building met his ears, but apart from that there were no sounds. Even more important, there was no one in sight. A short corridor led to a storeroom filled with empty shelves, and beyond that a doorway into a kitchen. Sam skulked through the kitchen, down another short hallway, and past what looked like a walk-in closet where two women dressed in white habits spoke quietly while arranging bundles of cloth on a shelf.

He continued down the hallway, which ended at a closed door beside a wide stairway. The door was more ornate than any he had seen and included a keyhole. He tried the handle and discovered it locked. His only option was the stairs.

The stairway held only a few steps and seemed to connect the end of the building accessed by the lower side street with the church proper. The music grew louder as he climbed, so Sam thought he would come out in the nave, but instead found himself in a small anteroom with two archway exits.

Peeking through the exit to the right, Sam looked out into the church's broad nave. Row after row of wooden pews filled the space, many of them occupied by lone worshipers or the occasional family. A soft, deep voice murmured against the background of organ music, but Sam couldn't make out any of the words. They didn't sound English. He risked stepping further through the archway so he could see down the length of the nave to the chancel, then hastily stepped back again. Behind a raised pulpit, gowned in white and reading from a book he assumed was the Bible, probably a Latin Bible since he couldn't understand the words, stood the Bishop of Hereford.

The other exit proved the better bet. It led into a narrow hallway populated by a series of empty offices. The room at the end was by far the largest and held more furniture than just a desk and a chair. There were closets and cupboards and bookcases. Even a couple of potted plants by the window. It reminded Sam a bit of his and Nora's office in Hartford. One thing it had that his PI office didn't, were the purple robes that lay over one of the chairs. Robes Sam had last seen worn by the Bishop when he had appeared in the Sheriff's Keep acting as one of Vaisey's advisors.

So, the Bishop of Hereford's office. Sam drummed his fingers together. He could work with this.

Moving quickly, Sam rummaged through the shelves, cupboards, and closets, looking for dirt. Dirt on the Bishop or Vaisey, that is. Something incriminating. Leverage Robin could use to get Vaisey thrown in jail or justice for Robin's father's murder. It wasn't until he turned to the Bishop's desk that he realized he was thinking too much like a private detective and not enough like an outlaw. His usual methods weren't going to work here.

The desk was littered with papers. An inkwell sat in one corner, and next to it a wooden stand with several quill pens. And there, on a thin gold chain, lay an ornate key. Sam had no idea what the key was for but figured it was important. He pocketed it, then looked through the various papers, none of which was a map of the Sheriff's Keep or instructions on where Robin and his friends were being held.

He was about to search the desk drawers when the organ music stopped. He paused and listened. He had no idea how church services were supposed to go, especially not in medieval England, but the last thing he wanted was Vaisey's evangelical advisor to find him going through his desk.

The silence lasted maybe ten seconds, then the organ started up again, louder than ever, but not before Sam heard the sound of people talking and feet moving. Taken together, it gave the sense of finality. The service had ended.

Sam rushed out of the Bishop's office, scurried down the narrow hallway, and into the anteroom by the stairs. Fortunately, the Bishop was nowhere in sight. Most likely he was bidding his parishioners farewell at the main entrance. Sam had seen that in movies.

At the bottom of the steps, he stopped and looked back toward the nave. Still no bishop. Then he turned his gaze to the locked door. It was the first locked door Sam had seen in Nottingham. Surely that meant there was something important behind it.

After an additional glance up the stairway, Sam pulled the pilfered key from his pocket and fitted it to the lock. He wasn't the least surprised when the key fit perfectly. The door swung open to reveal a new set of steps descending into darkness. Retrieving his penlight from his coat pocket, Sam closed and relocked the door before descending the steps.

He didn't know what to expect. He hadn't known old churches even had basements, never mind what they were used for. What he hoped to find were cells holding Robin, Marian, and Will Scarlet. A church basement a couple of streets away from the Sheriff's Keep was a perfect place to hide a hostage, but he couldn't imagine doing so without plenty of guards for security and to see to the hostages' needs. He didn't think they'd all be sitting in the dark, but perhaps there was a basement room with a lamp.

The steps ended in a spacious, windowless room remarkable only for the elaborately carved support pillars that rose up in rows to meet a low ceiling. He flashed his penlight around but could see no furniture or anything else to give the space purpose.

It was completely empty. After taking several steps, he looked down. Were those words and images engraved into the stone floor? He bent down and peered closer. Many of the images depicted skulls or what looked like coats of arms.

What was this? A crypt? Sam had heard of skeletons in the closet. Even skeletons beneath the floorboards, at a crime scene. But a basement graveyard? Why not? He wouldn't put it past rich folks to want to bury their dead somewhere out of the rain. Or maybe they figured under the church was closer to God.

Ignoring that he was quite literally walking on people's graves, Sam crossed the floor and searched the walls, looking for side rooms, closets, doors, anything to indicate the church basement contained more than the remains of past congregants. Behind the stairs, he found a walled-off area containing a furnace as well as a large bin filled with cut timber. Being mid-summer, the furnace hadn't seen use in a while. Behind the furnace, however, he found a soot-covered curtain hiding a false wall. Pushing the curtain aside, Sam discovered a narrow tunnel that led back into darkness.

"Now we're getting somewhere," Sam whispered.

Inside the tunnel, he had to hunch down somewhat so as not to hit his head against the low ceiling. The sides of the passageway were rough, and the floor uneven. Both appeared to be made from river stones and mortar. The tunnel didn't even go straight, but canted to one side then back again. It also seemed to dip lower in places, where small pools of foul-smelling water collected and the walls reeked of mould. Several times, Sam considered going back, but curiosity got the best of him. The passageway had to lead somewhere. Finding out might be important.

At last, the tunnel seemed to rise for a while before ending, this time at a locked door instead of a curtain. Sam tried the bishop's key again, with success. The door swung open.

Light emanated from the other side, so Sam turned off his penlight, slipped it into his pocket, and drew his Smith & Wesson M&P semi-automatic. Just in case there was trouble. Cautiously, he stuck his head through the doorway.

Stone walls greeted him. Several tiny windows near the ceiling were the source of the light, each window no larger than a bread loaf and lined with vertical iron bars. Sam glanced around, looking for a reason for the empty room to exist. Except for a long rain gutter beneath the windows and a wooden bench set against the wall opposite, there was nothing.

Sam put away his beanshooter and sat on the bench. A furnace room in a church basement. A secret tunnel. And an empty room. The only place he had seen in Nottingham under lock and key. What was he missing?

As Sam sat thinking, a murmur of voices whispered in his ears, too distant to make out the words. He listened and soon determined the sounds were not coming in through the windows, but from somewhere beyond the empty room.

Rising to his feet, he crept along the inner wall, searching for a ventilation hole through which the sound might be coming. What he found instead was an opening in the wall opposite the doorway. A second wall comprised of the same stone and mortar ran a few feet behind it. From further back, you couldn't tell it wasn't a single wall. Sam figured the optical illusion was intentional.

Slipping through the narrow gap, he found himself inside a room the exact opposite of the one he had left. Shelves and cupboards lined the walls. Chests and barrels covered the floor. All filled to overflowing with stacks of cloth, baskets of feathers, piles of metal rods, and numerous other things Sam could only guess at. So what was this? A secret storeroom for the church?

The voices here were louder. Sam worked his way through the mountains of riches to the far side of the room, where a door stood open into a hallway. He listened through the opening and made out two voices, a man and a woman.

"Guy is a fool," the woman said. "He fails at every task set before him."

Sam knew the voice and immediately realized the storeroom didn't belong to the church.

"Yes," the man agreed. Vaisey. "Guy is a fool. But he is my fool. I shall deal with him as I see fit."

How about that. The tunnel connected the church with the Sheriff's Keep.

Le Fay spoke again. "Guy is your cousin, is he not? Is that why you keep him?"

"I keep him because he does what I tell him. Or at least attempts to. Now he is injured, I require a new deputy. Perhaps that fellow Wincott."

"Sheriff! Sheriff!" A new voice. This one rising in volume as it approached.

"Hereford. What do you bother me with now?"

"The key," the bishop hissed. "It has gone missing."

"Key? What key?"

'To the tunnel," the bishop replied.

Sam knew this was his cue to leave. He navigated back through the crowded storeroom, slipped through the hidden gap into the empty room, and re-entered the tunnel, where he used the Bishop's key to lock the door behind him. Unless there was a second key, he was safe from pursuit from the keep. That didn't mean he was safe, however. Hereford could have men waiting for him at the Church.

That was the only play he had, however, so he hastily made his way through the tunnel, which he now realized ran beneath Castle Street, and came out behind the furnace in the church basement. Still holding his penlight, he traversed the basement graveyard to the stairs and climbed them. At the top, he pulled out his semi-automatic. He couldn't hear anything, but one couldn't be too careful.

Using the key, he unlocked the door and stepped out into the church hallway. He was alone.

Quickly, he made his way to the side door and out into the street. There was no sign of the Sheriff's men, so Sam put away his handgun and used his cane to hobble across town toward Pallium's Parchments.

39
LORD LUNDGREN

BY THE TIME Sam sat on the bench across the street from Effie's shop, he figured he'd avoided Guy of Gisbourne's assassins as well as any searchers the Sheriff might have sent after the thief who took his pet bishop's key. Sam didn't think anyone important had seen him enter or leave the church. And the only people he'd encountered inside were the two chatting women, who he felt confident hadn't noticed him. All the Sheriff had was a missing key. He couldn't know Sam had taken it. He might even believe the bishop had simply lost it somewhere.

But was he any further ahead? Sure, he'd found a back way into the Sheriff's Keep, if he dared use it, but he still had no idea where Robin was being kept. And, according to Vaisey, the wedding was set for tomorrow. Talk about your fast engagements.

Sam took a quick look up and down the street. Not seeing anyone suspicious, he crossed over and slipped inside the book shop's door.

As always, the inside of the shop was dark, the shutters drawn. Effie's voice whispered in the darkness. "Sam, is that you?"

Sam stepped across to the counter, reached out, and took Effie's hands in his. "I'm glad you're safe. I didn't know if Vaisey had come after you as well."

"Why? What happened?"

"Morgan Le Fay is here."

"What!"

During Sam's second visit to Camelot, he'd found Effie working as Le Fay's clerk. It was the only time he'd seen her frightened. "The wicked witch is working for Vaisey as one of his advisors."

Effie huffed. "Pulling the Sheriff's strings, you mean. What is she doing?"

Sam wasn't surprised Effie had reached the same conclusion he had. "Filling Vaisey's head with illusions of grandeur. Le Fay is somehow involved with John Lackland's rebellion against his brother Richard, and has convinced Vaisey he can get nearer the throne through marriage to Maid Marian."

"Marriage! To Marian, Robin's fiancée? I know she is cousin to the King, but she must be no less than eighth in line to the throne."

"I doubt Vaisey is above murdering a flock of relatives," Sam said. "Have you found out anything of where Robin and Marian are being held?"

Effie shook her head. "I have tried, but Mr. Lundgren had little to say regarding our Lord Sheriff or his doings. As for my customers, at the first hint of seeking information, they suddenly no longer seem to even know what day it is."

"They're scared," Sam said. "I don't blame them. By the way, the wedding is tomorrow."

"What?"

"I've just come from Vaisey. He pushed me again to goad Little John into attempting a rescue. With the wedding set for tomorrow, he'll be expecting the Merry Men to make their move tonight."

"What will you do?" Effie asked, her voice laden with concern.

"I'm not sure. Even if I find Robin's location, Vaisey's men will be prepared to kill anyone who approaches."

At that moment the door opened, letting in a shaft of light. Sam made out a lean man of less than average height, with some encumbrance on his back.

"Goodness woman, light a candle," the man shouted. "'Tis black as Hades in here."

Effie let go of Sam's hands and struck a match.

By the light of Effie's candle, Sam was able to take stock of the man in the doorway. A few years younger than himself. Fit. Dark hair. Clean-shaven. He also saw the encumbrance on the man's back was a bow and a quiver of arrows. Sam dug his hand into his coat pocket and gripped his semi-automatic.

The man's eyes paused briefly on Sam's face, which was still bruised and raw from the beating he'd taken two days earlier. Then they settled on Effie. "I know you are self-conscious about that scar, but trust me, no man is interested in a woman's face."

Effie ducked her head. "Yes, Lord Lundgren."

Lundgren. Effie's new boss. Sam feigned eager surprise. "Lundgren? Carol Lundgren?"

The man frowned briefly, then smiled. "You may think you have an advantage, but I know your name as well. Sam Spade. The Lord Sheriff has his eye on you."

Sam grinned and took a step forward. "Carol Lundgren. I had no idea you were a lord. Or is everyone who works for the Sheriff a lord now?"

The smile turned upside down. "Watch your tongue. I may not be a lord in land. Not yet. But I am a lord over people. Those in my employ must address me by my title."

"I see," Sam said, "so you can lord it over them."

"Sam!" Effie whispered.

"I've got this, doll." Sam drew his semi-automatic and aimed it at Effie's new lord. "Did you hear what happened to your Sheriff's errand boy, Guy of Gisbourne?"

Lundgren scowled at Sam's Smith & Wesson. "That?"

"Don't dismiss it," Sam said. "This baby may be small, but it can cost a man more than his leg."

"Guy has not lost his leg," Lundgren said.

Sam shrugged. "Not yet."

Lundgren glowered at the hand weapon and ground his teeth. "What is it you want?"

"The location of Maid Marian and Robin of Locksley."

"Is that all?"

"I'd also like to see one of your arrows."

A grin split Lundgren's face. "Which end?"

"The fletching will do."

With a snort, Lundgren pulled one of his arrows from the quiver on his back and offered it to Sam.

Keeping his semi-automatic levelled at Lundgren's chest, Sam examined the fletching without touching it. "I thought so. That was you on the roof three nights ago. You killed Joe Brody."

Lundgren smirked. "So what if I did? Joe Brody was a criminal. And I work for the Sheriff."

Sam chuckled and waved away the arrow. He continued chuckling while Lundgren passed it over his shoulder into his quiver. Then he ceased chuckling. "That's not how arrests are made. You didn't kill Brody for the Sheriff. Why'd you do it?"

Lundgren's face turned cold. "Arthur Geiger was a friend of mine. A good friend. Joe Brody killed Arthur. I killed Joe Brody."

"You're sure it was Brody who killed your friend?"

"Sure enough."

"Well." Sam shook his head. "I know for a fact the Sheriff frowns on his underlings killing people without clearing it with him first. So, back to the location of Robin of Locksley."

"You already know where Locksley is," Lundgren growled. "Why go through all this trouble with me?"

"He's in the Sheriff's Keep. Really?"

Lundgren nodded. "Of course, he is. The keep has the most secure cells in the shire."

"Effie," Sam said. "Give the man a clean sheet of paper and a pen, will you?"

"Uhm. Okay." Within moments, a blank parchment and a writing quill were on the counter.

Sam waggled his handgun. "Now, Lord Lundgren, draw me a map of the Sheriff's fortress. Be sure to mark where the cells are and the best way to reach them. Then we'll call our business finished."

40
A MOST UNUSUAL ESCAPE

SAM WATCHED THROUGH the window shutters of Pallium's Parchments as Lundgren retreated down Halifax Lane. The street seemed otherwise deserted, but that didn't necessarily mean there was no one lying in wait. There were plenty of shadows among the shop fronts where one could hide.

"Is there a back way out of here?" Sam asked.

"There is a drainage ditch," Effie responded. "Nothing like the wall tunnel behind Mr. Geiger's house, if that is what you mean."

"It'll have to do. Grab anything you don't want to leave behind."

"What? I cannot leave. My job—"

"—is too dangerous," Sam finished. "Your new boss knows too much of Vaisey's business. He has to know you and I are involved. Plus, he's a killer. You're no longer safe in Nottingham."

"Involved?" Effie asked. "You and I? You know I am not . . ."

"He knows you're helping me," Sam clarified. "If Vaisey doesn't have you killed, he'll throw you in jail to use as bait."

"Oh. Well. Such are the risks of being a spy."

"Your spying days are over. You gave it a shot. I suspect Lundgren was already onto you."

"But what shall I do?" Effie cried. "If the Lord Sheriff is after my head . . ."

"Join Robin Hood and his Merry Men," Sam suggested.

"You'll like Sherwood Forest. It's very homey."

Effie cast him an odd look. "Merry Men?"

"Yeah, yeah. Trust me. It's a good name."

Effie shook her head, then reached beneath the counter. When she straightened, she held a sack of coins. "If I am to be an outlaw, I suppose I should begin by stealing the midday book."

Sam grinned. "That's the spirit." He took one last look through the shutters, then stepped over to the counter and laid a hand on top of Effie's. "About that back exit."

"Through here," Effie said.

They moved through the single door behind the counter into a short hallway. A doorway to the right revealed a small kitchen with a cot against the wall. To the left, a curtained-off water closet. The hallway ended with a door that creaked when it opened. Unlike Geiger's house, there was no yard. Just a muddy trail that ran behind the row of shops.

"Is there an entrance nearby to the wall tunnel?" Sam asked.

Effie pointed. "At the end of the street."

"Let's go then." Sam stepped down onto the mud trail and felt his foot sink an inch.

"Is there a reason we do not use the street?" Effie asked.

Sam sighed. "I think I've made too many enemies recently."

"Lord Lundgren being the most recent?" she suggested.

"And Lundgren's not the most dangerous."

The ground was soft, but not wet enough that moisture soaked into his shoes. For that, Sam was grateful. They still had a long walk ahead of them, and he didn't know what moisture would do to his calluses.

As they made their way along the ditch, Effie asked, "How did you convince Lord Lundgren to draw you a map of the fortress? Did he really kill Joe Brody? Did you blackmail him with that knowledge? I hesitate to draw attention, but it seemed a weak threat."

"The threat was more complicated than that," Sam said, patting his Smith & Wesson that lay hidden beneath his trench coat. "Just be glad Lundgren broke when he did. Making good on the threat would have gotten messy."

"Messy?"

"You'll probably still get a chance to see what I mean."

"I hope so," Effie said.

"No, you don't. Not really."

The ditch ended at a junction where houses instead of shops backed against the wall. The street was different from Geiger's, but the houses looked much the same. Effie led Sam to a gate that opened into a side yard for one of the houses. Only, once they entered the yard, he couldn't see any way to access the adjoining house. The yard itself was small and lined on three sides with trees and bushes. A stone bench sat in the middle facing the street.

"Is this some kind of park?" Sam asked.

"Park?" Effie gave him a curious look. "Like the village green?"

"No, park as in a public space in suburban neighbourhoods where kids can play and adults can enjoy a touch of nature."

"You are describing the green. This is a commons."

"What's the difference?" Sam asked.

"The town owns the green, while this commons is owned by the residents along this street. We are trespassing."

"Then why are we here?"

Effie glanced around, seeming to make sure no one was in sight. Then she pushed aside the branches of one of the bushes, revealing a small cleared area behind the foliage. "This way. Hurry."

The space between the commons and the town wall would have been cramped for three, but for two was merely cosy. Trees and tall bushes blocked the early afternoon sun, creating an almost romantic ambience. Under different circumstances, Sam would have maybe said something. But in Geiger's shop, Effie *had* begun to say something, about how the two of them couldn't be involved. It was obvious nothing had changed in six years, so no point in trying. Instead, Sam asked, "Now what?"

"Do you not see it?" Effie asked.

Sam reached out to touch the grey-white stone of the wall. Most of it was covered by lichen and vines—some kind of creeping ivy maybe—but the place he touched seemed to have been brushed or rubbed free of growth. Effie looked at him expectantly, so he pushed against the wall, then jerked back slightly when it moved. Taking another go at it, he pushed harder, and kept pushing as a section of wall swung inward on hinges. He looked at Effie. "This is where you came out when you left Geiger's house?"

"It is the only street entrance I know about," Effie said. "I assume there are others, but I have only used this passageway three times. First, when Mr. Geiger showed me the way in the event I encounter trouble while delivering the book. Second, when he bid me take this route the night he was killed. And last, when Carmen and I escaped the Sheriff."

"Is this kind of thing usual?" Sam asked. "I mean town walls having tunnels and back doors?"

Effie shrugged. "I assume every city and castle has at least one bolthole. This wall tunnel seems overly elaborate, but Nottingham is a royal residence, after all. The King or his family members reside here at times, and hunt in Sherwood Forest."

Sam's cheek twitched. "I'm sure hunting isn't the only thing they did here. Which way to the town's back door?"

"You mean the one that opens to the eastern fields?"

"That's where we're going."

Effie's eyes widened. "That is suicide. There are archers on the battlements."

"They're taking the week off," Sam said. "On account of Vaisey's trap for Robin's Merry Men."

Effie looked doubtful.

"I've already gone that way a couple of times."

"Then you are the luckiest of men," Effie said.

"Trust me. Vaisey isn't going to shoot an arrow until he has all of Robin's Merry Men in his sights."

"Very well. But you shall leave the passageway first."

Sam tipped his hat. "I wouldn't have it any other way."

They encountered no one in the tunnel for the few minutes it took to reach the familiar exit. When Sam saw the beam still lying on the stone floor, and the door sitting loose on its hinges, he sighed with relief.

"I am surprised no one has resecured the door," Effie said.

Sam smiled. "A trap no one can enter isn't going to work." He then pulled open the door and stepped into sunlight and freedom.

Effie joined him a few moments later but hugged the town wall as she looked up at the battlements. "It is as you say. No archers. The Hospital of St John the Baptist is but a few minutes' walk from here."

"Only if we take the track along the wall." Sam pointed across the wheat field. "We should go that way, then circle around through the trees."

"If there is no one on the battlements," Effie asked, "why should it matter?"

"I'm sure there is someone," Sam said. "Lots of someones. But they've been instructed to watch from hiding instead of shoot."

Effie's gaze again scrutinized the crenels along the top of the wall. "I see no one."

"Why don't you stay inside the wall until I say it's safe," Sam said as he stepped out among the golden wheat. He walked backward, his eyes studying the battlements, his semi-automatic drawn and clutched at the ready. Just in case.

Effie watched him from the doorway. "You hold that curious device in your hands like it contains magic."

"It used to," Sam said. "But it can still get me out of a jam."

Walking backward, he saw nothing for several steps, then a head briefly popped up between two crenels before dropping back down. Sam waited. Nothing. He kept walking.

When he figured he was out of bowshot, he called to Effie. "Okay. You can come out."

Effie took one last glance upward, pulled the door back into place within the wall, then made a mad dash through the field.

Sam held his weapon with both hands, aimed up at the battlements, ready to provide cover fire. Just in case.

Effie ran past him, not slowing as she made her way to the treeline.

Sam resumed walking backward, his eyes vigilant for the slightest motion. When he figured Effie should be among the trees, he turned and jogged painfully across the remainder of the field. Together they stood concealed by the forest, watching the battlements for activity.

"That was a most unusual escape," Effie said.

"But less dramatic than it could have been," Sam suggested. "Vaisey doesn't want us. He wants Little John, David of Doncaster, and all the others. He needs us to come and go so we can lure the Merry Men into his trap."

"Then why all the subterfuge of escaping?" Effie asked.

"Vaisey can't know we know it's a trap."

Effie frowned. "I am confused."

"If you think you're confused, you should see me try to explain this to Little John. Also, while Vaisey isn't keen to see me dead just yet, Morgan Le Fay has already tried to kill me at least once. Guy of Gisbourne, maybe twice. And I'm sure your Lord Lundgren wouldn't mind putting a few arrows in me."

"You did incur that beating," Effie said. "Why have you not kicked the dust from your shoes and forsaken Nottingham?"

"I won't abandon my friends. And I certainly won't abandon you."

"You are too good to me, Sam Spade."

Sam's cheek twitched. "You deserve nothing but the best, angel."

By the time they reached St John the Baptist Hospital, it was midafternoon. As usual, Tuck greeted them.

"Lady Peregrine! Yours is a sight that warms my heart."

Conscious of her scar, Effie turned her unharmed cheek toward the portly churchman. "Friar Tuck. I see God has been bounteous in His dealings with you."

Tuck laughed. "Such a dignified way of saying I have accumulated more girth since last we met. At least you recognized me. That is a blessing."

The friar turned to Sam. "How went your meeting with the Sheriff? Did he permit you to see Robin? Marian?"

Sam snorted. "I could ask you to guess, but it would be no guess at all. As we predicted, Vaisey found yet another reason to keep me from seeing Robin. But plan B worked. I know where he and Marian are being held. And, I have a map."

Tuck clapped his hands. "That is good news. Little John will be pleased."

"No, he won't, because it's a trap. We can't use the map. Or attempt a rescue."

"But..."

"If we try, we'll all be killed."

Tuck wrung his hands. "Little John will be livid."

"Maybe not," Sam said. "I have a new plan. One that may not keep all of us alive, but it probably won't get us all killed either."

The friar looked doubtful. "What kind of plan can that be?"

"We're going to crash a wedding."

41

DEAD AND BLOODIED ON THE PRISON FLOOR

"NOT THE WEDDING!" Little John growled sometime later. "There can be no wedding. Marian is to wed Robin. We must attack tonight before the Sheriff carries out this heinous act in front of all the peoples of Nottinghamshire!"

"But that is exactly what the Sheriff expects," Tuck said. "Sam, you tell him. I find I am simply repeating myself."

Sam threw his fedora onto the refectory table and rubbed his eyes. Much to his dismay, the silent monks were already clearing away the remains of the late lunch or early supper or whatever it was they'd been eating. He had scarcely enjoyed a bite through all the nonstop interruptions from the Merry Men.

Did you see Robin? Is Robin well? Did you find the best route to his cell? How many archers does the Sheriff have? Do we need swordsmen?

David of Doncaster would ask the same questions as Much the Miller's son. Gilbert Whitehand would interrupt Reynold Greenleaf's question so he could repeat what he'd already asked, hoping for a different answer. Little John wouldn't ask any questions but kept interrupting to demand that everyone get ready to raid the Sheriff's Keep. And Sagramore. Sagramore stood leaning against the wall the entire time, anger and despair competing with each other to control his mood.

Eventually, Sam ignored them all so he could eat something, which left them to question and yell at each other. Now the argument had swung back his way.

"It's simple," Sam said. "Any assault on the Sheriff's Keep is suicide. You saw the map Lundgren drew. Vaisey's got Robin and the others in a cage, deep within a maze of tunnels and caves burrowed beneath Nottingham Castle. And there's a reason the Sheriff's Keep is called a keep. The place is designed to keep people out. And if anyone does get in, it's a slaughterhouse."

"But." Little John waved his hands in a near-apoplectic fit. "You found a passageway between St Peters Church and the Sheriff's Keep. They will not expect us that way."

"Of course they will. You need a key to use the tunnel, and Vaisey knows a key has gone missing. Besides, according to Lundgren, most of Vaisey's men are below the Castle guarding the jail. No matter how you reach the cells, you still have a hundred trained fighters to go through."

"We are willing to risk ourselves in the attempt," Little John insisted. "And we now have mercenaries—"

"Who will walk off the job once they know what they're up against," Sam finished.

Little John rose to his feet and clenched his massive hands into fists. Before he could speak, however, Azeem the Moor burst into laughter.

"You!" Little John shouted, his anger finding an outlet. "What is it you find funny about Robin being held captive?"

"But I, too, was once a captive," the Moor said. He leaned back in his chair and set his feet on the table. "Locked in a cage in Jerusalem. The cell next to me held two Christians. A cunning young man named Locksley and his friend Peter Dubois."

"We know all this," Little John grumbled. "Robin escaped, freed you as well, and brought you to England."

"Then you know nothing, Christian," Azeem said. "Robin did not bring me to England. I followed him here. I owe Robin my life, and will continue to follow him until the debt is repaid."

"Yes, yes," Little John said. "We all know your story."

"Yet you hear nothing. Robin and I escaped captivity. Robin's friend Peter did not. Peter perished during the escape."

"Your point?" Little John asked.

"The point is clear, Christian. Assume you assault the Sheriff's Keep, and fight through his hundred uncouth mercenaries. Assume you fight your way to the bowels of Nottingham Castle and break open Robin's cage. And that of Maid Marian. And of Will Scarlet. Assume you then fight your way again to freedom and make your way to Sherwood forest."

"Yes," Little John said, clearly impatient.

"Can you also assume that all three captives will escape with their lives?"

"Why would I not?" Little John demanded.

Azeem set his feet back on the floor and leaned across the table. "Because when three captives escaped Jerusalem, only two survived. The third was left dead and bloodied on the prison floor. And in Jerusalem, the jailors were fewer in number and had no warning of an escape."

Little John ground his teeth, then relaxed his fingers. He paced the floor and rubbed his chin. Then sat heavily on a stool and looked at Sam. "Tell me again this plan of yours for the wedding."

42
A REASONABLE AMOUNT OF TROUBLE

THE NIGHT PASSED slowly.

Unable to sleep, Sam sat for a while in a quiet corner of the hospital refectory with Effie, who without a job to report to, seemed lost.

"But what would I do in Sherwood Forest?" she asked. "Do bandits require clerks?"

Sam rubbed his ear. "How are you with cooking? And cleaning?"

Effie stared at him. "I am the daughter of a duke. We do not cook and clean."

"I don't suppose you serve tables, either."

"Certainly not," Effie said.

The conversation was going nowhere fast. Then he got an idea. "Would it be permissible to work for Maid Marian? As her personal assistant? She is the cousin of a king."

Effie's eyes brightened. "Of course. My father, were he still alive, would be pleased. Such a position would be most suitable."

"That's settled then. Once we rescue Marian, we'll offer her your services. I don't see how she could refuse."

Effie pursed her lips. "Should Maid Marian balk at the suggestion, Robin will convince her. The archer and I are friends, after all." Dilemma resolved, at least for the moment, Effie yawned. "I find myself suddenly tired. If you will excuse me, I shall take to my bed."

"Of course. Sleep well." Once Effie had gone, he added. "Now, if only *I* could sleep."

Most of the Merry Men sat at the refectory table, deep in conversation. It occurred to Sam that might be how the outlaws mentally prepared themselves for a mission.

He didn't have a ritual. He didn't think Nora did, either. If they had to be somewhere, they'd set a time to meet and she'd show up a few minutes early. Or, for all he knew, she did have a ritual and sacrificed a chicken or something before arriving. Sam figured if he had any ritual at all, it consisted of a shot of Bogart's Irish and a cigarette. Of course, cigarettes were now off the table. And he hadn't seen anything resembling whiskey in Camelot or Sherwood.

He noticed Nora sitting alone on the floor against one wall. Carmen had been with her, but Sternwood's daughter had gone off somewhere while he wasn't looking. Sam went over to sit beside his partner, his joints aching as he settled himself onto the floor. Nora didn't look up but sat with her sack of possessions in her lap. In her hands she held her wallet, which was open to display her driver's license. Nora stared at the photo.

"Not a bad picture," Sam said. "Mine always looks like a mug shot."

"Is that really me?" Nora asked. "She's beautiful."

"You are beautiful," Sam said. "And your name is Nora Clark. It says so right there beside your picture."

"Nora Clark. Such a plain name. I prefer Vivian."

"You can always change your name," Sam suggested. "Legally, I mean, but only after you get your memory back. At least you're talking better today. That's a good sign. Oh, here. I have something for you." Pulling Nora's cell phone from where it sat in his shirt pocket next to his, he hit the power button and was pleased to see the screen light up. The battery hadn't died yet.

"Do you remember your password?" he asked, passing Nora the phone.

Nora stared at it for a moment, then punched some buttons. The display changed to show an image of her 2016 obsidian blue Honda Accord and a *No Service* message. Nora pressed the power button and slid the phone into her sack.

"We're making progress," Sam said.

"Progress," Nora echoed. Then she closed her eyes, shifted sideways to lean against him, and began snoring.

Sam sighed. Putting beautiful women to sleep seemed to be one of his talents.

He sat like that for what seemed like hours, trying to sleep himself, but was too uncomfortable to make a go of it. During that time, the room emptied, some of Robin's men going to their beds, others venturing outdoors for fresh air or patrol duty. Finally, Tuck stood before him, shaking his head.

"No. No. This will not do. You need some rest, Sam. Tomorrow will be hazard enough without you falling asleep on your feet."

"Help me get Nora to her cot," Sam suggested.

He took hold of his partner's closest arm and climbed to his feet, while Tuck took the other arm and most of her weight. With his free hand, the friar scooped up Nora's sack of possessions. Somehow, Sam's partner managed to remain asleep.

"There is an unoccupied cot through that doorway," Tuck said, nodding with his chin. "We need not drag the poor woman further."

"You got that right," Sam said.

After Nora was safely tucked in, Sam rubbed his ear then stepped over to the sack Tuck had set on a nightstand. He opened it and searched the contents. "I thought so."

"What's that?" Tuck asked.

"Nora's Glock is missing."

"Is that important?"

"Maybe," Sam said. "I think I know where it is."

Tuck sighed. "You require rest. Not an egg hunt."

"It'll only take a minute," Sam said. He was tempted to ask the friar what an egg hunt was but decided he didn't need the distraction.

"See that it does," the churchman said. "Morning comes early."

"Before you go," Sam asked. "Where is Carmen making her nest?" He smiled at his choice of words but didn't think the friar caught the joke.

Tuck frowned. "I have some monks watching her. It is not an easy task."

"I'll bet."

The friar led Sam up a staircase and down a hallway to an area of the hospital he hadn't seen before. The rooms here had latches on the doors allowing them to be locked from the outside, and each door had a tiny window cut into it. When Sam peeked in through one of the windows, he saw an unshaven man sleeping on a cot.

"What is this place?"

"The lunatic wing," Tuck said. "Patients here suffer from poisons of the mind."

"Do you have treatments for them?"

"Not yet. We do our best to keep them comfortable."

"It's . . . quiet," Sam said.

Tuck nodded. "We add tincture of henbane and opium to their food. It usually settles the restless spirits."

"I bet."

"Ah. Here we are."

The hallway ended at a latched door like the others, only there was also a bench outside the door occupied by two of the silent monks. One of the monks made hand signals to Tuck, who shook his head.

"What?" Sam asked.

"Your Carmen has been requesting tincture of opium."

"Who's out there?" Carmen shouted from inside the room. "These idiot monks follow me everywhere. You can't treat me like a prisoner."

Sam stepped up to the small window and peered inside. Carmen stood with her back to one wall. Her blanket, pillow, and mattress lay strewn across the floor like she had thrown a tantrum. "If you'd behave like a reasonable adult, we wouldn't have to ask the monks to keep you out of trouble."

In response, Carmen let out a shriek and rushed toward the door, going so far as to push her hand through the window opening.

Sam reared back before he could lose an eye. "You're proving my point. Look, I don't mind a reasonable amount of trouble, but if you keep on this way, things are going to get ugly. Now, behave yourself, and we'll open the door."

The hand withdrew and Sam stepped forward to lift the latch.

"Is that wise?" Tuck asked.

"Probably not, but no one has ever accused me of being a genius." Sam pushed the door open into the room, and before he knew what was happening, Carmen pressed herself against him and engaged her lips against his.

It took a moment to recover from the shock, then Sam grabbed the young woman's arms and held her away from him. He almost felt sorry about it; Carmen was a great kisser. Before letting her go, he took a moment to make sure her hands were empty. He'd seen more than a few movies where a kiss was just a clever distraction for picking a pocket.

Sam felt his cheek twitch. "I didn't think you'd be so happy to see me."

"Take me with you," Carmen begged, almost crying. "They've got me locked up with the lunatics."

"That's only because you keep running off."

"I'll be good," Carmen pleaded. "I've got nowhere to go now."

"You make a good argument," Sam said. "Show me where it is, and I'll consider asking the monks to move you to a nicer room."

"What? Where what is?"

"Don't play games with me, sister. I haven't the patience for it."

A scowl crossed Carmen's face. Then she turned and pulled the nightstand away from the wall. Reaching behind it, she retrieved Nora's Glock.

"What did you want it for?" Sam asked, taking the weapon and pushing it into a pocket of his trench coat. "It's not worth much without bullets."

"You said we couldn't leave any modern metal behind when we went home. I didn't want Vivian to lose it. She's not all there, you know."

"Her name is Nora," Sam said. "And she's taken a liking to her possessions now that I retrieved them for her. Also, if I'm not mistaken, her memory is starting to come back."

Carmen let out a soft humph. "What's to stop you and Nora from leaving me behind when you go back to Connecticut?"

"So that's it. You figured if you had Nora's Glock, that we couldn't go back without you."

The young woman confirmed his words with a look.

"You'll just have to trust me. The last thing I have in mind is leaving you behind."

Carmen glowered at him. "How am I supposed to believe that?"

"I guess it's a matter of faith, isn't it?"

43
SHOOT ON SIGHT

AFTER A BRIEF night of fitful sleep, Tuck's words proved prophetic. Morning came early. Much too early.

"Porridge?" a cheerful voice asked.

Sam groaned, opened his eyes, and spied the friar standing in the doorway. "A double portion for me."

Tuck propelled himself into Sam's tiny hospital room, a steaming bowl cradled in his thick fingers. "I have brought you enough for four men. Today is a big day, with no guarantee when next we shall have opportunity to eat."

"Don't remind me," Sam said as he sat up in bed.

The porridge was hot, thick, and sweet. Sam ate all of it if only to give himself the strength to pull on his shoes. When he'd crept into bed, he hadn't removed his socks, mostly because he couldn't tell where cotton ended and swollen, healing skin began. If he did manage to make it home to Hartford, he'd have a doctor take a look. Surgery might be required.

The refectory, when Sam arrived, stank of sweat, honey, and beer. All of Robin's Merry Men looked to be there. Some ate porridge, while others checked over their arrows or adjusted their disguises.

Upon seeing Sam, Little John rose from his seat. "Men of Sherwood! Hear me!"

The big man's voice was anything but quiet; Sam had little

doubt everyone could hear him.

"We are all here friends of Robin and Marian."

"And Will Scarlet," someone called out.

"And, of course, Will Scarlet," Little John said. "Let us remember what we know. At noon today, the wicked Sheriff of Nottingham intends to wed fair Marian, not for love, not for support, but to use her good family name to worm his way onto England's throne."

Cries of anger and dismay rose throughout the hall.

To be heard, Little John spoke even louder. "The Sheriff claims that after Marian's final 'I do', he shall release Robin."

"And Will," a voice called.

"And Will. But we know the Sheriff's words are worth less than the breath it takes to utter them. Robin shall not be released. Yes," he added quickly. "Nor Will Scarlet. More than likely, both will be executed."

Again, cries of anger.

Now Tuck stood. "So let us away to Nottingham and see this wedding for ourselves. And should any of us have reason to not allow this joining to proceed, let us speak rather than hold our peace."

Everyone in the room cheered and rose from their seats.

Sam had to smile. The pep talk was great. Everyone was excited. But he knew nothing would go as easily as the friar had suggested. The first tricky part would be entering Nottingham town. Everything after that would only get more dangerous.

He continued smiling as he imagined the frown on Vaisey's face after waiting all night for the Merry Men to attack his fortress, only to have last night pass quietly into day.

Since capturing Robin, the Sheriff had instructed his guards to let Robin's men pass into the town, with the aim of encouraging an assault on Nottingham Keep where the outlaws would be slaughtered. Now, with the wedding mere hours away, that safe passage would be rescinded. Sam was pretty sure the new instruction was *Shoot on Sight*. The last thing Vaisey would want is his wedding interrupted. The hundred men he'd concealed in the keep would now be manning the battlements and watching the street corners.

Sam would have preferred to have moved Robin's men and their hired mercenaries into the town during the night, just as

Vaisey had expected. Instead of attacking the keep, however, he would hide them somewhere until the wedding. But that wouldn't work. Even if they could avoid being seen by Vaisey's spies on the near-deserted streets, there was nowhere several dozen men could hide and not be discovered. The Sheriff's men would surround them and indulge themselves in a slaughter.

Fortunately, Little John had convinced him that infiltrating Nottingham in broad daylight would not be a problem; they'd done it many times. So here they were the morning of the wedding, eating porridge for breakfast and assuming disguises.

Most of the Merry Men had once been farmers and simple craftsmen. They knew how to dress and act and duck their heads like peasants. Last evening, they had gone out and retrieved clothes, and carts, and chickens, and hay, and whatever else they needed to convincingly take goods to market.

The silent monks had also been busy, securing a wagon loaded with barrels of St Mary's Abbey ale, as ordered by the Bishop of Hereford. What was a wedding without beer and wine? When the monks brought the loaded wagon around, Sam wondered how one horse could pull so much weight. Each of the six giant oak barrels had to weigh at least three hundred pounds. Add the wagon, driver, and passengers, and that added up to maybe four thousand pounds. Sam didn't envy the tired-looking horse.

While he waited for his travel companions, he adjusted his borrowed monk robe to ensure it covered everything from his Burberry trench coat collar on down to his Thorogood Oxford shoes. Unsure of what to do with his felt fedora, he set it on top of one of the barrels in the wagon.

Tuck walked up and gave him a long appraisal. The large man shook his head. "No. You look nothing like a monk. Your hair is untonsured. Your shoulders too broad. You clearly wear bulky clothing beneath that robe."

"Also beneath this robe," Sam said, "I have a Smith & Weston Military & Police semi-automatic. I'll take my chances. Where's Sagramore? He doesn't look like a monk either. Or a farmer."

Tuck grinned. "The ex-knight is at our mercenary camp, teaching them all a few words in French."

"French?"

"We cannot have English mercenaries attend the wedding. As they do not work for the Sheriff, he would assume they are King

Richard's men. And they cannot pass as Celtic mercenaries. The Sheriff's own redshanks would name them frauds."

"And so, French?" Sam asked.

Tuck's grin widened. "The French are neutral in John's rebellion. They will say they are for hire. Sagramore intends to offer their services to the Sheriff."

Little John, dressed in the plain trousers and tunic of a farmer, joined them. "Is all here ready?" He looked at Sam. "You look nothing like a monk."

"I'll keep my head down," Sam said.

Little John shrugged and walked away.

Tuck laughed. "Little John and a few of the others will take their carts on ahead. They will set up outside the wall and hawk their wares to celebrants entering the town for the wedding. Should the gate guard refuse our wagon, they will be on hand to cause a distraction. Once we are inside Nottingham, they will make their way through the gate."

Sam wasn't particularly happy with Little John's plan to enter the town, but he couldn't think of a better one.

As Tuck moved off to converse with the silent monks, three women came around the corner of the hospital building and paused to look at the ale wagon, then at Sam. Though of differing heights, they could have been sisters as all were blonde, blue-eyed, and of similar complexion. Nora the oldest, then Effie, and finally Carmen.

Nora clutched her bag of possessions against her chest like it was a lifeline. She'd seemed happy when Sam returned her Glock that morning and had tucked it in with her wallet, phone, and penlight.

Effie held her head turned to one side, her scar partly obscured by loose hair and shadow. "You look nothing like a monk," she said. "It would be better should you join Sagramore's mercenaries."

Sam laughed. "Saggy's the one who suggested I join the monks. Said I wasn't tough enough to pass as a mercenary. Does this help?" He slipped his fedora back onto his head before reaching behind his shoulders and pulling up the loose hood that was part of the robe. The rough cloth covered his hat. And when he looked down, cast his face in shadow.

"You look like Death at Halloween," Carmen said. "All you

need is a plastic scythe."

"Not what I was going for," Sam said.

Tuck approached and nodded approvingly. "Maintain the cowl no matter how hot you may become. It is the only way you shall pass as a monk. And say nothing. Remember your vow of silence."

Sam raised one hand giving the universal thumbs-up gesture.

The friar mimicked him. "Yes. We are ready to fight." He turned to the three women. "Good ladies, you may ride with us as far as the town gates, but there we must part ways. It would be improper for monks to be seen entering Nottingham in the company of gentlewomen."

Sam saw a problem with the friar's invitation. The bench at the front of the wagon was wide enough for the driver and a passenger to either side, but not when the driver was Tuck. The only other place to sit was on the tailboard. He supposed that was how things worked in the country. He had to remember he wasn't in Hartford anymore.

When Effie volunteered to ride with the corpulent friar, Sam felt a moment of disappointment but realized it was for the best. He needed to spend as much time with Nora as he could. His familiar presence seemed to be helping to bring her back to herself, as did the presence of her few Connecticut possessions. Keeping an eye on Carmen wouldn't hurt either.

The three of them climbed up onto the tailboard and sat with their legs dangling. Sam vaguely remembered going on a hayride as a small child, some kind of family event put on by the city for police servicemen and their families. He'd sat on the back of a wagon just like this, only it had been pulled by a tractor, and there was snow on the ground to soften the blow if he fell. He hadn't worried about falling. Back then he hadn't a care in the world. Life had been so innocent once.

Tuck made a clicking sound with his tongue, and the heavily laden wagon shrugged into motion. Rather than pull out onto the track that ran along the town wall, the friar drove the wagon through a break in the trees and onto the York Road.

Sam figured it must be rush hour. All along the dirt road, people journeyed toward Nottingham, on foot, on horseback, or riding in small carts. Traffic seemed even heavier than on the day of the archery contest. He kept his face turned downward but shifted his gaze to one side to watch a train of covered carriages clatter past the slower-moving ale wagon. Commandeering a few of those might have been a better means of entering the town. Well, too late now.

They had been gone from the hospital only a few minutes when the wagon slowed to a halt. York Gate really wasn't that far, though on foot it seemed farther. Sam climbed up into the wagon so he could look out over the barrels, and was shocked to see a sea of visitors waiting to enter Nottingham.

"They must be real keen on weddings around here," he called to Tuck.

The friar shook his head and turned to look at Sam. "They expect a hanging."

"What?"

Effie also turned. "Have you not heard the chatter? The people on the road speak of a gallows being erected on the green."

Sam had to admit he hadn't been paying attention. His mind had been focused on Nora's progressing recovery, with maybe a few stray thoughts running to jealousy of Tuck sharing Effie's company. He had, however, noticed the travellers on the road seemed happy as they approached the town, but had assumed they were looking forward to a royal wedding, or whatever you call it when a tyrant forces a noblewoman to marry him.

"People are keen, as you say," Tuck told Sam, "on public executions."

Sam rubbed his ear. "I wouldn't put it past Vaisey to set up a gallows to reinforce his threat of hanging Robin should Marian decide to back out of their arrangement. It'll be a 'say *I do* or Robin dies' situation."

Tuck sighed. "Your plan had best work."

"No pressure," Sam said as he climbed back down onto the tailboard.

He turned to Nora and Carmen. "You ladies should set out on your own. Grab Effie and tell the gate guards you are bridesmaids for the wedding. Maybe they'll push you to the head of the line."

"Will you be all right, Sam?" Nora asked.

Sam smiled. "I'll be right as rain, angel. Right as rain."

With the bridesmaids on their way, Sam joined Tuck on the bench. His head was sweltering beneath the cowl, and sweat ran down his face. Tuck's cheeks were also slick with perspiration, even though his hood was down. Sam didn't know if the friar was sweating from the sun or from nerves.

The crowd moved at a snail's pace. Even so, Sam hoped the guards weren't giving everyone too detailed a looking over. As a cop, he'd worked check stops, usually smelling for alcohol and looking for glassy eyes, but sometimes comparing faces against wanted postings. It was a good thing photography hadn't been invented yet.

When the wagon finally reached the gate, one of the guards looked everything over, then peered up at Tuck. "Pleasant day, Holy Brothers. What have ye in yon barrels?"

Sam ducked his head, leaving Tuck to answer.

"Ale, my good man," the friar chirped. "By order of the Bishop himself. I have the paperwork here."

A second guard, taking charge, snorted. "Papers may say ale, but barrels mayhap hold anything."

"These barrels," Tuck said, all humour gone out of his voice, "hold St Mary's Abbey's finest sweet wine and honeyed ale."

Sam peeked out from his cowl and saw the unfriendly guard narrow his eyes. "Terryn," he told the first, "take an axe to one of the barrels. See if it holds wine or somewhat more sinister."

"Hold on now," Tuck cried, waving at the first guard. "If you break the barrel like that, you will ruin the wine. Terryn is your name? I shall report you to the Bishop. My back will not feel the lashes of his wrath for your ill manner. That shall fall to you."

Terryn hesitated, but the unfriendly guard held steady. "If we cannot verify the barrels' contents, then the wagon cannot enter the city. The Sheriff's words, not ours."

"The wine is for the wedding," Tuck scolded. "What is your name now, so I may tell the Bishop and the Sheriff why there is no wine?"

A moment's silence.

Finally, the unfriendly guard said, "Terryn, give one of those barrels a good shake and listen. What hear you?"

Sam turned his head sideways so he could watch the guard reach over the side of the wagon and rock one of the barrels.

"I hear wine," Terryn answered, looking relieved. "Or somewhat liquid."

"No arrows then?" asked the unfriendly guard. "No blades clanking?"

Sam heard wood scrape against wood as Terryn rocked a second barrel, then a third.

"It be heavy like wine."

"Fine then," the unfriendly guard ceded. "Off ye go. It be ten pennies for ye friars. And for the cargo, another forty pennies."

"Fifty pennies!" Tuck sputtered, the words getting tied in his tongue. "This is abbey wine. For the Bishop. It is not going to market."

"The Church be rich with gold," the guard said, sounding smug. "It can well afford fifty pennies."

"The Bishop will hear of this," Tuck roared. "As will the Sheriff."

The guard left his palm turned out. "The Sheriff will be paid. They can sort it out between them."

Tuck handed over a small fortune and got the wagon moving again.

Sam kept his head down as they rolled through the gate and into the crowded town. He whispered to Tuck, "They were so concerned about the barrels, they didn't give us too hard a look."

Tuck whispered back, "They were more interested in the pennies they could extort for the wagon."

The sheer noise of people filling the street reminded Sam to continue studying his shoes. Just because they made it inside the walls, didn't mean they were safe. The opposite, in fact.

As the wagon proceeded deeper into town, Sam knew they would need to turn toward the green. Eventually, they did. But when they came to a stop and he lifted his head, he saw they were on a sloped roadside next to a church. He almost laughed as the service door he had used the previous morning swung open, and several young monks stepped out. Sam ducked his head back down when one of them threw him a curious look.

"Ale for the wedding," Tuck called jovially. "No, I am not under the Bishop's censure of silence. Someone had to speak with the gate guards. Yes, lucky me. Here are the papers."

Sam heard, rather than watched, as the silent monks unloaded the wagon and carried the heavy barrels into the church. After they had finished and closed the door behind them, he whispered to Tuck, "What now?"

"The stables," Tuck whispered back. "Others will tend the horse and wagon while you and I get into position."

After travelling no more than two blocks, they reached a series of barn-like buildings that sat at one end of an open market. Tuck stopped the wagon in front of a building that included a cross above the door, then climbed down to negotiate with a silent monk.

Sam also climbed off the bench onto a cobbled street. Peeking out from beneath his hood, he spotted the north end of the green out past the market. It was hard to see much else, however, for the sheer crowds of people that filled the market, the green, and the surrounding streets.

"This way," Tuck murmured.

Sam followed after the friar in a direction that would take them back to the church, but then Tuck turned into a disused alley and held out his hands.

After a quick look around to make sure no one was watching, Sam pulled off the monk robe and handed it to Tuck.

"Good luck, Sam," Tuck said. Then the friar was gone.

"Yeah, I'm gonna need it," Sam told himself. Especially if Vaisey really did give a shoot on sight order.

44
THREE GOLDEN LIONS

SAM EMERGED FROM the alley intending to go back through the market and across the village green to the Sheriff's Keep. But as he got closer, he saw whole squadrons of soldiers keeping order as workers hauled chairs and tables and wooden beams from every neighbouring shop and building. The men carried their loads to the far end of the green and set them up as platforms and rows of seats. Sam rubbed his ear, then chose a roadway near the church that, though crowded with people, would take him to the keep without having to worry about the soldiers.

He noticed that people were everywhere, but didn't seem to be going anywhere. Instead, they stood or sat on crates, waiting to observe the wedding from the cheap seats.

Tuck had told the Merry Men that the village green was the only area large enough for such a wedding. Not even Nottingham's largest church, whose banks of pews Sam had glimpsed, could accommodate the anticipated audience.

"Everyone who is anyone will be there," Tuck had said. "Vaisey is marrying into the King's family and will have invited anyone not fiercely loyal to King Richard. The more witnesses the better. Many of the common folk will also wish to view the wedding as . . . well, a spectacle."

Sam could see that, if anything, Tuck had underestimated how many people would be at the wedding. Of course, the rumours of public execution may have played no small role in that.

As he worked through the mob of gawkers, Sam kept his hand in his trench coat pocket, his fingers clutching the grip of his semi-automatic. He didn't like to think what would happen if he had to use it, but he wasn't going to let some startled soldier with a sword skewer him, either.

When he reached the gate to the Sheriff's Keep, he counted six soldiers. Three were redshanks, legs bare beneath the bottom of their kilts, a round shield in one hand and a wide-bladed sword in the other. The remainder were English soldiers, with shields that were more square than round. The swords in their sheaths were the narrower kind Sam remembered from Camelot. Several archers also stood on the lower battlements above the gate. All of them gave Sam a hard look.

One of the redshanks snorted. "Th' Sheriff's bampot. Ye come alone this time?"

Sam smiled. "My lady friends are getting fitted for the wedding. Is the Sheriff in?"

"Th' sheriff, he prepares fur th' wedding," the redshank answered.

"I need to speak with His Overlordship. It will only take a moment."

"Efter th' wedding," the man answered.

"I suspect that after the wedding he'll be busy," Sam said. "Nuptials and all that. Perhaps it would be better if I pop in now."

"Th' sheriff isnae tae be disturbed."

"What I have to tell him is time-sensitive."

The man frowned. "Sensitive?"

"Has value now, but won't in an hour." When the man still didn't seem to understand, Sam added, "It concerns Robin of Locksley's band of men."

"How come did ye nae say so?" The redshank turned to open the door to the keep, then escorted Sam inside.

The keep's interior held its usual gloom. Strike that. It felt gloomier. Fewer candles burned in the chandelier, and there were at least twice the number of armed men than his last visit. None of the soldiers spoke, but stood like statues waiting for a command to draw their swords. Vaisey sat upon his throne, conferring with Guy of Gisbourne, who stood to one side favouring his leg and fondling a noose.

"Is that a local custom, then?" Sam asked. "The throwing of the noose after the wedding ceremony?"

Guy pulled the noose against his chest and scuttled behind the throne, as well as he could scuttle dragging one leg behind him.

"I am the Sheriff," Vaisey growled. "Nooses are my stock and trade. What do you want? I told the guard no visitors."

The redshank took a step forward. "He says he has information aboot Robin's outlaws."

Vaisey straightened his posture. "Little John and the others? What news? Have they accepted my invitation to the wedding?"

"They send their regrets." Sam turned his head this way and that to take in as much of the darkness behind the throne as possible. "Is Marian all right? I don't see her."

"Of course you do not see her. She is with her maids getting dressed."

"And by maids you mean Nora, Effie, and Carmen?"

Sam had argued against the ladies accepting Vaisey's demand that they serve as bridesmaids, but Effie had insisted they go through with it. The Sheriff would be suspicious otherwise. Sam's plan relied on the Sheriff moving forward with the wedding as planned.

Vaisey leaped down from his throne and slapped his palms together, a single clap, an expression of his good mood. "Lady Nora Clark of East Hartford. Lady Euphemia Peregrine of Earl. And Lady Carmen Sternwood of Codfish Falls. This is to be a proper wedding, and you shall use their full titles. Do you have information about Robin's outlaws or not?"

"Right," Sam said, sliding his semi-automatic back in its holster and drawing his hand from his pocket. "I saw them on my way here, camped off the highway maybe a mile outside of town. They seem to have acquired some new friends."

"Friends?"

"Knights, if I'm not mistaken. The men wore armour and carried shields and swords."

"You are mistaken," Vaisey said, stepping toward Sam and pausing just short of the life-size statue of himself. "Every knight able to hold a shield is in Jerusalem, fighting the King's third crusade."

"That's what I thought," Sam said. "But these were definitely knights. Oh, and there was an emblem on their shields, too. Three golden lions against a red background."

Vaisey's face blanched. "The Lionheart crest." He shook his head. "As much as I do not believe you, how many knights did you see?"

Sam rubbed his jaw. "No more than twenty. But I was only passing by on the road. I may have missed a few."

Vaisey paced the floor a few steps. "Even should you be right, twenty knights are no threat. Robin's men number no more than a dozen. At worst, we are looking at three dozen men."

"It looked like more than three dozen to me." Sam began counting on his fingers. "Must have been at least fifty men. But I was never good at math."

Vaisey's pacing was interrupted by one of his soldiers, who approached and whispered in the Sheriff's ear. Vaisey waved him away.

"News?" Sam asked.

Vaisey glared at him. "Little John has been seen within the walls. He did not have any knights with him."

"Probably doing reconnaissance," Sam said. "That's what I'd do."

"Reconnasssess . . ." Vaisey mumbled.

"Taking the lay of the land," Sam explained. "Selecting targets for his men and the knights."

Vaisey frowned. "Perhaps it is a good thing I received an offer of additional mercenaries today. Frenchmen. Are you familiar?"

"I've never had the pleasure," Sam said.

"I am told they are fierce fighters," Vaisey added, preening.

"I'm told they fight dirty," Sam said.

Vaisey looked at him. "Really? Excellent!"

Sam's cheek twitched. "You've told me where Maid Marian is. What about Robin?"

A villainous smile spread across Vaisey's lips. "Did you not see him outside? On the green? Unlike his band of outlaws, Robin did accept my invitation."

Sam wondered if that were true. If Robin was on the green, Little John and Tuck could have seen him already. "Well, I'm sure you have a lot of last-minute things to do. I just wanted to make sure the womenfolk were okay, and to tell you what I saw on the way here. I'll head out to the green myself. I wouldn't want to miss the start of the wedding. It is almost noon."

"You should have a place of honour," Vaisey said. "My men will escort you."

"There's no need for that."

Several soldiers stepped forward.

"Oh," Vaisey said, "but I really must insist."

45
A WEDDING AND A HANGING

AS SAM CROSSED Castle Street to the village green, one bullyboy on either side and several more at his back, he couldn't help but think things were working out rather well. People were everywhere, sitting on chairs, standing shoulder to shoulder wherever there was space, or forcing their way through the crowd seeking a better vantage point. Yet the sea of onlookers grudgingly parted to allow the Sheriff's mercenaries passage.

Sam kept his eyes peeled for Robin and any of the Merry Men, as well as anyone with a weapon who looked like they might be Little John's recruits. He knew nothing about the hired mercenaries except they were Englishmen whose families and friends had been displaced by Vaisey's machinations, and who now were pretending to be French.

He didn't look for armoured knights. That was just a tall tale he'd told, meant to confuse and distract Vaisey and his men.

The parting of spectators revealed a raised platform at the far end of the green, the same wooden framework Sam had seen being constructed. Now finished, it was a dreary affair, with a potted plant on either side, and a wooden cross propped up toward the back. Vaisey had certainly spared every expense.

Row upon row of mismatched chairs sat before it on the green, most of them occupied by notable townsfolk and visitors. Sam figured it was the unnotables sitting on makeshift stools or standing crowded together back on the street.

As Sam and his escort neared the platform, it became apparent the place of honour Vaisey had in mind was a chair in the first row. Sam was familiar enough with weddings to know the front row was reserved for immediate family of the bride and groom. He figured none of Marian's family had been invited, or possibly even informed of the wedding. As for Vaisey, Sam didn't think vipers had family.

The bullyboy escort growled at him to sit, and Sam shook his head. He had the entire first row to himself. Maybe the rest of the seats were reserved for the Merry Men.

The rows immediately behind him were filled with men and women, mostly men, dressed to the nines, tens, and an audacious few to the elevens. Nottingham's one-percenters and the most elite of the visitors.

Sam squinted, then rose to his feet for a better look. Behind the many rows of wedding guests, at the other end of the green, stood a large wooden cage. Inside that cage, a young man stood gripping the bars. Robin.

So far, so good. Vaisey really had brought Robin of Locksley out from his impenetrable keep and put him in plain sight on the village green. Did the Sheriff still expect the Merry Men to attack the keep? Or had he ordered his men to let them nowhere near the wedding? Sam made a careful study of the soldiers standing around the cage, as well as those hanging about the last few rows of onlookers. Celts.

With most of Vaisey's English soldiers manning the town walls, stationed inside his keep, and mixing among the people in an effort to spot the Merry Men, that left his redshank mercenaries to prevent anyone from rescuing Robin.

Sam watched as reinforcements joined the Celtic mercenaries—swordsmen dressed in a mix of leather and cotton. Not redshanks. They could be some of Vaisey's English soldiers. Or they could be Sagramore's newly hired faux Frenchmen.

A heavy hand fell on Sam's shoulder, and one of his bullyboy escorts hissed in his ear. "Sit!"

Sam plunked back down onto his chair and began taking serious stock of his surroundings. He didn't know when he'd need to move, but he wanted to be ready. Three of the five bullyboys who had accompanied him from the keep had disappeared. That left two, who stood at the foot of the platform glaring at him. He could handle two mooks.

There were also three redshank mercenaries toward the platform's other side. The distance between the English and Scottish, as well as the unfriendly glances the redshanks occasionally cast toward their counterparts, suggested there wasn't a lot of love lost between them. It reminded Sam of the rivalry between East Hartford and Connecticut State Police. Same job. Overlapping jurisdictions. Stepping on toes. Maybe he'd get a chance to use that.

Only five hard numbers. That would likely change when the wedding party arrived.

He noticed there were no chairs on the platform. No wedding arch. No table with a register book on it. Just the two potted plants and a cross made from wood scraps.

His gaze wandered further afield, taking in the crowds of people who sat or stood on the green to either side of the rows of seats. People seemed to number among the thousands. Once Little John set things in motion, the place would be bedlam. Sam suspected more injuries would result from stampeding wedding guests than from swords and arrows. This could be bad. Real bad.

A horn sounded, and Sam swivelled his head in the direction of the keep. The crowd watching from Castle Road parted as two columns of redshanks marched toward the wedding platform. Between the columns strutted the Sheriff of Nottingham, his expression a silly grin, and his trademark black leather attire accentuated by a circle of gold nested in his unruly hair. A crown? Vaisey really was getting ahead of himself.

This would be an ideal time for Little John to attack. He and his men could surround Vaisey, put down his redshank guard, and hold a knife to the vile man's throat until Robin and Marian were freed. The pounding of Sam's heart echoed in his ears as Vaisey strode down the now-cleared aisle that ran along one side of a bank of chairs. Where was Little John? The Merry Men?

His hand gripped his semi-automatic beneath his coat as Vaisey and his honour guard approached and strode past him. It would be an easy thing to pump some lead into the Sheriff, but then what? Sam didn't see any way to rescue the women, free Robin from his cage, and escape to Sherwood Forest, without a lot of help. Which is why the plan was for Little John to call the attack once he knew everyone was in place. Did Little John's silence mean something had gone wrong? Or just that everyone wasn't in position yet?

The redshanks came to a halt near the end of the platform, while the Sheriff continued on and mounted the steps. At some point when Sam wasn't looking, the Bishop of Hereford had ascended the platform and now stood waiting. The impious priest was once again bedecked in white, adorned only by a collar of gold and some kind of ornate staff.

Vaisey approached the priest, then turned and waved at the crowd, who responded with half-hearted applause. Undaunted, the contemptuous villain attempted a smile. Smiling wasn't a good look for the Sheriff.

Sam turned his head and peered out over the crowd. No sign of Robin's men, but he did spot Vaisey's lackey, Guy of Gisbourne, hobbling toward Robin's cage, dragging his bad leg behind him. The bootlicker clutched a heavy sack in his hands. A sack just the right size to contain the noose Sam had caught him fondling a short while earlier.

A dozen or more redshanks from the keep followed after Guy and joined their companions who were already guarding the cage. Several of the mercenaries bent down to lift up something heavy. A beam of wood. They hauled up one end, raising it, until the base slid down into a hole, causing the beam to stand upright. A shorter beam stuck out from the top end. Guy retrieved the rope from his sack. After several attempts, he succeeded in throwing one end over the shorter beam. He pulled it tight, then stepped back as one of the redshanks set a stool beneath the dangling noose. It was a hanging post.

Cheers rose from the crowd. Though they'd ostensibly come for a wedding, the rumours were now confirmed. There'd be a wedding and a hanging.

The horn sounded again, followed by a chorus of flutes. The crowd grew quiet, then loud again, as a new procession approached from the keep. Sam had to admit Maid Marian looked very much the bride in her long, pastel-blue gown that trailed behind her for what seemed a mile. Nora, Effie, and Carmen followed behind, clutching edges of the train in their hands to keep it from touching the ground. The bridesmaids also wore blue, but of plainer design and with no train.

The procession approached and ascended the platform, and the ladies glanced curiously at Sam when they saw him sitting alone in the first row of chairs, but most of their attention remained focused on the cage across the green. Sam figured he had never witnessed an unhappier bride. Marian confirmed his impression when she spoke loud enough to Vaisey for Sam to hear her angry words. "Why is Robin in a cage?"

"To ensure your cooperation," Vaisey replied smoothly. "We wouldn't want our wedding disrupted in any way, would we?"

Sam figured the nearest guests could also hear the conversation, but at the same time supposed they consisted of Vaisey's most ardent supporters.

"And what of the gibbet next to the cage?" Marian demanded.

"Insurance," Vaisey said. "As I promised, once we are wed, your friend will be released. However, should you begin to have second thoughts..."

"And why should I trust you?"

Vaisey grinned. "Because, my dear, you have no choice. Now chin up. Smile for the people. This is supposed to be a happy occasion."

Sam watched as Marian forced a smile, her complexion an odd mix of purple and pale. He then shifted his gaze to Effie, who mouthed at him, "What are you going to do?"

Sam could only force a smile himself, and nod his head. He thought about saying something. Something witty that would tell Effie everything was going to plan, while at the same time, not make Vaisey suspicious. Unfortunately, he couldn't think of any words that would do that, witty or otherwise. Especially when Little John had missed his first and best opportunity to rescue Robin. Sam hoped nothing had gone wrong.

The flutes that had accompanied the bridal procession fell silent, and the Bishop of Hereford stepped forward. "Lords and ladies," the pompous weasel drawled. "Citizens and servants. All who have come to witness the sacred joining of our beloved Sheriff and Lady Marian Dubois, cousin of Good King John."

The officious cleric pointed one hand above his head. "As the sun sits high in the sky each day, so shall the bond between man and wife remain, everlasting. What the Lord our God brings together, let no man put asunder. If any of you have reason why this joining should not be made, speak now or—"

A cry rose up from Robin's cage, immediately extinguished by the sound of a fist meeting flesh.

"Ah, yes," mumbled the Bishop. "As I was saying, speak now or forever hold your peace."

"I choose to speak," a voice called out.

Gasps rose from the crowd of onlookers.

Sam craned his neck and saw Azeem the Moor some distance away, standing on a barrel, shirtless, his dark, tattooed skin gleaming in the sun.

"This wedding is a farce," shouted the Moor. He pointed at Robin. "A good man in a cage." Then to Marian. "A woman forced to wed." Then finally to the Sheriff. "The Devil himself in disguise. Englishmen, behold! I am Azeem Edin Bashir Al Bakir. A Moor. A foreigner. A stranger to this land. Yet, I fight. With Robin Hood. Against this *worm* who sets himself as king above you. I am a free man. If you would be free also, join me. Join Robin. Join Robin Hood!"

Vaisey sounded like a strangled man as he shouted a response, "Arrest that man! No. Ignore that. Kill him!"

But Azeem was already gone, the barrel standing empty among the crowd.

"Worm!" someone in the crowd shouted.

"Worm!" came another voice. Sam thought he recognized it as Little John's.

Shouts of "Worm!" rose from all around.

Vaisey stood as tall as his limited height allowed, looking this way then that, trying to see who had called. But now almost everyone was shouting. "Worm!"

Sam waved for Marian and her bridesmaids to flee the platform and join him in the front row of chairs. The redshank guards, spooked by the bellowing crowd, did nothing to stop them.

"This is going to turn into a riot," he shouted at Effie. "But there's nowhere to run. For now, this looks like the safest spot. Besides," Sam couldn't stop himself from smiling, "we have the best seats in the house to watch the Sheriff of Nottingham throw a fit."

And it was true. Vaisey's face had become purple with rage, and froth spilled from his lips as he tried to call out instructions to his confused soldiers. Finally, Vaisey pointed to the cage. "Kill him! Kill Robin Hood!"

"Enough of this," Marian growled. Reaching beneath her wedding gown, she pulled free a small knife, probably something she had been saving for the marriage bed. Growling, she hacked at her wedding train, freeing her dress above the ankles. Then she lunged toward the platform steps.

Sam leaped out of his seat and grabbed the back of Marian's expensive blue gown, pulling the young woman aside in the nick of time. Two of Vaisey's redshank mercenaries had spotted the knife and were coming at her with swords. Sam let go of Marian and reached for his semi-automatic. Somehow, he managed to free it from his coat and shoot the nearest redshank in the face without getting himself stabbed first.

The other mercenary was so startled by the noise of the gun and the spray of blood from his companion, that he froze in mid-step. Sam's jaw dropped as the blade of Marian's knife brushed against the man's throat. The redshank stiffened, then dropped his sword and shield. With both hands, he grabbed at his neck. Hot blood gushed between his fingers. He was already dead. He just didn't know it.

Marian threw down the knife and picked up the dropped sword. Then she began making her way back past the rows of chairs toward Robin. Vaisey's Lords and Ladies, those who hadn't already fled, cringed in their seats as the wrathful bride ran past.

Waving for Effie, Nora, and Carmen to follow, Sam took off after Marian. Vaisey had surrounded himself with his remaining mercenaries, so there was no point going after him. It was time to run.

It took several minutes of pushing through panicked wedding guests and onlookers to reach the wooden cage, which was already open. Little John and David of Doncaster were helping a bruised and beaten Robin Hood to stand, while the rest of the Merry Men engaged the Sheriff's mercenaries. Marian pushed her way through them all and crushed herself against Robin, who grinned ear to ear. "It is a joyous day after all."

"We should be joyous someplace else," Sam said. "This village green has the makings of a killing field."

Robin gave Marian a final tight hug, then stepped back. "Right you are, my friend. To Sherwood Forest. There to hold a real wedding, if Maid Marian will have me."

"I do!" Marian cried, the sword in her hand half-forgotten. "I do. I do. I do."

"I can hardly wait," Sam muttered. Could things get any more Disney?

"This way looks safest," Little John said, pointing through the shifting crowd.

"Hey! What about me?" wailed a voice.

Everyone turned, and Sam noticed a second cage hidden behind the one that had held Robin.

"Will Scarlet," Little John said. "I did not see you there. David, go open Will's cage."

46
THE PUPPET TALKS

PEOPLE WERE RUNNING everywhere. As Sam had expected, many were falling underfoot. There was little he could do about it, however. The Sheriff's mercenaries, those the Merry Men hadn't dispatched at the cages, continued to pursue Robin and his people, which included Sam, Nora, Effie, Marian, and Carmen.

"This way!" Little John shouted. The giant outlaw had just fired an arrow and taken down a redshank mercenary who blocked their path.

Sam scanned the faces of Robin's men, and couldn't see any he didn't recognize.

"Where are your hired mercenaries?" Sam yelled.

Little John glanced back at him. "Some man the battlements above the York Gate. That is where we shall make our escape."

"And the rest?"

"On the streets between, eliminating the Sheriff's men."

"Then what's that up ahead?" Sam asked.

Further up the narrow roadway, a cluster of English soldiers waited with shields and swords.

"We must seek another path," Robin said.

"St Peter's church," Tuck cried. "The service entrance is over there."

It was only then Sam recognized the sloped street they were on and the tall church steeple with its ornamental battlements that dominated one side.

"Quickly," Robin cried.

They rushed toward the unassuming side entrance and began pouring through.

"This way." Sam led them through the kitchen and down the hallway to the steps leading up to the nave. "Keep going," he said, pointing to the steps. "Tuck knows the way."

"What are you going to do?" Robin asked.

"I'm going to unlock this door." From a trench coat pocket, Sam retrieved the ornate chain and key he had pilfered from the Bishop's desk. Once the door leading down to the basement stood open, he pocketed the key and joined the others fleeing up the steps.

"Should we not flee through this doorway?" Robin asked. "And lock it behind us."

Sam shook his head. "It leads to a tunnel that ends inside the Sheriff's Keep. If we go that way, we'll be trapped."

Robin cast him a confused look. "Then why unlock and leave the door open?"

"So they'll think we went that way."

A smile crossed Robin's face. "You are a devious man, Sam Spade."

"Only on my good days."

Sam and Robin now trailed behind the others as they fled through the nave, their footsteps echoing against the stone floor. When they caught up with the Merry Men at the vestibule, Tuck bid them wait while he determined a safe way out.

"The street appears clear of soldiers," the friar announced in a hushed voice when he returned from looking out the main entrance. "Many frightened townsfolk, but no soldiers."

"Then let us make haste," Robin said and was first to exit into the street.

The Merry Men fled south from the church square onto Lister Gate, then turned east on Low Pavement.

"The Sheriff's men will not look for us this far south in the town," Robin said. "From here there is no place to escape apart from Fisher Gate and Leen Bridge to the southeast. We shall not travel that far before turning back north toward York Gate."

"I'm just along for the ride," Sam said.

Sam had been on Low Pavement before and recognized the

market area more by its smell than its stalls. Instead of continuing east to the church on High Pavement, Robin led the band at a steady run north on a street called Fletcher Gate, then turned east again on Pitcher Gate. There was no sign of any of the Sheriff's men, and few townsfolk, apart from a few rushing home to their houses from the green.

At St Mary's Gate, they turned north again, and Sam was thoroughly lost until they met up with Stoney Street, which he knew led to their destination—York Gate. The street, which in the past had been crowded with people leaving or entering the town, or frequenting the various shops near the town wall, was now deserted.

Robin raised a hand signalling his men to slow, then stop. Up ahead, several men with swords or bows stepped out from doorways or between buildings.

Almost immediately, one of them collapsed in the street, an arrow protruding from his chest.

In response, several bowmen fired arrows at the Merry Men who, because of their disguises, were dressed in cotton shirts and pants, and carried no shields. Sitting ducks wasn't a bad description for them.

Sam grabbed Nora by the hand and led her to the questionable safety of the side of a house. Effie and Carmen followed.

The Merry Men, and Marian, remained in the street, firing arrows at the Sheriff's soldiers. Gilbert Whitehand let an arrow fly, taking down another bowman, while Little John and Marian took down a third and a fourth.

Sam had no idea how Robin's men had smuggled bows and swords into the town. Possibly they acquired them from friends already inside Nottingham. That didn't explain Marian, who'd had a knife concealed in her dress before picking up a redshank's sword.

"When did you get a bow?" Sam called to her after the Sheriff's men had either died or fled.

Marian grinned. "Alan-a-Dale lent me his as I am the better shot."

"I think it best we resume running," Little John said.

"Please, no." Tuck leaned against a wall, his chest heaving and sweat pouring down his face. "I am spent."

"Call upon your God," Azeem the Moor suggested. "The

Sheriff is on our heels. And he is not alone."

Sam looked back and saw at least two dozen redshanks, each with a wide sword and a heavy shield, marching toward them from the other end of the street. He couldn't see Vaisey but could hear the villain spurring his mercenaries on from the rear.

"We are less than a street from York Gate," Little John said to Tuck. "Were you a smaller man, I would carry you."

"Alas," the friar wheezed. "Were I a smaller man, I would not require carrying."

"You all go on ahead," Sam told the Merry Men. "As fast as you can. I'll delay them."

"You?" Tuck's brows rose high on his forehead. "By yourself? That is death."

"I won't be alone," Sam said. "I'll have two friends with me." He raised his semi-automatic. "Mr. Smith and Mr. Wesson."

"Are you right in the head?" Tuck asked.

"Don't worry, I'll be fine."

With no time for further debate, the friar shook his head. "Take care, my friend." Then he urged the others on, moving much faster than Sam had expected. Which was just as well. Sam's beanshooter only had so many bullets.

The redshanks slowed when they saw Sam standing alone in the middle of the street.

"What are you stopping for?" Vaisey shouted. "Kill him and go after the others."

Sam wagged the semi-automatic in the air. "Come out from hiding, Lord Sheriff. Do all English generals lead from behind? Or is that just how they do it in Scotland?"

The mercenaries all growled and likewise wagged their swords in the air. "Ye dare insult us?" one of them demanded.

"Actually, it's the Sheriff I'm insulting. But if he won't show himself, I'll have to kill one of you instead."

The redshank who had spoken laughed. "Whit? Wi' that stane in yer hand? Whit—"

That was all the mercenary got out before Sam plugged him between the eyes. The retort from the weapon echoed like thunder along the street as the Scottish soldier dropped like the stone he was asking about.

Sam wagged his firearm. "Anyone else have a question?"

"Kill him!" Vaisey shouted, his voice muted by the wall of

flesh, leather, and wood. "Do not forget who is paying you."

"You pay us tae kill," a redshank yelled back at their master. "You dinnae pay us tae die. Baigh wis a guid lad."

"You knew the risks when I hired you," Vaisey shouted. When that garnered no response, he added, "I'll double your pay." Still nothing. "Live or dead, you get paid. The living can divide it up."

Suddenly the redshanks were moving again.

Sam considered shooting them. Ducks in a barrel at the Durham Fair. But they were now being more strategic with their shields, holding them up to cover their heads. And there were more mercenaries than he had bullets. He looked around, trying to decide where to run.

"This way," Nora cried from further up the street. "I know a place."

"Where did you come from?" Sam called to her.

But his partner didn't answer. Instead, she began running down a narrow side street.

Sam didn't have to think twice. He bolted after Nora as fast as his sore feet could carry him. From behind, the pounding of boots on cobbles told him he'd soon have company.

The nice thing about heavy wooden shields, Sam decided as he fled down the empty side street and into a wider street after that, was that they were heavy. Unencumbered, he and Nora outdistanced their pursuers. But the Celtic mercenaries wouldn't give up. They continued to follow, encouraged by Vaisey's shouted promises of riches.

"I hope it isn't much further," Sam puffed. He could run faster than the men looking to kill him, but given the sorry state of his feet, he didn't think he could run further.

"Just up ahead," Nora said.

Sam noticed she was barely breathing hard. He knew Nora went to a gym regularly and was in better physical condition than him. She also hadn't lived the last ten years of her life as a chain smoker. Sam figured he could learn a thing or two from his partner beyond the fine art of private investigation.

They turned a corner and Sam felt he was on a street he recognized. Then Nora ran up to a door, pushed it open, and ducked inside. Sam followed, throwing the door shut behind him. He knew exactly where they were. Geiger's house.

Leaning forward, Sam pressed his hands against his knees and tried to catch his breath. When he could speak, he turned to Nora. "Do you think they saw us come in here?"

In answer, Vaisey's voice barked from outside. "Come out and face us like a man. Otherwise, we shall be forced to burn you out."

Sam shuffled over to a window and pushed aside a curtain. Redshanks lined the street. If anything, there were more of them. Reinforcements. "You still hiding behind your hirelings?" Sam shouted.

"A torch is on the way," Vaisey said in reply.

"Do your Scottish trouble boys know who they're working for?" Sam called out the window. "That you currently support John against his brother, the rightful King, but that you also intend to take John's place, and set yourself up as the King of England. That's why you needed to wed Marian. To get close to the throne."

Vaisey laughed. "You think mercenaries care one whit who rules England? They care only that they are paid."

"But England isn't enough for you," Sam said. "Once you have the throne, you'll want Scotland as well. And Ireland. And Wales."

"As th' Sheriff says," one of the redshanks called out, "one bloody laird is th' same as anither. It matters nae who pays me, sae lang as ah'm paid."

"But once the Sheriff is king," Sam countered, "he won't need mercenaries. He'll have more soldiers than he can use. In fact, mercenaries will be a problem. He'll probably have his soldiers hunt you down."

While the redshanks mulled that over, Sam turned to Nora. "Go check out the back. There's a gate that opens into a tunnel."

"There is?"

"Make sure the way is clear. I'll find something to block this door."

Nora left, and Sam looked around. There wasn't much that was heavy. The couch. Maybe the cabinet.

Nora came back. "There is a gate. But it's been blocked off with large stones."

"Can we move the stones? Or climb over them?"

Nora shook her head. "If we had an hour. Maybe."

"Well, that's just swell."

Nora frowned. "I was hoping they wouldn't see us enter the

house."

"You can blame me for that," Sam said. "I'm not as quick on my feet as I should be."

The grumbling outside grew louder, then Sam heard Vaisey cry, "You uncouth idiots! I am in charge here. It matters not if I am Sheriff or king."

"But John is nae a real king," a redshank cried. "He stole th' throne fae Richard."

"It matters not," Vaisey insisted. "John and Richard both have to die. And several of their cousins. When Marian is next in line and is my wife, I shall be king!"

"Bit ye'r nae wed tae Marian. Th' wey ah see it, Robin Hood wull be th' future king."

Several of the mercenaries laughed.

Vaisey's voice rose an octave, a picture of exasperation. "You insolent oafs! That is why I am paying you!"

Sam almost laughed. Most men didn't sign on as mercenaries because they were geniuses. They signed on because they had difficulty matching up socks.

"Ah think ye shuid pay us noo," said an indignant voice. "Ah'm hearing a lot a gab aboot bein' paid, bit ah hae nae seen a scabby coin."

A chorus of voices rose in agreement, and the next thing Sam knew the door burst open and Vaisey and Guy of Gisbourne stumbled inside. Vaisey slammed the door shut and Guy threw himself against it.

"Well," Vaisey growled at Sam. "I hope you are proud of yourself."

"I don't know if proud is the best word," Sam replied.

"You have got us all killed now," Vaisey screamed.

Sam continued to look out the window, where the redshank mercenaries stood arguing among themselves. "You know, I think I've got it all worked out."

"What?" Vaisey said. "Worked what out?"

"Who killed who," Sam said. "Your man Lundgren killed Joe Brody because he thought Brody killed Geiger. Only it was Carmen who killed Geiger. Sure, she pointed a finger at Brody, but she's a compulsive liar. I'll bet a twelve-year-old bottle of Scotch that Carmen is our killer. The only thing I'm still unsure about is Regan."

"Who?" Vaisey's crossed eyes suggested his brain was still stuck on Lundgren.

"Sean Regan," Sam explained. "He's the guy Nora and I were hired to find. I don't even know if he's alive or dead."

From Vaisey's vapid expression, Sam figured the explanation hadn't helped.

"Regan is dead," Nora said.

"Really?" Sam was intrigued. "How do you know?"

"It's obvious. Carmen killed him."

"She told you that?"

"No, but have you looked at her? I mean, really looked? Carmen wants what she wants when she wants it, and she's not going to let Daddy's soldier get in her way. Regan went to Sternwood Castle to take one of Carmen's toys away, or to cut off her allowance, or something, and Carmen wouldn't stand for it. Maybe they got in a fight. Or maybe she did him in with little provocation. Whatever happened, Carmen solved her problem with murder. I bet Regan's corpse is still back at the castle. Maybe hidden in the basement, and that's how Carmen found the passage here, just like we did."

"I'm sure you're right," Sam said. "That girl is trouble with a capital T."

"The puppet talks," Vaisey said, staring at Nora.

Nora smiled at him. "I was asleep for a while, but I'm awake now."

Vaisey snorted. "Asleep or awake, we are still about to die."

"Exactly," Sam said. "Since we have nothing to lose, we might as well get things off our chest. I'll go first. For me, it's dying leaving a case unresolved. Thanks to Nora, we can safely say what happened to Sean Regan. I feel a lot better. How about you, Vaisey? Anything you want to get off your chest?"

Vaisey frowned, and Sam could see the villain's gaze turn inward. Then, suddenly, the Sheriff of Nottingham turned and slammed himself against Guy of Gisbourne. Guy's mouth flew open and his tongue lolled out. Gagging sounds choked from his throat, and his eyes spun in their sockets. Finally, the vile toady fell forward against Vaisey's shoulder.

The Sheriff pulled back, and slowly withdrew a blade from Guy's abdomen. "You blithering idiot," Vaisey grumbled. "You may be my cousin, but you were always an incompetent fool."

"That's, uh, not really what I had in mind," Sam said.

"But I do feel a lot better," Vaisey insisted.

"Maybe I shouldn't tell you that Gisbourne was dead anyway. That leg of his is full of poison." Sam didn't think it was possible, but Vaisey's expression soured even further.

"Sam," Nora said. "It's grown quiet outside."

They all listened. It was true. Sam peeked out the window. "They're still there. I think they've settled their differences and are ready to storm the door." Sam pulled his Smith & Wesson semi-automatic from its holster and looked at Nora. "Maybe you should do the honours. You're a better shot."

Nora shrugged. "What do you suggest? Do I shoot us before they enter? Or shoot the first few of them that come through the door?"

"You people are insane!" Vaisey shouted. The murderous sheriff then shoved Gisbourne's dead weight aside, pulled open the door, and made a run for it.

Sam pushed the door shut again, while Nora pushed aside the curtain and looked outside. "One. Two. Thr—. Nope. He never made it to three. I think Vaisey's redshanks have the same sentiment toward Nottingham's Sheriff as he had toward his cousin. Ooh." Nora winced. "They've cut off his head. Now they've lifted his corpse into the air and are carrying it down the street. Looks like we're off the hook."

"Let's give it a minute," Sam said. "Then we can skulk away."

"You don't want to wait for nightfall?" Nora asked.

Sam shrugged. "Those mercenaries could get bored with the Sheriff and come back."

"You've got a point."

He joined Nora at the window and pushed the curtain further aside. Together, they watched as the redshanks carried Vaisey's remains to the end of the street and around the corner.

"We're clear," Nora said.

"Okay. But before we go, how about you tell me when you started remembering who you were."

"It's been a while now," his partner admitted. "But I couldn't seem to express myself. It was a struggle just to get a few words out. But after that craziness with the wedding, my brain seemed to start working again."

"I'm glad you're back."

Nora smiled and touched his arm. "I'm glad I'm back, too."
"Right." Sam glanced at Nora's hand. "Let's go then."

47
LOST IN A FOREST

THE STREETS REMAINED mostly empty as Sam and Nora made their way to the York Gate. They saw no sign of the Sheriff's men in the town or on the battlements and left through the gate unmolested.

"I think everyone's had enough for one day," Sam suggested. "First the riot at the wedding, then the shootout on Stoney Street a little while ago, and finally Vaisey's corpse carried through the streets by jubilant Scotsmen. It's enough to make you lock your door, turn out the lights, and crawl under a blanket."

"Are we really in the Middle Ages?" Nora asked. "And that was Robin Hood and his Merry Men? I thought that was just a story."

Sam laughed. "I can't be sure of what happened last week, never mind hundreds of years ago."

"And you really went to Camelot? And saw King Arthur?"

A black bird broke out from the trees and flew up and onto the town wall. It sat there, looking down at Sam, and let out a loud caw.

"Is that a crow or a raven?" Sam asked Nora.

"Is this a test?" his partner asked. "I think it's a crow."

"Me too." Sam's cheek twitched. "You know, I think King Arthur is the only person in Camelot I didn't see. It's funny—"

"And you'll get us back home?" Nora interrupted. "To Hartford?"

"I'm still working on that," Sam said.

They arrived at St John the Baptist Hospital, and though most of the beds were filled with patients, people injured in the stampede at the wedding, there was no sign of Robin and his Merry Men. Sam tried asking the silent monks if they knew anything, but couldn't interpret their hand signs. Sam figured he'd be lousy at charades.

"What now?" Nora asked. She had retrieved her small sack of possessions and abandoned her bridesmaid dress in favour of farmer pants and a men's shirt.

Sam rubbed his ear. "I can probably retrace my steps to Sherwood Forest. I'm sure that's where they've gone."

Nora looked at him. "Probably?"

"There aren't any road signs," Sam explained.

Outside the hospital, another black bird hopped along a tree branch. Or maybe it was the same bird.

Nora sighed. "The day isn't getting any younger. We'd better start walking."

Sam led Nora along the path through the trees that joined the York Road. The track continued through the forest on the other side and eventually brought them to The King's Great Way.

"Now we go north for maybe four hours," Sam said.

"And then?" Nora asked.

"Then we get lost in a forest."

"Lost?"

"Robin's Merry Men will find us."

"If you say so," Nora said.

They walked along the hardpacked dirt road, seeing little traffic. An older man on a tired-looking horse gave Sam an odd look but asked no questions. A little later, a party of maybe a dozen middle-aged women smirked and giggled, but one disapproving look from Nora sent them on their way.

"It's the clothes," Sam said. "My *mean streets* getup makes quite the fashion statement."

When they reached the spot where Sam figured he had encountered the two young men on horseback that first day he walked to Nottingham, he stopped and looked about. It was morning when he had come that way the first time. Now it was almost dark.

"Is this it?" Nora asked.

"I think so," Sam answered. "Call me metropolitan, but all these trees look alike."

"The trees here look older and taller than those by the hospital," Nora suggested. "And the grass is thicker. There are more bushes."

"Yup. Sherwood Forest. We may as well enter here."

"And become lost," Nora said, echoing Sam's earlier words.

Sam waved at the trees. "Lost in an easterly direction."

The going was rougher in the forest, with fallen branches and rocks hiding beneath tall grass and sprawling bushes. Sam tried to step where shade made it difficult for plants to grow.

After what felt like an hour, the birdcalls changed.

"I think we've been spotted," Sam said.

"You're referring to the bird calls," Nora suggested. "Our feathered friends are no longer singing. What we hear now are the mating calls of forest outlaws."

Sam smiled. "You really are your old self, aren't you?"

"I think so." Nora lifted a hand to the side of her head. "My skull still feels pretty soft right here. I wish I could remember how that happened."

"It'll come back to you," Sam said. "Give it time."

The forest had grown deathly quiet while they spoke. No more bird calls. Not even the chirp of a cricket.

"Maybe we should introduce ourselves," Sam said. He cupped his hands around his mouth. "Hello! My name is Sam Spade. This is Nora Clark. We're friends."

Nora looked at Sam. "Sam Spade?"

"It's a long story."

A few minutes later, a youth no older than twelve appeared from out of the forest. "Not *the* Sam Spade?"

"The one and only," Sam said.

The boy waved a hand. "Come with me."

They traipsed through the forest for another ten minutes, then Robin's camp opened up before them.

"Sam! Sam Spade!" Tuck was the first to see them, but soon they were surrounded by all the Merry Men, who hounded Sam to describe what had happened after they'd left him inside York Gate.

"I still do not understand how you escaped the Sheriff," Tuck said, once he'd finished.

Sam pulled off his fedora and ran the fingers of one hand through his hair. "Sure, I make it sound easy, but it took a lot of luck. And if those redshank mercenaries hadn't turned on their paymaster, the story would have had a different ending."

"So the Sheriff of Nottingham is dead? Truly?"

Sam's cheek twitched. "Unless Vaisey survived his head being separated from the rest of his body, I'm pretty sure he's dead."

A wide grin split Tuck's face. "Then we have additional cause for rejoicing. Robin is freed, and is to wed Maid Marian on the morrow—"

"Wait. What? Isn't that a little hasty?"

"Hasty? No, my friend. They have been engaged since before Robin went to Jerusalem with King Richard two summers ago. A wedding is long overdue."

"You mean to tell me Marian was going to marry the Sheriff, even though she was already engaged to Robin?"

"To save Robin's life!" the friar admonished. "The heart is a harsh mistress."

Sam glanced across the clearing to where Nora now sat with Effie and Carmen. He'd been in love with Euphemia Peregrine when she was seventeen, and again at twenty-three, and now again at twenty-nine, scar and all. All that while she'd been untouchable, incapable of loving any man, never mind a simple gumshoe from Connecticut. He shook his head at Tuck. "You can say that again, brother."

"Come drink by the fire," Tuck said. "The mead flows freely this night."

"I'd take you up on that," Sam said, "but I've been on my feet all day and I've yet to recover from walking all over England for the past week. You don't happen to have any of the silent monks' salve, do you?"

Tuck grinned. "I procured an ointment pot at the Hospital of St John the Baptist for this very moment."

48

AND FINALLY, WE DANCE!

HUNKERED BENEATH A blanket, the bottoms of his feet smeared with the silent monks' miracle salve, Sam fell asleep almost instantly. When he woke, the sun was high in the sky, and his stomach growled with hunger. The smell of meat roasting over a fire inspired him to dress quickly.

"You overslept, my friend," Tuck said. "Breakfast has come and gone."

Across the clearing, Sam could see a makeshift table covered with bread, cheeses, and apples. "There must be something to nibble on."

Tuck noticed his gaze. "You must not consider eating. The wedding shall soon begin, and we shall eat and drink for an entire afternoon."

Sam rubbed his face. "How about something to drink, then?"

The friar's eyes twinkled. "Of course!" He produced a bulging wineskin from the belt at his waist. "I always carry something with me."

Sam twisted free the wooden stopper and took a sip, expecting mead similar to what Tuck had provided when he first came to Robin's camp. Instead, all he tasted was water. "Thanks," he said, handing back the leather pouch.

"Of course," Tuck suggested, "at the wedding we shall have mead and a bit of ale for the ceremony."

"I can hardly wait," Sam said.

The friar nodded. "I have preparations to make. Such a joyous day!"

As the jolly churchman weaved a trail through the camp, Sam noticed Nora, Effie, and Carmen sitting on a log. Now that his partner had regained her memory, or most of it, he noticed Carmen had become silent as a mouse. It made him wonder what the younger Sternwood daughter was hiding, but didn't question it in case the asking turned her back into a lioness.

The only space remaining on the log was between Effie and Carmen, so Sam settled himself there even though sitting between Effie and Nora would have been more apropos. The woman he loved on one side, and the woman who could possibly love him on the other, if Nora's touch the previous day had meant anything. Sam had no clue if there was a chance of either working out.

Sadly, it was Carmen who leaned toward him and whispered in his ear. "You've rescued your friend. Can we go back to Connecticut now?"

As far as sweet nothings went, Sam gave Carmen's words a one out of ten.

"You don't want to stay for the wedding?" Sam murmured.

"I stayed for my sister's wedding," Carmen said. "And went back for the divorce. Marriage is overrated."

Sam felt his cheek twitch. "I'm pretty sure that in the Mel Brooks movie, Robin and Marian live happily ever after."

"Whatever. When do we go back to Connecticut?"

"I'm working on it," Sam said.

Carmen growled in her throat, then slid away a few inches along the log.

"I have good news," Effie said.

Sam turned his head, coming face to cheek with Effie's scar. Unlike Sagramore's, which ran like an angry red canal down the ex-knight's face, Effie's was a thin, dark seam that could have been painted on with a delicate brush. He didn't think it in any way reduced her natural beauty.

Effie turned toward him and smiled. "Maid, soon to be Lady, Marian has accepted my proposal to come work for her."

"I told you it would work out," Sam said.

The smile faded. "It means I shall not be available to work for you, should you establish yourself here."

"That's still up in the air," Sam admitted, the words eliciting an additional growl from Carmen.

"You intend to take your friends back to Connecticut?" Effie asked.

"If it's possible," Sam said.

Silence descended, and the four of them sat and watched as the Merry Men and their camp followers constructed an altar of sorts from branches and string, and set it against the base of the giant oak tree that dominated the clearing. From the great oak's lower branches, they hung streamers made from bright-coloured cloth. Wherever a flat surface could be found in the camp, a fat candle was placed, ready to be lit when the sun went down.

Fortunately, Sam didn't have to wait for nightfall before he could eat. When the preparations were finished, everyone in the camp gathered before the great tree. He and the ladies climbed up from the log bench and joined them.

Silence fell, then Alan-a-Dale produced a small harp. Grinning, the minstrel-turned-outlaw began strumming a cheerful tune. One by one, voices rose from the camp to add to the song, which grew in strength and ferocity. The words sounded English, sort of. Perhaps they were an older dialect.

Once everyone was in full chorus, Robin Hood, dressed in layers of verdant green cloth, stepped out from behind the great oak. Grinning from ear to ear, he added his voice in perfect harmony while walking among his followers, who grinned and gave him congratulatory slaps on the back.

When he arrived in front of the altar, the voices stopped, and Alan-a-Dale switched to a different tune. Sam almost recognized it as "Here Comes the Bride", only he was pretty sure the familiar wedding march hadn't been written yet.

He was still trying to make sense of it when all heads turned. Sam also looked. From behind a stand of trees, Maid Marian appeared, dressed in a white gown and veil, a wreath of young twigs set on her head like a crown. She strode among the crowd, receiving smiles and cheers, but fortunately, no back slaps.

Sam, along with Nora and Effie, cheered with the rest, and when the music ceased, Marian stood facing Robin. Tuck had also appeared from somewhere and now stood behind the happy couple at the altar.

"People of Sherwood," Tuck began, "today is a great occasion. Almost three years ago, the man and woman who now stand before you exchanged a promise to wed. But the time was not yet. A holy war stood in the way, calling upon many of our Lord's young men, including Robin of Locksley and Peter Dubois." The friar paused to acknowledge the absence of Marian's brother. "Other obstacles arose, most of them laid at the feet of King Richard's younger brother John, and the Pretender's tool, the Sheriff of Nottingham. And though not all of our troubles are passed, the time for this young couple has at last come."

The friar smiled. "Here, now, before God and all present, I ask you, Robin of Locksley, do you take Maid Marian to be your wedded wife, to have and to hold from this day forward, for better for worse, for richer for poorer, in sickness and in health, to love, cherish, and obey, till death do you part, according to God's holy ordinance?"

Robin took Marian's hands in his and gazed into her eyes. "I do. I give thee my troth."

Tuck then repeated the words for Marian.

Maid Marian squeezed Robin's hands and took a deep breath. "I do. I give thee my troth."

The friar nodded. "Then in the name of our Lord, those whom God hath joined together let no man put asunder. Forasmuch as Robin and Marian have consented together in holy wedlock, and have witnessed the same before God and this company, and thereto have given and pledged their troth each to the other; I pronounce, therefore, that they be Man and Wife together, in the Name of the Father, and of the Son, and of the Holy Spirit. Amen."

As one, the crowd cheered. Even Carmen forgot herself and raised her voice. Robin and Marian turned away from Tuck to grin at their friends. No kiss, apparently, but they did raise their joined hands in the air like champion prizefighters.

Tuck let out a hearty laugh. "Now we eat. Then we drink. And finally, we dance!"

Sam's stomach growled in appreciation, but he waited with the others for a turn to congratulate the bride and groom before making his way to the food table.

A short while later, Tuck laughed into Sam's ear. "'Tis the best of days!"

Sam wouldn't swear on it, but he suspected the friar was inebriated. He'd seen enough drunks during his time as a cop, but he also knew excessive joy could sometimes pass as too much to drink; a natural high.

"Indeed," Sam returned. He'd sampled all of the various wedding dishes, finding few that interested him. Perhaps they were delicacies made especially for the wedding. Sam was more of a steak and potatoes kind of guy. "It was nice to see you put that burlap robe of yours to good use."

The friar's mirth faded, and Sam could see the churchman was less intoxicated than he appeared. "Robin and Marian deserve a bishop's ministrations. And a church wedding. I suppose a forest cathedral and the service of a humble friar must suffice."

Sam let out a chuckle. "Don't be absurd. They were lucky to have one of their best friends perform the ceremony. I suspect given a choice between you and the Pope, they still would have chosen you to officiate."

Tuck's jaw dropped. "You think?"

"I know."

The friar straightened and thrust out his chest. "Well, one thing I do know is that Sam Spade would not lie to me, so I must believe you. Come, the dancing has started. We must join in."

"I'm not really much of a dancer," Sam said. "Besides, these shoes and these feet. What I really need is more of that fancy salve of yours, and to sit down."

He was about to do just that when Will Scarlet crashed through the trees into the glade. The young outlaw immediately hunched over, his hands on his knees. Breath came from his lungs as though from a bellows.

"My friend," Tuck said. "What is it?"

Scarlet looked up and swallowed. "Trouble," was all he managed, before adding, "in Nottingham. Lord Furnival. With his soldiers."

49
THE VILE SNAKE WHO MURDERED MY FATHER

"Furnival!" Robin shouted, striding toward Will Scarlet. "Apparently, we need not go to Locksley on the morrow. Furnival has come to Sherwood. To arms! To arms!"

"But Robin," Little John said, coming up behind his friend. "'Tis your wedding night."

"No," Marian contended, joining them. "Every night shall be our wedding night. Furnival—I refuse to name him lord—murdered Robin's father. Robin must take his revenge."

"We ride to Nottingham," Robin said, calling out to his men. "I know you fought yesterday and are yet tired, but if you love me, you will join me."

As with one voice, everyone in the camp shouted, "We ride!"

Sam found himself in a dilemma. If he walked, he would arrive at Nottingham hours after the Merry Men. Plus, his feet were not in the best shape. If he rode . . . well, he still remembered what that had been like. Whoa. Was it just a week ago?

Nora made the decision for him. She stepped up beside him leading two horses. "Tuck says this one is pretty tame."

Sam saw that one of the animals was tall and so black he could barely see it in the evening gloom. The other was shorter and tan coloured and looked half asleep. Both were saddled and ready to go.

"I assume you're referring to the tan pony," he said. "I suppose riding is one of the many talents you haven't mentioned to me yet."

"I rode as a child," Nora admitted. "But it's like riding a bike; you don't forget. Do you need a boost up?"

Sam did, but he wouldn't admit it. "I'll manage."

It took several tries, but Sam finally managed to hoist himself into the saddle and wedge his feet in the stirrups. Soon they were on their way, riding at the tail end of a convoy that wound through the forest. Because it was dusk, they didn't ride at a fast pace. Sam let his horse decide where to go, and focused on moving with the sway of the animal instead of bouncing in his saddle. Once they were on the road, Nora rode beside him, eyeing him appraisingly, but saying nothing.

Nora and Marian were the only women to ride with the Merry Men. Effie had insisted on coming, but Sam asked her to stay in the camp and keep an eye on Carmen. He didn't think Carmen would run off again, but he didn't see any reason for Effie to put herself in danger. Nora, he knew, could handle herself, especially now that she was thinking clearly and carried her loaded Glock 19 at her waist.

Darkness fell swiftly. The sky, unfortunately, was overcast, and not even the moon made a hazy appearance. As the light failed, several of the Merry Men lit torches. It wasn't enough to see by, but the grouping of horses managed to stay on the road, travelling at a steady walk. After what seemed, and probably was, hours, they slowed and the torches were extinguished, leaving Sam blind.

Or at least blinder than the Merry Men. Whispers floated on the night air.

"The gate is open."

"'Tis a trap."

"I see no archers on the battlements."

Then a voice called out, "The way is clear."

"Sagramore?" Little John asked.

A laugh. "No. I am the Sheriff of Nottingham's ghost. Of course it is I."

Then Tuck called out. "You missed the wedding."

"Was that not the point?" Sagramore replied.

"Not that wedding."

"Ah! Then, congratulations are in order. But first, we have a keep to subjugate."

"Lord Furnival?" This time Sam recognized Robin's voice.

"Aye," Sagramore said. "Our hirelings hounded the Sheriff's men through the town, preventing them from following you into Sherwood. Then word reached our ears that the Sheriff was dead, executed by his own redshank mercenaries, who then fled. We watched for a ruse, but felt the claim vindicated when Celts began leaving the town carrying spoils from the keep."

"'Tis true," Robin said. "Sam Spade witnessed the deed."

Sam knew it was Nora who saw the beheading, but it was the wrong time to split hairs.

Sagramore continued. "We were in the act of reclaiming some of our taxes from the fleeing redshanks when a troop of horsemen descended from the north along The King's Great Way."

Robin interrupted. "Furnival must have heard rumour of the Sheriff's wedding, and come to witness if his co-conspirator truly plotted against John the Pretender."

"No honour among rebels," Sagramore agreed.

"Where is Furnival now?" Robin asked.

"Holed up in the Sheriff's Keep." Sagramore let out a chuckle. "He left men at the gates and along the walls, but that is no longer a problem."

"Then let us carry on to the keep," Robin said.

The horses resumed moving.

"How," Sam whispered to Nora, who rode beside him, "do these men do all this in the pitch dark?"

Nora laughed. "I assume they're used to it."

After riding through Mansfield Gate, Sam hoped to at least be able to see the street. He knew there were no streetlamps, but candles and lanterns from inside the buildings should seep through the window curtains, making some difference. But he saw no lamplight. No candles. Maybe it was too deep into the night. Or maybe the residents didn't want to attract notice. Even so, he realized he could make out the shape of cobbles in the street. Maybe his eyes were getting used to the dark, after all.

As they neared the keep, his vision continued to improve. So much so that Sam figured what he was experiencing was predawn. Though the sun was still well below the horizon, light was seeping over the edge of the world. Soon he could make out the shapes of the buildings abutting the street, as well as the horses ahead of him. The sky above the town wall grew purple with an edge of pale white.

Though morning was on its way, the streets remained deserted. No brave souls up before dawn to collect milk, empty bedpans, or do whatever medieval townsfolk did first thing. The village green appeared in the distance, a flat grey plain in the poor light. Then shouts came from ahead, and Sam heard the flight of arrows. Some distance away, he could just make out the battlements above the Sheriff's Keep, and the main tower of Nottingham Castle beside it.

One of the horses slowed and eased back beside Sam and Nora. Tuck.

"Does Robin have a plan?" Sam asked the churchman.

Tuck looked at him and rubbed his tonsured head. "I suspect Robin shall challenge Lord Furnival to a duel."

"Is Furnival likely to accept?"

The friar laughed. "Not if he wishes to live. Robin will best him at blade or bow. More likely, Lord Furnival shall throw his redshanks at us. We shall have to kill them all in order to reach the cowering fopdoodle."

"This happens a lot around here, does it?" Sam asked.

Tuck shrugged. "Rare is the man of war who dies peacefully in his sleep."

As if to punctuate that statement, Sam's horse stepped carefully over a corpse with an arrow sticking out of it.

"From yesterday, do you suppose?" Sam asked.

The friar shook his head. "Either Lord Furnival's man, freshly killed just now, or some poor fool who attempted to defend the town in the wake of the Sheriff's death."

"You think Furnival has set himself up as Sheriff?" Sam asked.

Tuck snorted. "Possession, it is said, is nine-tenths of the law."

Sam found himself rethinking the mean streets of Hartford. Maybe they weren't so mean after all. People might throw obscenities at each other on a daily basis, but at least they rarely threw knives or bullets. Then again, the Dark Ages weren't called the Dark Ages because they didn't have incandescent lighting.

More shouts came from ahead, followed by a flight of arrows and the clash of swords. Minutes later, the line of horses in front of them spread to either side, and Sam saw they had reached the entrance to the Sheriff's Keep. He was surprised to see the portcullis raised, and bodies littering the small courtyard. Checking the horses, he saw many of the saddles were empty, and that Robin and Little John were nowhere in sight. Then Will Scarlet walked out from beneath the portcullis.

"Did we miss the fighting?" Tuck demanded.

Will Scarlet grinned up at him. "Could scarcely be called a fight. Sagramore's hirelings stormed the courtyard moments before we arrived. They secured the portcullis, allowing us to simply walk in. Robin waits for you inside."

"Waiting for us?" Sam asked.

Scarlet shrugged.

Sam managed to climb down off his pony without falling, then he, Nora, and Tuck stepped around the corpses in the courtyard and entered the Sheriff's Keep.

The inside was as dark as Sam remembered, perhaps darker, with so little light entering through the open doorway. Few candles burned in the wall sconces and chandelier, though the broad firepit in front of the throne was lit, adding more heat than light.

Seated on the high chair, an older man dressed in brown pants and a white shirt glowered at them. His expression was firm, but Sam could see his hands trembling.

"Ah, Sam," Robin said from where he stood near Vaisey's statue. "You have arrived. I wanted you to meet the man who sent his redshank mercenaries to beat you senseless without even knowing who you were. We can remedy that now. Lord Furnival, this is Sam Spade, a pie from Connecticut."

The haughty man sneered at the introduction.

"Sam," Robin continued, "this is the vile snake who murdered my father and claimed his estate—Lord Furnival of Sheffield."

"It was hardly murder," Furnival stated, his tone blasé. "Your father was given a choice. Join Prince John in his bid for the throne, or remain true to King Richard and live with the consequences." The older man smirked. "Or die with the consequences, as the case may be."

"You also have a choice," Robin announced, his voice almost a growl. "You may die at the end of my sword, or at the end of an arrow. Which do you prefer?"

Furnival leaned forward in the throne, and from somewhere acquired a backbone. "Listen, you ignorant little—"

That was as far as he got before an arrow poked through his throat. The older man jerked in his seat and grabbed both ends of the arrow with his hands. He struggled to speak but only succeeded in making a choking sound. Then he fought for breath. No joy there either. Falling forward off the throne, he caught himself on unsteady legs and danced a brief jig before toppling to the floor.

"Well, that is one task off my list," Robin said. "Next, we ride to Locksley and reclaim my father's castle."

Sam wasn't so sure. "Have you looked behind the throne?"

Robin blinked. "What? No. Why?"

"No tyrant stands alone," Sam said. "Vaisey had two advisors. I suspect they may still be here, hoping to continue in their positions with whoever becomes the new Sheriff."

Robin began walking toward the throne, stepping to one side so he could see behind it. "You there. Come out. Come out here now."

Slowly, a shadow emerged. Tuck let out a roar of laughter and approached the deceased Sheriff's one-time advisor. "Well, who have we here? Not the Bishop of Hereford? And what is that in your hands?"

"Wha-What?" stammered the bishop. He glanced down at his hands, and jerked backward as though surprised to see the ornate chest he was clutching. "It-It is . . . Why, I have no idea."

"You have no idea?" Tuck took two additional steps toward the clergyman who had ordered the monks at the Hospital of St John the Baptist to silence, and who later attempted to wed Maid Marian to Vaisey against her will.

The bishop stumbled backward, and in doing so dropped the chest, which spilled open, throwing coins and silver chains and assorted jewels across the floor.

"So now your sins extend to thievery!" Tuck cried.

The bishop's wild eyes searched left, then right. Suddenly he made a run for it, a vain attempt to outflank Tuck, after which he would need to deal with Robin, Sam, and the majority of Robin's men. It never came to that, however. As the bishop trundled past, Tuck threw him a bodycheck that would make any hockey fan proud. The bishop went flying sideways, smashing into a tall standing mirror, shattering the leaded glass, and stumbling through to the other side.

"Seven years bad luck," Nora said from where she stood at Sam's elbow.

Sam, favoured with a slightly better angle than his partner, shook his head. "More like seven seconds. Looks like the bishop sliced open an artery."

"What?" Tuck appeared frightened. "I killed him?"

"Accidents do happen," Sam said. "Shame about the mirror, though."

Robin, seeming undisturbed by the bishop's death, looked at Sam. "You said there were two advisors."

"Right." Sam took a deep breath, then called out in a sing-song voice, "Morgan Le Fay, where are you?"

Silence.

Sam let out a heavy sigh. "Don't make us come looking for you."

A small sound, then a short, thin woman dressed in red and black sauntered out from behind the throne. "Please, call me Mortianna. And I was only the Lord Sheriff's spiritual advisor. I never told him how to do his business."

"But," Tuck said, his face still pale as he stood by the broken mirror, "the Bishop of Hereford was the Sheriff's spiritual advisor."

Le Fay nearly purred. "We both were, darling. I advised on pagan matters while Hereford muttered all that Christianity nonsense. Vaisey liked to hedge his bets, that one did."

Sam's cheek twitched. "That's a nice story, but we've been here before. Back in Camelot, you were wheedling your way onto the throne by manipulating Mordred to do your dirty work. You were doing the same thing here with Vaisey, weren't you?"

"Your words are absurd," Le Fay said. "Were that my plan, I would be in Prince John's bed, not grovelling before his snake of a sheriff. No. I am innocent. I was merely biding my time here in Nottingham until magic returned."

"Returned?" Sam's cheek twitched again. "I was told magic was gone forever."

Le Fay laughed. "How could it be gone? You cannot destroy magic. It is bigger than all of us. And you are here, are you not? Only magic could have brought you. I must admit, I was shocked when I first saw you in this very hall. It was then I knew the magic had begun to return. Indeed, it was I who urged Vaisey not to have you killed. You have no idea how difficult that was. I was forced to lie and say you were necessary to seal his ascension to the throne."

Sam rubbed his ear. "Let me get this straight. You told Vaisey not to kill me?"

Le Fay smiled. "Oh, he wanted to. So very badly. Hereford also encouraged him. Nothing excited the poor bishop more than bloodshed." She glanced at the broken mirror, and at the blood pooling on the floor. "I hope he enjoyed his own."

"But Vaisey almost did kill me," Sam growled.

Her smile widened. "As I said, the Sheriff wanted to. And the Sheriff usually got what he wanted."

Sam rubbed his ear again, puzzled.

"What should be done with this woman?" Robin asked, apparently equally puzzled.

Azeem the Moor stepped forward. "She is a witch. She must not be suffered to live. So says the Qur'an."

"Let us not be hasty," Le Fay said. "I am not a witch. I am a sorceress. There is a big difference."

"You smell like a witch," Azeem said. "And you were in league with the Sheriff. And that man." He pointed at Bishop Hereford's corpse.

"The bishop," Robin said to Le Fay, "accused my father of devil worship to justify his murder. What did you accuse my father of?"

"Me?" Le Fay took a step backward. "Nothing. Back in Camelot I always saw you as a sweet boy. I had nothing against you or your father. Word of his death came as a complete surprise."

"Not true," said a warbling voice from behind the throne.

Sam watched as an aging, grey-haired man hobbled out from the shadows. His eyes were white, and he stretched his hands out before him. Blind? "Merlin?"

Robin laughed and rushed forward. "Do not be ridiculous, Sam. This is Duncan, my father's butler." Robin swept the old man into his arms. "Duncan! I thought you were dead!"

"I would prefer death," the old man croaked, as he awkwardly freed himself from Robin's grasp, "given what I have endured these past months."

The greybeard cast his blind eyes about the interior of the keep. "The Sheriff, his bishop, and his witch. All were at Locksley Castle when Furnival murdered your father. The good man that he was, Lord Locksley refused Furnival's insistence that he join Prince John's rebellion. When your father could not be swayed, it was Mortianna who first suggested he must die.

"Furnival argued he could not simply kill a peer without cause. That was when Hereford accused Lord Locksley of consorting with demons. No evidence, of course, and your father denied it, but it provided Lord Furnival the excuse he needed.

"Once the deed was done, Sheriff Vaisey pointed at me and said, 'We cannot have a witness.'

"The witch let out a shrill cackle, then said, 'I can remedy that.'"

Duncan lowered his head. "Suddenly I could no longer see."

Le Fay snorted into the quiet. "I have a spirited laugh. 'Tis hardly a cackle."

Sam noted she didn't deny causing the old man's blindness.

"The Sheriff," Duncan continued, "said he would make of me a servant, to remind him of his wonderous day at Castle Locksley. Since then, I have scrubbed pots in the keep's kitchen and emptied bedpans."

Robin again wrapped his arms around his father's butler. Sam suspected Duncan had played a role in the outlaw's early upbringing.

Le Fay stood watching. Maybe she was working up to another spell. "You did magic," Sam accused.

The sorceress from Camelot smiled. "I told you magic could not be destroyed."

"She is a witch," Azeem cried and ran toward her with his giant curved blade.

Le Fay waved a hand, and the Moor stumbled backward like he had bounced off an invisible wall.

"A witch!" Azeem cried.

Yup. Working up a spell. Sam levelled his Smith & Wesson and fired.

Though Le Fay looked fatigued from dealing with Azeem, she waved again, as though swatting a fly. The bullet changed course, grazing the cheek of the Sheriff of Nottingham statue instead of striking her cold, calloused heart. But the bullet wasn't done. It bounced off a wall sconce, shot upward to reflect off the chandelier, and ultimately flew back toward Le Fay, who let out a shriek when it grazed her own cheek as well as the statue's.

The witch threw her arms in the air, and all at once the keep began filling with smoke.

As everyone ran toward the doorway, Sam paused to pull Azeem to his feet. Then the two of them struggled through the roiling dark until they made their way outside.

Sam did a quick look about and found Nora leaning against the courtyard wall, coughing.

"What happened?" Robin asked. The outlaw stood closer to the gate, holding up his father's butler.

"Morgan Le Fay happened," Sam said. "The only good news is that she seems to have some magic. Maybe that means Nora and I can get home."

50
A CHANCE TO SAY GOODBYE

IT WAS LATE afternoon by the time they returned to Robin's camp in Sherwood Forest. Exhausted, Sam climbed into his blanket and immediately fell asleep. He woke in the wee hours of the morning, and sat, wondering about magic. It was back. Or on its way back. He'd have to tell Robin that he and Nora needed to return to Sternwood Castle, or Locksley Castle, as it was currently called. And Carmen, of course. The three of them had to find a way to return to their proper time.

He found himself thinking about Effie. He'd seen nothing to indicate that sometime in the past six years she'd changed her feelings about men, or at least one man. If he couldn't get back to Connecticut, there was nothing Sam would like more than to settle down with Lady Euphemia Peregrine and raise a few junior detectives. It didn't have to be in Nottingham. They could go anywhere. Or, why not take Effie with them back to Hartford? She wouldn't have to be self-conscious about her scar there. Or at least could be less self-conscious. If she wanted, she could have plastic surgery to make it less obvious.

But what about Nora? Had his partner decided to take their business relationship closer to the personal side? Had she flirted with him before losing her memory, then again after she regained it? Or was he reading more into it than what was meant?

Sam was still pondering various *what-if*s and *what-could-be*s when the sun finally rose, and with it, Robin's Merry Men.

"I fear we have another ride ahead of us," Robin announced when Sam sought the newly married bandit out.

"Oh?"

"Lord Furnival is dead, but his men still control Locksley Castle. I plan to take it back. You need not come with me if you have other plans."

"I have to come," Sam said. "Your father's castle—your castle now—is how we got here. In my time, it's been moved to Connecticut."

Robin grinned. "You jest, surely."

"No joke. Carmen's father had it shipped overseas stone by stone, and reassembled near a forest not too different from where it sits now."

"But my family?" Robin asked. "My children's, children's children. Do they not dwell in Locksley Castle?"

"Ah, well, no," Sam said. "They must have moved on somewhere along the line. I wish I could tell you what happens with your children's, children's children. But I don't know."

"Perhaps they go to London and rule all of England," Robin mused. "Marian is cousin to Good King Richard, though far in line from the throne."

"Maybe that's what happens," Sam said. "I'm not all that familiar with British royalty. Anyway, I'd like to ride with you to Locksley and see what happens when we get there."

Sam didn't mean that, of course. If he never saw a saddle again it would be too soon. But there was no avoiding it. The distance was too far to walk.

Despite being given the same docile pony he had ridden overnight to Nottingham, by the time they reached Locksley Castle it was early afternoon, and Sam's backside felt like it had gone through a meat grinder. Without him asking, Nora helped him down off the animal. He didn't complain. Dismounting on his own would have been a train wreck. Even with Nora's help, Sam could barely stand unaided.

Carmen Sternwood, in contrast, dismounted like she had been born in the saddle. As did Effie, who had taken her role of chief babysitter seriously and hadn't let Carmen out of her sight.

Sam's first order of business was to find somewhere to sit down. Preferably on a pillow. Only as he looked around did he remember why they had come to Locksley Castle. To retake it from Furnival's redshank mercenaries. Only he didn't see any mercenaries.

"Where is everyone?" Little John demanded. Robin's first lieutenant stormed up and down in front of the castle entrance.

"The place seems deserted," Sagramore said as he returned from peering inside the stable. "Not a horse, chicken, or grain of wheat."

"Furnival's redshanks have fled," Tuck concluded. "Word must have arrived of their master's tragic accident in Nottingham."

"Ah, well," Robin said. "Enough bloodshed for one summer. Eh, boys?"

The Merry Men all nodded and grunted agreement, except for Little John, who looked like he needed to bash in a few skulls after the long ride.

"You are all welcome to stay," Robin said to his men. "You are my family now. The castle is big enough for all of us!" He nodded to Will Scarlet. "Ride back to Sherwood to collect the rest of the camp. Take Alan-a-Dale with you."

Will looked a little put out as he climbed back onto his horse, but the band's minstrel merely grinned, then whistled a jaunty tune as they rode away.

The remainder of the Merry Men began settling the horses in the stable and moving their saddlebags into the castle.

Robin didn't join them but took Sam aside. "Your help has been instrumental in defeating the vile Sheriff. I am unsure how we would have succeeded without you, Sam. It saddens me that you are leaving us."

"You'll be all right. I'm pretty sure the movie I saw ended with you and Marian getting married. End of story. So all the craziness must be behind you."

The outlaw rubbed his chin. "True, the Sheriff is no more, and Furnival has come to an appropriate end, but the Pretender still covets the throne and has many supporters. Your aid may be all that could turn the tide."

Sam's cheek twitched. "You don't need me, otherwise the movie I saw would have had a sequel. No, something tells me your King Richard will be back to put his brother in his place. It's time now for happily-ever-afters. You and Marian have earned it."

"Very well," Robin said. "If you feel you must leave, so be it. But I am curious. How do you intend to use my father's castle to return to your home?"

Sam leaned forward and lowered his voice. "There's a bolthole around back."

When Robin frowned, Sam added, "You can't see it, but it's there. It's probably best if I show you."

Nora joined them, and Effie herded Carmen along as Sam led Robin around to the back of the castle. When they reached the place where Sam knew the door was, like before, there was nothing to see.

"It is here," Sam insisted. "We were in the lower level of the castle when Nora disappeared. Then I pushed against a place in the wall and a door opened. I went through and came out here."

"This is where I came out as well," Nora said. "I marked the wall there."

They all looked and saw a wound in a patch of moss.

Nora ran her gaze along the length of the wall and out into the forest. "Now that I'm looking at the castle and my mark, I remember. There were men with swords hanging around the front entrance, so I returned back here and headed out through the trees, hoping to find Codfish Falls Road or Highway 44 and flag down a car. I didn't know what had happened. I thought maybe I was suffering from carbon monoxide poisoning or been exposed to some kind of hallucinogen.

"I wandered for hours, I think, finding only trees and dirt tracts that had never seen a steel-belted radial tire. I finally found a cabin. I could hear someone humming a song I didn't recognize, and came around the side of the building, stopping when I saw a woman hanging wet laundry on a line strung between two trees. Before I could say anything, a rock came flying out of the woods and hit the woman on the head.

"I drew my Glock and waited. The next thing I knew, Carmen Sternwood came strolling out of the trees, proud as you please, and began collecting clothes off the line."

"I should have waited until they were dry," Carmen said, interrupting. "But I needed to get back to Nottingham to place a bet."

"What happened after that?" Sam asked Nora.

"I confronted Carmen. She seemed surprised at how I was dressed. Even more surprised that I knew who she was. And that I held a gun on her. She asked if I'd come to take her back to Connecticut.

"Everything after that is a bit foggy. I remember holstering my weapon. Asking her where we were. But that's all."

"I'll fill you in," Sam said. "When you weren't looking, Carmen picked up the rock she'd beaned the washerwoman with, and cracked you on the side of the head."

"I was aiming for the back of your head," Carmen said. "You turned before I could get a good swing in."

Sam continued speaking to Nora. "Then Carmen took your Glock and everything else in your pockets. And waited, wondering what to do. She probably planned to interrogate you. But when you woke up, you had amnesia."

"Isn't that a kicker," Carmen said. "I was going to threaten you with your own gun to take me back home, but you couldn't even remember where home was."

Robin was shaking his head. "This is all . . . interesting. Confusing, but interesting." He pressed a hand against the castle wall. "You say there is a bolthole here? My father never mentioned one, and I don't see it."

"Nor will you," said a voice from the forest.

Sam turned and saw someone emerge from among the trees, an older man not unlike Robin's father's butler, Duncan. Only this old man wasn't blind. He looked worse for wear than the last time Sam had seen him, older than the passing of six years could account for. He looked ancient. And frail.

"The Merlin," Robin whispered.

Effie was already rushing forward and gave the old man a crushing hug.

"Gentle now." Merlin chuckled. "I am not as spry as I once was."

"You have returned," Robin said.

"Aye." Merlin nodded. "Magic is returning, and I with it."

"But the Lady of the Lake is dead," Sam said.

The wizard sighed. "Aye. But she, too, will be back someday. And she will not be happy. Arthur really screwed the pooch this time."

Robin frowned.

"A phrase I picked up in the future," Merlin said.

The old man turned his eagle gaze on Sam. "You and your golden-haired friends cannot go back this way. When I made this bolthole for Robin's grandfather, it was so the castle residents could flee should the need arise. Its design prevents attackers from sneaking in the back way."

"A one-way door," Sam said. "So we'll have to go inside and come out again."

Merlin shook his head. "You would just arrive back here. No, I shall have to send you back as I have in the past."

"Like you brought us here in the first place?" Sam accused.

The wizard laughed. "No, you and your friends did that on your own. Quite the coincidence you finding this castle's enchanted bolthole just as magic began to return. And odd it would let you out here instead of in your own time. Yes, quite the coincidence."

"I don't believe in coincidences," Sam said.

Merlin shrugged. "Magic cares little for what you believe. It is what it is." The old man looked up at the sky, licked an index finger, and waved it around. "An hour, I should think. Magic is still weak and, frankly, a bit wild. I should be able to send you back in an hour or so. I hope you do not mind the wait."

"No," Sam said. "Not at all." He was just happy they could go back. Period.

"Let us go round to the front, then," Merlin said. "Shall we? Mayhap Tuck will have some mead hidden away."

"Tuck always has mead hidden away," Robin said.

Nora touched Sam's arm, holding him back. "That's Merlin? The wizard?"

"He was the last two times I was here," Sam said.

"And he can get us back to Hartford?"

"He has before."

"Okay."

"That's it? Okay?"

Nora cocked her head. "What? You want a parade?"

Carmen spoke up. "Yeah, I want a parade. That old man is going to get us home? How? By saying abracadabra?"

"More or less," Sam said.

Carmen shook her head. "You people are crazy."

Sam ignored Sternwood's feral daughter and focused on his

own thoughts. He had an hour before he went back home. That hadn't happened before. He'd always been whisked back to Connecticut in a hurry. For the first time, he had a chance to say goodbye. And so he made the rounds, bidding farewell to Tuck, Robin and Marian, Sir Sagramore, even David of Doncaster and Azeem the Moor.

"You have an unusual aura," Azeem said, rubbing his dark fingers against his tattooed face. "This is not your place. The old man speaks truly when he says he must send you elsewhere."

"What about you?" Sam asked. "I think your speech at the Sheriff's wedding was enough to fulfil your obligation to Robin."

"Perhaps," the Moor said. "Perhaps not. We shall see."

Finally, the only person he hadn't spoken with was Effie. What to do about Effie? Try to woo her? Convince her to go to Hartford with him?

But Euphemia Peregrine seemed glued to Merlin's side. Would he even get a chance to speak with her alone? Sam edged closer to hear what they were saying.

"Are you certain?" the wizard asked. "I could heal it. Maybe not today, but soon."

"I have hated this mark," Effie said, running her finger the length of the scar she had received as a spy in Mordred's camp. "But I no longer mind it for some reason. No, I do know the reason. Sam Spade. Sam accepted me for me, even with the scar."

"As well he should," Merlin said. "As all men should. We are not the face we show the world. We are something more, something essential. Our essence is who we are. And you, my dear, have a beautiful essence."

"I shall keep the mark," Effie said. "I earned it. It is part of me now."

And there, then, Sam knew that Effie would never be his. She was who she was. No interest in men. No interest in a life with Sam, here or in Hartford. He took a deep breath, and let out a heavy sigh.

Effie and Merlin both heard the sound and turned toward him.

"I'm going to miss you," Sam said. "Both of you."

Merlin grinned. "But not for long. Not for you, in any case. Six months shall pass in your Connecticut, six years for the rest of us, and then, perhaps, we shall meet again. But our hour is almost up. I shall gather my strength while you fetch your companions."

51
THE END OF ANOTHER CASE

ONE MOMENT, SAM stood in front of Locksley Castle with Nora and Carmen by his side, the wizard Merlin and Euphemia Peregrine a few feet away, and Robin Hood and his Merry Men gathered in a circle like an audience in the round. The air was still and the forest quiet except for the circling of a large black bird overhead.

The next moment, Sam was still standing in front of Locksley Castle. Only it was now called Sternwood Castle, and it was in Connecticut instead of England. Nora stood beside him working her jaw, while Carmen Sternwood lay twitching on the ground, inarticulate sounds passing between her lips.

"Yeah," Sam said. "Time travel would never make a good amusement ride."

The *Caw! Caw! Caaaawwww!* of a bird made Sam look up to see a large crow wheeling overhead. Could that . . . ? No, it couldn't.

Nora interrupted his thoughts by pressing a hand against his arm, maybe to assure herself he was real. Or maybe as a suggestion they could be more than partners?

"Are we really back in Connecticut?" she asked.

Sam rested his opposite hand on hers and offered his partner a smile. "Look around, angel. Merlin and Effie are gone. No more Robin Hood, Tuck, or Little John. The construction isn't finished.

And there's Owen Taylor's truck."

"Hey!" The Hawks Development workman came walking around from the side of the castle. "Oh, it's you. Man, you've been inside for hours. I was going to come looking for you." Then he looked down and saw Carmen. The younger woman had ceased her spasms and was catching her breath. "Miss Sternwood! Are you all right?"

"She was having a fit of some kind," Sam said. "But it appears to be over. Say, you don't happen to have any rope in that truck, do you?"

Owen's eyes rose against his forehead. "I'm sure I can rustle something up. But maybe I should help Miss—"

"We've got it." Nora let go of Sam's arm and bent down to help Carmen to her feet.

The Hawks Development employee shrugged, and returned a minute later with a length of yellow nylon cord.

"Perfect." Sam took the rope and turned toward Carmen, who was still looking a little shellshocked. "Could you put your hands behind your back please?"

"Wha-What? Where am I?"

"You can play that game if you like," Nora said. "You're still going to have to answer a few questions." Grabbing one of Carmen's arms in each hand, Nora wrenched them behind the young woman's back.

"Wait! What? You can't do this!"

"I can and I am," Nora said, holding Carmen's hands in place.

Sam looped the yellow cord into a handcuff knot, then tightened it around Carmen's wrists. "That should do it."

Owen stood there saying nothing, his mouth hanging slightly open.

"What do you think you're doing?" Carmen demanded. "My father will—"

"Your father hired us to find Sean Regan," Sam interrupted. "You know where he is, so maybe you should just tell us."

Carmen pushed against Nora with her shoulder, then kicked out, hoping to strike a knee, but missed as Nora stepped sideways.

"Try that again," Sam's partner said, "and Mr. Taylor will have to find us more rope. It's been a while since I hogtied anyone."

"You wouldn't dare," Carmen growled. "Do you know who I

am?"

"You're the person who murdered Sean Regan," Sam said.

Carmen turned her head to stare at him.

"Where's the body, sister?" Sam had studied enough criminals to recognize the subtle guilt in the young woman's eyes. He knew he'd called it true.

Carmen's mouth opened, but no words came out.

Turning toward Owen, Sam pulled out his phone. The battery was almost dead, but for the first time in a week, it had a signal. He displayed the photo of Regan he had shown the Hawks Development workman when they first met. "You sure you haven't seen this guy?"

"I, uh," Owen stammered.

"Lie to me," Sam said, "and you'll be charged with accessory to murder."

"Murder!" Owen pointed at Carmen. "She told me he was a boyfriend, and she didn't want her father to find out."

"When did you see him?" Sam demanded.

"It's been three or four days." The workman frowned at Carmen. "He went inside with her. Neither of them came out, not that I saw. Well, she's here now, but I haven't seen him again."

Sam turned back to Sternwood's daughter. "The jig's up, sister. I know Regan wasn't your boyfriend, so what did you do with him?"

Carmen's eyes blazed. "How do you know he wasn't my boyfriend? He could have been."

"Because he was your father's boyfriend, that's how. I can't think of another reason a chauffeur would pose in a painting with his boss."

"My fa—" Carmen fell back into Nora's arms.

Nora blinked her eyes. "Did she just faint?"

"I guess she really didn't know," Sam said.

It took an additional twenty minutes of arguments and threats, including a call to the police, before Carmen reluctantly led them down into the lower level of the castle.

"Regan followed you into the basement?" Sam asked as he turned on his penlight.

The young woman smirked. "I can make men follow me anywhere."

Sam almost laughed. Not only was he following the attractive young femme fatale into the great abyss, but so was Owen Taylor. The Hawks Development workman had retrieved a full-on flashlight from his truck. When he turned it on, it was like a searchlight running across the steps and walls.

Even so, Nora retrieved her own penlight from the small bag of possessions she kept tied to her waist.

Neither penlight was probably needed, but Sam liked to be in control of his destiny. Nora probably did as well.

The musty darkness and stone everything of Castle Sternwood's lower level brought to Sam a strong sense of déjà vu, not just of his first visit there, but of Nottingham's underground tunnel that connected Bishop Hereford's church with the Sheriff's Keep, and the privacy tunnel that ran within Nottingham's eastern wall. He could see himself avoiding underground structures for the next little while.

Carmen glanced around, then led them down the hallway toward where Sam had found the bolthole. Was she maybe trying to escape? Would she make a run for the hidden door? Hoping to flee back to Sherwood Forest? Or would the door lead somewhen else this time? Robin's grandfather's day? Or maybe World War II England?

Sam tucked his penlight into his trench coat pocket and prepared himself to grab the young woman should she try anything.

Before the hallway ended, however, Carmen stepped into an empty side chamber. "Behind there," she mumbled, pointing to a section of wall.

"You buried Regan behind a wall?" Nora asked. "How Edgar Allan Poe of you."

"This room is smaller than it should be," Owen said, shining his flashlight from floor to ceiling and side to side. He looked at Carmen. "You hauled extra stones in here by yourself?"

Carmen shrugged. "Sean helped. I told him I wanted a safe room, a place to hide valuables, and didn't want the contractors to know about it. He helped me break apart a wall back down the corridor, and rebuild it here."

"Sounds like a nice guy," Sam said.

Carmen harrumphed.

Owen ran one hand along the false wall. "This is good workmanship."

"Why did you kill Regan?" Nora asked.

Carmen set her jaw, and a small pout formed on her bottom lip. "He was going to tell Daddy how I gambled away the money that was supposed to go to the contractors."

Sam shook his head. "Your father would have found out anyway if he hasn't already. What's the real reason?"

"I suggested an arrangement," Carmen admitted. "Sean refused."

"An arrangement?"

Carmen's eyes narrowed. "A friendly arrangement. To give me time to win back the money."

"He refused your advances," Nora suggested.

Carmen glowered at Nora, then at Sam. Even in the poorly lit basement room, Sam could see the young woman's rage. "He said no. To me. Me! Have you seen him? Not in his entire life could Sean ever get a woman like me!"

"No," Sam said, "but he didn't really want to, did he?"

Carmen's sails lost their wind. "Sean was really my father's lover?"

"That's the impression I got when we met with your father," Sam said.

Carmen sniffed. "So I messed up. Daddy will bail me out. He always does."

"He may not be able to this time," Nora said.

Sam nodded. "And he may not want to."

Nora grabbed Sternwood's younger daughter by her bound wrists, and the four of them retraced their steps through the castle basement and up the stairs. As they stepped outside into the crisp, clean air of rural Connecticut, the cry of approaching police sirens heralded the end of another case.

THE END

ABOUT THE AUTHOR

RANDY MCCHARLES is a full-time author of speculative and crime fiction.

He is the recipient of several Aurora Awards, and in 2013 his short story "Ghost-B-Gone Incorporated" won the House of Anansi 7-day Ghost Story Contest.

Randy's most recent publications include *A Connecticut Gumshoe in King Arthur's Court* from Tyche Books, five novels in the Peter Galloway private detective series, the 2017 Aurora Award shortlisted novel *The Day of the Demon*, and the 2016 Aurora Award shortlisted novel *Much Ado about Macbeth*, also from Tyche Books.

In addition to writing, Randy organizes various literary events including the award-winning When Words Collide Festival for Readers and Writers.

www.ingramcontent.com/pod-product-compliance
Lightning Source LLC
LaVergne TN
LVHW040040080526
838202LV00045B/3413